USA TODAY bestselling  books and writing even tions, she finally sold h she has written fifty-plu lives in Tennessee with h hiking, travelling and fan

You can connect with Janice at
www.janicemaynard.com
www.Twitter.com/janicemaynard
www.Facebook.com/ janicemaynardreaderpage
www.Facebook.com/JaniceSMaynard
and www.Instagram.com/TheRealJaniceMaynard

A lover of storytelling in all forms, **Susannah Erwin** worked for major film studios before writing her first novel, which won RWA's Golden Heart® Award. She lives in Northern California with her husband and a very spoiled but utterly delightful cat.

3524 912

Also by Janice Maynard

Discover more at millsandboon.co.uk

A CONTRACT SEDUCTION

JANICE MAYNARD

WANTED: BILLIONAIRE'S WIFE

SUSANNAH ERWIN

MILLS & BOON

First Published in Great Britain 2019
by Mills & Boon, an imprint of HarperCollinsPublishers,
1 London Bridge Street, London, SE1 9GF

A Contract Seduction © 2019 Janice Maynard
Wanted: Billionaire's Wife © 2019 Susannah Erwin

ISBN: 978-0-263-27181-2

0519

MIX
Paper from
responsible sources
FSC™ C007454

This book is produced from independently certified FSC™ paper to ensure responsible forest management.

For more information visit: www.harpercollins.co.uk/green

Printed and bound in Spain
by CPI, Barcelona

A CONTRACT SEDUCTION

JANICE MAYNARD

For Charles, my one and only—thank you
for being my hero in every way!

One

Tumor. Inoperable. Cancer.

Jonathan Tarleton gripped the steering wheel, white knuckled, and stared unseeingly through the windshield. The traffic on the 526 beltway that surrounded Charleston was light in the middle of the day. Even so, he probably shouldn't be driving. He was undoubtedly in shock. But all he could think about was going home.

Like an injured animal seeking its den, he needed to go to ground. To hide. To come to grips with the unimaginable.

Thank God, his sister was recently married and living with her new husband, Jonathan's best friend. If Jonathan had come face-to-face with Mazie at the big house out at the beach, his sibling would have known instantly that something was wrong. The two of them were close.

Under ordinary circumstances, neither Jonathan nor Mazie would still be living under the roof where they had grown up. But their father was all alone and getting more and more feeble day by day. Though a number of the old man's friends had moved to communities where they had companionship and medical care close at hand, Gerald Tarleton clung to his fortress of a home on a barrier island.

Jonathan pulled into the under-house parking and rested his forehead on his hands. He felt weak and scared and angry. How the hell was this going to work? He was the sole force that directed the family shipping company. Even though his father's name was still on the letterhead, Jonathan carried the weight of the entire enterprise.

His twin brother should have been here to help, but Hartley was nowhere to be found. After inexplicably stealing a million dollars from the company and then vanishing, Hartley had been written out of the will and out of their lives.

The betrayal had cut Jonathan to the bone. It was a secret hurt that ate at him like the disease in his body. He and his father were the only ones who knew what had happened. They hadn't wanted to break Mazie's heart or tarnish her image of her big brother.

With a shaking hand, Jonathan turned off the ignition. Instantly—now that the AC was unavailable—humidity began to filter into the vehicle. Jonathan was a South Carolina lowlander to the bone, but the summer heat could be brutal.

He gathered his things and headed upstairs. Because of security concerns, the Tarletons had two high-tech offices inside the house in addition to those at Tarleton Shipping headquarters. Not only did the arrangement ensure privacy when necessary, but it meant that Jonathan could keep tabs on his father. The situation sometimes cramped his style, but he had a condo in the city where he could escape on occasion.

For a man of thirty-one, almost thirty-two, his social life was a joke. He dated occasionally, but few women understood the demands he juggled. His family's decades-old shipping empire was both his great privilege and his curse. He couldn't even remember the last time he'd felt close to any woman, physically or otherwise.

But he made the sacrifices willingly. He was proud of what the Tarletons had built here in Charleston. Proud, and absolutely determined to see it thrive.

He paused for a moment in the living room to stare out through the expansive plate-glass windows to the ocean glittering beneath a June sun. The view never failed to soothe him. Until today.

Now, the immensity and timelessness of the sea mocked him. Humans were little more than specks in the cosmos. Grains of sand on the immense sandy beach of the infinite universe.

All the old clichés were true. Facing one's mortality turned everything upside down. *Time*, that nebulous resource that once seemed a cheap commodity, was suddenly more precious than anything he had ever stored in a bank vault.

How long did he have? The doctor said six months. Maybe more. Maybe less. How was Jonathan going to tell his sister? His father? What would happen to the company, his family's legacy? Mazie had her own interests, her own life.

She would be the sole owner of the family business once Jonathan and Gerald were gone. Since she had never shown any signs that she was interested in being a hands-on partner in Tarleton Shipping, maybe she would sell. Perhaps that would be for the best. The end to an era.

The thought pained him more than he could say. Until today he hadn't realized exactly how much he was emotionally invested in the company. It wasn't merely a job to him. It was his birthright and a symbol of his family's place in Charleston's history.

Moments later, he found Gerald Tarleton dozing in a chair in the den. Jonathan didn't wake his father. He felt raw and out of control. And his head hurt like hell.

The debilitating headaches had started almost a year ago. At first they were infrequent. Then the episodes increased. One doctor said it was stress. Another wrote it off as migraines.

A dozen medications had been tried and discarded. Today his doctor had given him a handful of sample pills, along with a prescription for more. Right now Jonathan could take one, climb into bed and hopefully sleep off the throbbing pain.

But that wouldn't solve the bigger problems.

The prospect of drugged oblivion was almost irresistible. He didn't want to face another minute of this wretched day. But when he reached the kitchen, he grabbed a tumbler, filled it with tap water and downed a couple of over-the-counter acetaminophen tablets.

He had responsibilities. Responsibilities that weren't going anywhere. The only thing that had changed was the time line.

Jonathan always thrived under pressure. Give him a project, a deadline, and he would leap into motion. The adrenaline rush of achieving the impossible drove him to labor, to excel, to work harder than he had to.

Those traits would stand him in good stead for the next few months.

Grimly he leaned his hip against the marble countertop. In that instant, he made his first postdiagnosis decision. He would keep this news under wraps for now. There was no reason for his family and friends to be upset. To grieve. There would be plenty of time for that when he was gone. Right now, all he wanted was to preserve the status quo.

The first order of business was to make a plan. He would figure this out. Vague, desperate ideas flitted through his brain, each one more flawed or untenable than the last. There had to be an answer. He couldn't simply walk off into that final great sunset and let everything sink into ruin.

He needed time to process, to come to terms with the sword of Damocles hanging over his head. His money and power and influence were worthless currency now. He couldn't buy his way out of this...

Lisette Stanhope punched in the alarm code, waited for the large gates to slide back and then drove slowly onto the

Tarleton property. Even after working with Jonathan Tarleton for six years, she never failed to appreciate the magnificence of his family home.

Tarletons had lived for decades on the tip of a small barrier island just north of the city. Their fifteen acres were more than enough for the compound that included the main house and several smaller buildings scattered around.

An imposing gated iron fence protected the enclave on land. Water access was impossible due to a high brick wall at the top of the sand. The beach itself was public property, but no one could wander onto Tarleton property, either out of curiosity or with dangerous motives. Hurricanes and erosion made the wall outrageously expensive to maintain, but the current Tarleton patriarch was by nature paranoid and suspicious, so security was a constant concern.

When she saw Jonathan's car parked beneath the house, her heart sank. He was usually not home this time of day. She'd been hoping to slip in, say hello to Gerald and put the envelope in her purse on Jonathan's desk.

She could have carried out her errand at the main office where she worked most of the time, but this particular scenario demanded privacy. The decision to turn in her resignation had her stomach in knots. Jonathan would be either furious or perplexed—or both.

After reading her brief note, he would demand an explanation. Naturally. She had been practicing her speech. *In a rut. New challenges. More time to travel.* When she said the words in front of her bathroom mirror, they almost seemed believable. The part that made her wince was acknowledging how good Jonathan and his family had been to her.

Lisette's mother had suffered a debilitating stroke when Lisette was in grad school. For almost seven years, Lisette had worked two jobs and barely managed to keep food on the table and pay the stable of women who helped care for her mother's considerable needs.

Being hired by Tarleton Shipping six years ago had literally changed her life. The generous salary and benefits package had relieved her financial worries to a great extent and had enabled her to spend quality time with her mother.

When her mom had a second stroke and passed away last fall, Jonathan had insisted that Lisette take ample time to mourn and to handle her mother's affairs. Not many other bosses in a corporate setting would have been so generous.

And now Lisette was about to repay Jonathan's immense consideration by abandoning the company...by abandoning her boss.

He wouldn't see this coming, but it was her only choice.

She wanted marriage—a husband and a baby and a normal, ordinary life. Mooning over her boss for another year or two or five was never going to bring those dreams to fruition. She'd had a silly crush on Jonathan, but he'd never once given any indication that he felt the same. She needed a fresh start, a new setting, a chance to meet another man and get Jonathan out of her system once and for all. Her personal life had been on hold for so long she barely knew how to begin, but she knew instinctively that she had to move on.

Her heart slugged in her chest. She didn't want to face him. Guilt and other messier emotions might derail her plan.

When she opened the door at the top of the stairs, again with a code punched in, she stepped into a house that echoed with quiet. Maybe Jonathan wasn't here after all. Maybe a friend had picked him up. Or maybe he was with Mazie and J.B. The newlyweds loved entertaining.

Finding Gerald Tarleton dozing in his favorite recliner was no surprise. Lisette tiptoed past, careful not to wake him. Perhaps if Jonathan was gone or at least upstairs, she could slip in and out without a confrontation.

The upper levels were the family's living quarters. At the back of the main floor, overlooking the driveway, were two rooms that had been outfitted with every conceivable feature to make the offices here as good as or better than the ones downtown.

The smaller of the two was Lisette's domain. She had started out with Tarleton Shipping in accounting but quickly moved up the food chain until she became Jonathan's executive assistant, a title she had held for the past three years. Her job was to do anything and everything to make his life run more smoothly.

And she was good at it. Very good.

A quick visual exploration confirmed that no one was in either office. Now that she was here, her misgivings increased tenfold. She reached into her purse for the crumpled envelope and extracted it. The door between the two offices stood open.

Last night she had composed and revised a dozen versions. Resigning via a letter was cowardly. Jonathan deserved to hear her decision directly. But she couldn't do it. She was afraid he would try to change her mind.

Her hands were sweating. Once she did this, there would be no going back. Just as she was ready to approach his desk and place her missive in a prominent position, a deep male voice came from behind her.

"Lisette. What are you doing?"

Rattled and breathless, she spun around, managing to stash the envelope in her skirt pocket. "Jonathan. You startled me. I thought you weren't home."

He cocked his head, giving her a quizzical smile. "I live here," he reminded her.

"Of course you do." She wiped her hands on her hips. "When you weren't at the office, I thought I might come out to the house. You know. In case you needed me." The lie rolled off her lips.

Jonathan barely seemed to register her awkward phrasing. For the first time she saw that his face was pale. And he seemed tense. Distracted.

"Jonathan? Is something wrong?" He couldn't have known what she was about to do...could he?

He stared at her. "It hasn't been a great day."

"I'm sorry. Is there anything I can do to help?" Maybe fate had saved her from really bad timing. This was not the look of a man who would take her resignation with equanimity.

"I don't know." He spoke the words slowly, almost as if he were in a daze.

Now his demeanor began to worry her. The Jonathan she knew was sharp and decisive, a brilliant boss who ran his massive company with an iron fist but was also scrupulously fair.

She touched his forearm briefly, mostly because she couldn't help herself. "What's going on? Did we lose the Porter deal?"

He shook his head. "No." He shuffled a few papers on his desk. "I sent you some emails last night. Why don't you handle those? Then I might dictate a few letters." He winced and put a hand to his head, his pallor deepening.

Lisette knew about the headaches. She and Jonathan worked together closely, and she was well aware that he had been plagued by the pain for months now. "Have you taken anything?" she asked quietly. "I can see that you're hurting."

His grimace spoke volumes. "Yes. But not long ago."

"Why don't you go upstairs and lie down? You can forward your cell to the phone here. I'll come get you if it's anything urgent."

Even hurting and not at his best, Jonathan Tarleton was handsome and charismatic. He carried an aura of absolute control. Seeing him so vulnerable was both shocking and unsettling.

"An hour," he said gruffly. "No more. I'll set the alarm on my phone."

Jonathan climbed the stairs slowly. Reality began to sink in. This situation wasn't going to improve. He could get another opinion, but what was the use? He'd been to multiple doctors. This last set of tests was the first time he had received a definitive answer.

In his large, well-appointed bedroom, he cursed beneath his breath and admitted to himself that he needed the pills. He had to think clearly, and right now his head felt like someone was using it for a bongo drum.

Once he was sprawled on his comfortable mattress, he lay very still and waited for the meds to work. Knowing that Lisette was downstairs helped. Though he didn't doze, he let his mind wander. Slowly his body relaxed. Stress was a killer. The irony of that didn't escape him.

Thinking about Lisette was both comforting and arousing. She had been a part of his life for a long time now. His personal, rigid code of ethics meant that he never acted on his attraction to her. They were work colleagues. Nothing more. He had regretted that at times, but now he should be glad. He was going to need someone in his corner who could be objective about what was to come.

Lisette was a soothing personality. Her competence and complete ability to handle any and every crisis were what had won him over in the beginning. He trusted her with any number of confidential work details, everything from high-level negotiations to financial secrets.

Some men might overlook her. Her brown hair and quiet personality were unremarkable. She had a feminine shape, but she didn't dress to impress. Her sexiest trait was her brain. She challenged him, kept him on his toes. The truth was, she was as capable as he, though she was always careful not to overstep her position.

Jonathan wouldn't have cared even if she had. He knew she could go to any company in the country or even abroad and land a prestigious job. For that reason, he had increased her salary in regular bumps to show her how much she was appreciated. And he had given her more and more responsibilities as she proved her loyalty to Tarleton Shipping.

Gradually the tension in his muscles began to ease. The pain in his head subsided to a dull ache instead of stabbing torture. As he began to feel more like himself, an idea bubbled to the surface.

What if he negotiated with Lisette to sub for him over the next few months when he wasn't able to function? He never knew from one day to the next how he was going to feel. If Lisette was deputized to make unilateral decisions, Jonathan would be able to mentally relax.

Better still, what if she could be the one to save Tarleton Shipping for the next generation? She had the brains and the people skills. And he knew she cared deeply about the company.

It would also mean he could postpone telling his family for a little bit longer. The prospect of hurting the people he loved flayed him. How could he dump that kind of news on them? It might kill his father. Mazie and J.B. were struggling with fertility. They sure as hell didn't need grief on top of that.

The doctor had said he *might* have longer than six months. Eating well and getting plenty of rest were supposed to be key. Jonathan was willing to fight, but the odds were definitely not in his favor. If a cure was out of the question, then all he could hope for was time enough to secure his legacy and the company's future. The more he contemplated the next few months, the more he became convinced that Lisette was the key to it all.

At last he stood and raked his hands through his hair. After splashing water on his face, he studied his reflection in the mirror. He'd taken some hard knocks in his life, but this was the worst. Grimly he weighed the cost of bringing Lisette in on the secret. He couldn't stand to be pitied or coddled.

There would have to be ground rules. And she had to know this new role was optional. If she said no, he would go it alone.

By the time he padded back downstairs in his stocking feet, almost two hours had passed. Both offices were empty. He found Lisette perched on an ottoman chatting with his father. She always went out of her way to make the old man feel special.

Gerald Tarleton had become a father late in life. Which was why Jonathan, at thirty-one, now bore the sole responsibility for running a mammoth enterprise. He strode into the room, watching both of their faces. Lisette's was serene. His father tried to give him a hard time.

"Napping in the middle of the day, son? That's my job."

Jonathan ruffled his father's hair and perched on the arm of the sofa. "I had a devil of a headache, but I'm feeling better now."

"Are you really?" Lisette asked, her gaze troubled.

He nodded. "Really." After a moment of chitchat about the weather, Jonathan stood. "You'll have to excuse us, Dad. Lisette and I have a few things to wrap up before she goes home."

"Of course. Besides, I've got to make sure the housekeeper has all the food ready. The boys are coming over for poker at six."

The "boys" were all Gerald's age. Jonathan was happy to see his father pursuing social interests. Both Mazie and Jonathan had been encouraging him to get out of the house more. He'd been depressed over the winter, but things were improving.

Lisette followed Jonathan back to the offices. "I took care of everything you sent me so far. Is there anything else you need today? If not, I'll see you downtown in the morning."

Jonathan stared at her intently, allowing his customary reserve to dissolve for a moment. Lisette was everything he liked in a woman and more. Beautiful, insightful, funny. And subtly sexy in a way some men might miss. Was he hatching this plan to save his family's business, or was his libido steering the ship?

He was about to find out.

Two

Jonathan knew this was an opening he couldn't pass up. But he had no idea how Lisette would react. He'd never felt uncomfortable around her before today. Then again, he'd never faced the prospect of shifting their relationship to a different footing.

She was the one person outside his small family circle whom he trusted completely. Not only with his secrets but with the future of his company and his personal legacy.

In order for such a fledgling plan to work, Lisette would have to be personally invested in what he was about to propose. She would have to be confident in her power and autonomy.

His burgeoning idea was a lot to dump on a woman. He would have to ease into it.

Maybe this was a stupid idea.

Lisette eyed him with curiosity in her gaze. Perhaps he wasn't as stoic as he had hoped. Or as guarded.

"I need to speak to you," he said carefully. "But not here. And it's not about work. Or at least not entirely."

Now her curiosity turned to confusion. "I don't understand."

Jonathan felt his neck heat. "If you would feel more comfortable, I could ask someone from HR to sit in on this conversation."

Her eyes widened. "Are you firing me?"

He gaped. "God, no. Are you insane? Why would I fire the best employee I've ever had?"

"Then what is this about?"

Jonathan swallowed. "Will you come to dinner with me?" he asked quietly. "We'll drive up the coast. Where we won't be seen. The matter I want to discuss with you is sensitive. I don't want to take advantage of your kindness, though, so feel free to say no."

Lisette shook her head slowly, her expression wry. "I've known you for a very long time, Jonathan. Dinner is fine. And we don't need a chaperone. Clearly, whatever you have to say is important. I'm happy to listen."

"Thank you."

She glanced down at her khaki skirt and sleeveless top. "Is what I'm wearing okay?"

He nodded slowly. "We might even take a picnic instead of going to a restaurant." There would be more privacy that way. No chance of anyone overhearing the conversation.

Though Lisette was clearly flustered, she didn't quibble over the plan. "I'm ready whenever you are. Do I need to drive?" she asked. "Because of the meds you took?"

"No. Not this time. I would never do anything to endanger you."

After quick goodbyes to Gerald, they exited the house. Jonathan tossed a couple of beach chairs into the back of the SUV. Being in the car together was definitely awkward. Her body language said she was uncertain of his intentions.

It didn't help that he was not big on small talk.

As he drove up the coast, he formulated a plan. Thirty minutes later, he pulled into a small fishing town and parked near a shed adjacent to the pier. This particular spot was more popular with locals than tourists. They ordered two shrimp baskets with large lemonades and took it to go.

Lisette teased him. "I pegged you as more of a beer than lemonade guy."

He shrugged. "Can't drink with the headache meds."

She winced. "Ah. Of course. Sorry."

Jonathan remembered a stretch of beach that was not particularly crowded. And this was the time of day that families headed inside to shower and clean up for dinner. As he suspected, there was plenty of open sand to be alone.

He carried the chairs. Lisette brought the food and drinks. The tide was headed out, so they picked a spot near a tidal pool and set up camp.

A light breeze blew in from the water. The sea was gunmetal gray, the sky streaked with golds and pinks, though sunset was a couple of hours away. Neither of them spoke as they opened their bags of food.

Jonathan sat back with a sigh. He'd lived near Charleston his entire life. The water was a part of him. The sand. The steady inexorable pull of the tides. Why did he spend so much time inside working?

It was human nature, he supposed, to take things for granted. After all, the sea would always be there. What had never occurred to him was that *he* wouldn't. He was measuring his life in months now, not years. Soon the parameters would be smaller than that. Weeks. Days.

Choking anger swelled in his chest. He didn't want to die. It wasn't fair. He felt as if he had only begun to live. But if he had to go, he wanted Lisette to protect his reputation and everything he had worked so hard to build.

Beside him, she ate her meal in silence, her gaze trained on the horizon. What was she thinking?

He had to speak his piece. But how? Even now, the words seemed ridiculous. Overly dramatic. *By the way, I'm living on borrowed time. Thought you should know.*

Part of him wanted to take off running down the beach and never stop. Perhaps if he ran fast enough and far enough, the grim reaper couldn't keep up. Perhaps this was all a bad dream.

Lisette leaned forward and set her cup in the sand, twisting it until it stayed upright. She tucked her trash in the bag and sat back, eyes closed. "That was lovely," she said. "I should have dinner at the beach every day."

"Not a bad idea."

The silence built between them, but it wasn't unpleasant. The ocean lulled their senses, washing away the stresses of the day.

Lisette reached out one leg and dabbled the tip of her sandal in the tidal pool, not looking at him. "So what's this big secret? Talk to me, Jonathan."

His stomach clenched. His jaw tightened. "I have a brain tumor," he said flatly. "Inoperable. Terminal."

Icy disbelief swept over her body and through her veins as if she'd been doused with winter rain and left to shiver and convulse in a stark landscape. No. It couldn't be true.

Slowly she turned to face him. Her shaking hands twisted in her lap. "Are you positive?" It was a stupid question. No one tossed around statements like that unless they were sure.

His bleak profile matched his body language as he stared at the water. "Oh, yeah." His low laugh held no humor. "The latest test results came in this morning."

"I'm so sorry," she whispered.

"I don't know how long I have," he said. "And I don't know what to expect. Which is why I'm having this conversation with you. I don't want to tell my family yet. I thought you could be an impartial…"

He trailed off, clearly searching for a word.

"A friend? A colleague?" The impossibility of what he was asking staggered her.

"You're more than that," he said huskily. "I trust you implicitly. I want to give you the authority to step in and make decisions if I'm having a bad day. I realize this is asking a lot of you, but I'll change your title and compensate you accordingly."

"Shouldn't Hartley be the one to fill this role?" She had never quite understood why he disappeared.

Jonathan's expression turned glacial. "My brother is gone and he's not coming back. It's not something I can discuss with you."

"But surely your other family members need to know. You can't keep this a secret, Jonathan."

"I realize that." His fists were clenched on the arms of the chair. "But I have to find the right time. I'll wait as long as I can."

She wanted to argue with him. For everyone's sake. But once Jonathan Tarleton made up his mind, you'd have better luck moving a giant boulder than changing his decision.

The enormity of what he had told her began to sink in. Her heart was raw and broken. She loved him. That's why she had planned to leave. How could she stay with him day after day and witness the unthinkable? It would destroy her. But how could she say no when he needed her?

"I'd like to think about it overnight," she said. "I'm not sure I feel comfortable trying to insert myself into company politics. There are a lot of people who won't take kindly to this setup."

"I'm the boss. What I say goes."

"But what about the board of directors? And your father, Gerald? And what happens when you become too ill to work?"

Her throat tightened with tears, tears she couldn't shed. He thought she was an impartial bystander. How much more wrong could he be?

"I need to walk," she said.

"Okay." Jonathan stood as well, shrugging out of his sport coat and rolling up the sleeves of his crisp cotton dress shirt.

They took off their shoes and headed down the beach.

Jonathan matched his long stride to her shorter one, because he topped her by six inches. His chestnut hair was burnished by the setting sun. The dark brown eyes, which could be fierce or good-humored, were hidden behind sunglasses.

His arms were deeply tanned, his hands masculine.

He was a beautiful human being. It was almost impossible to imagine that vitality and charisma being snuffed out.

At last, after half an hour passed, the tension dissipated and re-formed into something else. Awareness.

At least on her part. Being with him like this was a physical pain. When had she first realized he was the one? Long before she became his assistant. The fact that he was completely out of her orbit had kept her crush in check. But working together day after day had turned her fluttery feelings into something far deeper and more real.

She not only loved him, she admired and respected him. In a world where men in power sometimes abused their positions, Jonathan Tarleton had never treated his employees, female *or* male, with careless disregard.

If he had any faults at all, and he surely did, the most visible was his careful aloofness. He kept to himself, never blurring the lines between his authority and those who worked for him.

That fact made today's revelations all the more stunning.

They were walking shoulder to shoulder, so close she could have reached out and touched his hand. The beach was almost deserted now, the daylight fading rapidly as the sun kissed the water at the horizon.

Taking a deep breath, she halted and waited for him to follow suit.

He turned when he realized she had dropped back. "Time to go home?" he asked lightly.

"I'll do it," she said recklessly. "I'll do what you asked."

"I thought you needed to think it over."

She shook her head. "You and your family have been very good to me. It's only right that I should return the favor."

Jonathan removed his sunglasses and tucked them into his shirt pocket. "We sent flowers and gave you time off when your mother passed." He frowned. "It's not the same thing at all. What I'm asking you to do is nebulous and tricky and burdensome."

Burdensome. The word made her want to laugh, but not in a good way. Walking beside Jonathan for the next weeks and months would tax her emotional strength and her acting ability.

"I'm honored," she said slowly, trying not to give her secrets away. "I care about you, Jonathan. You're facing some very dark days. So, yes, I'll help you any way I can."

She saw his chest rise and fall. Had he been so uncertain that she would agree to his proposal?

His throat rippled as he swallowed. His gaze held a bleak acknowledgment of what he faced. "Thank you."

The two words were little more than a croak.

Tears stung her eyes. Without overthinking it, she went up on her tiptoes and kissed his cheek. Then she wrapped her arms around his stiff body in a brief hug. "I'm so very sorry," she said.

He might as well have been a statue. "I have rules," he said gruffly.

"Oh?" She shoved the hair from her face. Standing with the wind at her back made her feel disheveled.

"I won't be coddled." He snapped the words. "And I don't want your pity. Understood?"

She recoiled inwardly, but she kept her expression calm. "I can live with that. But when I see that you need help, I'll give it. So that's my rule, I suppose. I won't stand by and let you suffer if I can do anything about it."

He blinked. Apparently the kiss and the hug hadn't

shocked him as much as her talking back to him with belligerence in her voice.

A tiny smile tilted the corners of his mouth. "I've spent most of the day thinking I'd never have anything to laugh about again. You just proved me wrong. Have I had a lioness in my midst disguised as a kitty cat all this time?"

Her face heated. "Things are about to change between us," she said quietly. "Are you sure this is what you want?"

He leaned forward and brushed his lips against her cheek, barely a touch at all. "I am. I do."

Something made her legs go all wonky. For a moment, she thought she might faint. If that was how a kiss from Jonathan affected her when he was being amused and affectionate, God help her if she ever experienced the real thing. She tried to suck in more air. "Okay then."

Jonathan looped his arm through hers and turned them around. "It's late," he said. "We need to get you home."

She would have slept in her car on the street if it had meant not ending this extraordinary interlude. His skin was warm against hers. She wanted to lean her head against his shoulder, but of course, she did not.

Something had happened here on this beach. The tides in her relationship with her boss had shifted to something far more real, more intimate. Unfortunately, she couldn't even be glad about that change, because it meant she was losing him.

Back at the car, they dusted off their feet and used a water bottle for their impromptu cleanup. When Jonathan started the engine, he glanced sideways at her. "Dessert and coffee before we head back?"

Yes, her heart cried. Yes!

She shook her head. "It's been a long day. I'd better not."

"Of course." He paused. "I think it goes without saying, but you must promise not to talk to anyone about my condition. *No one*. If the truth were to come out, our stock prices might plummet. Until I have a plan in place to handle the gossip and the fallout, there can't be a whisper that anything is wrong."

"I understand. You have my word."

They barely spoke during the drive back. Without the beauty of the ocean and the beach to distract them, the enormity of Jonathan's diagnosis filled her with aching compassion and raw regret. How could this be happening? It wasn't fair. Not for him, not for his family, not for anyone.

But whoever said life was fair?

When they reached the Tarleton house, she exited the vehicle and stood beside her own car. In the unflattering glow of the security light beneath the house, Jonathan's expression was grim, his skin sallow.

He seemed so damned brave and alone. She couldn't leave him like this.

Rounding the car, she went to him and slid her arms around his waist. He wasn't her boss at this moment. He was a man nearing a perilous cliff, a human being with little more than sheer grit and determination to help him face the days ahead.

At first, he was unresponsive. Maybe her emotion was only making things worse. Finally, a great shudder racked his frame. He buried his face in her hair and clung to her tightly.

Her tears wet his shirt. "I'm so sorry, Jonathan. So very sorry."

They stood there like that for long moments. It might have been a minute or five or ten.

At last he straightened. He used his thumb to catch a tear on her lower lashes. "Don't cry for me, Lizzy. I'd rather it be me than someone else. Hell, I probably deserve it."

She stepped back reluctantly and stared up at him. "Don't joke," she said. "There's nothing remotely funny about this situation."

His smile was both weary and beautiful. "Isn't that what they say? I have to laugh to keep from crying?"

"I can't imagine you crying. You're tough and resourceful. Very macho, in fact."

"Is that how you see me?"

She shrugged. "You've been my boss. I only looked at you one way."

"And now?"

Was this some kind of trick question?

She hesitated. "I know you're human, Jonathan. Just like the rest of us. But I never wanted to test that theory. I'd rather think of you as a superhero than admit the truth right now."

His wince echoed her honesty. "You and me both. This won't be easy for me. And I'm not talking about the physical part. The prospect of not being in control scares the hell out of me."

"I'll be here, Jonathan. But you *have* to tell your family. They'll be so hurt if you don't and they find out another way."

He shoved his hands into his pockets. "I'll tell them. I swear. I just need a little time to wrap my head around this."

"Have you thought about seeing a counselor or a priest… someone like that? It might help."

He cupped her cheek in one big palm, his touch burning her skin and sending shivers of sensation in every direction. "I have you, Lisette. That will have to do."

Three

Lisette cried herself to sleep. And then had nightmares. Waking at dawn was a relief for half a second until the truth came rushing back with a vengeance. Jonathan was dying.

Thank God, she hadn't turned in her resignation before he told her about his illness. He needed her. She was determined to give him all the love and care she could muster…but without letting on that she had loved him for a long time. That news would make things worse. She knew it instinctively.

The only reason he had asked for her help was because she was an outsider he could trust. So—not family.

Walking into the downtown office that morning was anticlimactic. Jonathan was on a conference call with someone in England. The entire floor was abuzz with the usual ebb and flow of projects and activities.

Lisette loved working for Tarleton Shipping. As hard as it had been to make the decision to leave, it was impossible to imagine this place without Jonathan. She pressed a hand to her stomach where nervous butterflies performed a tango.

Last night at the beach house had changed everything.

Somehow, she was supposed to carry on as if nothing was out of the ordinary, but at the same time she had to monitor Jonathan's behavior and be ready to step in whenever he needed her. She wondered if he was regretting that he had told her the truth.

Yesterday had been an extraordinarily hard time for him.

Hearing news like that would rattle anyone. The fact that Lisette had shown up at his house in the wake of his crisis might have had something to do with him asking her to take on a role that was so personal and critical.

If she knew him well—and she did—it was probably best to pretend nothing had changed. It was going to be very hard not to hover and treat him like he was sick. She couldn't help feeling responsible, especially because he was keeping his family in the dark for now.

The day spun by, entirely unremarkable in its *ordinariness*. People came and went. Meetings happened. Jonathan whirled from one thing to the next, barely speaking to her in the interim.

She could almost believe that last night was a dream.

Occasionally, though, she caught his eye across the room, and a connection quivered between them. The feeling of intimacy startled her. He had let her in on something intensely personal. There would be no going back from this.

She had craved a personal connection with Jonathan. But not at this price.

How was she going to face the days ahead?

On her lunch hour, her friend Rebekah coaxed her out of the building. "Let's walk," she said. "It's not quite so hot today, and I've been wanting to try that new restaurant over near the market."

There was nothing unusual about the situation. Still, Lisette felt Jonathan's gaze searing her back as she exited the executive suite of offices. Did he expect her to dance attendance on him 24/7?

Rebekah called her out on her odd mood while they ate. "What's wrong with you?" she asked, frowning. "You've barely said a word. Are you feeling okay?"

"I'm fine," Lisette said. "A lot on my mind."

Her friend's expression softened. "I just realized. Today

marks eight months since your mother died, doesn't it? I'm sorry, hon."

Guilt swamped Lisette. Her friend had metaphorically and literally held her hand during some very dark days. "I'm getting used to her being gone. I find new reasons to be happy every day. My mother wouldn't have wanted me to be gloomy all the time."

"Well, good," Rebekah said. "Because Robbie's friend who just moved here from Memphis wants to meet you. I thought we could go to dinner together Friday night."

Lisette winced inwardly. Rebekah had been on her case for months to start dating. Caring for her mother and working full-time had not left any room for a social life. Now that her mother was gone and months had passed, it made sense for Lisette to get back in the game.

She was torn. The trouble was, she didn't want to meet a string of strange guys, even though she knew her dream of marriage and a baby required some kind of change on her part. She didn't need clubbing and dancing to be happy. The only man she wanted was Jonathan. Their new situation would give her a little piece of him. Would it be enough to justify putting her dreams on hold?

"Sure," she said, trying hard to appreciate her friend's enthusiasm. "That sounds great."

The following two days passed in much the same manner, at least when it came to Jonathan's behavior. He didn't *look* sick. Aside from downing the occasional over-the-counter meds, his bronzed skin and boundless energy seemed to belie his diagnosis.

When Friday afternoon rolled around, Lisette was almost glad Jonathan was away from the office. Their new relationship made her both tense and uncertain. It was a relief to step out into the sunshine and walk to her car. She had just enough time to dash home, shower and change before she met Rebekah and the others at the restaurant.

It was a shock to run into her boss in the parking garage. He looked frazzled, but otherwise normal. "You're leaving?" he asked.

She nodded her head. "It's five thirty. Was there something you needed?"

His small frown took her by surprise. "I thought we might have dinner together," he said. "To talk about how we're going to handle this new work situation."

She flushed, feeling the heat creep from her breasts to her hairline. "I'm sorry," she said stiffly. "I have plans."

He seemed shocked. "A date?"

"That's a personal question," she snapped. His obvious surprise nicked her pride. It was true she had lived like a nun while caring for her mother. And, yes, she was five years Jonathan's senior. But she was hardly a pariah.

His gaze darkened. "I'm sorry to have held you up," he said, his tone stiff and formal. "I'll see you Monday morning."

The bleak expression in his eyes caught her heart and squeezed it hard. She was trying so desperately to protect herself, to avoid letting him hurt her, that she was forgetting the hell he was facing.

"Wait," she said impulsively as he turned to walk away. "What about lunch at my place Sunday? I'll cook for you."

Some of the starch left his spine. At last a smile tilted those gorgeous masculine lips. "That sounds great, Lisette. If you're sure it's not too much trouble."

"Not at all. And by the way, I've moved since my mother died. I'm in a condo in North Charleston now." Her salary was generous, but it didn't stretch to upscale places in the historic district.

He nodded. "I'll get the address from your file."

"Noon?"

"I'll be there."

The unexpected encounter meant she had to rush like

crazy to go home and then meet her friend. She made it to the restaurant with two minutes to spare. Her blind date for the evening was overly chatty, but all in all a decent guy. Under other circumstances, she might have hoped for a second date.

As it was, though, she found her mind wandering time and again during the pleasant meal to Jonathan. What was he doing? How was he feeling?

When the two females left the table to visit the ladies' room, Rebekah leaned in to whisper conspiratorially. "Well, what do you think of him? He likes you. I can tell."

Lisette made use of the facilities and then washed her hands. "I don't know, Rebekah. He isn't really my type."

Rebekah snorted. "You don't *have* a type," she said. "This is the first time I've coaxed you out of the house. At least give him a chance. It's not like you've got your heart set on someone else."

"I'll keep an open mind, I swear."

Lisette had been careful at work to hide her feelings about Jonathan, from Rebekah in particular. She'd kept her hopeless crush a secret from everyone. When Lisette had been planning to resign, she was going to tell her friend that she was in a rut after her mother's death and that she needed a fresh start. Now those heavy-handed explanations weren't going to be necessary.

But there would be other questions when she began spending more time with Jonathan. She would have to spin the story somehow to protect his secret. And if her so-called promotion became public knowledge, the situation would definitely become awkward.

At last the interminable evening wound to a close. She had never been more glad to head home and crash. Even then, she couldn't stop thinking about her boss. He had chosen to confide his secret in her. She couldn't pretend any longer that she didn't want to be much more than his stand-in at work.

He was ferociously smart and driven. The man *did* have a sense of humor, but it was dry and often kept under wraps. Because his father had been forced to step down as president when his health deteriorated, Jonathan bore a heavy load of responsibility.

All day Saturday Lisette obsessed about what to cook, what to wear. She was terrified of letting her boss know that her emotions were involved. If she was going to be able to help, she had to let him think she regarded this as a job and nothing more.

By Sunday morning, she had worked herself into a full-blown tizzy. When her curling iron failed to do what she wanted it to do, she gave up styling her thick, straight hair and put it up in a ponytail.

She didn't want to look like she thought this was a date, so she put on an older pair of jeans, black ballerina flats and a cute teal top with a lemon print. A dash of lip gloss and some mascara took care of the rest.

By the time her tomato sauce was ready and the simple fruit salad cut and arranged in crystal bowls, she felt mildly nauseous. What was she thinking? She should have resigned as she had planned.

She was weak when it came to her boss. This was a chance to be with him in a way she wouldn't otherwise. It "was" an intimacy of sorts. A dangerous intimacy she both yearned for and feared.

Instead of getting *over* Jonathan, she was only going to fall more deeply under his spell and end up having her heart broken into a million unmendable pieces. Broken because he couldn't love her back, and broken because soon he would be gone from her life forever.

Her buzzer rang at exactly eleven fifty-nine. That was *so* Jonathan. The man made punctuality a religion.

She opened the door and managed a smile. "Good morning, or I guess it's officially afternoon now. Come on in."

Her knees wobbled when the scent of his crisp aftershave teased her nostrils. His broad shoulders were encased in a simple white cotton shirt. Rolled-up sleeves revealed muscular arms tanned from years in the sun. An expensive watch gleamed on one wrist.

He was dressed more casually than she had ever seen him. Jeans, too, like her. Leather deck shoes that drew attention to his sexy feet.

When she realized she was getting turned on by the man's feet, she knew she was in big trouble.

Her big, sexy guest smiled. "Smells amazing in here."

Jonathan was gobsmacked and trying not to show it. What had happened to the prim and proper woman who managed his business affairs with such aplomb? Suddenly… today…she looked barely twenty. Her smooth, creamy skin was unadorned. That perky ponytail bared the nape of her neck.

Her lightweight summer blouse fit her generous breasts snugly. And those skinny jeans? Hell. A man could be excused for wanting to cup that heart-shaped butt in his two hands. His libido, which in recent days had been squashed, roared back to life in a big way.

Was his reaction inappropriate? Should he try harder to ignore the attraction? Or, under the circumstances, could he be excused for wanting to let himself finally get closer to Lisette?

He shifted from one foot to the other. "This is very nice of you," he said. "I've been looking forward to a home-cooked meal."

Lisette gave him a look, one eyebrow raised. "You have the best housekeeper and chef in the state of South Carolina."

"It's not the same as having a woman cook for me."

He hadn't intended to bring flirtation into the mix, not at all. But the comment slipped out.

Far from being offended, Lisette gave him a shy smile. "Sit down at the table," she said. "Everything is almost ready."

He sprawled in a trendy retro chair that reminded him of something his great-grandmother might have used back in the 1950s. The Formica-top table was aqua and white. In the center sat a white hobnail vase filled with daisies. Yellow place mats had been set with flatware and cloth napkins.

"I like your condo," he said.

"Thanks. I needed a change of scenery after Mom died. This building is very friendly, and I like the neighborhood."

"Does the guy you were out with Friday night live here?" The question popped out of his mouth before he could censor it. Entirely inappropriate from boss to employee. Entirely understandable from a man who felt like he was losing everything. His whole life had shifted. Inappropriate feelings he had suppressed for so long in the past were coming to the fore.

Lisette had her back to him, grating fresh parmesan cheese for their spaghetti. He saw her go still. But she didn't turn around. "No," she said quietly. "That was a blind date my friend Rebekah set up."

"Rebekah in Purchasing?"

"Yes."

He drummed his fingers on the table. "Sorry," he muttered. "None of my business."

She turned to face him with an unreadable expression on her face. "This is not going to work unless we can both speak freely. Under the circumstances, I understand that you want to know more about my life. If I'm going to help you, you have to trust me."

"I *do* trust you," he said quickly. "Completely."

"But?" Her half smile called him out.

Clearly she was reading his ambivalence. "I think you were right about the possibility of people resenting you if I suddenly give you carte blanche to make decisions."

She nodded slowly. "It *will* look odd. Does this mean you've changed your mind?"

He stood to pace restlessly, shoving his hands in his pockets. Second-guessing himself was a novelty he didn't enjoy. In almost any situation he was able to cut through to the center of a matter and make decisions...good decisions. But that was business.

This new scenario with Lisette comprised a hundred more layers of uncertainty. "I haven't changed my mind," he said. "But I've had more time to think about this, and I've come to a few conclusions."

"Sounds important," she said lightly, pouring each of them a glass of iced tea.

"It will keep until after we've eaten. I always think better on a full stomach. And have your wine," he said. "You don't have to abstain on my account."

She shook her head. "I happen to love iced tea. Mine is very good, if I do say so myself. My grandmother taught my mom, and my mom taught me."

"I know very little about your family," he said.

"Not much to tell." Lisette set white porcelain salad bowls, dressing, and the two plates of steaming pasta on the table, along with a smaller plate of fragrant garlic bread. Jonathan held out her chair as she seated herself. Then he took the spot opposite her.

"Is your father still living?" he asked. "I don't remember hearing you say."

She shook her head. "My mother never spoke of him. As a kid I fantasized that he was a secret agent or a prince in some foreign country. Unfortunately, I think the truth is that he just didn't care and walked away."

"Were they married?"

"I believe so. There's a name on my birth certificate. And it's the same last name as my mom's and mine. But she could have made him up."

"Haven't you ever wanted to track him down?"

Lisette grimaced, a bite of spaghetti halfway to her mouth. She set the fork on her plate and sighed. "According to all the books and movies, I should. Want to, I mean. But the truth is, I don't."

"Why not?" Jonathan had cleared most of his plate. He was starving, and the meal was amazing. Lisette had barely picked at her spaghetti. Was it because she was nervous? He hoped not. He wanted things between them to be comfortable. Easy.

Maybe that was an impossible task under the circumstances.

She curled her fingers around the stem of her crystal goblet and wrinkled her nose. "My mom did the best she could for us, but I was a latchkey kid from the time I was eight or nine. Our house wasn't like my friends' houses. It was quiet and empty and lonely. I decided that I would make my own home someday and fill it with color and sound and happiness."

Jonathan nodded and smiled. "You're off to a good start." Inwardly he groaned. His needs and wants were going to be in direct opposition to hers. Was it fair of him to ask so much when he could give her so little in return?

"Thank you." Her cheeks were flushed. It could be the heat from the kitchen, or perhaps she was as aware of him as he was of her. Before today, he would have said that he knew Lisette Stanhope extremely well. Now, here in her cozy, peaceful home, he was finding out how wrong he could be.

Away from the office, she seemed a different person to him. Younger, more vulnerable. Again his conscience

pricked him. Lisette was conscientious and compassionate. Last year when one of their employees suffered an extended illness, Lisette was the one who organized meals
for the family.

She had been a devoted daughter and caretaker to her
mother for a decade or more. Jonathan didn't want to be another burden she had to carry. To be honest, he didn't want
to be *anyone's* burden, but especially not hers.

If they were to enter into this arrangement, the benefits couldn't and shouldn't be one-sided. It was becoming
more and more clear to him that there was only one real
way for this new relationship to work. A drastic step that
would change everything.

As the silence between them lengthened, Lisette finished most of her meal. Jonathan had a second helping of
everything.

"Thank you for cooking," he said. Something about the
simple, hearty meal fed his soul as well as his stomach.
Food was one of a man's appetites. Sexual intimacy was another. The fact that he felt jittery and hungry for his hostess
was as much a shock to him as what he was about to say.

They cleared the table together. Lisette started the dish-
washer, and then she touched him lightly on the shoulder.
"Let's go into the living room. We'll be more comfortable."

The few steps between the two rooms did not give him
time enough to prepare a speech.

Lisette kicked off her shoes and settled onto one end
of the sofa, her legs curled beneath her. "Well," she said.
"Don't keep me in suspense. If I'm not to have a promotion, what's your answer?"

He sucked in a breath, feeling more rattled and off his
game than he had since the day of his diagnosis. "I think
you should marry me."

Four

Lisette blinked, trying not to react. "Um…" Maybe the brain tumor had begun to affect his reasoning. Or maybe she had misheard him.

Jonathan witnessed her shock despite her efforts to play it cool. His neck heated beneath his collar. "I'm not crazy," he muttered. "But it would solve a lot of problems. No one at the office would complain if I make my *wife* my partner. We could work side by side. This is the Tarleton empire. For you to pull off the kinds of decisions you'll be required to make, you need to be family. It's the perfect solution."

Except it wasn't. The mere fact that her emotions went all gooey at the prospect meant she would be seriously crazy to accept such an offer. She wanted him. She wanted to be married, but not like this.

When she had attempted to turn in her resignation last week, she had been imagining a future with an ordinary guy. Maybe a teacher…or an accountant like herself. Two babies. Perhaps three. A small house with toys in the yard and even the proverbial picket fence. Everything she had missed growing up when it was only a single mom and a lonely daughter.

Now fate, or a deity with a messed-up sense of humor, was offering her a skewed version of that dream. "I don't know what to say." It was true. Jonathan had left her speechless.

He sprawled in an armchair, looking masculine and gorgeous and moody. "Say you'll think about it."

She chose her words carefully. "It seems like an extreme measure."

"But you have to admit it's a practical solution."

"Where would we live?"

"Out at the beach house."

"But I just bought this place, and I love it."

"You could sublet it. Or leave it empty and come here when you need a break from…" He waved a hand. "I'll pay for whatever you need. Money won't be a problem. We'll have a prenup that outlines everything you're entitled to when I'm gone."

He was talking about his illness. Addressing the elephant in the room. She didn't want to think about that.

Other issues weighed as heavily. "I'll be hated and vilified," she said. "When the truth comes out. Your family and your friends and your employees will think I deliberately married a dying man to get my hands on a chunk of Tarleton Shipping."

"It doesn't matter what anyone else thinks," he said, his tone truculent. "Our private arrangement is no one else's business. Dad won't question anything, and Mazie isn't going to squawk. She has plenty of her own assets, not to mention the fact that she married J.B."

Jonathan's best friend and his sister had gotten engaged last Christmas. Everyone assumed the two of them would plan a huge Charleston wedding, but the couple had surprised everyone by jetting off to Vegas in the middle of January and tying the knot in a private ceremony. The groom's mother had thrown the party of all parties when they returned.

Lisette had been invited and had attended despite the fact that she hadn't been in a celebratory mood. The gray days of January had exacerbated her grief. The new year had stretched ahead of her, long and lonely.

In the end, the party had done her good. It was fun, for

one thing. It had warmed her heart to see Jonathan's sister so happy and in love with her rakish husband. *J.B.* as he was called, Jackson Beauregard Vaughan, was a real estate tycoon. He and the Tarletons had been friends since they were all children. Only Hartley Tarleton had been missing from the festivities.

Jonathan, himself, had been resplendent that night in a conservative tailored tux. He'd had women flocking around him like so many chattering mynah birds. That had been Lisette's first inkling that she was going to have to either get over her desperate crush somehow or move entirely out of his orbit and find herself a new life.

Now he stared at her so intently her nipples beaded beneath her top. She crossed her arms over her chest. "You can't just toss this at me and expect an instant answer."

His smile was unexpectedly sweet. "I know you, Lizzy. You're a lot like me. Pragmatic. Decisive. You don't dither. I've always admired that about you."

"Flattery will get you nowhere."

He chuckled. "Admit it. My plan makes perfect sense."

Lisette chewed the inside of her lip, far more tempted than she should have been. He hadn't mentioned marriage between them in any context but work. Yet there were a lot of hours in the day when the two of them *wouldn't* be working. How did he foresee that part of their relationship unfolding?

Was this to be a marriage of convenience? A paper commitment that she would look after him and have his back when he asked for assistance? She didn't require a sham marriage to do that. Jonathan was in a very bad situation, and he needed her help. She would give it gladly.

"There must be another way," she said.

"Why make it more difficult than it has to be? I'm asking a hell of a lot, I realize. And to be honest, it will soothe my conscience to know that you'll have financial security when I'm gone. It's the very least I can do considering what you're offering me in return."

"I don't want your money, Jonathan."

"Maybe not, but that's my condition. Life won't be easy for whoever takes over Tarleton Shipping. It will either have to be you or Mazie, and I'm almost a hundred percent certain she doesn't want that responsibility."

"Neither do I," Lisette protested. "I'll help you all I can in the short term. Because we're friends and you're a decent human being who is in a terrible spot. But I won't profit from simply doing the right thing."

"So what happens to the business when I'm no longer able to look after things?"

"I don't know, Jonathan. I really don't. Maybe we both need to give this some thought before we make any irrevocable decisions."

"I'd like to work on the legal documents soon." A bleak look flashed across his face. "The uncertainty of my condition compels me to get things nailed down as quickly as possible."

"How long do I have to decide?"

He shrugged. "Forty-eight hours?"

It wasn't much time. She inhaled, her fingers digging into the arm of the sofa. "And what about the physical side of our relationship?"

For the barest of moments, his jaw dropped. Perhaps her candor had shocked him. But he recovered quickly. His gaze was calm though his eyes flashed hot. "That will, of course, be entirely up to you. I don't think it's the kind of question that should be addressed in a prenup. You're a very appealing woman. We'll be living together. Our arrangement can be platonic or physical. I won't ask anything of you that you aren't prepared to give."

The intimation was unmistakable. He would be *interested* in taking her to bed. Hearing such a thing destroyed

Lisette's ability to think clearly. It had never occurred to her that she was the kind of woman to attract Jonathan's attention under *any* circumstances. To have him address the subject so matter-of-factly stunned her.

"Very well," she said slowly. "I agree to think about all this for forty-eight hours."

Jonathan's nod was terse. "I'll get my lawyer started on the nuts and bolts of the contract. You should be considering anything specific you want included in the document."

"Like what? Movie-star demands? Orange M&M's on my desk every morning? Water from the French Alps? A personal assistant?"

At last Jonathan ceased wearing a path in her rug and sat down at the opposite end of the sofa with a weary grin. "Very funny. But the details are important to me. If we go through with this, your whole life will change. Any personal dreams you have will need to be put on hold. It hardly seems fair, but I'm desperate enough to ask."

He was right. The truth was sobering. She would be giving him six months of her life or—if Jonathan were lucky—maybe a year.

All the reasons she had wanted to resign still existed. Jonathan was almost thirty-two years old. She was thirty-seven. Far too old for him under normal circumstances, at least by her reckoning. Over the long years of caring for her mother, Lisette had missed out on all sorts of coming-of-age experiences. The carefree vacations abroad. The fun and frivolity of a weekend social life. Casual dating. She didn't regret it. She would never regret the time she had spent with her mother. And she would do it again in a heartbeat.

When you loved someone, you gave whatever the situation demanded in order to make that person a priority. Jonathan had chosen her because he thought she could be objective. It was her task to prove him right. She would make the sacrifice gladly, but he could never know why. He could never know she loved him. That knowledge would only add to the burden he carried.

It seemed so damned unfair to become part of his life and yet still never have him. Not completely. Her throat was thick with tears.

She sensed he needed assurance that she was taking him seriously. "Don't worry, Jonathan. I'll obsess about this day and night, and then I'll settle in for the long haul. I'm not flippant about the situation, honestly."

"Fair enough." He glanced at his watch. "I've got work to do, so I'd better head back to the beach."

"It's the weekend. Don't you think you need to rest?"

"I'll rest when I'm dead."

It was the kind of comedic one-liner workaholics used all the time, a way to describe and justify a manic schedule. Today Lisette found no humor in it.

She stood when he did, a good six feet of real estate between them.

Jonathan rolled his neck and shoved his hands into his pockets. "Thanks for the meal. It was fabulous."

Suddenly, she knew that she couldn't enter into this unconventional agreement without at least a few answers to questions that were...*sensitive*. She and Jonathan were going to be very close. Especially as the months passed and he leaned on her more and more.

She was tired of living like a nun...tired of denying she was a woman with needs and desires like everyone else. She wanted Jonathan, had wanted him for so very long. If his oblique remarks were revealing, he wanted her, too.

Before she could lose her nerve, she went to him and put her hands on his shoulders. Though she felt him tense, she continued her experiment.

"Will you kiss me, Jonathan?" she whispered, her throat tight. "I need to know if we have a spark, or if I'm only going to be your stand-in at work and possibly your nurse. I'm not making light of this. It's important to me."

His eyes could range from cognac to dark chocolate. Right now they were lit with a flame that took her breath and made her knees go weak. "As you wish," he said quietly.

Carefully he cupped her neck in two big hands and tilted her head slightly to one side. After that—as their breath mingled—he found her mouth and covered her lips with his. "Oh…" Her startled exclamation was involuntary. At first, the kiss was awkward and slightly embarrassing. He was her boss. She was his assistant. Before today, she would never have dreamed of crossing this line.

His kiss was firm and perfect, but her body was rigid, uncertain.

Jonathan made a sound low in his throat…a groan. A ragged sigh. "Relax, Lisette."

She tried, she really did. Her universe was cartwheeling out of control. He dragged her closer, deepening the kiss, pressing her to him in such a way that she couldn't miss the evidence of his body responding to hers. His sex rose and thrust against her abdomen.

Pulling back was the correct thing to do. Breaking the connection. Reclaiming sanity.

Neither of them chose to be wise.

Jonathan tugged the tie from her ponytail and sifted his fingers through the thickness of her shoulder-length hair. When his fingers brushed the nape of her neck, she shivered.

She was within seconds of pulling him down onto her sofa when her dormant sense of self-preservation shouted a warning. This wasn't a fairy tale. She was about to travel a road that ended in disaster.

Reluctantly she stepped back, breathing hard, trembling in every cell and trying not to show it. "Well," she said, trying for amused nonchalance. "I suppose we answered that question. If we decide to be friends with benefits, the spark is there."

Jonathan's frown was dark. With his hair disheveled where her hands had raked through it and his face flushed with the remnants of arousal, he looked dangerously disgruntled.

"It's not something to joke about. I won't be with other women if you're my wife. I'd expect the same courtesy from you."

She wanted to laugh. The thought of sleeping with another man while married to her boss was ludicrous. But Jonathan would probably misunderstand her reaction. So she pressed her lips together and tried to look penitent.

"Of course," she muttered. "One step at a time. First we have to decide if marriage would be convenient or impossibly convoluted."

He folded his arms and took a stance that was definitely more stubborn male than obsequious suitor. "There's nothing to decide. You know I'm right. It's the only way. Unless you've changed your mind about helping me."

She lifted her chin, matching him glare for glare. "I won't be bullied. I want to examine the pros and cons from every direction. You're correct in saying that I'm decisive as a rule. But I've never been an impulsive person. I don't plan to start now."

He would have been well within his rights to point out that her recent behavior was damned impulsive. Fortunately for her, he held his tongue on that matter.

"Tuesday night," he said firmly. "My father is taking an overnight fishing trip with J.B.'s dad. They've been planning it for months. I'll have the housekeeper fix us a meal, and then we can walk the beach."

Lisette nodded slowly. "Okay. I like the sound of that. And just so we're clear, *you* can change your mind, too. I know the news of your diagnosis threw you into a tailspin. It would have knocked anyone on their butt. Give yourself more time to think this through. You won't hurt my feelings if you see another way out of your situation."

She didn't tell him that if he did, she would soon be gone.

Jonathan shook his head doggedly. "I've already come up with the perfect plan. Now it's simply a question of implementation."

"Very well."

He reached for his wallet and keys. "You'll be at work in the morning?"

She raised an eyebrow. "Of course. Where else would I be?"

Nodding tersely, he strode toward the door. "I'll see you then." It was a small condo. He was on the doorstep in moments.

"Wait," she cried.

He turned and stared at her. "What?"

"Jonathan…" She trailed off, not entirely sure how to say what she wanted to say.

"What?"

Impatience was painted all over his face. For a man who had seemed very happy to spend part of the afternoon with her, he was now clearly itching to leave. Maybe he had regrets, too.

"You don't seem all that sick," she said slowly, not wanting to anger him. "I know about the headaches, but what if the doctor was wrong?"

His jaw jutted and his hands fisted at his sides. "You don't understand," he said. "I've been to see half a dozen highly respected medical professionals in the last nine months. I even missed Christmas with my sister because one of those damn doctors suggested I spend a week in the desert learning meditation techniques."

The disgust in his voice made her grin. "That doesn't sound like you at all, no offense."

"None taken. The point is, no one thought my headaches were anything terribly serious until I went back for a second series of visits with my doctor here in Charleston. I wasn't getting any better. The senior radiologist read my MRI and CT scans. The report details were all there in black-and-white, Lisette. The doc told me flat out. I can't keep grasping for hope when there is none. I've decided to deal with this the best way I know how. If you can't live with that, then I'll simply hire a nurse when the time comes."

"And Tarleton Shipping?"

"Mazie will have to come up with a plan."

Lisette understood the futility of empty hope. She had certainly dealt with the phenomenon on multiple occasions during her mother's illness. But to imagine Jonathan dying was more than she could wrap her brain around.

"I'm sorry," she said quietly. "I won't mention it again."

"Thank you."

Once more she was struck by how alone he seemed. He did have family, but no one could walk this road with him. Her heart twisted. "I'll give you my answer Tuesday night, I swear."

Jonathan grimaced. "I shouldn't even be bringing you into this."

"I'm sort of the perfect choice," she said. "With my mother gone now, I have no demands on my time. We'll figure this out, Jonathan. We will."

His gaze seemed to settle on her lips. Or was it her breasts? "And you won't say anything to anyone?"

"No. It will be our secret, no matter what happens."

Five

Jonathan went home and hid himself away in his office, studying spreadsheets…making plans for a future he might not experience. More than anything, he wanted to talk to J.B. They had been best friends since grade school. J.B. wouldn't coddle him or shower him with false sympathy.

But once J.B. knew, there would be no keeping the secret from Mazie. Jonathan wasn't ready to break his sister's heart. The two of them had always been close, and they were even closer now that Hartley had abandoned the family.

Jonathan wrestled with unanswerable questions. How long did he have? Would he live to see Christmas? No matter how many novels he had read or movies he had seen, when the bitter news came to a man personally, it was a hell of a lot different from fiction.

He didn't want to die. He wanted to live.

Maybe the Tarletons had been cursed from the beginning. His mother's mental instability. His father's wavering health at a relatively early age. Hartley's betrayal. And now this.

Jonathan had read his share of pirate legends. Tales of buried treasures that were never found. The very spot of land on which the Tarleton home stood was reputed to have been the lair of the famous buccaneer Bloody Bart, an aristocratic Englishman who had been exiled to the New World after bringing shame to his family during a fatal duel.

Unlike the seventeenth-century pirate, Jonathan had no-where to run. He would have to face his demons head-on.

After dinner with his father and a few games of chess, Jonathan escaped the house to walk the beach. The night was wild and windy, the tiny grains of sand scouring his exposed skin. The minor discomfort did not deter him.

Here in the privacy of his own company, he allowed himself to remember the afternoon with Lisette. Her home was warm and welcoming. Even walking through the front door had made him feel a sense of hope.

His reaction made no sense, not really. Hope was a com-modity in short supply. He was a bastard for asking his ex-ecutive assistant to give up months of her life to make *his* more palatable. She had been through so much.

But as guilty as he felt for involving her, he couldn't bring himself to rescind his request. He was bone-deep scared. He *needed* Lisette.

Her light and positivity and her ability to break monu-mental tasks into manageable pieces would keep him sane as uncertainty dogged his waking hours over the weeks and months to come. She would secure the Tarleton legacy, and thus give him peace.

The fact that Lisette had so matter-of-factly brought a potential physical relationship into the mix told him more than anything that he had been right in thinking she could handle what was to come.

Of *course*, sex would rear its head. A man and a woman. Legally wed. Friends who trusted each other and liked each other.

For his part, it was more than *like*. His body had re-sponded urgently to her kiss. He didn't think he had ever before let on that he was attracted to her. At work, he had been scrupulously circumspect.

Yet when she bravely addressed the possible physical nature of their potential agreement, his libido had jumped in immediately. Reliving the moment when his lips claimed hers in a searing kiss made his breathing unsteady and his sex hard. If he had known what it would be like to hold her in his arms so intimately, he might never have been able to keep up the guise of boss and assistant as long as he had.

He craved Lisette.

Could he in good conscience allow their agreement to include physical intimacy? As much as he wanted to say, *Hell yes*, the more rational side of his brain urged caution.

If Lisette agreed to his unconventional proposal, both of their lives would change significantly. If they married, soon the world would look at both of them differently. Look and wonder...

Jonathan was hiding an enormous secret, and he had demanded that Lisette keep his secret, too. He was expecting a lot from her. Some would say too much.

Still, when he imagined having her in his bed each night, the terrible weight that had rested on his shoulders when the doctor delivered the grim news seemed not quite so terrible. She would stand beside him when things got tough. She would have his back.

What did he have to offer her in return? She claimed not to care about his money, and from what he knew of her, that was certainly true. He'd tried to give her an unexplained bonus when her mother's medical bills mounted precipitously. Lisette had seen through his ruse and declined politely.

She was a proud woman. And self-sufficient. He had no idea what her financial circumstances were. Had her mother's extended illness been a monetary stress? And were there perhaps still bills outstanding?

Then and there, he decided on two of his nonnegotiable points for the prenup. First of all, he would pay off any of his new wife's debts, whether or not they stemmed from her mother's care. Secondly, he would buy Lisette a beach

house…something relatively small and cozy and charming…with ample hurricane insurance to ensure that she
would always be able to rebuild after any kind of natural
disaster.

After those two decisions, his mental gyrations ground
to a halt. What did he really know about his self-possessed
assistant? Not much of a personal nature. Did she want to
travel the world? Explore places off the beaten path? Take
culinary lessons in France? Go back to school and get a
doctorate in something?

He wanted to shower her with evidence of his gratitude,
but he had no clue where to start. If he was successful in
persuading her to marry him, perhaps his immediate goal
should be to establish an emotional relationship with Lisette. Learn her likes and dislikes. Dig deep into the personality of a woman who was in many ways a mystery to him.

When his legs were aching, and his throat was dry with
thirst, he finally turned around and made his way back
home. Tuesday night. It seemed an eternity to wait.

Still, nothing good could come of this unless Lisette decided to help him of her own free will. No pressure from
Jonathan. No emotional manipulation.

For a man accustomed to shaping the world and his destiny with bare hands and unflinching determination, this
wait-and-see approach was sheer torment.

His customary store of patience had run out.

He wanted to call her right now. Show up on her doorstep again. Demand that she see things his way.

Instead, he let himself into the big, silent house, ate a
cold roast beef sandwich and then climbed the stairs to
his bedroom. He paused in the doorway, trying to view
the masculine furnishings and dark colors from a female
perspective. The first order of business would be to insist
that Lisette redecorate. If she became his wife, this suite
of room would be *theirs*, not his.

It was an important distinction.

The wind on his forehead during the beach walk had brought the headache back, but it was bearable. He showered and climbed beneath the covers.

Instead of contemplating his own demise, he closed his eyes and tried to recreate the memory of Lisette's lips beneath his. Her taste. The alluring shape of her body.

Physical arousal was almost a relief despite the lack of a partner. How long would he feel like himself? He couldn't imagine a night where he slept beside his wife and didn't want to make love to her.

Groaning and cursing, he rolled to his stomach and buried his face in his arms. One slender woman held a great deal of his fate in her hands. She couldn't save him ultimately, but her answer would have a huge impact on how the next six months unfolded.

He knew what he wanted. Now he could only hope that she wanted it, too...

When Lisette arrived at work Monday morning, the boss was not in the building. No one seemed to know where he was, in fact.

She should have been relieved. Not having to face him meant she could get her work done. But her imagination ran amok. Had he suffered some kind of collapse? Was he regretting that he had shared his secret with her? Had his lawyer cautioned him about marriage under these circumstances?

Was Jonathan, even now, wondering how to tell her he had changed his mind?

By lunchtime he still had not made an appearance. No phone calls. No texts. No emails.

Only a visit from Rebekah managed to derail Lisette's escalating worry.

The other woman glanced at her watch. "You ready to

eat? The cafeteria downstairs actually has a couple of good choices today."

Lisette shook her head. "I'd rather grab a yogurt and peanuts and take a walk, if you don't mind."

Rebekah was easygoing and cheerful. "Suits me," she said. "Let me get my sneakers out of my desk, and I'll meet you down front."

Thirty minutes later, warm and breathing hard, they found a shaded bench in the park and sat down to eat their brown bag lunches. Both of them had small fridges in their offices for just such an occasion.

Lisette's friend sighed, lifting her face to the leafy canopy overhead. "It's days like this I almost wish I were a carriage driver. I could spend the whole day outdoors."

"Sure you could. Educating grumpy tourists with history they don't care about. Wiping gum off the seats half a dozen times a day. Breathing horse sweat and car exhaust fumes."

Rebekah lifted both eyebrows. "Wow. What put you in such a prickly mood?"

"Sorry." Lisette grimaced. "I didn't sleep last night."

"You should try melatonin. I hear it works wonders."

Probably not under the current circumstances. "Maybe I will." Rebekah never had insomnia, to hear her tell it.

Her friend stood up and stretched. "I suppose we'd better be getting back. I hear the big boss frowns on slackers."

Her silly jest made Lisette squirm inwardly. "I wouldn't know. I've barely had time to breathe today. And that's with him MIA. It's worse when he's actually around. The man's brain never stops."

They took their time walking back. Rebekah tucked her sunglasses on top of her head when the sun went behind a cloud. She waved at a kid in a stroller and then glanced at Lisette. "Tamara and Nicole want us to get together soon and do some planning for the Alaska trip."

Lisette's heart dropped. How could she have forgotten?

The four women had put down hefty deposits for a fabulous Inside Passage adventure in early September. "Um, I may have to bow out. Something has come up."

It was a clunky excuse at best. Rebekah stopped dead in the center of the sidewalk and gawked. "What are you talking about? This whole thing was your idea from the beginning."

It was true. Lisette had wanted to do something big and exciting to mark her new unencumbered lifestyle. She grieved her mother deeply, but for the first time in her adult life, she was now free to go and do and try things she had missed for so long. The Alaskan cruise had seemed like the perfect choice.

"It may seem crazy, and I don't know how to explain, but I can't be gone this fall."

"Why?" Rebekah's furrowed brow and perplexed expression were entirely justified.

"It's a secret," Lisette said weakly. "And it's not mine to tell."

Rebekah's face tightened with hurt. "I see."

"You don't," Lisette said urgently, taking her friend's arm. "I'd tell you if I could, but I swear it's important."

Rebekah pulled away. "You do realize that you sound ridiculous?" She shook her head in disgust and continued walking.

Lisette hurried to catch up. "I'll be able to tell you sometime, but not yet. Please don't be mad."

The Tarleton Shipping building loomed in front of them. Rebekah sailed through the front door without pause. They both boarded the elevator in silence. Unfortunately, three other employees stepped in as well. Purchasing was on the third floor. Lisette had to go all the way to the top.

When the quiet ding sounded and the doors slid open at three, Rebekah didn't say a word. Lisette's heart clenched. "I'll call you tonight," she said, trying not to sound desperate.

Rebekah's nod was curt. "Whatever."

And then the doors closed.

For the remainder of the afternoon, Lisette's stomach clenched in turmoil. This thing with Jonathan had blown up so quickly, she had not thought about the impact secrecy would have in her social circle. With no family to speak of except for a handful of distant cousins, her tight-knit group of friends in Charleston *was* her family. She couldn't afford to lose a single one of them over this charade, and certainly not Rebekah.

At four thirty, Jonathan still hadn't made an appearance.

Screw that. If the two of them were going to be partners in this terrible, sad experience, she wouldn't be pushed aside. Either she was central to Jonathan's life or she wasn't.

With her hands shaking, she pulled out her phone and sent a text to his private number. Where are you? I'm worried...

Ten minutes passed. Then twenty. She shut down her computer and tidied her desk. Anger and frustration began to edge out the worry. Jonathan couldn't expect her to be fully involved in his life and yet treat her like an afterthought. That wouldn't work. Period.

Just as she was about to head home, her phone finally dinged.

Sorry. I got a call before sunrise about a crisis at the New Orleans shipyard. They needed me on-site immediately. Everything has been resolved. I should be back in town before midnight.

Even as relief eased the knot in her chest, her misgivings grew. Was this the kind of thing Jonathan might expect her to handle in the upcoming weeks? She knew the workings of Tarleton Shipping inside and out, but that didn't mean she was adequately prepared to play his role. Her repeated assurances to him that she would be happy to help now made her feel trapped and anxious.

She wasn't the boss. Even if she married Jonathan, what did she know about imitating a man who was an alpha leader, a charismatic figure who could calm storms with his mere presence? Signing checks and directing meetings was one thing. But what about moments like today? Could she handle it?

All evening she brooded, wondering if it would be cowardly to back out. Jonathan was not alone. He had his sister and his father, and even his friend and brother-in-law, J.B.

Jonathan Tarleton wasn't without resources, emotional or otherwise.

Though it would seem cruel and unfeeling, she could still submit her letter of resignation. End the relationship. Walk away while she still had her pride and most of her heart.

Again she asked herself why Jonathan had suggested marriage. He claimed it was so that no one would question her legitimacy when she acted on his behalf. At some level, the explanation made sense. But what if he wanted marriage so he could manipulate her? Maybe he thought a legal union would give him more control.

In the privacy of her own home, her apprehension grew. After years of heavy responsibilities, she was now free to live her life on her own terms. Why would she give that up, knowing that to get entangled with Jonathan meant pain and heartache?

Deep in her heart, she knew why. She loved him desperately, and she wanted this time with him, however short it might be.

In the midst of her soul-searching, her cell phone rang. The number was all too familiar.

She hit the button. "Hello?"

Jonathan's voice rumbled in her ear. "It's me." He sounded tired.

"Are you home?"

"I am."

The stilted conversation was wince-worthy. He was her boss. She was his executive assistant. Despite their recent interactions, nothing had changed. Yet. She cleared her throat. "Did everything go well?"

"It did. Eventually. One of our foremen was accused of taking a bribe to use a Tarleton Shipping container for unlawful transport in exchange for drugs. The Feds were there. It was a huge mess. Fortunately, one of our solid guys reported what was about to happen. I've promoted him, by the way."

"Is he in danger now?"

"Thankfully, no. It wasn't some big international cartel. Just a local boy trying to make a buck."

"Ah. I'm glad it's over."

Silence fell.

Lisette jumped in before he could say anything else. "If you don't mind, Jonathan, I'd like to take the day off tomorrow. I have a lot to think about."

Six

Jonathan's gut clenched. He could hear it in her voice. She wasn't going to stick with him. Grinding his jaw, he tried to force normal, soothing words between clenched teeth. "Of course," he said. "Whatever you need."

"Thank you for being patient with me." Her tone was an attempt to placate him. The condescension only solidified the bleak disappointment that crushed his chest and made it hard to breathe.

"Why wouldn't I?" he said lightly. He wiped sweat from his brow and shrugged out of his jacket with his free hand. "I knew going into this that our potential agreement was a long shot. Your job isn't dependent on your answer. Surely you know that."

"I do," she said softly.

Damn, he hated telephone conversations. He wanted to see her face…read the expression in her eyes. Her irises were the light green of summer moss, but flecked with amber. Now that he thought about it, her eyes were definitely her best feature. A drowning man could find his way home in those eyes.

He glanced at the clock. "I should let you get to bed," he said gruffly. "It's late."

Lisette murmured her agreement and broke the tenuous connection.

The word *bed* hovered in Jonathan's brain like a symbol of all that was problematic with his marriage of convenience idea. Even given the definite spark between him and Lisette, she was not the kind of woman to enter into a casual relationship, marriage license or no marriage license.

He was momentarily taken aback to realize how very badly he wanted to see his ring on her finger. Were his feelings real, or was he creating an emotional connection in his brain to excuse the fact that he was trying to conscript her life to make his own easier?

It was too late to walk on the beach. Exhaustion rolled over him in a crushing wave. It was all he could do to shower and tumble into bed. Unfortunately, as soon as he turned out the lights, he began to see all the problems with his current situation.

Mazie and J.B. hadn't taken a real honeymoon back in January when they got married, because they were both tangled in business situations needing their attention. Now that things had settled down, his sister and his best friend had airline tickets and premium hotel reservations for a three-week getaway in Hawaii. They planned to leave Charleston the first of July. Mazie had talked about nothing else for days.

Originally, Jonathan had decided to tell them his news when they got *home* from the islands. He didn't want to ruin their trip.

However, now, if there was any possibility Lisette was going to agree to marry him, he needed to talk to Mazie sooner than later. Jonathan sure as hell couldn't get married without telling his sister. She would be deeply hurt. Mazie would want to be there.

Could Jonathan do the wedding and save the bad news for later? Probably not. His sister would have too many questions about the speedy union.

His brain raced in circles. His head ached damnably despite the medication he had taken.

In an attempt to coax sleep, he shoved away all the questions about logistics and decisions and, instead, focused his thoughts on Lisette. A better man than he was would cut her loose. Absolve her of any responsibility for his future.

She deserved to be free. He had nothing to offer that would make up for the sacrifice she was considering. The fact that he was asking at all made him question his own honor.

Sleep came eventually. But it only visited in fits and starts, and was hardly restful. The following morning, he headed downtown an hour before his usual commute. Lisette wasn't going to be there. He needed to stay ahead of the curve today.

The hours dragged by.

He had a sandwich at his desk for lunch and continued working. Because he couldn't count on the future, he felt compelled to labor twice as hard as usual to make up for the uncertainty.

The only thing that sustained him throughout the afternoon when he wanted to sleep at his desk was the knowledge that Lisette would be with him tonight. She had promised.

At four there was a quiet knock on his office door. With no Lisette to stand guard, whoever it was had found him in his lair.

"Come in," he said.

The woman who entered was familiar… Lisette's friend. He gave her his best nonthreatening smile, because she seemed extremely nervous. "What can I do for you—Rebekah, isn't it?"

"Yes." She shifted from one foot to the other. "I'm sorry to intrude, Mr. Tarleton, but I'm worried about Lisette. She's been acting very odd lately, and she's not at her desk."

He winced inwardly, feeling more guilty than ever. His deceit was compounding expensive interest. "I'm sure she's fine," he said, perhaps a shade too heartily. "I would have heard if there were a problem."

"Oh." Rebekah hesitated. "Sorry I bothered you."

"No bother at all.

She smiled weakly and backed up. "Thank you."

Before he could say anything else, she was gone. Rebekah's visit was a stark reminder that Lisette had a life which didn't include Jonathan. He was asking a hell of a lot to drag his assistant into his personal crisis.

One glance at the clock told him he needed to leave. Earlier, he'd notified Lisette that he was sending a car service to pick her up at five thirty. Jonathan had exactly enough time to head home for a quick shower and change of clothes.

Oddly, now that the moment of decision was at hand, a feeling of peace wrapped him in calm. One way or another, tonight would give him the answers he needed. By the end of the evening he would know if Lisette was prepared to help him.

If her answer was one he didn't want to hear, Jonathan would find his way alone.

Lisette decided, in retrospect, that taking the day off might not have been the answer to her problems. At least at work she would have been too busy to overthink the situation with Jonathan.

As it was, she ran five miles after breakfast, her apartment was now spotless and she had even baked a cake for the Tarleton Shipping receptionist whose birthday was tomorrow.

She had also spent far too much time wrangling with a decision that had no clear-cut answer.

The first hurdle in confronting the upcoming face-to-face with Jonathan was deciding what to wear. She had been to his beach house a hundred times. Tonight was different. Tonight was an occasion. Tonight she wanted to look her best.

Because there had been no let-up in the string of blistering, muggy days, she chose a pale green sundress splashed with poppies. It was new, and it was definitely not office attire. The fitted waist and flared above-the-knee skirt made her feel feminine and comfortable at the same time.

Cork-heeled taupe espadrilles with ribbons tied at the ankle completed her look. A bit of light makeup and she was done.

She hadn't argued when Jonathan offered to send a car to pick her up. Her nerves were shredded. Driving in this condition was not advisable.

At the Tarleton front gate, the driver lowered the window so Lisette could punch in the code. Then he dropped her at the center of the driveway and departed the way he had come.

Lisette put a hand to her stomach, hoping she could even manage to *eat* dinner. She climbed the imposing curved staircase, pausing on the landing to admire the double mahogany doors inlaid with stained glass. Starfish and dolphins and sea turtles gamboled in bas-relief amid swirling hues of blue and green.

It occurred to her in an instant that if she married Jonathan, this would also be *her* house. The idea was bizarre... absurd. She was an ordinary person, the product of a single-parent home where money had always been tight, and an exciting evening out was popcorn and a movie.

This...this luxurious beachside mansion was the stuff of fantasy. Though she had worked here time and again when Gerald Tarleton or Jonathan needed her on-site, the prospect of being mistress of such a place was almost as daunting as that of being Jonathan's wife.

On an ordinary day, she would have used her key and let herself in. The senior Mr. Tarleton had mobility issues, and the chef and housekeeper were often too busy to play butler.

But tonight Lisette couldn't simply enter unannounced. This was Jonathan's home. The workday was over. He had

invited her here for a special dinner to discuss his future...
their future.

With her heart thumping like a wild bird in her chest
and her hands damp, she rang the bell.

Moments later, Jonathan himself opened the door. His
warm, intimate smile soothed some of her nerves. His gaze
raked her from head to toe, missing nothing. "Lisette. Right
on time. I hope you're hungry. Mrs. Rackham has outdone
herself."

"The house smells amazing." As he stepped back to
allow her to enter, she inhaled *his* familiar scent. Starched
cotton. Warm male skin. A whiff of aftershave. The combination made her dizzy.

At the office, Jonathan invariably wore a suit. Despite
Charleston's reputation for laid back hospitality, the head
of Tarleton Shipping carried himself with formal reserve.
Lisette often wondered if it was because he had inherited
the helm of the business at a young age and needed to establish his dominance among employees who were often
two decades his senior.

Tonight Jonathan was dressed more casually, though he
still wore a navy sport coat over dark gray trousers and a
crisp dress shirt. He'd done without a tie. Where the top
buttons of his shirt were open, she glimpsed tanned skin
and a hint of collarbone.

She had to remind herself to breathe.

"We'll go on into the dining room if that's okay with
you," he said. "There's a cheese soufflé on the way, and I
promised we wouldn't linger over drinks."

Lisette lowered her voice. "Well, since you *can't* drink
and I'm not much of a wine connoisseur, I think we can
live with that."

She caught her breath when she saw the table settings.
Whatever instructions Jonathan had given the two ladies

who ran his house so well had resulted in a spread worthy of the most elegant dinner party.

Fine, pale ivory china edged with silver. Heavy sterling flatware in an intricate pattern that looked as if it might have been antique. And a blush-pink linen tablecloth. In the center of all that magnificence sat a low crystal bowl overflowing with dahlias and white roses.

Jonathan held out her chair. "I hope you're hungry."

"I am now," she said, wondering if his fingers had brushed her bare shoulder by accident.

They were sitting at one corner of the table in a cozy arrangement that gave them both a spectacular view of the ocean. Jonathan lifted his crystal water glass. "To new beginnings."

She touched her goblet to his, meeting his bland gaze with suspicion. If this largesse was supposed to sway her decision, it was doing a great job. A woman could get used to this. "To the future," she said quietly. "May it be long and happy."

A shadow crossed his handsome face but was gone in an instant. He seemed determined to make the evening more social than serious. Lisette was okay with that. For the moment.

The meal was fabulous, as good or better than anything she had ever enjoyed at one of Charleston's many fine restaurants. Jonathan was a master at conversation. He'd learned at his father's knee perhaps. The fate of poor Mrs. Tarleton was somewhat of a mystery. She was still alive. That much Lisette knew. But rumor had it that she lived somewhere far away in a mental facility.

By the time dessert rolled around—coconut cream pie in a featherlight crust—Lisette had relaxed enough to actually enjoy herself. It was rare that she spent an evening like this with a man who was both intelligent and charming and far too sexy for his own good.

Her recent blind date couldn't compare.

As the housekeeper began to clear the table, they stood. Jonathan took Lisette's elbow in a light touch and steered her toward the den.

Here, too, huge windows brought the outdoors inside. A fat, golden-red sun had begun its descent toward the horizon, though it was still several hours until dark.

"I've always loved this room," she said. "You're lucky to have grown up here."

"I probably take it for granted more than I should."

She couldn't read his expression. When she sat on the sofa, Jonathan remained standing, though not in one place. He paced restlessly, his body language jerky and uncoordinated, very different from his usual suave sophistication.

Her heart twisted. "If you've changed your mind, Jonathan, it's okay. Really. I won't be insulted."

He stopped and glared. "I haven't changed my mind, though I could give you the same speech."

Lisette shook her head slowly. "I've done little else but think about your situation from the moment you told me. I'm still not convinced that marriage is the answer, but you know your company better than I. If you believe you need a wife to conceal your condition in the short term, I'm willing to help you."

He exhaled deeply, as though he hadn't been at all sure she was going to cooperate. "That's good to hear."

"It might be easier, though, to simply *pretend* we got married. There wouldn't be as many layers of complication."

He stood at the window, his back to her. "The legalities are important." After a long moment of silence, he came and joined her, but on the opposite end of the couch. "If you're acting as my stand-in, the decisions you make will have to be binding."

"I hadn't considered that." After all, this was exactly why he needed her. To handle the reins of Tarleton Shipping when the CEO became too ill to function. The prospect speared her with regret and pain. "How long will you wait to tell your family?"

Jonathan grimaced. "I know it has to be soon. But I don't want to hurt them. I don't want to disrupt their lives."

She slipped off her shoes and propped her arm on the back of the sofa, head on her hand. "You're not God, Jonathan. You can't protect them from this. They're adults. Part of the way they'll cope is by being there for you when things get difficult. I understand it's hard. Being in control is who you are. You like taking charge. You're the boss."

"You say that like it's a bad thing." His joke fell flat.

"I *get* being a control freak. Honestly, I'm right there with you. During my mother's extended illness, I had to learn that setting impossibly high expectations for myself and life in general was a huge stress producer." She paused, uncertain how he would take her next words. "You're ill, Jonathan. You'll have to let down your guard, your reserve, for people to help you."

His dark frown told her he hadn't completely come to terms with what was ahead of him. "I hear what you're saying. I'll try. That's all I can promise."

"Fair enough."

His fingers tapped a restless rhythm on his thighs, drawing attention to the beauty of his fit body. The seemingly relaxed masculine sprawl made her want to scoot across the cushions that separated them and curl up in his lap.

She had to keep telling herself this was business. Or at the very least, her good deed for the year. Her stupid crush would only complicate matters. She had to ignore the fact that she wanted Jonathan to fall in love with her.

The *loving* thing for her to do was keep her feelings in check and concentrate on him and what he needed. But what about her needs? Did she dare open up to him about what she really wanted? He was in a mood to offer her the moon. Maybe this was her chance to make part of her dreams come true.

Suddenly, he leaned forward and put his head in his hands. "I owe you an apology," he said, sighing.

"I don't understand."

"Your friend. Rebekah. She came looking for you and was pretty upset that you hadn't let her know you were going to be out of the office today. I didn't think about the ramifications of asking you to keep my secret."

"Oh." Lisette gnawed her lip. "She's bummed because I backed out of a trip we had planned for the fall. I couldn't explain. I suppose my not being at work today only compounded her confusion."

He sat up and frowned again. "Why would you cancel your vacation?"

Lisette stared at him. "For one, I can't take off on a girl trip if I just got married to you, and more importantly, September is three months from now. A lot of things could change."

She saw on his face the parade of emotions. First, the realization that she was right and, second, a grim distaste for having to plan an uncertain future. His jaw worked. "I want you to bring her in on the secret. You'll need someone, too, Lisette. For support. I'll ask her to sign a nondisclosure agreement."

"Thank you," she said quietly. "I wouldn't want to lose my best friend over this."

"I'm sorry I didn't look at your perspective sooner. I don't mean to be selfish. This entire situation has turned me into someone I barely know."

Lisette felt an urgency to reach out in this moment. She leaned toward him and touched his arm. "We're both finding our way, Jonathan. You're not a selfish person. Not at all. No matter how off kilter you may feel, you're the same man I've always admired and respected."

Seven

Jonathan jerked away, angry and embarrassed. It didn't help that Lisette looked as if she had stepped out of a spring garden. A man in his prime should be anticipating a night of pleasure with an appealing, sexy woman. Not preparing to go over dry legal documents.

But legal documents were the reason Lisette was here.

The concern in her eyes felt like acid on a raw wound. He didn't want her sympathy and her kindness.

He was a man, damn it. He wasn't weak, and he wasn't helpless.

"I'll get the paperwork," he said curtly, wishing he could put an end to this. He leaped to his feet and strode across the room to the armoire that discreetly disguised the television and other devices. Instead of keeping the documents in his home office where someone might have stumbled upon them today, he had stashed them in a shallow drawer that held batteries and extra cords.

The legal-size folder was cream colored with the name of his lawyer's firm embossed in gold. Even the weight of it in his hand felt momentous. He glanced over his shoulder at Lisette. "Shall we go to the office where you can spread out the papers and read them carefully?"

She shook her head, patting the seat beside her. "The coffee table will work. Why don't you come sit by me so you can explain stuff? Besides, I trust you. I don't have to read every word."

"Well, you should," he grumbled. "You're far too trusting."

Her gaze narrowed. "I told you I don't want your money. So there's nothing for me to worry about, now is there?"

Her snippiness restored his sense of humor. "Duly noted." He sat down beside her and was immediately assailed by an array of sensory delights. Her hair smelled like lemons. Her bare knees peeking out from beneath the hem of her sweet yet sexy dress struck him as unbearably erotic.

He cleared his throat and opened the folder, leaning forward slightly to place it in front of her on the polished wooden surface. "Take your time," he said. "There's lots of legal speak, but I think most of it is understandable in context. Let me know if you have questions."

Lisette leaned forward as well. They were sitting hip to hip. In better days, the two of them had gone over contracts together a hundred times. But never one like this.

Staring down at the sheaf of papers did little to distract his attention from how close she was…how good she smelled. Lisette was a *woman*. A woman he was hoping to marry.

For convenience, surely. And because she *could* and *would* keep his secret. But, try as he might, attempting to look at this situation as just another legal transaction didn't compute.

It was clear to him she was at least skimming the contents of the document and making note of the headings. He had included a generous posthumous settlement for his widow-to-be, as well as monthly payments to her personal account for the time that she would be his wife.

The lengthy silence on her part unsettled him. Perhaps the reality of seeing everything laid out in black-and-white was causing second thoughts.

At last she closed the folder, sat back and gave him a long, searching stare. "You can't give me five million dollars in exchange for six months of my life." The tone was flat.

"Of course I can. And we both know it might be longer than six."

Lisette's eyes flashed. "Six, twelve, eighteen…it doesn't matter. Your inheritance should go to your sister. Or your brother. Or both."

His fists clenched. "Hartley gets nothing from me. If you want to be noble and stupid, you can give your share to him. But not until I'm dead and gone."

"Do you know how irrational you sound when the subject of your brother comes up?"

Now his jaw was as tight as his fists. "Stay out of this, Lisette. I mean it. It has nothing to do with you."

"So I'll be your wife, but not really? You're the one who told me I would be family. Was that a lie?" Her dark gaze judged him and found him wanting.

"Quit twisting my words. You know what I mean."

"What happens if I don't sign your precious prenup?"

"Then no marriage."

Her jaw dropped the tiniest bit. Just enough to make him want to kiss those soft pink lips that had formed a tiny O of surprise. "But you need me."

He nodded. "I do. On my terms, though. My honor and my reputation are very important to me. In the end, that's all a man really leaves behind. If you choose to do this enormous, crazy thing for me, I'm determined to take care of you, Lizzy, even from the grave."

During his admittedly pompous speech, her eyes grew bigger and bigger. Moisture sheened that beautiful sea-glass green gaze. "I keep thinking this isn't real," she whispered.

His throat tightened, making it hard to speak. "So do I."

"Oh, Jonathan." She wrapped her arms around him, obviously seeking to offer comfort.

But he was far beyond being pacified by a simple hug. He craved the oblivion of physical passion. With his heart slamming in his chest, he rested his chin on top of her head.

Then, because his self-control was tenuous at best under the circumstances, he eluded her embrace and stood. His forehead was damp with sweat. His mouth was dry. "There's nothing in the contract about physical intimacy. I want you to have time to get to know me. To decide if a *marriage* in every sense of the word is something you want. But those considerations are strictly between you and me. Whether or not we decide to live together as man and wife in the same bed, the terms of the contract are binding."

Lisette stood as well. In her bare feet, she seemed small and vulnerable. Yet the woman he knew so well was resilient and resourceful.

He followed her when she went to the window, though he kept a safe distance between them. The ocean was gray and dark now, painted with a vivid stripe of gold and red cast by the sun trying valiantly to stay above the horizon. The room was becoming dim. No one had turned on a light.

Lisette shrugged. "In other circumstances, I might have enjoyed becoming your lover."

With her back to him, she couldn't see his shock. "And now?" he asked, the words strained.

She whirled and leaned against the glass, her arms crossed below her breasts. "I don't want to fall in love with you and have my heart broken."

Disappointment flooded his chest. "I see."

"I doubt you do. You're an extremely handsome man. I'm sure that any number of women have wanted to seduce you. And yet I don't even know if you've been in a serious relationship recently."

"I haven't," he said brusquely. "Nothing but work and family. I'm a very dull boy."

She rolled her eyes. "Nice try." After a hushed breath, she let her gaze slide over him from head to toe. As if she were sizing up an item she meant to purchase. It was not the look of an innocent who was curious. Nor was it particularly flirtatious. Instead, her frank assessment was intense. Personal.

Her shoulders lifted and fell, drawing attention to creamy skin and a delicate collarbone. "I think you forgot something."

He lifted an eyebrow. "Surely not. My lawyer is very thorough."

Lisette actually chuckled. The feminine sound made the back of his neck tingle. "You told me I could ask for anything I wanted," she said. "Don't you remember?"

"Ah, yes. The orange M&M's. Is that it?"

She shook her head slowly, pale green eyes filled with a million secrets he couldn't decipher. "Of course not."

"Then what?"

As he stared at her, half aroused, half alarmed, her tongue came out and wet her lips. In that moment, he realized she wasn't calm at all.

"Lisette?" He prompted her, trying to break the long gap in the conversation.

She shrugged, her expression both wary and intent. "I want you to give me a baby."

Lisette winced when Jonathan actually stumbled backward a step, his shock almost palpable. When he didn't respond, her stomach clenched, and her face and throat burned. "Say something," she muttered, mortified that she had actually gone through with her proposition. The idea had come to her in the middle of the night. At 3:00 a.m., it had even made perfect sense.

"Umm…" Jonathan rubbed his chin where the faint shadow of dark beard said he might not have shaved since early morning. She liked the way he looked. A lot.

"That's not an answer."

He cursed beneath his breath. "Good Lord, Lisette. You

can't drop a bomb like that and expect an immediate response. Is this for real?"

"Of course it's for real," she snapped. "I don't go around asking men to get me pregnant for the heck of it."

"But why?"

His befuddlement made her angry. "You have no clue, do you? I'm thirty-seven, Jonathan. Five years older than you, almost five and a half."

"Five years is nothing."

"Says the man who's not even thirty-two. I've spent all of my adult life caring for my mother. Thankfully, she's at peace and no longer in pain. I'm free to make a life for myself. But there's no significant other on the horizon, and now I'm contemplating being with you for a year, give or take. My stupid biological clock is ticking. I don't think I should wait any longer."

"A baby…" He said it with wonderment and concern as if he actually had no idea at all how the process started.

"It's not so farfetched," she said quietly. "You're a decent man, and if I did get pregnant, you could look at it as leaving a piece of yourself behind."

His face darkened. "It? The baby? It wouldn't be an *it* though, would it? Your baby would be mine, too. A precious little one I'd love. And grieve all the more to have to say goodbye. What you're asking isn't fair, Lizzy."

She hadn't thought of it in those terms. Of course he would love a baby. And not living to see his own child grow up would be a terrible burden to bear.

Still, something inside her said this was the perfect time, the perfect man, her last chance.

Was she fooling herself to think she wouldn't come to love Jonathan exponentially more as his wife, as the mother of his child? How could she bear it? Unless, when her heart was broken and aching at losing Jonathan, she could find comfort in a baby… a tiny version of him to love.

"I suppose not," she said, trying to put herself in his shoes. "But promise me you'll think about it. I wouldn't ask if it wasn't important to me. Very important, Jonathan."

He nodded slowly, his expression grim. "I promise. Though I have to be honest with you… I can't imagine changing my mind. My sister and brother-in-law are struggling to get pregnant. What would they think if I deliberately tried to get *you* pregnant knowing I won't live to raise my own child?"

"If they eventually conceive, this baby…*our* baby… would be a cousin. That's special and sweet."

He shook his head slowly. "You make a persuasive argument. I'll think about it. I can't give you more than that."

She nodded, though something told her he wouldn't be easy to convince. "Hand me something to write with. Let's do this, and then I don't want to see these papers ever again."

Jonathan's expensive fountain pen was weighty in her hand. She signed her name again and again…everywhere a small yellow flag denoted her input. Finally, she capped the pen, straightened the papers and closed the folder.

Her husband-to-be had stared at her the entire time as if afraid she might bolt. Now he smiled. "You're doing a good thing, Lisette. I'm grateful. I swear you won't regret it."

That was a vow he likely couldn't keep. She felt sick with nerves. She was signing her life away in order to watch the man she cared for deeply abandon her in death. She was in love with him, planning to build a life—albeit temporary—with him, and then would ultimately watch it disappear. Was she crazy to go through with the marriage?

But then again, life in general was nebulous and uncertain. She had to take this chance. "What next?" she asked quietly.

"I've spoken to the judge. He's a family friend. We can get married in his chambers Saturday morning."

She sucked in a breath. "So soon?"

"No reason to wait."

"Will it be just you and me?"

"We'll need witnesses. You'll bring Rebekah. I'll have Mazie and J.B."

"Which means we have to tell them tomorrow."

"Yes."

"And what about your father?"

For once, the decisive head of Tarleton Shipping appeared unsure. "I'm still wrestling with that one. Most days he's fine, but his mental faculties slip in and out. I'm not sure he'd be capable of keeping either secret—my health *or* the real reason for the marriage. I think it may be best not to say anything at all to him for the time being."

"Don't you think he'll notice someone new is living in his house?"

Her sarcasm rolled off Jonathan without hitting its mark. "Dad's quarters are on the main floor. He won't have a clue what you and I are doing upstairs."

Suddenly, a startling vision flashed in her brain. Jonathan's bed. The two of them naked between the sheets. Her breathing quickened. "People will expect us to take a honeymoon," she said, trying not to think about what traditionally happened on post-wedding trips.

"True." He frowned. "I suppose we could go somewhere for a few days."

"Or simply say that things at work are too busy for you to be gone right now...that we're planning a big romantic getaway for later in the year."

"Unfortunately, we just finished a series of seminars on work/life balance. Remember?"

"Ah..." He was right. Jonathan was a great employer. The benefits package at Tarleton Shipping was second to none. He encouraged his staff to take their vacation days...

all of them. Research underscored that a happy, well-rested work force was more productive.

How would it look if the boss himself didn't even take time off to get married?

Jonathan punched something into his phone. "A week in the Caribbean should do it, don't you think?"

She blinked. "The Caribbean?"

"One of my buddies owns a villa in Antigua. He's offered it to me half a dozen times. Comes complete with a household staff. Nothing to do but relax in the sun. I just sent him a text."

"Wouldn't it be booked by now?"

"Maybe not this time of year. Winter is high season."

Seven days and nights in a tropical paradise with a fake husband who just happened to be her boss. What could possibly go wrong?

Before she could come up with a believable objection, Jonathan's phone dinged. He held it up triumphantly. "We're in for the entire week. He says the days are available."

"Do you really want to be gone that long?" Jonathan rarely took any time for himself.

He dropped his phone on the desk. "We need this, Lizzy. A chance to get used to each other away from prying eyes. The fiction of a honeymoon will make things that much easier when we go back to work."

Now he crossed the room and took her shoulders in his hands. His thumbs caressed her collarbone. He was so close she couldn't breathe.

"That makes sense, I suppose," she said.

"Look at me, Lisette."

Reluctantly she tipped back her head and met his brown-eyed gaze straight on. "What now?"

"You don't seem like a woman who's excited about taking a break from work."

"I haven't taken a real vacation in a very long time. I'm not good at relaxing. A definite character flaw."

"Are you worried because I'll be with you?"

She felt naked beneath his intent stare. "I'm sure we can do our own thing and not get in each other's way."

His chest rose and fell in a mighty sigh. He tucked her hair carefully behind her ears. Then he pressed a gentle kiss to her lips. "Thank you, Lisette. For everything."

Her immediate instinct was to pull back. Not because she didn't want the kiss, but because she wanted it far too much.

But she didn't jerk away, and she didn't refuse his overture. This was the man she was going to marry on Saturday.

When she kissed him back, he was the one who seemed startled.

He made a noise low in his chest. A groan. Then two big hands came up and cupped her cheeks. "God, you're sweet," he muttered.

The kiss deepened. Lisette allowed herself to relax in his embrace, to enjoy the novelty of having a man—this man in particular—hold her and let her know without words that he wanted her. She felt the urgency of his arousal.

Men could enjoy sex without involving their emotions. She knew that. Even so, Jonathan's desperation slid beneath her defenses and made her believe this marriage might have a chance of becoming real.

His tongue moved between her lips and stroked hers, taking the starch out of her knees and stealing her breath. Her arms encircled his neck. Her fingertips found the silky hair at his nape and played with the baby-fine strands.

Jonathan took the kiss deeper, more dominant now, less afraid perhaps that she might not want what he had to offer...that she might not want him.

She moaned, pressing ever closer. She wanted this and so much more. But how could she protect herself?

Suddenly, she saw the clock on the wall behind his shoulder. Like Cinderella, her time was up. She pulled away, smoothing her hair awkwardly. "I have to go," she said. "The driver will be waiting at the gate."

"You asked him to come back? Why? You knew I would take you home." His frown was black.

"I wasn't entirely sure how the evening would go," she confessed. "It seemed better this way."

"You're afraid of me?" He was visibly insulted.

She touched two fingers to his lips, lingering there for a moment before stepping back from temptation. "I was afraid of us," she said.

Eight

The next day, Jonathan sat opposite his sister and his best friend and watched them process the news. He'd tried to phrase things diplomatically. He'd wanted to spare them the worst of what he knew. But despite his best efforts, it was what it was. The end.

Mazie wept openly. J.B.—his arm around his wife—looked as if he'd been kicked in the chest by a horse.

The three of them had just finished dinner. When Jonathan had phoned his sister and told her he wanted to come over, she had insisted on cooking…claimed she rarely had the chance anymore.

Her business kept her tied up most days.

Now they all sat in the beautifully appointed living room with the veranda that overlooked Meeting Street, and Mazie cried.

J.B. cleared his throat. "Are you sure?"

It was the same question Lisette had asked in the beginning. Maybe it was the question all families asked when faced with a difficult diagnosis. A plea for a help and a way out.

Jonathan nodded. "I'm sure. Multiple doctors. Multiple tests. I didn't want to tell you both yet. I didn't want to ruin your trip. But Lisette insisted."

J.B. narrowed his eyebrows. "Lisette?"

"His executive assistant," Mazie croaked, wiping her eyes.

"I know who she is. Nice lady. Smart enough to keep *Jonathan* in line."

"I hope so," Jonathan said. "Because I'm marrying her on Saturday. And I need you both to be there."

J.B. snorted. "Has your brain started shutting down? You can't get married Saturday. That's ridiculous."

Mazie slugged her husband's arm. "Not funny." Then her expression faltered. "But I don't understand, Jonathan. You've never given me any hint that you thought of Lisette romantically. Besides, isn't she quite a bit older than you?"

He shrugged, irritated by that same stupid argument. "Five years. It's not a big deal. But no. We're not in love. I asked her to marry me so I could appoint her as a partner in the company. As my health fails, Lisette will be deputized to make decisions. And in the short term, she can cover for me if I have bad days. It's imperative that we stave off news of my illness as long as possible so our stock prices aren't affected."

J.B. folded his arms across his chest, for once his expression deadly serious. "What's to keep her from ruining you financially? I have some experience in this arena. How well do you know her? Can she be trusted?"

Jonathan reached for patience. J.B.'s first wife had been in it for the money and had made his life a misery. It was understandable that J.B. had issues when it came to women and marriage.

"I'd trust her with my life," Jonathan said. "I suppose I literally am. But there's a prenup, so you can stand down. I love you both, and I want you to be with me Saturday when I tie the knot. The only other person who's going to know the whole truth is Lisette's best friend. Rebekah will there, too."

Mazie stood and wrapped her arms around him. His baby sister's tight hug threatened to shake Jonathan's hard-won composure.

"So do I throw you a big reception?" she asked, the

words muffled against his shirt. Her wet face had dampened the fabric.

He leaned his cheek on the top of her head. "Thanks, sis, but no. We're heading off immediately for a honeymoon in Antigua. I want the whole newlywed thing to look as real as possible."

J.B. stood as well, grim faced. "What if your health takes a bad turn when you're out of the country?"

Jonathan straightened and patted Mazie on the back. He didn't need sympathy right now. He needed everyone to treat him like normal; otherwise, he'd never make it through these next few months.

"It won't be that fast, according to the doc. Even the headaches have been irregular. Some days I feel fine."

"But you're definitely *not* fine." His sister pulled herself together visibly. "We should contact Hartley."

"No." Jonathan shouted the word, his neck tight with rage and the deep hurt he had felt ever since his brother's betrayal. At Mazie's stricken expression, he tempered his tone. "I can't deal with him right now. I'll need all my energy to keep the company afloat and to deal with whatever physical symptoms come my way. My brother is not part of the equation. Promise me you won't try to contact him, Mazie."

He could see the struggle on her face. At last she nodded. "If that's what you want. And Daddy?"

Jonathan shook his head. "I have no idea. He'll have to be told…eventually. But I think in these early days it's best to pretend everything is normal."

"You're probably right."

The three of them stood there in a small circle. For a moment, Jonathan could almost glimpse the children they had been so long ago. These were two of the most important people in his life.

He sighed. "I want you to be kind to Lisette. This will

be extremely difficult for her. She'll need your support and friendship."

"I wasn't going to run her out of town," J.B. groused. "But I'm still not comfortable with you giving her so much power."

Mazie patted her husband's hand. "We'll have dinner together. You'll see how great she is." She glanced at her brother. "As soon as you get back? We won't go to a restaurant, though. It needs to be here. So we can talk freely."

"I'd like that, Maze," Jonathan said. "Honestly, right now I'm taking things one day at a time. It's not a great feeling."

The conversation gradually moved to other topics, but Jonathan wasn't fooled. His illness was the enormous elephant in the room.

The news had changed both his sister and his best friend. Mazie was shocked and subdued and very upset, but trying not to show it. J.B.—who was the life of any party— had morphed into an unusually serious man, one with pain in his eyes.

Jonathan struggled with inexplicable guilt. He was strong. He would handle whatever was coming. But hurting the people he loved was a consequence no number of pep talks could soothe.

As the evening wore on, he realized he needed to leave them alone to process the difficult news he had shared. Besides, it was late, and he was exhausted. Not from any physical exertion today. But from the effort to carry on as normal when his emotions were all over the map.

He didn't want emotions. He didn't trust them. From the time his father had tucked his so-very-ill mother away in an institution, Jonathan had learned that life was easier when he bottled up all his pain and refused to acknowledge its existence.

J.B. walked him down to the car. The two men stood in silence beneath the neon glow of a security light.

J.B.'s expression was equal parts angry and determined. "Are you holding anything back? You can protect Mazie, but I won't have you lying to me, even if you think you have a damned good reason."

Jonathan leaned against the car, jingling keys in his hand. "Swear to God, that's it. No cure. No hope. And worst of all, no timetable. They'll repeat my scans every two months. So we'll know where things are."

"Son of a bitch." J.B.'s vehement curse was weirdly helpful. It expressed the utter outrage and incredulity Jonathan felt, the gut-level response he hadn't allowed himself.

"I'm heading home," he said. "Dad will wonder why I'm so late."

"And your bride-to-be? What about her?"

"We'll see each other at work in the morning. Back off, J.B. She's doing a wonderful thing for me."

"And she'll be a wealthy widow in the end."

The sarcasm wasn't veiled. Jonathan's temper boiled. "Of course she will. Because that's the way I want it. I have no idea how this is all going to go down. I asked a woman who's been through hell with her own mother to do it all over again. That makes me the villain in this scenario, not Lizzy."

"Lizzy? You're cozy enough for nicknames?"

"We've worked together a long time. We're friends."

"Just friends?" J.B. didn't bother to hide his skepticism. "Or is there more to this than you wanted Mazie to know? Have you and your executive assistant hooked up now and again?"

"Not that it's any of your damned business, but no. It's not like that."

"Sorry, bud. You don't sound convincing at all. I'm guessing you have a *thing* for her, and when your world got caught up in this wicked undertow, your subconscious grabbed onto the nearest lifeline."

Jonathan sucked in a sharp breath. J.B. had known him since they were both five years old. J.B. was smart and extremely perceptive, despite his genial, good-ole'-boy demeanor. There might be a kernel of truth in his summation of the current situation.

"Well, hell."

J.B. chuckled, this time with no sympathy at all. "You want her, don't you?"

Jonathan rubbed the back of his neck. "I'd be lying if I said I hadn't fantasized about her now and again. But I swear I never stepped over any line at work. Never. Not once."

"Settle down. I believe you. But the bigger question is, what does Lisette think about you?"

"Hell if I know. She has a big heart. And she feels sorry for me."

"It wouldn't be entirely surprising if she had a thing for you. Some women go for the buttoned-up, way-too-serious type."

Jonathan choked out a rusty laugh. Trust J.B. to make him see the humor in a dire situation. "Thanks for the ringing endorsement."

"When you remember to smile and you tear yourself away from spreadsheets and budgets, you're not half-bad."

"I'll put that on my tombstone."

"Shit, Jonathan. This can't be happening." In a completely atypical move, J.B. grabbed him close and gave him a crushing bear hug. "I'm here for you, man, day or night. You know that, right?"

Jonathan pulled away, both deeply touched and deeply despairing. "I do."

They stood there in silence, forever it seemed, neither of them willing to walk away. J.B. finally cursed beneath his breath. "If I fly in another specialist, will you see him or her? I've got the money. You know I do."

"And so do I. Your generosity is duly noted. But I swear I've seen the best. No one thought the headaches were anything serious, because they come and go. I'm healthy as a horse by any other metric. It took this last round of tests to get at the truth. My doctor is a professional. It's hard to miss a giant fucking tumor..." His voice cracked embarrassingly.

J.B. stared at the ground, and then his jaw thrust out the same way it had every time he'd been thwarted as a kid. "You're the best damn man I've ever known, hands down. If there's even a shred of a chance, you'll find it. I'd lay money on it."

Jonathan's eyes burned. "Oh, crud, J.B. If this is some kind of wind-beneath-my-wings speech, quit embarrassing yourself. Besides, I'm not riding off into the sunset yet."

"We're a team, bro. Wherever it takes us."

The team had once included Hartley. Jonathan shoved the random, painful thought aside. "I'll see you Saturday," he said gruffly.

"We'll be there."

"I'll text Mazie the details."

"You know she's going to smother you, don't you? The woman is a born nurturer."

"She definitely is. No news on the fertility front?"

"Not yet. But it's early. We're supposed to relax. The doctor says that's important."

"It will happen."

"I think so, too."

"I wish I could have kept this from her. The worry can't be good when she's trying to get pregnant."

"Mazie would have killed you herself if you'd kept her in the dark and she found out. We'll be fine."

Jonathan climbed into his car, started the engine and lowered the windows. Immediately, the scent of roses seeped into the hot interior. "Take care of my sister, J.B."

His friend's nod was curt. "Always."

* * *

Thursday morning at ten, Lisette brought Rebekah downstairs in front of the Tarleton Shipping building to meet Jonathan. After a brief, awkward round of greetings the three adults piled into Jonathan's car. Lisette sat in the back with Rebekah.

When Lisette's eyes met Jonathan's in the rearview mirror, his intense gaze made her stomach flip. Yesterday had seemed a million years long. Though Jonathan had been in and out of the office, they barely spoke to each other. She knew he had met with his sister and brother-in-law last night, but she hadn't found the opportunity to quiz him about how things had gone.

And as for Rebekah… Lisette's poor friend was confused and apprehensive and trying not to show it. All Lisette had been able to tell her was that she was going to be brought in on some company secrets and that it would require her to sign a nondisclosure agreement.

The trip to the lawyer's office was little more than ten minutes, even in traffic. Jonathan's lawyer was an extremely attractive blonde who might have been Lisette's age. Maybe even a bit older. After she greeted Jonathan, he volunteered to step into an outer office while the three women met.

Lisette appreciated his courtesy. Rebekah's eyes had grown wider and rounder with every step of the process. She would be more comfortable without the head of Tarleton Shipping in the room.

When the three women were alone, the lawyer jumped right in. "Thank you for coming today, Rebekah. Jonathan and Lisette want to share some information with you, but the subject matter is sensitive. If you choose not to be brought in at a higher level, you may say so, and we won't go any further."

Rebekah looked at Lisette. "Do you need me to do this?"

For a moment, Lisette felt the weight of guilt. Keeping secrets was not easy. She desperately wanted to be able to talk to her friend about all that was going on. "I do," she said. "We've always shared everything. This is important, or I wouldn't ask."

Rebekah turned back to the lawyer. "Give me the papers. I'll sign whatever Lisette wants me to."

The document was at least a dozen pages long…legal-size pages. The lawyer flipped; Rebekah signed again and again.

When it was done, the lawyer gathered the document into a folder. "I'll have my staff make copies. Each of you will receive one, as will Jonathan." Her businesslike demeanor softened. "I'll leave you two to talk for a few minutes. With the door closed, no one will disturb you."

The room was silent. Rebekah put her hands to her flushed cheeks. "Say something, please. I'm freaking out over here. I feel like I'm in a spy movie. What the heck is going on?"

Lisette started talking and couldn't stop. She hadn't realized what an enormous relief it was going to be to finally share the details of the past few days with someone who really cared and could actually help her work through the morass of personal and ethical dilemmas she faced.

When she explained Jonathan's illness, Rebekah looked stricken. "Oh, God. I'm so sorry."

"There's more," Lisette said. "He wants to keep the news under wraps as long as possible so the company stock won't be affected."

Rebekah nodded. "That makes sense. And you're his assistant, so you'll have to be in the know." She paused, frowning. "But why me? What do I have to do with anything?"

Lisette chewed the inside of her lip until she tasted the tang of blood. "You thought I was acting weird and selfish, and rightly so. You're my best friend. I *needed* you to know so that our relationship wouldn't be in danger."

"But there's more, surely. I signed my life away a moment ago. What's it all about?"

Lisette couldn't sit still any longer. The lawyer's personal office was spacious and beautifully decorated, but there wasn't much room to pace. Lisette was shaky and tense. Saying these things out loud made her decision seem more real, more radically dangerous.

"Jonathan has asked me to marry him," she said slowly. "So that when his condition begins to deteriorate, I can make decisions and step in as his proxy."

Rebekah's expression intensified every one of Lisette's doubts. Her friend looked either incredibly shocked or horrified, or maybe a mixture of both. "That's insane," she said. "He can't ask that of you. It's too much."

"Well, he did," Lisette muttered. She had never breathed a word about her crush on her boss. As far as Rebekah knew, Jonathan was nothing more than an employer. "He'll be going through hell, Rebekah. I can't stand by and watch him suffer if I can help."

"What about his family?"

"They'll be supportive, of course. But because of my position, I'm uniquely suited to help him run Tarleton Shipping. The fiction of our wedding will deflect any grumblings about why I'm being given so much latitude in decision-making."

"I still don't like it," Rebekah said, her gaze troubled. "It sounds like he's taking advantage of you. It's not fair."

If there was ever a time for truth, it was now. "I care about him, Rebekah."

"As a human being, you mean?"

"As a man. I love him. No matter how hard this is, I want to be with him for however long he has left."

Nine

Lisette's life became both easier and harder in the hours that followed. Easier, in that Rebekah was now her confidante, her sounding board. Harder, because the plan that had been set into motion accelerated rapidly.

Rebekah was tucked into a cab to return to the office without them. Lisette and Jonathan went to the courthouse for the marriage license.

Producing a photo ID and watching Jonathan hand over cash for the fee was certainly not romantic under the circumstances. Lisette felt the noose of inevitability tighten around her neck.

Any woman would want to marry a man like Jonathan. But the speed and the matter-of-fact way he was ticking off items on his list was a little too clinical for Lisette's taste. She wanted to be more to him than a convenience.

As she penned her name alongside his, her hand shook. The wet ink smudged, making her handwriting almost illegible. "Do we need to start over?" she asked the clerk.

The young woman shook her head. "Nope. It's still legal. That's all that matters."

Outside on the courthouse steps, Lisette paused to pull her sunglasses from her purse. The day was bright and sunny, but mostly she wanted to be able to hide behind them. With each moment that passed, she was becoming more and more aware of her handsome fiancé.

"Are we going to grab lunch?" she asked. "I'm starving. I was too nervous about Rebekah and the lawyer to eat breakfast."

Jonathan grimaced. "I'd love to, but I have a meeting. I can drop you at the office, though."

His gaze was trained on the throngs of tourists passing by on the street. Charleston was a popular vacation spot.

Once again his habitually aloof mask was firmly in place.

Lisette's heart sank. Was this how it was going to be between them? Cold and distant whenever he couldn't handle the emotional aspects of the situation? Suddenly, she couldn't bear to be near him. "I'll walk," she said curtly.

She took off down the steps at a breakneck pace, considering the fact that she was wearing heels. Tears stung her eyes. She blinked them away angrily. How could he treat her like nothing more than a coworker when he had begged her to marry him?

"Wait. Stop."

She ignored him, walking faster. Her throat and her chest were tight. Forty-eight hours. She had forty-eight hours to decide if she could go through with this charade.

A large, masculine hand grabbed her shoulder, spinning her around. Jonathan tugged her into a patch of shade at the entrance to an alley. "I'm sorry," he said, his gaze contrite. "I've never been in this situation before. I'm making a mess of it. I don't know how I'm supposed to act." Without asking permission, he removed her sunglasses and wiped tears from beneath her eyes.

The stupid, dense man was so close they were breathing the same air. She felt naked without her polarized protection. "Give me those." She snatched for the sunglasses, but he held them away, out of reach. She glared at him. "Just pretend you're getting married for the *normal* reasons," she said, infusing the words with all the sarcasm she could muster. "Pretend some poor deluded woman actually cares about you." Her voice escalated to an embarrassing octave.

His gaze settled on her lips, the hot stare almost tangible. "And do you, Lisette? Do you care about me?"

"That's not a fair question," she mumbled, finally retrieving her sunglasses from his grasp. She settled them on her nose. "I need food. Go away."

Those gorgeous masculine lips quirked upward in a smile that stole her breath. "I care about you, Lizzy Stanhope. I have for a long time. In fact, I almost asked you out on half a dozen different occasions. But in the age of #MeToo, I decided it wasn't the thing to do. Because I had no clue if you were even interested."

"*Why* do you care about me? Or how?"

He shrugged. "You're cute and funny and smart. I enjoy your company."

His calm pronouncement destroyed her composure. The aloof Jonathan might be better for her in the long run. "I'm sorry I yelled at you," she said meekly. "You should go. You'll be late for your meeting."

He said a rude word, a word she'd never heard him use. Then he slid his hands beneath her hair and cupped her head. When he lowered his mouth to hers, his lips firm and warm and demanding, everything spun in a dizzying arc behind her eyes. Maybe she had heat stroke.

Was it possible for a really good kiss to short-circuit a woman's brain? When she finally regained her senses, Jonathan was breathing hard. His face was flushed. Her sunglasses were tucked in the breast pocket of his jacket. When had that happened?

She swallowed. "Was that supposed to be an apology?"

He grinned. "I don't know. Did it succeed?"

"Yes, damn you. But don't expect to bamboozle me so easily every time we get in an argument."

"*Bamboozle?* Maybe you *are* too old for me."

That he could tease her so easily moments after they had kissed each other senseless told her he felt comfortable with her. Or something. *Comfortable* was definitely a misnomer.

This crackling awareness between them was not exactly relaxing.

She waved a hand. "Go take care of business. I'm not mad at you. I know it's hard for a high-powered businessman to be gone for a week."

He glanced at his watch and muttered an imprecation beneath his breath. "I'll see you in the morning."

"Probably not. You're not the only one with plans to make."

"I stand corrected. At the courthouse then? Saturday? Two o'clock?"

"Yes. I'll be there."

He kissed her again, long and slow and sweet as honey. "Thank you, Lisette. I swear you won't regret it."

She already did, but that was grief for another day. In the here and now, she would pretend nothing was wrong. Putting her palms against his hard, warm chest, she shoved. "Go. We're good. I won't be a no-show. You don't have to worry about me, Jonathan."

Backing away slowly, he lifted a hand. "Saturday. Don't be late." Then he shifted into a loping run and disappeared around the corner.

Though Lisette and Rebekah were in the office for the remainder of Thursday, they each decided to burn a vacation day on Friday so Lisette could find a dress to wear for the wedding.

It was a tall order on short notice. Fortunately, Rebekah was a hard-core reader of glossy bridal magazines and a devotee of every wedding-themed show on TV. She picked up Lisette at nine the next morning and was prepared with a list of Charleston's boutiques and bridal salons to hit up.

Lisette couldn't help wishing her wedding was going

to be different. She had always assumed that one day she would walk down the center aisle in a big church with violins playing "Pachelbel's Canon."

Grow up, kid, she lectured herself sternly. During the years of her mother's lengthy illness, she'd had to learn time and again that special occasions couldn't be planned too carefully. Circumstances dictated change. Life was unpredictable.

She thrust her girlish daydreams into a mental lockbox and reminded herself why she was really going through with this wedding.

Jonathan Tarleton needed her.

Forty-eight hours after the meeting in the lawyer's office, Jonathan stood in the judge's chambers and felt his pulse rate increase. Lisette was late. Not terribly so, but enough to tighten his stomach.

Mazie fiddled with the silk pocket square in his charcoal suit. "You look so handsome," she whispered. Tears filled her eyes and spilled over. "I know why you're taking this honeymoon, but I don't want you to go. I'll worry about you every minute of the day. Promise you'll call and text."

He kissed her forehead. "Of course I will. Besides, I'm feeling fine right now. Haven't had a headache in three days."

"You don't have to be brave for me." She put her arms around him. "Hartley should be here. It's not right."

"Don't start with me, Maze. Today is hard enough without you heaping sentimental guilt on my head."

She pulled back, looking hurt. "You're my brother and I love you, but sometimes you are so damn stubborn I could smack you."

He pinched her chin, a maneuver she had hated since childhood. "That goes both ways, little chick."

J.B. waved an arm between them. "Hey. Break it up, you two. I think the bride has arrived."

Jonathan spun and watched the door swing open wide. Rebekah entered first, wearing a flattering summer dress that was the green of Lisette's eyes. Behind her stood the woman who made his heart race. A wide-eyed, pink-cheeked bride-to-be. His feet carried him across the room, though he didn't remember telling them to move.

"Lizzy," he muttered, stunned and moved. "You look amazing."

Her wedding gown was exactly right. Not too casual and not too traditional. It was perfect for a marriage of expedience in a judge's office. The ivory lace made her skin glow. The strapless bodice emphasized her beautiful breasts and her narrow waist.

The slightly flared skirt skimmed her hips, ending just above her knees. Maybe he had been wrong about her eyes. Now that he thought about it, her shapely legs might be her best asset.

Her smile was confident, though a bit wobbly. "You're not so bad yourself, Mr. Tarleton. Sorry I'm late. I forgot my suitcase, so we had to turn the cab around."

His gut eased. She wasn't changing her mind, thank God. "You're here now. That's all that matters."

He stood back and let Lisette introduce her friend to Mazie and J.B. Soon the judge cleared his throat, signaling his readiness to begin. Everyone took their places. Jonathan was surprised to realize that his palms were damp. It wasn't every day a man got married.

For a moment, regret speared him. This surely wasn't the scenario Lisette had imagined and anticipated as a young girl. At least he had bought her a bridal bouquet. The lilies and red roses were extravagant and over-the-top, but they lent a much-needed festive note. Lisette clutched the flowers in her left hand and slipped her right hand into his.

He blanked out after that. The occasion was surreal. Never in a million years had he imagined he'd be married in such a fashion. Not quite a shotgun wedding, but close. The judge's sonorous voice resonated in the small room. *Wilt thou take... Do you promise...* When the man in the black robe reached the part about "in sickness and in health," Lisette squeezed his fingers.

He clutched her hand, incredulous that she had agreed to his plan. He was deeply grateful for her huge heart and inherent practicality.

When it came time for the rings, he felt a sharper pinch of regret. He'd spent so many hours yesterday dealing with Tarleton Shipping business that he had completely forgotten a wedding ring. Fortunately, this morning he'd been able to rifle through the safe at the beach house and find a small signet ring that had belonged to his great-grandfather. Because the gold circlet was designed to be worn on a man's pinkie finger, the fit should work for Lisette until Jonathan could select something better.

He waited for Rebekah to relieve the bride of her bouquet. Then Jonathan took Lisette's left hand and slid the time-worn band onto the appropriate finger. *With this ring, I thee wed... With my body, I thee worship.*

The import of the ceremony slammed into him without warning, destroying everything he thought he had wanted. This was wrong. He hadn't meant to make a mockery of marriage. He'd been so focused on keeping his empire afloat he'd practically demanded Lisette's cooperation. And she'd been too kind to point out all his selfish shortcomings.

When he glanced down at her, expecting to see reproach in her gaze, her clear-eyed smile washed over him like a benediction.

The judge continued. *By the power vested in me...*

The next words penetrated the haze in Jonathan's brain

and jerked him fully into the moment. "I now pronounce you husband and wife. You may kiss the bride."

He was married. Lisette Stanhope was his wife.

She looked up at him shyly, waiting. The other four adults in the room waited as well.

His body felt clumsy and uncoordinated. Jonathan Tarleton—who knew exactly what to do in any situation—was frustrated and disconcerted. Because he saw no other choice, he lowered his head and captured Lisette's mouth with his. Not the kind of erotic kiss that prompted raucous catcalls or wild applause, but a quick peck on the lips. The barest nod to convention.

When he released her, there was a split second of silence, and then everyone rushed in at once to share their congratulations.

Lisette smiled and laughed and accepted the good wishes with grace. But her gaze never met his. Not once.

It was a measure of his complete discomposure that he found his hands fisting at the sight of J.B. kissing the bride.

Then it was over. The judge had places to be. There was no wedding meal. No reception. Mazie and J.B. had offered to drop Rebekah at her condo. A hired car was waiting down below to whisk Jonathan and Lisette to the airport. Jonathan had chartered a small jet to fly them to Antigua.

Because it was far too hot to linger on the street outside, they all said their goodbyes in the lobby. Except for the large bouquet Lisette carried, there was nothing particularly festive about the moment. Rebekah and Mazie looked worried. J.B.'s gaze was guarded.

Jonathan knew they were all staring at him, trying to decide if he was going to keel over. Their unspoken concern raked his nerves and made him snappy. "We should go," he said. "The pilot will be waiting on us."

While he and J.B. retrieved Jonathan's and Lisette's luggage from the building's concierge, the women huddled together, deep in conversation.

The car was summoned. One last round of hugs. Then Jonathan found himself in the back seat of an air-conditioned sedan, seated beside his wife. *His wife*. God in heaven…

He cleared his throat. "Are you cool enough?" He adjusted the vent.

"I'm fine." Lisette's response was subdued.

They had worked in tandem for three years and had known each other much longer than that. Right now, though, she seemed like a stranger.

What was he supposed to say to her? How was he supposed to act?

Fortunately, the drive to the airport took less than half an hour. Traffic was relatively light on a Saturday afternoon.

"I think you'll enjoy the flight," he said. "No changing planes in Atlanta or Miami. Our own personal crew…two pilots and one attendant."

Lisette twisted the signet ring on her finger. "Sounds expensive."

"It's our wedding day. I thought we should splurge."

As it turned out, he was right. Lisette was visibly impressed with the plane's amenities. While the pilot finished his preflight checklist, the flight attendant—who happened to be male—served them champagne and English biscuits.

The cookies were delicious. Jonathan didn't bother explaining that he couldn't drink the champagne. Instead, he handed his flute to Lisette when she finished hers. After a moment's hesitation, she downed the second glass. Good. If she was as nervous as he was, the Dutch courage might help.

When they were airborne, Lisette kicked off her shoes

and curled her legs beneath her. She had carefully placed her wedding flowers on the empty seat beside her. Jonathan sat mere inches away, though across the small aisle.

Only the attentive presence of the flight attendant saved them from an awkward, extended silence. But after an hour that included meal service and various other polite interruptions, the flight attendant excused himself and retreated to a small cubicle at the back of the jet, leaving Jonathan and Lisette alone.

Lisette reclined her seat, reached for the small pillow and blanket and closed her eyes.

Jonathan studied her as she slept. Or maybe she was *pretending* to be asleep. Who could tell? Their honeymoon was off to a stunningly bad start. If this was how it was going to be for the next seven days, he might as well call the whole thing off.

Not that he really had that option. He and his new wife were headed to the Caribbean for a week that the outside world thought was all about sex, sex and more sex.

He snorted inwardly. He'd hoped he and Lisette could use this time to get to know each other on a more intimate level, not sex *necessarily*, but he had at least entertained the notion.

Even now, his body stirred at the thought of taking his new wife to bed. At one time, it had seemed like a possibility. Not today.

With nothing to occupy his time, he reached for the copy of the *Wall Street Journal* that had been tucked in the seat pocket in front of him prior to his arrival. The usual financial predictions and analyses failed to hold his interest for more than a few minutes.

At last he snapped the paper shut and tossed it aside, muttering his displeasure with the newspaper in particular and the situation in general.

His travel companion stirred, sitting up and yawning.

"What's the matter with you? I've traveled with toddlers who were quieter."

"Sorry," he said, not bothering to hide his sulky tone.

She glared at him. "If you have something to say, say it. You've been in a bad mood all afternoon. Is it the wedding? Are you regretting what we did earlier? Is the old ball and chain cramping your style?"

"It's everything," he said.

Ten

Lisette blinked in shock and her temper began to boil. "*You're* the one who insisted on marriage. Is the big, bad alpha wolf having second thoughts?"

His ill humor dented her feelings though she wouldn't tell him that for the world. She wasn't a real bride. If her husband chose to behave like a bear with a thorn in his paw, she shouldn't take it personally.

Jonathan stretched his arms over his head and sighed lustily. "I hate flying," he muttered.

"But you can't drive to Antigua."

"Exactly."

His scowl should have intimidated her, but she was tired of pretending this day was about love and romance. "Feel free to ignore me," she said sharply, staring out the window where white puffball clouds put on a show.

"I can't ignore you, Lizzy. That's the problem."

She spun her head so quickly her neck protested. "What does that mean?"

"You're temptation personified in that dress. I've wanted to strip it off you all afternoon."

Her jaw dropped. Heat spread from her throat to her face. "You can't be serious."

He shrugged. "I'm a man. You're my legally wed wife. No red-blooded male I know could entirely ignore the ramifications."

"I thought you were second-guessing our agreement," she whispered, her throat tight.

"I was. But not the way you're thinking. I'm frustrated that I ruined this day for you. No matter what happens next in your life, this will always be your first marriage. And as celebrations go, this one was a bust."

His wry honesty soothed some of her hurt. She waved a dismissive hand. "I wouldn't worry about it. My expectations were pretty low."

"Ouch." His shocked laugh restored her confidence. The odd balance of power between them was unprecedented territory. In their roles at Tarleton Shipping, the lines had been crisp and clear. No gray areas.

Now their entire relationship was one big gray area.

"How are you feeling?" she asked, studying his face for signs of pain or discomfort.

The scowl returned, though not as dark and brooding as before. "I don't want to talk about my health, remember?"

"So I'm never allowed to check on my husband's welfare? That seems cold. I'd do the same for an acquaintance who was ill."

"I'm not ill," he snapped.

"I don't understand."

He unfastened his seat belt and stood up to walk the aisle. Back and forth. His energy and passion, momentarily chained by circumstances, nevertheless vibrated in the close confines of the jet's cabin.

Without warning, the plane jolted and Jonathan staggered.

The attendant stuck his head out at the back of the plane, intercom phone in hand. "Rough weather up ahead, sir. You'll have to take your seat."

Jonathan nodded and sat down, belting in with quick, practiced movements. He glanced at Lisette. "You okay?"

"I'm fine. You never answered my question."

"It wasn't really a question as I recall."

"Don't play with words. Why did you say you aren't ill?"

He stared straight ahead, his classic male profile carved in grim lines. At last he exhaled. "I have a time bomb inside my skull. But I won't tiptoe around, always worrying about when and if it's going to blow up and kill me. I have a life to live. A future to plan, though it might not be as long as I had hoped. I'm not going to spend every waking day assessing my slow decay. I can't do that. I won't. Do you understand?"

His hands gripped the armrests so tightly his knuckles turned white. She knew he wasn't afraid to fly, so his turmoil came from another source.

Lisette reached out her right hand and linked her fingers with his. "I do," she said quietly. "I won't ask again, or at least I'll try not to. As far as I'm concerned, you're going to live until you're ninety. Does that work for you?"

Some of his tension winnowed away. He shot her a sideways glance that was both sheepish and relieved. "Thanks." His thumb caressed the back of her hand. "I swear I'll ask for help when the time comes."

"Fair enough." She hadn't realized that holding hands with her husband on her wedding day was going to affect her so strongly. She had reached out to him in a gesture of comfort and understanding. Now she was reluctant to let go. But she did. She was a wife in name only.

Gradually the turbulence outside the plane subsided. The flight attendant reappeared with coffee and sodas and snacks. "We'll be on the ground in forty-five minutes," he said.

"So soon?" She was startled.

Jonathan's smile was smug. "And now you know the benefits of chartering a private jet. Hassle-free. Besides, nothing is too good for my new bride."

The flight attendant smiled, so their charade must be working. Maybe no one would be able to tell they weren't really a couple.

Landing in St. John's and deplaning was smooth and easy. Jonathan had planned this end of the trip as well. Instead of a private car, he had arranged to rent a four-wheel-drive vehicle that would handle the sometimes precipitous roads leading up to his friend's hillside villa just below Shirley Heights.

The air was lush and humid, but not more so than Charleston, and the wind off the ocean was heavenly. Flowering trees and shrubs scented the air with exotic fragrances.

After loading their things into the back of the Jeep, Jonathan helped her up into the high passenger seat, and soon they were off on the next leg of their journey. He handled the narrow, rough road with confidence. When they pulled up in front of the beautiful home that was to be their own private retreat for the week, Lisette was speechless. She wasn't sure what she had expected, but it wasn't this lavish, stunning luxury.

A uniformed maid met them and gave them a brief tour before excusing herself to finish preparing their dinner. The house overlooked English Harbour, a glittering field of blue dotted with a hundred sailboats. Colorful bougainvillea surrounded the property and draped over railings.

"We can have dinner here," Jonathan said, indicating the elegant glass-and-rattan table on the wide veranda. "A bird's-eye view for our first sunset."

"That sounds perfect."

His gaze raked her from head to toe. "You look beautiful in that dress, but would you like to change into something more comfortable for the rest of the evening?"

She searched his words for hidden meanings, but found none. The thought of a cool shower after a busy day of wedding preparations and travel sounded wonderful.

"I would," she said. "If it's just us, we don't have to be formal, do we?"

"Not at all. This week is ours."

His quiet words and the intimacy in his smile sent a thrill through her body. Spending time with Jonathan under any circumstance would be enjoyable. He was a charismatic, fascinating man. But he was also intensely virile and masculine, and she dared not let herself think about what might unfold here in this tropical paradise.

The maid had shown them the master suite with its hedonistic glass-walled shower. Jonathan fetched both large suitcases from the Jeep and placed them on matching teak chests at the foot of the massive king-size bed. Its carved posts reflected the English colonial influence in Antigua, as did the vibrantly colored watercolors depicting points of historical interest, which were spread around the room.

Lisette set their carry-ons beside the dresser. Being here with Jonathan in this lovely room that was so obviously created for couples to enjoy rattled her considerably. "I'll use the bathroom across the hall," she said, trying not to look at either the bed *or* her new husband. "We don't want to be late for our first meal. The maid said half an hour." She grabbed what she needed and tried to smile as if her nerves weren't escalating by the minute.

Jonathan nodded, his gaze hooded. "Sounds good."

She clutched her toiletry kit and clothes and fled. In the other room she locked the door and collapsed onto the bed, her heart pounding in her chest. Did Jonathan mean for them to be intimate tonight?

The prospect filled her with a confusing mixture of anticipation and dread. The sexual attraction between them was no longer veiled. Jonathan didn't even try to hide the hunger in his gaze. But he had said they needed time to get used to each other. Was that only for her benefit?

Probably. Men rarely missed a chance to be physically intimate with a woman when the woman was available and interested.

As his wife, she was definitely available. And she had been interested for a long time.

Though she needed breathing space to find her bearings, the clock was not her friend. She undressed and jumped in the shower, keeping the water frigid. The brisk jolt of cold against her heated flesh revived and refreshed her. Wrapping up in a thick terry robe afterward felt wonderful.

She had worn her hair up in a complicated knot for the wedding and the flight. Now she took it down and brushed it out. Carefully she caught back the sides in gold clips and stared at herself in the mirror.

Jonathan claimed he'd had no serious relationships recently. She had no reason to doubt him. Even so, the prospect of getting naked with him was intimidating. Her own sexual experience was fairly limited, and she certainly couldn't match his innate confidence.

Nevertheless, she had made a monumental decision on her own behalf. After being halfway in love with her handsome boss for a very long time, now they were alone together, sharing a faux honeymoon. If the moment seemed right and Jonathan was receptive, she was going to let him know she wanted a real marriage in every sense of the word. And she was going to revisit the baby idea whether he liked it or not. She was giving up a lot for him.

Sighing deeply, she picked up the outfit she had chosen for this first evening. The garment was loose and flowing, with a halter neck. What made the dress provocative was the partially sheer lawn fabric. The color was ecru, adding to the impression that she was seminude. Tiny gold threads sifted through the cotton from throat to toe, catching the light with each movement.

She dropped the robe to the floor and debated the available undergarments. Dispensing with her bra wasn't a hard choice. She slid the lovely dress over her head and let it fall to her bare feet. The incredibly soft material caressed her sensitive skin. Though her rigid nipples pressed against the cloth in a provocative fashion, the look was certainly appropriate for an intimate dinner, particularly during a honeymoon.

The impulse to go full commando was strong, but she wasn't quite that brave. So she stepped into the brand-new pair of undies she had bought yesterday afternoon at a lingerie boutique. The lacy thong matched the color of her skin and did nothing to disturb the pleasing flow of the dress.

Her light eye makeup still looked good, though she added a bit of dramatic color for the evening. Then, all that was left was to add some gloss to her lips.

When she was ready, she stepped back and tried to study her reflection as a man would. The dress flattered her body and hinted at more curves beneath.

Would her new husband like the way she looked?

Her heart rapped in her chest as if she had run a mile. She tried to take a deep breath, but it didn't help.

She was nervous as a skittish Victorian virgin on her wedding night.

When she could delay no longer, she opened the guest room door and peeked out into the hall. Jonathan had left the master suite open, so she was able to see that the room was empty. Unless he was still in the bathroom, which seemed doubtful.

She had spent far too long getting ready. Jonathan was probably on the terrace waiting for her.

Her instincts were correct. She found him standing at the low stone wall, staring out at the idyllic scene below as if he hadn't a care in the world. His appearance surprised her. Instead of his customary dark suit and tie, he wore lightweight khaki pants and a crisp white linen shirt that stretched across broad shoulders. Leather deck shoes with no socks completed the look of a man on vacation.

For some reason, this relaxed version of Jonathan made him seem like a stranger.

She inhaled sharply. "I hope dinner is ready. I'm starving."

Jonathan spun around. All the blood in his body rushed to his groin in a painful arousal that left him unsteady on his feet. "Lizzy," he muttered. "You're here." Her tentative smile dazzled him. Why had he ever thought of her as average? Now that they were on intimate terms, her subtle, understated beauty caught him by the throat and wouldn't let go.

She was wearing some kind of sultry dress that was designed to make a man drool and stutter. It clung to her stellar breasts and slid over her body like a raw caress. Was she naked underneath? The possibility consumed him.

The maid appeared at exactly the wrong time. Jonathan wanted to curse at her and send her away, but the tray she carried was laden with culinary delights that made his stomach rumble even in the midst of his desperate desire for his bride.

The table was situated so that both parties had an unobstructed view of the ocean. He held Lizzy's chair and waited for her to be seated. Her hair brushed her bare shoulders. He wanted to run his fingers through it.

Instead, he took his place across from her and listened with half an ear as the maid/cook explained each dish. There were fried plantains and local grouper with pineapple chutney. Toast points with a Creole dipping sauce and a beautiful key lime pie.

Lisette chatted animatedly with the older local woman, at last coaxing a smile from her dour, expressionless face. Jonathan was struck suddenly by how different he and Lizzy were in temperament. She opened herself up to everyone, while Jonathan kept himself in check.

His recent diagnosis had only exacerbated his instinct to hide behind his CEO persona. Even so—sweet, generous, compassionate Lisette had agreed to his outlandish plan. Perhaps unconsciously, he had known she would. Which made him an opportunist and a user.

The realization shamed him, because it was too late for second thoughts.

Once the maid was assured that Jonathan and Lisette had everything they needed, she disappeared, leaving the newlyweds to their private wedding-night feast.

Jonathan forced himself to eat and talk and smile. Everything a normal groom would do. Some of his turmoil subsided, winnowed away by the sheer magic of a tropical night.

Lisette leaned back in her chair, meal forgotten, when the sun neared the horizon. "I can't imagine this would ever get old," she whispered. She reached across the table and took his hand. "Watch it with me," she said. "And make a wish."

He gripped her fingers, feeling how slender and delicate they were in contrast to his larger hand. "I don't think that's a real thing. Isn't it only shooting stars?"

"It can be whatever we want it to be. Look," she said urgently. The sun seemed to sink more quickly now. The bottom rim kissed the ocean. The sun melted into a fatter, wider ball, and then it was gone.

Jonathan stared at the colors swirling on the horizon. How many more sunsets would he live to see?

He cleared his throat. "I understand now why my buddy bought this place. It's more than a tax write-off."

Lisette grimaced. "A tax write-off? Oh, Jonathan. Surely you have a tiny bit of romance in your soul."

"Maybe. Did you make a wish?"

"I did, but I'm not telling you."

"I'll bet I could make you talk."

She blinked, perhaps as surprised as he was by the blatantly sexual comment. He hadn't even known he was going to say it.

"Um…" She released his hand. "May I ask you something?"

He waved a hand. "I'm feeling pretty mellow at the moment. The floor is yours, my beautiful bride."

"We've danced around the issue of whether or not this marriage, *our* marriage, is going to include physical intimacy. And we talked about having time to get used to each other…to know each other in a different way than we do at work."

Her pause was so long he felt compelled to say something. "Yes."

"You said it would be up to me."

"Yes." The word was more of a croak.

"Well…" She hesitated. Though he couldn't be sure with only candlelight to illuminate her face, he thought she had blushed. "Waiting for the shoe to drop makes me nervous and jumpy around you. I think I'd rather go ahead and get it over with. If you don't mind."

Eleven

He scowled. "Like a root canal or tetanus shot? Pardon me if I'm not flattered." In fact, he was downright insulted. No woman had ever approached sex with him as a hurdle to be overcome. "I told you, our marriage doesn't have to include physical intimacy at all."

"That came out wrong. This is my first wedding night, and I don't have a script."

"I haven't ever been married either, but I'm pretty damned sure a real husband and wife would have had sex *before* dinner. Or maybe skipped dinner altogether." He was practically shouting at her and he didn't know why. Except that he wanted to slide that tantalizing dress from her body and see what Lisette Stanhope would be like in bed.

"I'm sorry," she said, the words stiff. "I didn't mean to make you angry. Forget I said anything."

He stood abruptly. Arousal coursed through his veins, pulsating and urgent. If he didn't get some space—some breathing room—he was going to take her right here on the dinner table. "Excuse me," he muttered.

"Don't you want dessert?"

"Screw dessert," he snarled.

An hour later, Lisette sat with her bare feet propped on the railing and toyed with a piece of key lime pie. It was actually one of her favorites, and this particular version was the best she had ever tasted. But her stomach was tied in knots.

The maid had cleared the table not long after Jonathan's stormy exit. A short while later the silent woman climbed into her car for the trip home. Lisette had heard the steady chug of the old engine as it made its way down the mountain.

She replayed the evening in her head, wondering how she might have approached things differently. She hadn't expected problems to crop up so soon. It looked like the honeymoon period was over. She couldn't even laugh at her own joke.

The sky was dark now, punctuated with a million stars. The night wasn't quiet. Birds and other unseen animals spoke to each other in interesting choruses. Because she had napped on the plane, she wasn't sleepy at all. It was far more entertaining to stay out here and absorb the Caribbean magic than it would be to toss and turn in an unfamiliar bed.

Besides, she couldn't share a bed with Jonathan. Not now. Had he put her suitcase in the guest room? Or moved his own? She was too much of a chicken to go inside and find out.

She had to get through six days and six more nights of this before they could go home. The villa had a jewel of a swimming pool, and she had brought two brand-new swimsuits. Maybe she could read and work on the summer tan she never seemed to manage.

Tears of regret stung her eyes, but she refused to let them fall. Jonathan's rejection of her awkward overture had hurt. It still hurt.

All she'd been trying to tell him was that she was ready. She wanted him. Instead, she had made it sound like sleeping with her new husband was a chore and an obligation. No wonder he lost his cool.

She set the small china plate with the pie crumbs on the wall and leaned back so she could see more of the sky. Never had she been more confused or more unsure of herself. Helping Jonathan through these next weeks and months was something she *wanted* to do…something she needed to do.

He was a decent, kind, hardworking man who had been dealt an abominably bad hand. He was also exactly the kind of man she had always looked for in a life partner. But none had ever come along until Jonathan. Or at least not one who made her body quiver with desire. She wanted him. Desperately.

What did *she* know about seduction? Apparently nothing. She and Jonathan were married and planted smack-dab in the midst of a tropical paradise, and yet still she had bobbled it. She hadn't wanted to be a passive female, waiting for him to make the first move. She'd wanted to assert her femininity, to be bold and fearless.

Maybe men didn't like that in a woman. Maybe they always wanted to be the aggressor. At least in the beginning.

It was late. She should probably go in.

Before she could follow through on that thought, a deep male voice sounded behind her.

"Lisette…"

That was all. Just her name.

She stood up and faced him. "Yes?"

He shrugged. "I'm sorry."

"I'm sorry, too."

Without saying another word, he took his phone from his pocket, tapped a few icons and set the device on the table. A slow, sultry cascade of music filled the air. Jonathan held out his hand. "Will you dance with me?"

Never in a million years would she have pegged Jonathan Tarleton for a dancer, but he proved her wrong. He was both light on his feet and moved with natural rhythm. As he swept her into his arms and twirled them across the flagstone patio, it seemed as if they were dancing on clouds.

With her cheek pressed to his chest, she noted his ragged breathing, his thudding pulse. He held her tightly, close enough for him to know that she was essentially naked beneath her dress. They danced in bare feet. The differences in their heights made her feel cherished and protected.

One song ended. Another began. She couldn't ignore the way his aroused sex pressed against her abdomen.

She didn't know what to say, but there was no real need for conversation. Their bodies communicated without words.

After a few more songs, the music ended. Before she could do more than inhale a shocked breath, she felt Jonathan's fingers play with the knot at her nape. "May I?" he asked, his breath warm on her ear.

A hard shiver rocked through her body. "Yes."

Moments later, with a gentle tug from him, her dress fell in a pool at her feet. He took a step back and stared. "I want a do-over," he said hoarsely.

She wrapped her arms around her breasts, equal parts excited and uncertain. "Me, too. I want to sleep with you, Jonathan. Very much."

He raised an eyebrow. "Sleep?"

"Don't tease me. Not now. I'm trying to play this cool and sophisticated. But I'm at a definite disadvantage."

Her wry comment coaxed a grin from him. "What if I take off my shirt?" He tackled the buttons so fast she laughed out loud. But when his chest was bare, her levity dried up.

She cocked her head. "If I had known you were hiding a six-pack beneath those hand-tailored suits," she said, "I would have hit on you a long time ago."

He scooped her up in his arms, his gaze hot and hungry. "No, you wouldn't. You've always been the consummate professional. You never even hinted that you were interested in me."

"Of course not," she whispered. "You were my boss."

He kicked open the door, carried her into the house and bumped the door shut with his hip before locking it. "And now I'm your husband."

"Yes, you are." She cupped his cheek with her hand. "I'm glad you changed your mind. I'm sorry I made sex with you sound like something I was tolerating. I didn't want to wait, but my words came out all wrong."

"I'll let you make it up to me." He strode in the direction of the bedroom. In the doorway, he paused. "I have a confession." He dropped her onto the mattress and settled beside her, placing one hand, palm flat, on her stomach. His dark eyes glittered. "I'm very much afraid I came up with the marriage idea because I was obsessed with you... not because I cared about Tarleton Shipping."

Being mostly naked with Jonathan in a huge, hedonistic bed should have embarrassed her, but all she could think about was how very much she wanted him. "Maybe it was both," she said. "I'm okay with that."

He stood up and stripped off his pants and boxers. The sight of his aroused sex dried her mouth. His body was intensely masculine and incredibly beautiful. For a man who purportedly worked long hours, he surely did *something* to maintain that physique.

When he reached into his pants pocket for a trio of condoms, she realized that the reason he had come out to the terrace to make peace was because he wanted more than a platonic wedding night.

His crooked smile found its way into her heart and made her eyes sting with emotional tears. She loved him. It was the only reason she had said yes to this inconvenient marriage.

She still wanted a baby, but since they had come close to ruining this first night, she wouldn't bring it up. Yet...

She flipped back the covers and held out her hand.

"Come get warm." The tile floor was icy with the AC running.

Though the bed was large, when Jonathan joined her, his big, masculine body dominated the space. She tried to scoot farther to one side, but he grabbed her wrist. "Come here, Ms. Tarleton." Leaning over her on one elbow, he brushed the hair from her face. "I want a real honeymoon," he said softly. The words were not particularly provocative, but the expression on his face made her tremble.

She touched his shoulder, stroking the hard planes where smooth, taut skin stretched over muscle and bone. "So do I."

He let her explore for several long moments, not moving at all. But the flush on his cheekbones darkened. "I like having you touch me, Lizzy."

When he cupped her breast and teased her nipple with his thumb, she gasped. Heat bloomed and streaked through her body like an erotic pinball, flipping switches she didn't even know existed.

She tried to say something, but he bent his head and tasted the furled flesh, raking it with his teeth. Her hands clenched in his hair as all the breath wheezed out of her lungs.

It was almost laughable to think about how she had imagined this moment. In her mind, the first time with Jonathan was going to be tender and gentle. Why she'd held that notion, she couldn't say.

The reality was totally unlike her fantasies. It was far more visceral, more powerful. He staked his claim without apology.

He touched her everywhere.

And all along the way, he muttered praises and pleas and demands. He allowed her neither timidity nor inhibitions. His hunger ignited her own, taking her to places she hadn't experienced.

They tumbled across the mattress, wrestling for the

upper hand, both determined to drive the other to the edge. Jonathan dragged her lacy undies down her legs, careful not to tear them. She wouldn't have minded.

Now he moved lower in the bed. "I want to taste you," he said. "Spread your legs." Three words. Three little words, and she was his slave.

His intimate demand shocked her. For a moment, her thighs tightened instinctively.

As he moved to his elbows and nudged her ankles apart, he lifted his head, staring at her challengingly. "Too much, Lizzy?"

She forced herself to relax. "No," she said softly. "Never."

Jonathan was skilled at more than dancing. He shot her over the edge of her first climax with dizzying speed. Her body was his. He played it like a master, demanding her total submission to his will.

Though she wanted to give him the same pleasure he was giving her, she barely had time to breathe or choke out a cry of completion. He gave no quarter, drawing out the incredible bliss of orgasm until she was weak and spent.

At last he let her rest. "You're amazing," he said, resting his cheek on her upper thigh. "Maybe we'll never leave this room."

With his hair tumbled across his forehead and his pupils dilated with arousal, he looked very different from the man who controlled a huge business empire with cool confidence. Tonight he was naked and voracious, utterly male, completely devoted to pleasing his bride.

She still trembled from their recent excess. "I've waited a long time for this," she said. The words were only slightly unsteady. "I want you on your back, Jonathan, so I can have my way with you."

The muscles in his throat rippled as he swallowed. His erection bumped her knee. "Should I be scared?" he joked as he rolled away from her and sprawled on the empty side of the bed.

"Very."

He tucked his hands behind his head. His cocky grin made him look young and carefree. For a moment, her heart wrestled with the reality of the future, but she shoved the bad thoughts aside. No time for tears or mourning now.

Despite what had just happened, she was shy about him seeing her naked. While she debated how best to play with him, she wrapped the coverlet from the foot of the bed around herself and clutched it with one hand.

Her gaze landed on a beautiful azure-glazed urn filled with dry grasses. She plucked one out of the container and brushed the fluffy tip against her arm. "This will do," she said.

Jonathan's eyes widened. Perhaps he had been expecting oral sex. Everything in its time. She wanted to keep her new husband off balance. He leaned toward arrogance at times. It wouldn't be a bad thing for him to wonder what she was up to.

Trying to climb back onto the bed without losing either her weapon of torment *or* her covering was virtually impossible.

Jonathan smirked. "I've seen all there is to see. No reason to be shy with me now."

The challenge in his voice tipped her decision. She dropped the soft throw and stood at the side of the bed, naked and in charge. Or at least that's what she was shooting for. Jonathan's searing gaze, intense and bold, was almost enough to melt her into a puddle.

"I'm not shy," she lied. "I was merely planning my assault."

"Sounds dangerous."

She ran her hand down his thigh, carefully avoiding

the interesting territory nearby. "Close your eyes, Jonathan. Relax."

He obeyed the first command, but choked out an incredulous laugh. "Relax? You can't be serious. You've got me so tightly wound I might go up in flames."

"I have faith in you," she said, leaning down to kiss his sculpted lips. She let the tip of her tongue push inside his mouth and brush *his* tongue. "Whatever you do, don't open your eyes. Just glide on a sea of pleasure. One muscle at a time." She lowered her voice to a murmur. "I want you to feel *everything*. Do you understand?"

He nodded, his jaw tight. "I'll try."

With the feathery end of her long frond, she started at his ears and his cheeks, caressing one at a time. He gasped once, sharply, and his hands fisted at his hips. Slowly she moved the seagrass along his sternum and over his belly. When she neared his erection, his entire body went rigid and a ragged moan escaped him. "Not yet," she murmured. "You're too tense. You want to be in control, don't you, Jonathan?"

"Hell, yes."

She slid the fluffy tip across the tops of his thighs, *accidentally* brushing his vulnerable sac in the process. Then it was on to his calves, his ankles and his big, unabashedly male feet.

"Letting go can be wonderful," she promised.

The word he said made her smile. He was clearly trying to indulge her and so very clearly losing the battle.

Now she hovered the stalk of seagrass over his body and let the soft tip toy with his erection. His sex was swollen and hard, flat against his belly. Importunate. Ready for action.

When she touched him like that, a giant shudder racked his frame. "Please," he muttered. "No more."

She dropped the dried plant and climbed onto the bed, taking his sex in her hands and squeezing gently.

Before she could taste him intimately, his control snapped. He reared up and took her head in his two hands, dragging her mouth to his, kissing her desperately. "I can't wait," he groaned. "Now, Lizzy. Now."

He reached blindly for one of the condoms. A fleeting regret swept through her. Would he ever change his mind about the baby?

But then he was on top of her and in her and her world exploded. When she grabbed his shoulders, her nails sank into his flesh. He grunted in pain, but didn't stop. She didn't want him to. Ever. The feel of his body taking hers would be imprinted in her memory forever.

Canting her hips, she urged him deeper and deeper still until the blunt head of his sex pressed her womb. "Jonathan…" she cried out. Suddenly she was both elated and terrified. She would never be able to protect her heart. Not if things were like this between them.

There was no room for subterfuge, no opportunity for self-defense.

"Relax, Lizzy." It was his turn to say the word. He must have felt her moment of indecision. His lips nuzzled her ear. "I want you every way there is to want a woman," he said. His voice was rough, almost inaudible. "You're mine," he said. "For as long as we have."

Even the fact that he brought reality into their bed couldn't stop the headlong rush into abandon. "Yes," she moaned. "Yes."

Stunned fulfillment caught her yet again and swept her into the currents of his passion. Jonathan went rigid and thrust inside her forever, it seemed, until he found his own release and collapsed on top of her.

Twelve

God in heaven. What have we done? Jonathan was groggy and satiated. His limbs were numb, his brain fogged with a jumble of thoughts that didn't quite coalesce into reason.

When he could open one eye, he determined that his new wife slept...draped over him like a soft, curvy boa. And that vision, only that, was enough to have his sex stirring again.

If he had known it would be like this, he might never have been able to leave her alone for these last three years. Tonight had shown him a whole new side of Lisette Stanhope. She was strong and capable. He knew that much, of course. But she was also sexually adventurous and fun in bed.

She'd been hiding behind sensible skirts and tops and boring colors. Here, in Antigua, her sexuality had blossomed. Or maybe it had been there along, and she had simply kept it from him.

Suddenly an unpleasant thought occurred. His new bride wasn't a virgin. He knew that, of course. She was thirty-seven years old. But where had she learned how to turn a man into a drooling idiot? Jonathan liked being able to drive *her* wild, but when she turned the tables on him and used a pseudomassage to push him to the edge of his control, the experience was less comfortable.

Incredibly arousing and erotically eye-opening, but still a disturbing moment. He'd never had sex like that with *any* woman. Not that the mechanics were so very different. But it was the mood, the way his body responded as if his arousal and his sexual response had been conditioned by the scent of her skin and the sound of her voice.

He slid out of bed and visited the facilities. Lisette was still deeply asleep, so he grabbed a quick shower. When he walked back into the bedroom—towel tied at his hips— her eyes were open.

She lifted up on her elbows. The sheet slithered below her breasts. His towel tented in the front. "Good morning," she said huskily.

"Good morning to you." He couldn't do a thing in the world about the lewdly fashioned terry cloth at his groin.

Lisette pretended not to notice. "Does the maid come first thing?"

"I was told there would be plenty of food in the fridge for breakfast and lunch. Sunday is her day off. We're all alone."

Those incredible pale green eyes studied him intently. "Is that information I need to know?"

It was impossible to miss the challenge in her gaze. He nodded slowly. "I didn't want you to worry."

"Worry?"

"You know. About being interrupted. This bedroom is entirely private. Off-limits."

"Ah."

He sat down on the edge of the mattress. "Did you sleep well?"

"I must have. I don't really recall last night. I think I was dead to the world."

"That's a shame. Parts of it were pretty damned spectacular."

Her lips twitched. "Oh, *that* part. Yeah. I remember that."

He ditched the towel and reached for her. "How hungry

are you on a scale of one to ten?" Lifting her on top of him, he stroked her bottom.

Her chest heaved in a sigh. "I had my heart set on an omelet, but an appetizer might be nice."

He took a moment to enjoy the view. With her hair tousled and her pale skin warm from their bed, just looking at her gave him an odd ache in his chest. She was easier with him now, less tentative. Last night had cemented something in their relationship.

"At the risk of sounding like a sex-obsessed male," he said, "I have to tell you your breasts are spectacular." Firm, smooth flesh. Raspberry tips. A sudden vision of his wife nursing their child flashed into his mind. He knew Lisette wanted a baby. She had made that very clear. The prospect of trying to get her pregnant fried his brain. It was too soon to make a decision like that, but suddenly, it wasn't out of the question.

"Be honest," he said, breathing heavily. "You wore that dress last night to drive me insane."

"It was a hot evening." Her smile was innocent.

He snorted. "It's hot in Charleston, but I've never seen you in anything remotely similar."

"You only see me at work. Maybe I dress like that all the time when I'm out on the town."

He pulled her down for a quick kiss. "Do you?"

"No."

Lisette realized that things were escalating rapidly. Unfortunately, she badly needed to visit the bathroom and freshen up. "Jonathan?"

"Hmm?" He nibbled the side of her neck, just below her right ear.

She shuddered. "Give me three minutes," she said, scrambling off her provocative perch and fleeing. In the bathroom, she closed the door, hoping he didn't hear the quiet snick of the lock. She needed privacy, but more than that, she needed a moment to steady her thoughts, to find solid ground.

After taking care of urgent needs, she did a few quick ablutions, then leaned forward on the vanity and studied her face in the mirror. She was a married woman now. A legal part of Jonathan's life. Whatever faced them, she would be with him day after day. His wife, for better or worse.

When she had awakened a little while ago and spotted him standing in the doorway, he almost seemed like a stranger. In all the years she had known him, never once had she seen him unshaven. Today, dark stubble shadowed his firm jaw, giving him a rakish air. The change was unexpected, but she definitely liked it. Scruffy Jonathan was even more appealing than tuxedo-clad Jonathan.

She returned to the bedroom with a mix of anticipation and trepidation. Daylight sex was different. Harder for a woman to hide an extra five pounds or pretend to be a seductress when in reality she was anything but.

Jonathan was looking at his phone, but he tossed it aside as soon as she appeared. His smile made her toes curl against the cool tile. "Hey," he said, his greeting warm and husky. "Come join me."

Though she felt shy even now, he didn't have to ask her twice. She chewed her bottom lip, trying not to notice the way her stomach flipped and went into free fall when Jonathan pulled her close and stroked her arm. Her *arm*, for Pete's sake. When he eventually moved to other body parts, she would be a goner.

She cleared her throat. "What would you like to do today?" she asked, wincing inwardly at hearing herself. She sounded like a perky travel agent.

Her husband's low chuckle didn't help her embarrassment. "You mean after sex and breakfast? At the rate we're going, there won't be much of the day left."

"Are you complaining?" She laid her hand on his hair-roughened upper thigh, feeling the taut muscles.

"Lord, no. I'm even willing to give up breakfast if my wife keeps me busy all morning."

As if on cue, Lisette's stomach growled. She curled into his side, putting her hand, palm flat, right over his heart. One of her legs trapped both of his, but there was no question as to who was in control.

He shifted without warning and put her beneath him, kissing her lazily. His lips were firm and persuasive. "How hungry *are* you?" he asked, nuzzling her nose with his.

Feelings rose in her chest, wild poignant emotions that choked her, making it hard to breathe. How was she supposed to be blasé about this? Most normal honeymooners would be planning their future. Instead, Jonathan was asking her to live only in the moment. It was far harder than she had thought it would be to pretend.

She managed a smile. "Hungry for you," she said lightly. "The other can wait."

Maybe Jonathan sensed her ambivalence, because after reaching for protection, he stroked her body so carefully and so gently she nearly cried for real this time. How was she going to protect herself? Being with him like this was too real, too devastatingly sweet. The thought of losing him was more than she could bear.

He entered her slowly, so slowly she was forced to wrap her ankles behind his back and urge him deeper. The more she tried, the more he taunted them both.

His voice was rough, unsteady. "Tell me how you like it, beautiful girl. Slow and infinite? Or hard and fast? I'll give you whatever you ask."

Her good intentions cracked. "Give me a baby, Jonathan. Please." The words slipped out of their own volition, born of a need to keep part of him with her forever. As soon as she spoke, she knew she had ruined the magic.

Jonathan was close to the edge, but he rolled away, grim-faced, and disappeared into the bathroom.

Tears wet her cheeks as she grabbed her things and sought the relative safety of the guest room. She couldn't do this. It wasn't fair.

She buried her face in the pillows that didn't carry his scent and cried until her chest hurt and her eyes were puffy. They had barely made it twenty-four hours, and already their marriage was on the rocks.

He was asking the impossible. *Be his stand-in at work. His bed partner at home*. But don't love. Don't try to make any of this real.

This relationship wasn't working out as she had planned. She thought she could be satisfied with having a small bit of his life. That she could let him go when the time came.

But now, she wasn't at all sure she would be able to play her part. It was too damn hard.

At last she rose and showered. Afterward she put on one of her new bikinis and topped it with a modest cover-up. When hunger drove her to the kitchen, she found evidence that her husband had dined earlier. For her part, a banana and yogurt with granola were all that she could manage… that, and hot black coffee with plenty of sugar.

Unlike yesterday evening, today there were no mutual apologies in the hours that followed. No dancing on the terrace.

Lisette swam and sunbathed. Jonathan appeared eventually and claimed a lounger at the opposite end of the pool. He buried his face in a business magazine and occasionally slept.

What he did *not* do was make any attempt to converse at all.

She was hurt and angry, but she wouldn't apologize for feeling the way she did. It wasn't unreasonable of her to ask for a baby, or even to demand one. She was giving up her dreams for Jonathan. He had promised to consider the pregnancy. Had he not really meant it?

Perhaps there was a better way to smooth over their mutual wounds. Something very basic and elemental like the need between a man and a woman.

When the heat from the late-afternoon sun became intense, she removed her cover-up and applied more sunscreen. With her back to Jonathan, she twisted her hair into a messy knot and then bent over to pick up the brush she had intentionally dropped. Was he watching? She had never done anything so physically manipulative in her life, but desperate times and all that.

Instead of using the diving board as she had earlier, she donned her sunglasses and entered the water via the shallow steps…which just happened to be on *Jonathan's* end of the pool. After that, she did lazy laps, one after the other. On each return trip, she peeked at her companion. Hiding behind her darkened lenses allowed her to observe him without his being entirely sure that she was.

He definitely wasn't sleeping any longer.

His board shorts meant she couldn't tell if he was responding physically to her deliberate teasing, but at last she noticed that his hands clenched the arms of the lounger.

Bingo… He couldn't ignore her. That was what she was counting on. They might not have everything going for them that a normal couple would, but there was plenty of room for progress.

Jonathan couldn't stonewall her about this baby thing. He wanted her too badly, and she felt the same way about him.

Righteous indignation and lust were a dangerous combination. Jonathan was not happy with how things had unfolded today, but he refused to go crawling to his bride. She understood how he felt. He'd made his position very clear.

He was a master negotiator, and he knew from experience that it was always better to make an adversary come to him, not vice versa.

So he stayed where he was and told himself he was in the right.

Which was cold comfort when Lisette stood up in the shallow end and sluiced water from her curvy body with both hands.

By Caribbean standards, her navy bikini was probably puritanical, but damn it, her breasts were about to pop out of that top. And as for the bottom half, well, he couldn't get his mind off the gorgeous erotic secrets that were his for the taking, barely covered. Wet and warm. Perfectly feminine.

When she turned her back on him for the hundredth time, it seemed, and swam lazily toward the other end of the pool, he'd had enough. He lunged to his feet, strode down the steps and bulleted toward his prey as silently as a shark. He'd been on the varsity swim team in college, and he had lived at the shore his entire life.

Lisette Stanhope Tarleton didn't have a chance.

A heartbeat later, he glided up beneath her and wrapped his arms around her legs, dragging her under. The water at this end was deep. The sudden move knocked her sunglasses loose. Her wide-eyed gaze met his under the water. Sunlight showered down on them through the ripples in the pool.

He put his hand behind her neck and pulled her close for a hard kiss. Then he kicked hard and shot them both back to the surface. When they could breathe, he put his hands at her waist and lifted her as high as he could. "Grab the diving board, Lizzy."

She obeyed, but her face mirrored her confusion. "What are we doing? Some kind of kinky yoga?"

"Call it whatever you want, Ms. Tarleton. But don't let go." Lazily, as if every nerve in his body wasn't scraped raw by the lust pounding in his limbs, he reached out and dragged her bikini top below her breasts.

It was a dicey game he played. Staying afloat required him to move his legs continually. He curled an arm around her waist. That was better. Now he could take one berry-colored nipple into his mouth without drowning.

Her skin tasted of chlorine and coconut oil. He might as well have been tasting her sex, so visceral was his reaction. With his free hand, he tugged the bottom half of her suit to her ankles, freed it completely and tossed it up on the side of the pool. The bikini top followed. Gently he entered her with two fingers. Her inner muscles tightened.

"Jonathan?" The single word was breathless.

"I don't know what to do with you," he muttered, stunned enough by his own weakness to be completely honest.

"We could try the shallow end."

It took him half a second to realize that while he was pondering the greater questions of life, Lisette had taken his comment at face value and was offering a practical solution.

"Yes, we could," he said. "You can let go now, sweetheart. I've got you." He tugged her through the water to the center of the pool where the water was neck deep. Her arms were still linked around his shoulders, even though she no longer needed his support.

Her eyelashes were spiky and wet. Her almost translucent green eyes stared deep into his soul. Or that's how it seemed for a hushed moment.

She rubbed a drop of water from his chin. "I like this pirate look," she said softly. "Too bad he has to disappear when we go home."

"Being the boss does occasionally have its downside." He kissed her nose and her bare, pink lips. "I want to take you right here. Just like this." The notion consumed him.

A shadow danced across her face. "No condoms, remember?"

"I won't come inside you."

She shook her head slowly. "I can't take that chance. Not when you're so adamant about not having a baby. I want you to make me pregnant, but it has to be a conscious choice on your part."

Damn it. Nothing like having a lover throw your own words back at you. "Put your legs around me," he coaxed. Lisette was blissfully naked, but Jonathan was still wearing his swim trunks. Nothing could happen.

The water made her buoyant. She granted his request easily. Now her breasts were snuggled into his chest and those long, gorgeous legs wrapped tightly around his waist.

She nibbled his earlobe. "We have a wonderful, comfy bed inside. I bet we could get there if we tried."

His body quaked. He rubbed his hardened sex against her center, tormenting them both. Lisette buried her face in his shoulder and moaned.

"I want you," he said, the words hoarse and raspy. For a mad moment, he almost caved. Making Lisette pregnant was a titillating idea, one that messed with his head. He could do it. Right now. Give her a baby. His child.

But his will was stronger than his desire. Because he cared about her. Being a single parent was hard and lonely. When he was gone, he wanted Lisette to be free. Unencumbered.

He pulled her arms from around his neck and made her stand. "Inside," he said. "Now. Please, Lizzy. Hurry."

Her eyebrows went up. *I can't get out yet. I'm naked. Grab my suit.*

"There's no one here but us. C'mon, Miss Priss. I'll guard your modesty. If anybody shows up unexpectedly, I'll throw myself on top of you so they can't see a thing."

She took his hand and followed him out of the pool, laughing. "You'd do that for me?"

He turned on the outdoor shower. "Anytime, day or night. All you have to do is ask."

They took turns rinsing off and then wrapped up in huge fluffy towels from a heated bin. Jonathan was nearing the edge of his self-control. It had been hours since he had made love to his brand-new wife, and he intended to make up for lost time.

Thirteen

Several hours after they left the pool, Lisette found herself standing with her sexy husband in a crowd of people at Shirley Heights, a restored military lookout and gun battery. This particular spot—just above their honeymoon villa—afforded incredible sunset views of English and Falmouth harbors. Every Sunday night the locals staged a huge barbecue, serenaded by a collection of home-grown musical talent.

Since it was the maid's day off, Jonathan had suggested this as a casual dinner plan. He held her close to his side as they made their way through the press of people. The tantalizing smells wafting from open grills and the pulsing rhythms of steel drums created a definite party atmosphere.

When they had eaten, they staked out a spot at the edge of the hilltop to witness the famed sunset. Lisette felt safe in Jonathan's embrace. She leaned against him, hoping to see the elusive green flash as the sun slid below the horizon. From this vantage point, it was fairly common, or so they had been told.

As they stood amid the throng of affable tourists, she felt the strangest combination of relaxation and arousal. Being here with Jonathan was the first truly carefree thing she had done for herself in years.

He smelled wonderful, a mix of warm male skin and elusive aftershave…something expensive, no doubt.

When someone bumped into them from behind, Lisette stumbled forward.

Jonathan steadied her. "You okay?"

She stretched her arms over her head, yawning. "I'm great," she said. "Oh, look. There it goes." The sun disappeared and, unmistakably, a brief burst of emerald lit the horizon.

"Maybe it's a good omen." Jonathan nuzzled her ear, standing behind her and sliding his arms around her waist.

"I never saw you as a superstitious kind of guy," she teased. It was true. The Jonathan Tarleton most people knew was logical and not given to flights of fancy. Yet here they were in a most unusual circumstance.

Darkness fell rapidly. They slowly made their way back to where Jonathan had parked the Jeep. "Ready for home, Ms. Tarleton?" he asked, helping her into the passenger seat. He paused to kiss her.

His lips were firm and warm, and tasted like cinnamon from the dessert they had shared.

When he pulled back at last and went around the Jeep to his own side, she put a hand to her chest, breathless. They'd had sex twice so far today, and yet she trembled with wanting him.

At the house, she showered while Jonathan checked all the outer doors and turned on the overnight pool filter. When he returned, she was sitting in bed wearing another new purchase. The coffee-colored satin made her feel sexy and playful.

The flare of heat in Jonathan's eyes said he approved, as well. "I won't be long," he promised.

While she waited, she realized the two of them had a problem. They shouldn't use sex to manipulate each other. It wasn't productive, and it wasn't healthy. Jonathan had promised to think about the baby thing, but she didn't see any indication that he was changing his mind.

Maybe she would have to insist. Jonathan was going to have to make a few concessions. He had married her, and she wouldn't be kept in the dark about how he was feeling. If she was going to be at his side, he had to trust her. Completely.

Her serious musings evaporated when he strode nude across the bedroom and climbed into bed. It was still too soon for her to be blasé about his big, aroused, decidedly damp-from-the-shower body.

"Did you even *try* to dry off?" she asked.

He slipped a hand between her thighs, finding her warm center. "I was in a hurry." His other hand found a satin-covered breast and stroked it. "You look hot in this." His pupils were dilated. His ever-ready erection bobbed as if it hadn't been satisfied in months.

"Thank you."

He sprawled onto his back and lifted her across his body. "We started off like this earlier today and got sidetracked. Seeing you from this angle takes my breath away. You're gorgeous, Lizzy." He shimmied the satin up her thighs until it bunched around her waist.

She leaned forward and put her hands on his shoulders. "I like where this is going."

When he reached for the condom and handed it to her, his smile was challenging. "Will you do the honors?"

She hesitated. "If you want me to." Having him watch her so intently made the whole process nerve-racking. She handled the foil carefully. When it was time to roll the latex down his shaft, her hands trembled.

Jonathan, on the other hand, didn't move at all. He was rigid, braced as if to withstand mortal torture.

Her relative inexperience in this arena made the act unintentionally provocative. His chest heaved and he closed his eyes, groaning.

She flushed, more than a little turned-on by how very much he liked having her touch him. "I'm done," she said.

He opened one eyelid. "Oh, no, sweet thing. We're only just beginning."

Nothing he did was what she expected. Instead of lifting her onto his erection, he used his thumb to caress her intimately. She was embarrassingly wet. "I'm ready," she muttered, mortified by the fact that all her intimate bits were on full display.

His wicked smile calculated every degree of her insecurity. "You should see this from my side," he drawled. "Sheer perfection."

Her eyes scrunched shut, no longer able to watch his big tanned hands on her body. It was too much. Since she was trying very hard not to come yet, she started reciting multiplication tables in her head.

Jonathan seemed in no particular hurry to move past the overture. Now both of his thumbs separated her swollen labia. "I'm insane with wanting you, Lizzy. I'd swear you spiked my drink tonight if we hadn't been teetotalers."

His words were like sandpaper, scraping at her composure, revealing layers beneath. Truths she didn't want to admit. She went up on her knees and tried to move things along. When she wrapped her fingers around his shaft and guided him toward her entrance, every atom of air in the room dried up, leaving her breathless and starved for oxygen.

Gently she lowered herself until they were joined completely. The sensation of fullness from this angle was indescribable.

Jonathan's fingers gripped her bare butt so tightly she knew she would have bruises tomorrow. "Ride me, Lisette," he begged.

She was tentative at first, self-conscious. But Jonathan's response spurred her on. With her every careful slide downward, his sex found pleasure points inside her. "Jonathan..." She dropped her head back and closed her eyes.

He took the reins, a position she offered gladly. After that, all she had to do was feel and feel and feel. Each time they were together was different and new. Tonight he pushed her higher and higher, calculating which caresses would excite her without sending her over the top.

His own self-control seemed endless.

She was still wearing her nightgown. Jonathan was completely nude. The juxtaposition of her satin-clad flesh and his taut, muscled frame was provocative. Naughty.

When she managed a peek at him, his gaze burned into hers. "You're mine, Lizzy," he said.

A slight furrow creased her brow. The words sounded oddly possessive for a man who had nothing to offer her but his body...and that only temporarily. She glared at him through half-closed eyes. "Goes both ways, Jonathan. I want all of you. Nobody else. Just you."

Her words did something to him. He growled. There was no other way to describe the sound he made low in his throat. Bracing his feet against the mattress, he thrust wildly.

Lisette crashed over the edge of the precipice where he had kept her poised for hours, it seemed. The pleasure bordered on pain, sharp and deep.

Jonathan's climax racked his body, left him rigid and groaning. It lasted forever.

When she collapsed on top of him, her husband pulled the covers over them both. "Sleep," he muttered.

Lisette nodded and buried her face in the curve of his neck and shoulder. "Yes."

Monday dawned bright and glorious. Lisette didn't actually *see* the fabulous blue skies and sunshine until almost noon. Jonathan had awakened her twice during the night. Now she was sore and satiated and groggy.

When she realized that her husband was not in bed beside her, she frowned.

Before she could do anything more than run a hand through her wild sleep-tousled hair, Jonathan appeared in the doorway, looking disgustingly fresh and handsome. She felt like a wreck.

His gorgeous smile had her tugging the sheet upward instinctively. She needed sustenance before the next round. Were all honeymoons like this?

Then she focused on what he carried. A breakfast tray. Filled with an array of tantalizing goodies.

"May I ask you a favor?" she said politely.

His lips quirked in a grin. "Of course."

"Give me five minutes to freshen up. Then come back. And FYI, one pot of coffee might not be enough."

Her indefatigable lover chuckled, turned around and disappeared.

Fearing his level of cooperation, she darted from the bed and into the bathroom. Since her sexy nightgown was crumpled on the bedroom floor, she put on one of the thick terry robes, brushed her hair and washed her face.

By the time she returned to the bedroom, she felt marginally more human. Jonathan showed up as she sat down on the bed. She scooted toward the headboard and waited for him to place the breakfast tray across her lap.

She patted the mattress beside her. "You going to join me?"

"I'll have coffee," he said, pointing at the second cup. "I ate earlier. You were so tired I didn't want to wake you." His smug smile made her face heat.

"And whose fault was that?"

He mimicked her pose from the opposite side of the bed. "Mine. All mine."

Though he professed to have eaten, that didn't stop him from stealing tidbits from her tray. They shared the meal in companionable silence. The screened windows were open, letting in the breeze.

Lisette studied her husband when she thought he wasn't looking. He was young and healthy and strong. At least that's what his outward appearance conveyed. She couldn't believe he was as sick as he said.

Maybe the culprit was stress. Here on vacation in a Caribbean playground he didn't appear to be in pain. His posture was relaxed, his color good. As soon as they returned to Charleston, she was going to try one more time to get him to another doctor for an evaluation.

People made mistakes all the time. Jonathan couldn't be dying. She wouldn't believe it.

When she declared herself stuffed, Jonathan removed the tray and sprawled beside her, head on his hand. In touching distance. Then he lifted one eyebrow. One sexy, inquisitive eyebrow.

"Oh, no," she said, laughing. "We need to pace ourselves. Besides, you promised me a tropical vacation. I've barely seen anything."

He put his hand on her ankle. "*I've* seen a lot," he smirked.

She stood before she could give in to temptation. After rounding the foot of the bed, she rummaged in her suitcase for a sundress. "What's on the agenda for today? And don't say sex," she warned, grinning in spite of herself.

The man had an enormous ego. It wouldn't be good for him to know how easily he could coax her into never leaving the house.

Jonathan pretended to be disappointed, but since he had showered and was wearing navy linen shorts and a collared shirt, she could tell he had an excursion in mind.

"I thought we'd go into St. John's," he said. "First of all, we need to buy wedding rings."

Her hands stilled in her suitcase. "That's not really necessary, is it?"

"We got married so quickly I had to improvise. But I want you look the part of the CEO's wife."

Any pleasure she had anticipated in the task, fizzled. "I see. That makes sense, I guess."

Inwardly she grimaced. The way he posed the shopping idea made it clear that his bargain with her was practical and not romantic. She knew that all too well. Still, disappointment soured her stomach.

Twenty minutes later they were headed down the hill and toward the capital. The city of twenty thousand plus was more cosmopolitan than Lisette had expected. Cruise ships docked regularly in the deep harbor. High-profile banks, upscale shops and malls all mingled with more traditional Antiguan enterprises. The spires of a cathedral dominated the skyline.

Jonathan parked and took her hand as they got out. "My friend who owns the villa told me where to find the best jeweler. I called ahead and told them we were coming."

Inside the small shop, well-lit cases were crammed with tray after tray of rings and necklaces and watches. Calypso music played from a room in the back. In a large cage dangling from the ceiling, a brightly colored parrot squawked a greeting. Unlike a glitzy establishment in the States, this enterprise was more pirate cove than Madison Avenue.

"Are you sure about this?" she whispered.

He nodded slowly. "I'm supposed to ask for Henry."

A large black man appeared from behind a curtain, beaming. "That would be me. And you, of course, are the Tarletons. Welcome to Antigua."

"Thank you," Jonathan said. "I'm Jonathan, and this is my wife, Lisette. We tied the knot in somewhat of a hurry, so we didn't have the appropriate rings. We're here to remedy that."

"Excellent. I have plenty of inventory, as you can see."

While the two men initiated a search, Lisette curled her fingers around the small signet ring on her left hand. She didn't really want to give it up. Jonathan had said vows to her and married her with this ring. It was special to her.

Reluctantly she slipped it off and tucked it into her small clutch purse.

When she joined the men at a case on the far side of the room, Henri had rolled out a red velvet cloth and was piling up choices, one after another. All the rings were in matching sets.

She shot Jonathan a startled glance. "*You're* going to wear a wedding band, too?"

"Of course." He seemed surprised. "Why wouldn't I?"

A dozen reasons came to mind right off. This wasn't a real marriage. He was only protecting his company and hiding his illness.

Fortunately, his question was rhetorical and didn't require an answer.

Henry spoke up, his British accent most appealing. "Do you see anything you like, little ma'am?"

"Those are nice," she said, pointing to a plain set, hoping they would be less expensive. It seemed both reckless and immoral to spend a fortune on a prop.

Jonathan nodded. "I like them, as well."

The shiny silver-colored bands were edged with the tiniest of beading design around the rims.

The jeweler handed both rings to Jonathan. "Platinum. Designer pieces. Excellent choice."

Before Lisette could protest the expense, Jonathan took her hand in his and slipped the smaller of the two rings on her left hand without ceremony. It fit perfectly.

He smiled at her. "What do you think?"

"It's lovely."

Instead of offering her the male ring—so she could return the favor—he put the second band on his own finger and nodded. "These will do nicely. Now we need to look at engagement rings."

Lisette pulled on his arm. "May I speak to you in private?"

Jonathan frowned. "Right now?"

"Yes, right now."

While Henry straightened the case, Lisette dragged Jonathan over toward the front door of the shop. She lowered her voice. "I don't want an engagement ring. Under the circumstances, it's completely unnecessary."

Jonathan's eyes turned glacial. He wasn't accustomed to anyone countermanding his wishes. "Under *what* circumstances?"

"Don't be deliberately dense. This is a marriage of expedience, of convenience. It's pointless to spend thousands of dollars on a meaningless romantic gesture."

He was stone cold now. *This* was the man she knew the best. The unflappable CEO. The hard-edged businessman.

"And what about the honeymoon?"

She cocked her head, confused. What about it?"

"Wouldn't you say the honeymoon has been real?" His icy gaze dropped from her face to her breasts. "Surely that deserves recognition."

Her temper flared. "When a man has sex with a woman and then pays her off in pricey baubles, there's a word for that."

His chin jutted. "You're my wife, not some random woman. I fail to see why my buying you a diamond makes me the bad guy."

"I'd rather have a baby than a diamond ring."

Here they were again. Back at square one. Arguing. Apparently, the only time they were both in perfect accord was when they were in bed.

Her throat was tight with sad, angry tears. And the truth

was even worse. She wasn't angry with Jonathan for being who he was; she was angry with herself for falling into the trap of believing any of this was real.

She lowered her head, not wanting him to see her anguish. "Fine," she muttered. "Pick one out. I'll wear it."

The standoff lasted for painful seconds. Then, with a low curse, Jonathan whirled around and went back to confer with the jeweler again.

Because Lisette refused to be part of the process, she lingered where she was, pretending to peruse the collection of watches. If Henry was puzzled by her indifference, he didn't let on. Fifteen minutes later, he and Jonathan completed their transaction.

Outside, the sun was blinding. Lisette donned her sunglasses. "Can we do lunch next?" she asked. "I'm getting hungry."

"Not yet." Without warning, Jonathan knelt in the street and took her hand. "Lisette Stanhope, will you do me the honor of being engaged to me?"

Fourteen

Jonathan knew he was in trouble. He had hurt his bride—not intentionally, but nevertheless true. Now he willingly made a fool of himself in hopes of bringing a smile back to her face.

She wanted a baby, and Lord knows, he'd enjoy making one with her. Something stopped him though. A certainty that it wasn't fair to tie her down when he wouldn't be around to share the parenting.

Lisette pulled on his arm. "Get up, for goodness' sake. People are staring at us."

He allowed her to pull him to his feet, but still he held the ring. "I asked you a question, Lizzy. My execution was faulty all along the way, but no less sincere. Say you'll marry me."

She gaped at him, and then her mouth snapped shut. "We're *already* married. This is ridiculous."

"When is your birthday?"

"It was three weeks ago, remember? I took the day off and went to Savannah with a friend."

"Ah, yes." Again he took her hand. "Then consider this a belated birthday present. It wouldn't have been an appropriate gift from your boss, but now it's perfectly acceptable." Before she could protest, he reached out and slid the ring onto the third finger of her left hand. "Happy two-day anniversary, Ms. Tarleton. Here's to many more."

For the first time, Lisette looked at the ring. Her eyes widened.

Jonathan had selected a stunning stone, emerald cut. Three carats. Virtually perfect in color and clarity. The delicate setting did nothing to detract from the diamond's beauty. As Lisette held up her arm, the sun caught facets of the once-upon-a-time carbon and cast rainbows in every direction.

"Do you like it?" he asked. "We don't have to keep it. We can get something else. But I want you to have something as beautiful as you are."

Lisette grabbed him around his neck, nearly strangling him. "How is it that I'm ready to murder you one minute and kiss you the next?"

Her aggrieved question made him laugh. He folded her close against his chest. "It's not an easy thing we're doing," he said, stroking her hair, the strands hot from the sun. "I plunged us into this arrangement without much thought. We'll muddle through, I swear."

She pulled back and kissed him sweetly, healing the rift between them. "I'm sorry I was so grumpy," she said. "Thank you for my engagement ring."

Every time he took her in his arms, he wanted her. In a bed. Standing up against a brick wall in a nearby alley. He shook his head, dislodging the fantasy. "Thank *you*," he said. "For wearing it."

Their détente lasted all through lunch. They found a place by the water and dined on fat prawns, sourdough bread and coleslaw. At his insistence, Lisette enjoyed a glass of wine with her meal.

Her eyes sparkled with happiness.

The truth struck him without warning. Like a tsunami barreling in from the sea, flattening every preconception in its wake.

He was in love with his bride. In lust, yes. But even more than that.

His heart hammered in his chest. The prawns rolled

restlessly in his stomach. This wasn't part of the equation, part of the agreement. Suddenly, the idea of making Lisette pregnant seemed the most logical thing in the world.

He had chosen her to be his temporary bride because she was an impartial bystander. It was a lie he had told himself instead of admitting the truth. He wanted her and needed her.

Since he couldn't promise her forever, maybe giving her a baby was the best way to show her how much he cared.

She reached across the table and touched his hand. "You okay?"

Even the innocent caress of her fingers made him hollow with need. He nodded jerkily. "Sorry. My mind wandered."

Lisette made a face. "Not to business, I hope. We'll have to deal with all of that soon enough."

He made himself return her smile though it felt false. "Indeed. Today, we play. Did I mention that my buddy has a cabin cruiser…a small yacht? I thought we'd take her out for a spin."

"I'd love that," she said, her enthusiasm infectious. "Now I know why you insisted we bring our beach bags."

He nodded. "I wanted to surprise you, but I didn't think you'd go for nude sunbathing, even in the middle of the ocean."

"Not enough sunscreen in the world for that," she said, chuckling.

They left the Jeep parked in a shady spot on a quiet side street and made their way to the marina on foot. The formalities were brief though thorough. Afterward they changed clothes in the public cabana-like restroom. Soon they were motoring their way out of the harbor at a snail's pace, heading toward open water.

Lisette shoved her hair up under a floppy cloth hat.

"Better tie it," he said. "Or the wind will snatch it away."

When he cleared the final no-wake sign, he opened the

throttle. Lisette had chosen to sit at the bow of the boat with her face to the horizon. When the vessel picked up velocity, practically dancing over the water as if the craft were airborne, the wind snatched her laughter and carried it back to him where he stood at the wheel.

He understood her response. It wasn't humor. It was the sheer exhilaration of speed.

For half an hour he ranged around the coastline. This vantage point gave them a new perspective. Antigua was a blue-and-green jewel dotted with white-sand beaches, 365 in all, or so the tourist bureau would have you believe.

At last he cut the engine and let the craft bob on the open water.

Lisette turned around. "Are you dropping anchor?"

"No. Too deep. But we're fine where we are. You want something to drink? Maybe you should get out of the sun for a little while. Your cute nose is turning pink."

She made her way back toward the rear of the boat, staggering once when a choppy wave slapped the hull. "Is *get out of the sun* code for fooling around? I've never had sex on a boat."

"Have a seat." He handed her a water bottle, grinning. "I might be persuaded. Though I warn you, the bunks below are narrow."

Lisette drained the bottle and rested her head against the back of the cushioned banquette. "I could live like this," she said, eyes closed, expression dreamy.

He studied her intently, noting the way her white lacy cover-up billowed in the breeze, giving him tantalizing peeks of bare skin. "I never can decide which I like best— the flat-out exhilaration of speed or the challenge of battling the wind in a sailboat."

She peeked over her shoulder at the harbor in the distance. "Sailboats are beautiful. But I'd probably be one of those people who misjudges the boom and gets bumped into the water."

She stood and padded toward him in her bare feet, wrapping both arms around his waist. He folded her close. "I'd never let that happen to you, Lizzy." He bent his head and kissed her lazily, enjoying the slow buzz of arousal, the perfect bliss of a summer afternoon.

There wasn't a cloud on the horizon. The only storms up ahead were the ones he faced personally. Holding her like this made him want to fight for his future. But what was the point? Trying to stave off the inevitable would only drag both of them through a painful, uncertain time.

It was better to stay with the course he had chosen. Live each day to the fullest for as long as he had. He would love her and care for her the only way he knew how. And if a baby came from that love, perhaps the child would be a far more lasting legacy than a shipping business.

When Lisette went downstairs to visit the head, Jonathan stared out to sea. For a brief moment, he flashed on a snippet of memory from his younger days. He and Hartley had been barely fifteen, thinking they ruled the world. A friend had offered them his sailboat for the afternoon.

Both boys were experienced boaters, but a storm had blown up out of nowhere, turning the ocean into a raging beast. They had barely made it back into dock. The near miss had sobered them.

Without Hartley by his side, Jonathan might have died.

And now he was going to die without his twin anyway. The sharp pain in his chest was bittersweet. Holding onto anger was exhausting and pointless. He'd closed the book on Hartley months ago. He no longer had a brother.

When Lisette reappeared, he shook off his melancholy. "You ready to move on?"

She pretend-pouted, looking adorably sexy and playful. "I checked out those bunks. They're not so bad."

His body tightened. "I'm listening."

He'd been keeping the boat in relatively the same orientation, idling the motor occasionally and adjusting their position relative to the island. But it wouldn't hurt to drift briefly.

Lisette took off her cover-up and swimsuit top. "A quickie to hold us over until we get back to the house? I'm pretty sure this is a bucket list item."

Her challenging smile was adorable. Did she really think he had any objections? Hell, no. The sight of her soft, full breasts—completely bare—dried his mouth.

He shut off the engine and locked the wheel. "Five minutes," he said. He scanned the horizon. "We're all alone at the moment. No danger in sight." Except his wife's delectable body. "Down the steps, woman. I'm right behind you."

Lizzy started laughing when he tried to undress and slammed his elbow into a cabinet door. Pain shot up his arm, but he was undeterred.

She shimmied out of her swimsuit bottom and scooted onto the nearest berth. The simple navy cotton comforter was covered with a white nautical print. The vision in front of him looked like some kind of erotic pinup girl from a sailor's calendar.

"Hurry up," she said huskily. "You said five minutes."

Fast wasn't going to be a problem. He was on a hair trigger. Suddenly he ground his jaw and kicked the side of the bunk, barely even flinching when his toes protested.

Lisette's eyes widened. "What's wrong?"

"No condoms, damn it."

"Oh." She pulled the covers over her naked body, clearly trying to mask her disappointment with a wobbly smile. "Then we'll wait. No worries."

He fought a battle with himself. He couldn't tell her how he felt. Not with his diagnosis. His love would be nothing more than a burden. There was one thing he could do, and that was give her the baby she wanted. It hurt like hell to think he wouldn't know his own child. But it hurt even more to know he wouldn't be able to love Lizzy the way she deserved.

"Jonathan?" She lifted up on her elbows, a familiar pose. It made her look like temptation incarnate, though this time she kept the covers clutched to her chest.

"Do you still want to get pregnant?" he asked bluntly.

The color drained from her face and then rushed back in a flush of red that covered her cheeks and throat and everything else he could see. "Is that a serious question?"

His arms hung at his sides, hands fisted. He was so hard he ached all the way from his balls to his teeth. "Completely."

Her smile was radiant, nearly knocking him on his ass with its voltage. "Yes, Jonathan. I do."

"Okay, then. Let's do this." His world shifted into a weird pinpoint focus. Time slowed. He levered himself onto the narrow berth alongside her, pausing to assess the situation. When he slipped a finger into her sex, she was ready for him. More than ready.

His options were limited. This boat wasn't built for Kama Sutra positions. Jonathan moved on top of his lover and entered her steadily. "Good God," he whispered, fully reverent.

She smoothed the hair from his damp forehead with a gentle caress. "What, Jonathan? Tell me."

He kissed her temple, her nose, her soft, perfect lips. "I've never been with a woman like this. Skin to skin."

Her gaze reflected the wonderment he felt. "I like it," she confessed almost bashfully. "But you know it will take more than once."

"We'll just have to work at it," he groaned. "I'm game if you are."

She stroked his back, her fingernails digging into his flesh when he surged hard inside her. The little hiccupped moan she made inflamed him. In this most elemental joining, he felt his control slip far too soon. *Hell.* The additional stimulation without a manmade barrier dragged him deep into a place of drugged pleasure so dizzying he might never find his way back to the surface.

His climax hit hard and went on forever, until he was drained. He slumped on top of his bride. Vaguely he remembered hearing her come.

They were both covered in sweat. In the distance, the mournful cry of a seagull drew him back to consciousness.

Grief hit him hard. He adored his bride and he didn't want to give her up. Ever. How could he say goodbye to her? How could he imagine another man stepping in one day and living the life that was supposed to be Jonathan's.

How could he lose everything he cared about?

He shifted to one side and cupped her cheek with his hand. "Did I crush you?"

Her green eyes stared up at him, dazed. "Wow."

"Yeah. Wow." That about summed it up.

He toyed with her navel. "I should probably make sure everything is okay on deck."

She nodded. "You do that. I'll just stay here and reminisce."

"Brat." He reached for his shirt and swim shorts and reluctantly abandoned her. Taking the ladder two rungs at a time, he vaulted upward.

Nothing had changed. The sea still moved mysteriously beneath the hull. The sun continued to beam down with heat and passion.

But, for Jonathan, everything had been upended. He was going to fight. He wasn't going to take no for an answer when it came to pursuing other treatment options. And he was going pray like hell that his make-believe wife might fall in love with him for real.

He wanted to *tell* Lizzy, to thank her for rescuing him

from despair. To prove to her that he wanted to make their marriage real. A forever kind of deal. But something held him back. In business, he never rolled out a new initiative unless he had studied every angle.

That's how he would handle this new decision. No point in getting Lisette's hopes up. It would only disappoint both of them if there really was no hope for his recovery.

He started the engine and studied the radar. Good depth. No problems.

When Lisette joined him, her smile was hard to read. It wasn't smug, and it wasn't jubilant.

If anything, she seemed cautiously pleased. Come to think of it, that was a pretty damn good description of how *he* felt at the moment.

She stood beside him and repaired her ponytail with practiced feminine movements. "Do we have plenty of gas?"

He glanced at the gauge. "Yes. Why?"

She sighed and leaned her head on his shoulder, wrapping her arm through his. "I want to go fast again."

His wife had a need for speed. He understood that desire perfectly. "All you had to do was ask." As she released him and headed for the bow again, he raised his voice to be heard over the revving motor. "Promise me you'll hold on to the rail. I don't want to lose you."

She half turned, gazing at him over her shoulder, her expression mischievous. "You're never going to lose me, Jonathan Tarleton. I'm yours until the last sunset. Now let's get going. See if you can make me scream."

The taunting double entendre made him laugh. "Challenge accepted."

When he was sure she was settled with one hand clenched around the railing, he let the beast loose. He would never be careless with his passenger. He knew exactly how far he could push the nimble pleasure craft.

The needles on all the dials quivered and moved to the

right. His eyes stung even behind sunglasses. The wind in his face was surprisingly cold.

He shouted at her. "More?"

She nodded, lifting one hand and pointing at the sky.

If he had his way, he would have taken Lizzy all the way beyond the horizon in search of a happy ending. Instead, he did the next best thing. He let her feel what it was like to fly.

Seconds passed. Minutes. He was vigilant. Eagle-eyed. One wrong move could mean a collision with another craft. But he kept them just inside the edge of reason. It was exhilarating and cathartic and utterly perfect.

He noted the rapidly dwindling fuel supply and realized that it was time to go back. One more minute. One more dose of immortality.

Disaster struck without warning. A stabbing pain crushed the back of his right eye. His vision blurred. Anguished incredulity shook him. *Please, God, no. Not now.*

Instinctively he backed off on the throttle. Too quickly, in fact. He stumbled and had to grab the counter for purchase. Lisette ended up in the floor of the boat, laughing. "You could have warned me," she called out.

He gripped the wheel, barely able to see. "Lizzy. I need you to come back here."

She waved him off. "I'm fine," she said. "Don't worry. It wasn't that much of a bump. I'm not hurt."

Sweat poured down his back. The pain made him want to throw up. But that would scare her.

Think, man, think.

Slowly, stifling a groan, he reached for a water bottle and uncapped it. He tried a sip, but his stomach rebelled. Instead, he poured it around his neck. His heart rate was in the stratosphere. Shock, no doubt.

They were too far from shore. Too damned far.

He raised his voice a second time. "Lizzy. I need you to come back here. Now. Please."

Fifteen

Lisette's head snapped around. Her stomach clenched in alarm. The note in Jonathan's voice was so utterly unlike him she knew something was badly wrong. After leaping to her feet, she ran back to where he stood.

"What is it?" she cried, panicked by his pallor. "What is it?" But she knew. Dear God in heaven, she knew.

He was gritting his teeth, gray and shaking. "Something happened to my right eye."

"You're in pain?"

His brief hesitation was telling. "Yes. I can't see much on that side."

She removed his sunglasses and put them in the cup holder on the dash. "Take my hand," she said softly, speaking to him as she would a frightened child. "Sit down, Jonathan."

He slumped onto the bench seat, barely upright. "You'll have to get us back in. I'll help you with the boat."

"I don't care about the damn boat," she yelled, forgetting her bedside manner. Tears stung her eyes. "Tell me you have medicine with you, damn it. Tell me you do."

He nodded jerkily. "Foil packet. In my wallet. I can't take both. They knock me out. The doctor gave them to me for emergencies."

Her hands were shaking as she riffled through the pockets of his windbreaker and found his billfold. Jonathan was in pain. She couldn't bear it.

At last she found the tablets and punched one through

the foil. When she handed it over and offered him water, he managed to swallow the medicine with a grimace.

"You feel sick, don't you?" she said.

"A little." The lie was not even close to being believable. What would they do if he couldn't keep the pills down? "Don't move for a few minutes."

"Okay." He slid until he was on his back with one arm flung across his eyes. The canopy protected them from the sun.

Suddenly she realized that the motor was still puttering at low speed. Instead of asking Jonathan, she studied the dashboard, located the appropriate controls and shut off the engine.

Now they bobbed in the water. Alone in a great expanse of blue.

"Do I need to call for help?" she asked quietly.

The muscles in his throat rippled visibly. "No."

Even ill and hurting, he was utterly masculine. He had one tanned leg extended on the seat. The other foot braced on the floor of the boat.

She knelt beside him and rested her cheek against his arm. "Take your time. We're not in a rush."

When he stroked her hair, she could tell his hand was shaking.

Minutes passed. Five. Ten. Thirty. Under other circumstances, this lazy summer float would have been relaxing. As it was, Lisette's stomach cramped in painful knots. She was so damned scared. Not for herself, but for Jonathan.

At last he struggled to sit up. A bit of color had returned to his face, and he no longer looked as if he were about to pass out.

When he had both feet on the floor, she put her hands on his knees. "Look at me, Jonathan. And don't give me some pretty lie. How bad is your head?"

He covered her hands with his. "Bearable."

"You swear?"

His smile didn't quite reach his eyes. "I swear."

She nodded. "Okay then. Tell me what to do."

Slowly he straightened, swaying only slightly, though that could have been the motion of the boat. "I'll be right here beside you. We'll take it easy. This dial needs to stay between these two lines. The only tricky part will be entering the harbor. It's going to be busy."

"I'm fine," she said. "I've always wanted to learn how to drive a yacht."

He winced, this time theatrically. "You don't *drive* a yacht."

She waved a hand. "Whatever. Now lie back down and rest.

Though they were only a few miles offshore, at the speed where Lisette felt comfortable, it was going to take at least half an hour or more. Gradually the island began to come into focus. She wasn't sure which was scarier—being in control of a huge watercraft in the middle of the ocean, or coming closer to land, and having to navigate an obstacle course of Jet Skis and sailboats and a dozen other yachts and speedboats of every shape and size.

Jonathan stayed upright the entire way, not standing but seated inches away from her, his mere presence giving her the confidence she needed.

Once they reached the mouth of the harbor, she cut their speed even more and clutched the steering wheel. "Here goes nothing," she muttered.

"You're doing great."

A few vessels honked at her for going *too* slow, but for the most part, her progress was unimpeded. When they approached the area of the marina where the yacht had been berthed, her nerves increased. "I hope your friend has insurance. This is worse than parallel parking."

"I'll help you," Jonathan said. "It will be fine." He rose to his feet and muttered something.

She shot him a look, alarmed. "What's wrong?"

The jut of his jawline was grim. "My depth perception is shot. We'll have to get close and drift in. The guys at the dock will tie us off."

The next fifteen minutes were a blur. Somehow, Lisette managed to get the boat close enough to the pier for Jonathan to throw a rope. His first try landed in the water. A second attempt worked.

When Jonathan reached over and cut the engine, Lisette exhaled a noisy sigh. "Never again," she said. Instead of feeling relief, now she was free to worry about her husband.

He kissed her sweaty cheek. "You were great." When he bent down and started gathering their personal items, she gritted her teeth. Stubborn man.

"Let me do that," she said, trying to elbow him out of the way.

"Lisette." The steel in his voice told her the CEO was back. "I'm fine." The unspoken message was *Back off.*

But he was definitely *not* fine. She knew that the worst part of today's ordeal for him had been feeling out of control. Now he was trying to take over again, though she was damned if she would let him collapse in the street.

Because he was ignoring her attempts to make him sit down, she got in his face and glared. "Here's the schedule, big guy. We're going to slowly stroll to our car. I'll drive us back to the villa. Then we'll have a peaceful, quiet dinner and make a game plan."

"Why do we need a plan? If you're insisting I rest, let's spend all day by the pool tomorrow. Problem solved."

She gaped at him, unable to tell if he was serious or merely trying to aggravate her. "The honeymoon is over, Jonathan. We're flying home to Charleston as soon as I can get that swanky jet back down here. I may need your help with the details," she conceded.

Jonathan picked up the large straw tote and motioned her ahead of him. "You go first. And take somebody's hand when you climb out. The boat can move unexpectedly."

A dozen strong feelings duked it out in her chest, not the least of which was the furious impulse to push her aggravating husband overboard and let him take his chances.

Because she didn't want to make a scene—and because several gorgeous dock hands were waiting to secure the boat and return it to its assigned slip—Lisette picked up the small cooler and climbed out.

She wasn't able to breathe until Jonathan was on dry land, as well. Of *course*, he hadn't asked for help disembarking.

The afternoon heat was blistering. Earlier she'd had the impression they parked close to the water. Now, the distance seemed to have multiplied.

Jonathan walked beside her, not saying a word. She wanted to ask how he was feeling, but she didn't want to get her head snapped off.

When they reached the car at last, she put a small towel down on the driver's seat to keep from burning her legs on the hot leather. Jonathan's movements were *careful* as he eased into the passenger seat. She had the impression he was trying to limit his range of motion to keep from jostling his head.

At the villa, she parked haphazardly and faced her silent passenger. "Go straight to the bedroom. Please, Jonathan. I'll check with the maid about our dinner. Then I'll come join you, and we can talk."

He nodded. His pallor had increased again, despite the humid temperature. When she found him half an hour later, he was sprawled on top of the mattress, facedown, as if the strength of his will had carried him that far but no farther.

She whispered his name. When there was no answer, she leaned down to make sure he was breathing. The fear she had kept at bay earlier came rushing back. The doctor had said six months. Jonathan had been feeling pretty good lately. Surely this was a momentary setback.

Or maybe it was the beginning of the end.

She gathered fresh clothes, went into the bathroom and locked the door. Then she stood in a hot shower and cried. Jonathan had married her because he needed someone calm and capable in his corner. Somehow she had to find it in herself to ignore her own grief and be the woman he needed.

When she finally returned to the bedroom, she was blissfully clean but puffy eyed, Hopefully, Jonathan wouldn't notice.

She found him on his back this time, staring at the ceiling.

Though it seemed impossible under the circumstances, she wanted him still. She needed the physical connection to reassure herself she wasn't losing him yet. Today had been both terrifying and illuminating. Jonathan had been an integral part of her life for many years. Now he was her husband. Whatever happened to him was going to impact every part of her existence.

She scooted across the bed, huddled into her robe, and curled up beside him, resting her head on the edge of his pillow. Immediately he shifted and put his arm around her, still silent.

When she found the courage to speak, there was no point in playing games. "You know we have to go home…right?"

"I know." The flat intonation in those two words could have masked anger or despair or both.

"We should call your sister and brother-in-law and ask them to come over for dinner tomorrow night. Mazie's going to realize something is up when we return home early. The explanations will be better face-to-face."

"That's why I married you," he said lightly. "The voice of wisdom."

"You don't sound glad. That was a pretty snarky comment."

He rolled to his feet. "How long till dinner?"

"Half an hour."

"I'll shower and meet you on the terrace."

As a dismissal, it was unmistakable. She swallowed her hurt. "I'll use the guest room to finish getting ready."

"Suit yourself." It was as if he couldn't bear to look at her. "I'll be out shortly."

Jonathan was being an asshole. He recognized the behavior, but he couldn't seem to do anything about it.

He wanted to hide from the world, from Lisette in particular.

His *episode* today had completely knocked the wind out of him. He'd thought he had time. He'd thought things would only get bad at the end. Apparently he'd been in denial all along.

How could he know what was right and what was wrong? Lisette wanted a baby. Maybe they had created a new life today. But if not, surely it was for the best. Time was running out for him. Bit by bit he was losing everything. Knowing that his future with Lisette was slipping between his fingers stabbed him with painful regret.

Though the last thing he felt like doing was eating some fancy romantic meal, he couldn't bring himself to abandon his bride in the midst of their honeymoon. He joined her as promised. It didn't escape his notice that Lisette downed three glasses of wine during dinner.

He wasn't the only one who had suffered today. Lisette must have been scared out of her mind, but the woman was a damned trouper. She'd kept her cool, and she had done what had to be done.

Tonight she looked like a weary angel. Her halter-necked sundress was pale peach, a soft color that made her sun-kissed skin glow. She had put her hair up, exposing the vulnerable nape of her neck.

As crappy as the day had been, Jonathan knew how he wanted it to end. With Lizzy beneath him, welcoming him home. He loved her. Truth be told, he was only now realizing how much. Faced with the prospect of losing her, his feelings were a riotous flood of thoughts and yearnings he dared not reveal.

But would she desire him the same way tonight?

A man liked to be a man. Today hadn't shown him at his best. Would she think less of him? The random thought didn't even make sense. His emotions were all over the place.

He ate enough to be sociable and then nursed a glass of water while picking at his dessert. The mango sorbet and shortbread cookie were delicious, though he'd lost his appetite along with his faith in the future.

The maid came been back and forth, serving and removing dishes. Her interruptions kept the awkward lack of conversation between bride and groom at bay. But now dinner was over and the silence lengthened.

Jonathan felt the weight of everything piling up on him. His wife. His company. His sister and J.B. and the old man. How was it all going to play out? Would Hartley try to swoop in and take over? His brother's motives were still a painful mystery.

Jonathan never should have asked for Lisette's help. She didn't deserve this. She needed a man who was whole. One who could give her multiple children and a home and a happily-ever-after.

His mood slipped lower. All the positive thinking in the world wasn't going to change a damn thing.

He stood abruptly and tossed his napkin on the table. "I'm going for a walk," he said gruffly. "Don't wait up for me."

"I could go with you."

His shoulders tensed as he stopped with his back to her. Tense seconds passed. "No. I'd rather be alone right now."

Lisette made some excuse to the maid and fled inside. To have her husband make it so embarrassingly clear he didn't want her company was a pain that left her breathless. She was no psychologist, but she recognized why Jonathan was pushing her away.

Perhaps it was the only choice he could make to deal with the changes happening in his life. The terrifying moment out on the water today would have frightened anyone. For a man who kept an iron grip on his destiny, the incident must surely have made the earth shift beneath his feet.

She gathered everything she needed and holed up in the guest suite across the hall from the master bedroom. The hollow feeling in her chest wouldn't go away. After changing into the soft feminine nightwear she had bought for her honeymoon, she sat on the bed, scooted up against the headboard and tried to read the novel she had brought with her.

The book was a bestseller by one of her favorite comedic writers. After she read the same page three times, she gave up.

Was she going to be reduced to playing online solitaire during her honeymoon?

She picked up her cell phone and nearly dropped it when it rang insistently. No contact was linked to the number, but it was a Charleston-area prefix, so she answered.

"Hello?"

After the briefest of pauses, a male voice on the other end spoke. "Lisette, this is Hartley Tarleton, Jonathan's brother."

Her gasp was loud enough for him to hear. "Why are you calling me? How did you get this number?" She had been with Tarleton Shipping long before Hartley disappeared, so she knew him, of course. But they weren't on casual phone-call terms.

"Mazie gave it to me. Listen, Lisette. I need to know about Jonathan. He's in trouble isn't he? Tell me what's going on. Mazie says he's sick."

"Why would you think he's in trouble?" Her mind raced feverishly, looking for sinister motives in the conversation.

Hartley's muttered curse was audible, even with a crackly cell connection. "He's my twin. We've always had that gut ESP thing. Quit stalling. I need to know."

"You shouldn't be calling me," she said, trying to sound firm when her insides were shaking. "Ask your sister."

"I did, damn it. Mazie gave me the bare bones, but she said you're the one who knows everything that's going on with my brother...all the details."

"Well, she's wrong. Your brother isn't big on opening up to people. Or have you forgotten that?"

"I haven't forgotten anything."

"I'm hanging up now," she whispered. "Jonathan would be furious if he knew I was talking to you. Whatever you did hurt him very badly."

There was a brief pause where she could hear Hartley breathing. Then he spoke softly. "Jonathan wasn't the only one who got hurt, Lisette. Think about that, why don't you. And if you have any heart at all, swear you'll let me know when the situation gets bad. I have to be there with him. Please."

"I can't promise that."

"I love him."

The three words were filled with such aching anguish that tears stung her eyes. "I do, too," Lisette said.

"Keep my number."

She knew she shouldn't. She knew it was wrong. But she felt a strong, empathetic connection to Jonathan's banished sibling. "I will. But that's all I can promise, Hartley. I'm sorry." She tapped the red button and ended the call before she could change her mind.

Sixteen

The adrenaline and stress of the day left their mark on Lisette. After the odd phone call with Hartley, she fell asleep almost instantly, though she tossed restlessly and turned the sheets into a tangled mess.

Sometime after one in the morning, a noise jerked her awake.

Jonathan's whisper soothed her fears. "It's me, Lizzy." He scooped her into his arms and carried her to their bedroom. "I'm sorry I was an ass. I can't sleep without you."

She curled against him, relief flooding her body. "Don't shut me out." She wanted to tell him she loved him, but she stopped short.

"I'll try," he said.

His arms were strong, cradling her to his naked chest. He smelled like soap and warm male skin and everything she held dear.

"Are you okay?" she asked. He'd told her not to do that... not to hover and ask questions about his health. But her need to know was stronger than her worry about his displeasure.

After a moment's pause, he kissed her forehead and deposited her gently on their bed. At some point he had carefully folded back the sheets before coming to the other room. Now he joined her and stretched out with a sigh. "I'm fine."

She raised up on one elbow, stroking the hair from his forehead, only then realizing that he was *completely* nude. "Truly?"

"Truly."

His expression was hard to read. A night-light burned in the adjoining bathroom, but the bedroom itself was shadowed and dim. "Did you make arrangements for the jet?" she asked. Surely that was a safe topic.

He nodded. "We'll need to be at the airport by ten thirty tomorrow morning for preflight security and screening."

Suddenly she knew what she had to do, what she *wanted* to do. "Then we have tonight," she whispered. If their honeymoon was to be cut short, she wanted him to remember these last few hours...to remember her as his bride. When they returned to Charleston, she couldn't bear it if he pushed her aside in his quest to be stoic. She needed him to understand they were a team.

She braced herself on one hand and bent her head to taste a flat, copper-colored nipple. With her free hand, she stroked the hard planes of his chest. His abdomen was roped with impressive muscles. "I love your body," she murmured, feeling the texture that was so uniquely male. Warm silk over taut sinew.

Jonathan shuddered when she touched him intimately. He tried to move on top of her, but she pushed him back. "Let me do this first, Jonathan. I want to...please."

He closed his eyes, his entire body rigid. She circled the head of his sex with her tongue, loving the sounds he made when she took more of him in her mouth. Here, in their bedroom, she breached his careful barriers. Here, in the dark of night, he let her see his wants. His needs.

Maybe his thoughts were still hidden from her. Maybe they always would be. But at least in this one place, they knew each other fully.

The hour was late. Though Lisette wanted to make the pleasure last for hours, Jonathan was too hungry, too reluctant to play the submissive forever. When he groaned and cursed and fisted his hands in the sheets, his control snapped so quickly it caught her off guard.

"No more," he rasped. He stripped her flimsy gown away. "On your back, woman. Let me see you."

She smiled up at him. "Nothing has changed. All the parts are still the same."

He shook his head slowly. "That's where you're wrong. Each time I take you, I swear you dazzle me more. Your body is soft and curved and perfect, but that's not even the best of it. You're smart and funny and strong, and all those things pale in comparison to your huge heart."

Her mouth dropped open. She had never heard him speak so poetically. In fact, she didn't know he had it in him. Her eyes misted. "What a lovely thing to say."

His smile was lopsided. "It's all true." He cupped her breast in his hand. "Now, at the risk of undoing all my fine words, I'm going to take you hard and fast, because I've wanted you for hours, Lizzy, and I'm afraid I might die if I don't get inside you soon."

It was just an expression. A funny way of expressing his arousal. But her throat tightened. "I want you just as badly, Jonathan Tarleton." She pulled his head down for a kiss. "I'm all yours."

Relief made him light-headed. Lizzy was being far more generous that he might have been were their situations reversed. She hadn't taken him to task for his grouchy behavior earlier. Her empathy made him want to be a better man.

Though his erection ached and throbbed, he made himself wait. He would show her how much she meant to him even if he couldn't say the words. After tucking an extra pillow beneath her head, he gave himself free rein to pleasure her until neither of them could bear any more.

He had rapidly grown addicted to the feel of her skin

beneath his fingertips. The fragrance of her shampoo. The way her spine arched off the bed when he found a spot on the inside of her thigh that made her tremble.

He tasted every inch of her skin, knew every soft, damp secret.

Deliberately he drove her higher and higher, holding her ruthlessly on the knife edge of release, denying them both what they wanted.

When she moaned his name and wrapped her arms around his neck, he knew the time had come. He settled between her thighs and fit the head of his sex at her entrance. "Watch," he said. "Watch me take you."

Her pupils were dilated, almost covering her irises. He had kissed her so long and so hard her lips were pink and swollen. When she looked down at the spot where their bodies joined, she nodded slowly, her expression arrested. "Yes, Jonathan. Yes."

He entered her slowly, perhaps more slowly than he ever had before. Each tiny increment was exquisite torture. Her body gripped his, knew his. The connection was more than physical. It was painfully real and encompassing, and if he hadn't been drowning in sheer physical bliss, he might have run screaming from the knowledge that he hadn't managed to hold anything back from her.

He was losing himself completely.

When he was lodged inside her all the way, he hesitated. Most of his weight rested on his arms so as not to crush her. "Lizzy?"

"Yes?" Her expression was unguarded. Open. Revealing. Was that love he saw there? He wanted it to be so. He wanted to believe that Lizzy was with him because she needed him, not the other way around. He had kept so much of himself closed off for so long, it was habit now. He craved her love. Yearned for it.

Fear held him back. Fear of being weak. Fear that he

would fail her by leaving her alone. "Never mind," he muttered. "It will keep."

He withdrew and thrust deep, sending both of them into delirium. It might have been hours or minutes that he moved wildly inside her, relishing the way her inner muscles clutched at him as if trying to link them forever. The sensation was exquisite and painful, and his body ached and shuddered and finally exploded.

Lizzy came, too. He heard her cry, felt the way her legs wrapped around his waist and her body lifted into him, trying to ride every last trembling wave.

When it was done, blackness overcame him. He slept instantly, their bodies still joined.

Seventeen

The return trip to Charleston was so uneventful and anticlimactic that Jonathan wished they had chosen to finish their week in Antigua. He felt completely normal, but it was too late now.

The only holdup they experienced was at the airport in St. John's. They were forced to wait on the tarmac for an hour past their expected departure time, which meant it would be late afternoon when they touched down in Charleston, later still when they made it to the beach house.

It wasn't really a problem. Jonathan's father was away on a weeklong golf outing with his friends. Though the old man did little more than ride the cart, he enjoyed the company.

The housekeeper and chef had been summoned from their breaks. Jonathan would have to make it up to them later. In the meantime, the capable women would have dinner for four ready at six o'clock.

Jonathan and Lisette barely made it. They had both slept on the plane, and the trip had gone smoothly after the slow start. But the traffic in and around the Charleston airport when they exited at rush hour was heavy.

Neither of them spoke much on the drive out to the house. They were probably going to arrive just as Mazie and J.B. showed up.

Lisette pulled out a comb and compact, and fretted over her reflection.

He put a hand on her leg. "Relax. You look beautiful. It's just my sister."

"Easy for you to say. You're not the one who has crazy hair."

He managed a chuckle though his chest was tight. He dreaded telling Mazie and J.B. what had happened in Antigua.

In the end, both vehicles swept through the gate at almost the exact same instant. They parked and Jonathan took a deep breath. "Let's leave everything in the car until later."

Lisette nodded and squeezed his hand. "It will be okay. The truth is always better than secrets."

He wasn't entirely convinced, but he didn't really have a choice.

The four of them got out, exchanged hugs and climbed the front staircase. Once inside, fabulous smells wafted from the kitchen. Jonathan and Lisette had only snacked on the plane. And Jonathan had eaten sparingly at dinner the night before. His stomach growled audibly, making everyone laugh.

Mazie grinned at Lisette. "Didn't you feed him down in Antigua?"

Lisette grimaced. "You know your brother. He does his own thing."

Ordinarily they might have all enjoyed appetizers and drinks on the porch. As it was, since Jonathan was on an alcohol-free regimen, they went into the dining room at the housekeeper's suggestion so dinner could be served hot.

The meal was incredible, especially for such short notice. Seared scallops. A light corn chowder. Spinach salad and angel food cake with fresh strawberries for dessert.

Mazie was remarkably patient. She endured the conversation about sports and movies and whether or not the upcoming hurricane season was going to be a bad one. But as soon as the last dish was cleared away, she shifted her chair back from the table, pinned Jonathan with a challenging gaze, and wrapped her arms around her waist. "Okay, big brother. Tell me what happened. Why did your honeymoon get cut short?"

Lisette's heart went out to Jonathan. He was stone-faced, trapped by his sister's interrogation. Lisette was positive that if he'd had his way, no one would ever have known what happened out on that boat. No one but Lisette.

When he didn't say anything at first, she tried to deflect the attention from her silent husband. "We had an incident," she said, trying her best to downplay what had happened. But the facts were damning, and the other two adults at the table weren't stupid.

J.B. frowned. "What kind of incident?"

Jonathan stared out the window, his jaw tight. The tension in the room was desperately uncomfortable.

Lisette tried again. "Jonathan experienced severe pain behind his right eye. It affected his vision for a number of hours."

J.B. cursed under his breath. Mazie, predictably, started to cry.

Jonathan stood, rounded the table and put his arms around his sister from behind, kissing her cheek. "Don't make a thing of this, sis. I'm fine now."

His assurance was cold comfort.

Lisette had had over a day to get used to the idea that Jonathan might be incapacitated sooner rather than later. His sister and brother-in-law had not.

J.B. leaped to his feet and paced, his body language communicating his turmoil. "You know you'll have to use a driver, right? You can't take chances."

Lisette expected Jonathan to reply angrily, but his half smile was resigned. "I know. We'll deal with it."

Before anyone could say another word, the housekeeper

appeared in the doorway. Lisette didn't know how much the woman had overhead, but she clearly hadn't wanted to interrupt.

"There's a car at the front gate, Mr. Tarleton. A Dr. Shapiro? He says he needs to speak to you. It's urgent."

Jonathan paled beneath his tan. "Buzz him in."

A deadly silence fell around the table. Then something clicked for Lisette. She looked at Jonathan. He's not your doctor…is he?"

"No." Jonathan shrugged. "I can't imagine what he wants."

A dozen scenarios flashed through Lisette's imagination, each one worse than the last. Maybe the cancer was further along than they had been led to believe. Jonathan's family doctor was a general practitioner. This other doctor might have been sent to deliver the news.

When the housekeeper ushered the newcomer into the dining room, no one said a word. The man was in his early sixties. Distinguished. Only a sprinkle of silver at his temples.

Jonathan stuck out his hand. "Dr. Shapiro? I don't think we've met. I'm Jonathan Tarleton. Call me Jonathan."

The older man wasted no time. "I'm the senior administrator at the hospital. May we speak in private, Jonathan? It's a matter of some urgency."

Jonathan's pallor increased. He looked around the room. "This is my family. They can hear whatever you have to say."

The doctor hesitated, clearly ill at ease. "Very well. There's no way to dance around this, so I'll just say it. You don't have cancer. There's no brain tumor."

All the oxygen was sucked out of the room by the incredible pronouncement.

"How do you know?" Jonathan's question was sharp.

Dr. Shapiro took a breath. "Our senior radiologist has

been removed from the hospital's roster. His credentials have been revoked by the state licensing board. For the past two years he has been abusing prescription drugs and other substances. He took on more and more cases, and in the process, misread or transposed results.

Jonathan spoke sharply. "So I'm not the only one involved?"

The other man winced. "Many patients have been affected, though none with such grave results as yours. Part of it was financial. The radiologist was billing insurance and siphoning off cash. He has incorrectly read and reported on dozens if not hundreds of test results. Yours was one case out of many."

Mazie frowned. "I don't understand. How could he rise to the level of senior staff under these circumstances?"

"He was one of our best. But apparently, he's had some untreated issues of his own. His wife left him three years ago. That led to his recent downward spiral. I'm very sorry."

Lisette's brain struggled to do the math, and something didn't add up. "But you're not here to deliver good news, are you? That's why you're not smiling." Her heart was beating so rapidly in her chest she thought she might faint. When she went to Jonathan and slipped her hand into his, her husband's fingers were icy.

Dr. Shapiro's expression grew grimmer still. "Your recent test results did confirm a serious problem. But it's not either of the things you were told. You have a large brain aneurysm, Jonathan. As far as we can tell, it's been leaking slowly. That accounts for the severe headaches that have come and gone."

Mazie took her brother's other hand. "But there's a cure, surely. This is better than cancer."

J.B. wrapped his arm around his wife protectively. "Easy, Maze. Let the man talk."

Still, Jonathan was silent. The four of them faced the unwelcome visitor.

Dr. Shapiro ignored everyone in the room but the patient. "You'll need surgery as soon as we can arrange it. A few more tests in the meantime, of course—just because now we know what we're looking for—but no time wasted."

Lisette bit down hard on her lower lip. "What's the big rush? It's been there a long time, right?"

The doctor glanced at her and then back at Jonathan. "It could rupture at any moment, son. In forty percent of cases, that event is fatal."

Jonathan stepped away from his circle of loved ones. "And if it's not fatal, I could end up comatose."

Dr. Shapiro winced. "Neurological damage is a distinct possibility. That's why we want to do surgery without delay. I've taken the liberty of contacting a specialist at Emory in Atlanta. He's willing to come if we can work around his schedule. You're young and otherwise healthy. Your prognosis should be positive. And of course—under the circumstances—the hospital will cover any and all associated costs not covered by your insurance."

J.B. scowled. "I hardly think money is the issue here. Criminal negligence is more like it."

Mazie, surprisingly, stepped up her game, appearing both calm and decisive. She kissed Jonathan and hugged Lisette. "You guys need time to talk. We'll get out of here and leave you alone. I'll text you first thing tomorrow. In the meantime, we're only a phone call away."

After they departed, Dr. Shapiro addressed Jonathan. "I'd like you to be at my office at ten in the morning. We'll go over all the options. Do you have any more questions at the moment?"

Jonathan shook his head. "No. I'll be there."

Lisette shook the man's hand. "Thank you for coming in person. It means a lot."

The housekeeper showed the doctor to the door. Jonathan prowled the dining room, his expression thunderous. "Of course he came in person. They're about to get sued by dozens of families. He's doing damage control."

"That's not helping," Lisette said.

"You know what would help?"

"What?"

"Having sex with my wife."

Jonathan loved the fact that he could still make her blush. She nodded slowly. "If you're sure you feel like it."

"I feel fine," he muttered. "That's the hell of it. C'mon. Let's get our stuff out of the car and go to bed."

By the time they grabbed their suitcases, the housekeeper and chef were finished in the kitchen. The two women bade them good-night. Jonathan locked up the house.

Outwardly, he was trying to act as if everything was normal. The reason for Lisette to be his wife had disappeared in an instant. No longer did he have to dread months of dwindling health. Either he recovered, or he would be gone.

Could he tell her he loved her? That he wanted to get her pregnant...to become a family for real? What would she say? Her deepest thoughts were still a mystery to him. He knew she cared about him at some level. She had a huge heart. But if he had this surgery and survived, would she want to stay?

The prospect filled him with jittery anticipation. He no longer faced a death sentence. There was a decent chance he was going to make a full recovery. For the first time in forever, he felt hope and jubilation effervesce in his chest.

He and Lisette went upstairs. It dawned on him halfway down the hall that tonight was another first. Lisette had never slept with him at the beach house.

He paused in the doorway to the bedroom and sighed. "Well, damn."

Lisette peeked around his shoulder and groaned.

Jonathan's walk-in closet was enormous, though he used barely a third of it. He had charged the assistant house-keeper and her teenage daughter with moving all of Lisette's personal belongings from her condo to her new residence. Obviously the two women had assumed they had the rest of the week to accomplish the task. Jonathan had forgotten to let them know about the change in plans.

At the moment, the big king-size bed was covered with stacks of Lisette's clothes that had been carried over from *her* closet.

Lisette elbowed past him and set down her bags. "No worries. We can just hang it all up, and I can organize later. It won't take us fifteen minutes."

She was right. They grabbed one pile at a time and hung garments on the empty rods. Jonathan had longer arms. He was able to take more with each trip. But near the end, he got too ambitious. A few things that were still in plastic dry-cleaning bags caused everything to shift, and he lost the lot of it on the floor.

He waved Lisette away. "I've got this. Go unpack your bag. Get ready for bed."

As he scooped up two hangars at a time, a white envelope fell out of a skirt pocket. He picked it up, ready to lay it aside, when he realized his name was neatly printed on the front. In Lisette's handwriting.

Curious, he opened the flap and scanned the letter. Everything inside him went icy cold. *She had been planning to leave him, to leave Tarleton Shipping.* He looked at the date on the letter. *This* was why he had found her in his office that fateful day. While he'd been reeling from his diagnosis, Lisette had been taking steps to change her life, to move on.

Despite his pretext of needing a decision maker in the office—someone to help him keep his illness a secret—he knew now that he had asked her to marry him because he'd been falling in love with her. He had believed there was a good chance she had feelings for him, too. Everything about their honeymoon had convinced him it was true.

After they slept together for the first time, he'd assumed the reason she'd accepted his outlandish proposal was because she wanted to explore the connection they shared. To be with him for whatever time he had left.

The truth was far worse. She had married him out of pity. Her compassionate heart and giving nature had convinced her to be his convenient wife, though the setup was *inconvenient* for her.

His stomach curled with nausea. If he truly loved her, he would have to let her go. She'd spent years of her adulthood caring for her mother. Judging from the letter, she had been on the verge of finally making a life that was her own. He sure as hell didn't want her to give up anything else for him.

Because he couldn't quite process this new information in the wake of everything else that had happened today, he shoved the letter into his pocket. He would deal with it later. When he knew what it was he wanted to say to her.

When she walked out of the bathroom wearing nothing but an Isle of Palms T-shirt with tiny bikini panties, her smile erased some of the ice encasing his heart. "Thanks for finishing that," she said.

His body tightened. Despite his stress and mental fatigue, the rest of him was raring to go. "No problem. Let me grab a quick shower and I'll meet you under the covers."

Her smile faltered. "Don't we need to talk about tomorrow? The doctor? Everything he said? You've had a shock, Jonathan."

Two shocks, he thought, remembering the letter. "To be honest, I'd rather have sex and then sleep with my wife.

Tomorrow will come soon enough. I've had about all the bad news I can handle at the moment."

As if on cue, her cell phone rang. It was on the dresser. He was the closest, so he picked it up to hand it to her. The caller ID on the screen was like a punch to the gut. Hartley Tarleton.

Jonathan felt weird. Like his body was heavy but the rest of him was floating above the room, observing. He stared at Lisette. "Why the hell is my brother calling you?"

Her ringtone was a familiar Beatle's lyric about love being the only thing a person needed. It went on and on. She'd been holding out her hand for the phone. Now her arm dropped to her side. She was dead white, her gaze anxious. "I can explain."

He hit the button that denied the call. Now the silence was deafening. "No," he said carefully. "I don't believe you can."

The enormity of the betrayal sliced through him with a pain greater than what had happened to him on the boat. Lisette knew how he felt about Hartley. Everyone in his family knew.

She wrung her hands, the action oddly ludicrous. "I put his name in my list of contacts so I would know never to answer that number."

"Try again." His hands and his arms were numb. Was he having a heart attack? First Dr. Shapiro. Next, a jubilant moment when he thought all his dreams could come true. Then finding the letter. Now this.

Lisette lifted her chin. "He called me yesterday in Antigua. Hartley said he knew something was wrong with you…that you brothers had always shared a weird twin connection. I told him I couldn't talk to him. I didn't give him any information about you, I swear. I hung up as quickly as I could."

"I see." He studied her words. His brain was doing some

kind of hyper supercomputer thing. Maybe Lisette was involved with Hartley somehow. And Jonathan had been stupid enough to sign a generous prenup, giving Lisette far more than Hartley had stolen from the company. What the hell was going on?

His bride stared at him. Tears brimmed in her eyes and rolled down her cheeks. "It's the truth. I swear." She swallowed visibly. "I love you, Jonathan. Let me help you. Don't push me away."

Let me help you.

"I don't need help," he said carefully. He no longer knew what to believe. But ultimately, her involvement with Hartley—or lack of—was a peripheral matter. Jonathan had to set her free. He couldn't let her sacrifice her life for his. If the only way he could push her away convincingly was to be harsh, he would do it, no matter how much it might hurt. He pulled the letter out of his pocket. "Remember this?"

"Oh, God."

"Indeed." He laid her resignation letter on the dresser. "I'm going to a hotel right now. When I get back tomorrow, I want you gone."

Lisette's face was ashen. "I know things have changed," she said. "But you married me to protect the company. We shouldn't be hasty. Let's take time to think things through."

"The reason I married you no longer exists. Either the surgery kills me—in which case my sister will take over all the decision making—or I'll recover and life will go on. But you have no place here. Not anymore."

"I told you I love you," she cried. "You have to believe me."

He shook his head slowly. "I don't know what to believe right now. Apparently nothing in my life is what it seems. I'm dissolving our arrangement, Lisette." He picked up the letter, his chest tight with despair. "Feel free to *pursue other opportunities* and *find new challenges*. It makes no difference at all to me," he lied. "I have more important things to worry about than your happiness and your future. That's up to you, I'm afraid." He heard the cold, cutting words leave his lips and watched them hit their mark.

Lisette trembled so hard her teeth were chattering. "I told you I love you. I want to be with you when you undergo this surgery. Please, Jonathan."

"No." He didn't dress it up.

She sucked in a deep breath, her gaze shattered. "Are you saying you want an annulment...a divorce?"

There would never be a baby. Not now. Knowing that was the most terrible blow of all.

"A divorce would be for the best. But we'll hit Pause on the details until after the surgery. After all, this whole mess may sort itself out if my brain explodes."

"Don't say that," she cried.

He shrugged. "You heard the doctor. Forty percent fatal. The way my luck has been going lately, even I wouldn't place money on *my* chances."

"Please don't go," she begged. "Come to bed with me. You'll feel better in the morning."

The giant wall broke, the one that had been damming up all the pain and screaming regret in his gut. He felt it drag him under, knew the moment he reached his breaking point.

She wasn't his to keep, never had been.

"No thanks, Lizzy. I'm done with you."

Four days after Jonathan Tarleton kicked her out of his house, Lisette paced the floors of the hospital surgical wing. Waiting. Waiting. She had company. Mazie and J.B. were there, too, but they were huddled together in the family lounge, promising each other that Mazie's brother and Jonathan's best friend was going to make it.

Thinking about the surgery made Lisette ill. Somewhere nearby a surgeon was drilling a hole in her husband's skull, attempting to clip off the blood supply to the bulging pocket in a vessel or an artery. The specifics were hazy. She had tried to research the procedure, but the information she found had been so terrifying she decided ignorance was the best choice for now.

Because Jonathan had been adamant about his decision to exclude Lisette, she had been forced to tell Mazie everything. Thankfully, J.B.'s and Mazie's kindness had soothed the edges of her wretched heartbreak.

Still, as soon as Jonathan was conscious, she would no longer be able to hang around. The thought was unbearable.

The more she thought about it, though, the more determined she became to ignore his edict. Jonathan was only half of this relationship. She had a right to fight for him, and she would. For a brief moment in Antigua, happiness had been in her grasp.

She would get it back if she had to beat the stupid man over the head. He loved her. She had to believe that. His body had told her so again and again, even if he hadn't managed the actual words.

At long last, the surgery was over and Jonathan was moved to ICU.

Mazie's red-rimmed eyes telegraphed relief. "You go in first," she said. "He's out of it, and it will make you feel better."

Lisette hugged her tightly. "Thank you." She slipped into the curtained cubicle and felt her heart shatter all over again. Jonathan looked so alone. So very far away. They had shaved a small section of his head, she knew that. A white bandage covered the wound.

Carefully she pulled the single small chair closer to the side of the bed. She picked up the large male hand that wasn't tethered to an IV. Curling her fingers around his, she spoke to him softly.

"It's me, Jonathan. Lizzy. Your wife. I know we played a

charade, but I so badly wanted it to be real. I've loved you forever, it seems. When I thought you were dying, I didn't know how I would go on. I decided I wanted to be with you for however long we had together. Now you're angry and hurt, and I don't know what to do. If you can hear me, please listen. You are mine, you stubborn man. I adore you, and I'm pretty sure you love me, too. I want to make a baby with you and a future. So I'm not letting you go."

She wanted to say more, but tears clogged her throat. Mazie had been generous to give her this time. Mazie and J.B. would want to come in, too.

When she thought she could leave without embarrassing herself, she wiped her face and stood. All around her, machines beeped and whooshed. Jonathan lay still as death, not entirely out of the woods.

Here and now, she resolved to fight. It would require patience and waiting for the right moment to help him see the truth. Not only that, she might have to play hardball to make him admit that he loved her. Maybe a little subterfuge on her part.

All's fair in love and war...

Though it took every bit of strength she could muster, she walked out of his room, out of the hospital—but not out of his life.

Eighteen

One month later...

Jonathan stood in front of Lisette's condo and knocked carefully. His recovery had moved far too slowly for his satisfaction. And there had been bumps in the road. Today was the first time he'd been allowed behind the wheel of a car. And only now because he had told his sister he needed to see his wife.

When Lisette opened the door, he drank in the sight of her. Her face was thinner, her gaze guarded. She didn't seem too surprised. Maybe Mazie had tipped her off.

"Hello, Lisette," he said.

"Come in." She stepped back and waited for him to walk toward the living room.

In the arched doorway, he jerked back, startled. There were moving boxes stacked neatly in two corners. "You're leaving? I thought you loved this condo."

Lisette sat down in a chair and motioned for him to do the same. "I'm moving to Savannah. I have three job interviews lined up next week."

He was stunned. What had he expected? That she was going to wait on him to quit being a giant pain in the ass? Her announcement left him off script and reeling.

When he couldn't come up with a response to her news, she pointed to a small pile on the coffee table. "The wedding band and engagement ring are in the boxes. Your lawyer drew up papers nullifying our prenup. I've signed everything. All you have to do is add your signature and file the documents. I cleaned out my desk at work and turned in keys. If I've forgotten anything, feel free to text me."

At last he found his voice. "You can't dissolve the pre-nup without my consent."

"Actually, I can. The agreement was predicated on your diagnosis of terminal cancer. Since that no longer applied, everything else was off the table. Your lawyer agreed, but of course, feel free to discuss it with her."

"And what about your termination package from Tarleton Shipping?"

Her eyelids flickered as though his barb had hit some unseen mark. "I turned in my original resignation letter. I wasn't entitled to severance."

He gripped the arms of the chair, trying not to grab her up and kiss her until her calm facade cracked. "I'm sorry, Lizzy. So damned sorry. That night we returned from our honeymoon was a terrible time in my life…even worse than the day they told me I had cancer. I wasn't myself. Please forgive me."

She stared at the rug. "Nothing to forgive. You were in shock. It's understandable."

"I love you," he said, feeling desperate because she was slipping away. Irrevocably.

This time she looked straight at him, but it was as if she hadn't heard what he said. "You should know that I've talked to Hartley multiple times in the last few weeks. He's been extremely worried about you, and I thought he should have as much information as possible."

Jonathan blinked. The old feelings of anger and betrayal tried to take hold. "I don't know why my brother did what he did, but I won't be batshit crazy about it anymore. Looking death in the face has a way of rearranging a man's priorities."

"I'm glad to know that. I hope the two of you can reconcile some day."

"Did you hear me?" Jonathan said hoarsely. "I told you I love you."

She shook her head slowly. Those translucent green eyes held pain he had put there. "You've had plenty of opportunities to tell me that over the years and you never said it. Even on our honeymoon when we were as close as two people can be, you didn't say it. You liked having sex with me. I know that. But it's two different things."

He stood up, no longer able to contain his nervous energy. "I do love you," he said. "The only reason I didn't say anything earlier was because I thought you would grieve more when I was gone if you knew."

"That's an interesting theory," she said, her smile more wry than sarcastic. "You're a closed-off man, Jonathan. Aloof. Afraid of letting anyone get close. You love your sister and your father and J.B., but even with them, you didn't want to share the news that you had cancer. You wanted to handle everything on your own. The only person who has ever really known you intimately is your twin brother. And now you've locked him out of your life, too."

"I asked *you* for help."

She shook her head slowly. "Only because you saw me as an uninterested bystander. You thought I could be impartial. Unbiased. You needed me to be a buffer between you and the rest of the world."

"It's not true." He scraped his hands through his hair, his fingers brushing unwittingly over the bumpy scar that would always be a reminder. "Okay, maybe I told you that. I may have even thought I believed it. But in Antigua, I let myself see the real you. I wasn't your boss anymore. I was your lover." He hesitated. "Do you remember that day on the boat?"

Lisette's eyes widened as if aghast he would bring it up.

"Of course I remember it," she said. "It was the best moment of our trip, right up until it wasn't. But I'm not sure why we're rehashing the details. You could have died in front of me. I've never been so terrified."

"I can't forget, either," he said slowly, pausing at the window but not really seeing the view. "I watched you sitting in the bow of the boat…laughing, beautiful, so damned happy. I knew then that I loved you. Whether you believe me or not, I decided that when we got home I was going to try one more time to see if there were any last-ditch treatments. Any hope at all."

He turned to face her. "I wanted to fight, Lizzy. Because I realized I loved you. When Dr. Shapiro told us the truth, I knew you and I had a chance."

"But then you found my letter."

He grimaced. "It was bad timing all the way around. I had admitted to myself that I loved you, but suddenly I realized you had sacrificed a portion of your life for me out of what appeared to be duty or compassion. I wanted to set you free. So I deliberately pushed you away."

He'd given it his all, every ounce of truth. He'd put his heart on the line. But nothing in her expression changed. If anything, she had retreated into herself. Perhaps she learned that move from him.

"Say something," he demanded.

"It doesn't matter," she said softly, her eyes shiny with tears. "Think back, Jonathan. You loved your life before you got sick. You adored the pressure-cooker environment, and you relished being in charge. You seldom dated, because you didn't have the time to give to a relationship. Your future was all mapped out, and you liked it."

"I liked it because you were there with me."

She inhaled sharply. "I can't be that woman anymore. Things have changed."

He crossed the room in two strides and pulled her to

her feet, gripping her hands tightly. "Then I'll change, too. The night I was so cruel to you, you said you loved me. Is it not true anymore? Is that one of the changes my selfishness caused?"

Lisette had used up her last reserves of courage. When Mazie told her Jonathan was coming to see her, it seemed like a personal challenge. Was she going to fight for him? She was tired of making sacrifices for other people, tired of hiding her feelings.

The moving ruse was a way to needle him, but if things didn't work out, it would become a reality.

The past month had seemed like a desert journey. She had grieved the loss of Jonathan endlessly...had scrounged for any tiny scraps of information about his recovery.

When he was dismissed from the hospital, it was even worse. Then all she could do was imagine him out at the beach house, sleeping in the bed that was supposed to be theirs.

Now here he was, saying things and doing things that were too enchanting to be true.

"Maybe I love you, and maybe I don't," she said. "But if you're here out of guilt —if that's all it is—you can go back to being you. I deserve to be happy. I deserve a man who cares more about his wife and his family than his need to be in control of everything."

He searched her face. "That man is gone. I wouldn't take him back, even if he came crawling. When I was in the hospital, I had to learn how to accept help. How to be grateful to doctors and nurses who were doing their damnedest to keep me alive. I wasn't in charge, Lisette. I wasn't top dog. I like to think I learned a bit of humility. But if I brag about it too much, it kind of defeats the purpose," he joked.

She stared at him, only now realizing that a new light shone from his eyes, a new peace.

He rubbed his thumb over her cheek. "Please, my love. Tell me you don't love me if that's what you want to say, but you're going to have to work to make me believe it. Because I remember what it was like to be inside you when you screamed my name. I still hear those moments in my dreams."

Her joy and her fear collided in her chest. "My period is three weeks late," she blurted out. "You didn't sign on for that."

He stared at her, trying to process the incredible words. He put a hand on her flat belly. "Of course I did. It was my idea on the boat that day, remember?"

"But only because you thought it would be all up to me later. You thought you were going to be dead and gone. Parenting is two decades or more of flat-out hard work."

He dropped his forehead to hers, his whole body shaking. "I adore you, Lizzy Tarleton. There's nothing in this world I would like more than to make a dozen babies with you and live happily ever after."

Lisette sobbed, wiping her cheek on his shoulder. "Truly?" Was this terrible nightmare really over?

He pulled her close. "We said vows. For better or for worse. We've gotten the latter out of the way early. Now let's plan our future together, my love." He scooped her up and sat on the sofa with her in his lap. "And you might want to stop crying, because I bought this new shirt just for today."

Her giggle was watery.

He bent his head and kissed her. Lisette wrapped her arms around his neck. "I do love you, Jonathan," she whispered. "I've loved you for a very long time. But…"

He reared back, alarm written on his face. "But what?"

"I think three babies will be enough."

His smile returned. "I'll wear you down."

She felt his sex pressing beneath her leg and knew that he wanted her every bit as much as she wanted him. "How do you feel about make-up sex?" she asked, stroking his bottom lip suggestively.

His grin was devilishly masculine and enthusiastic. "I thought you'd never ask."

* * * * *

WANTED:
BILLIONAIRE'S WIFE

SUSANNAH ERWIN

To Jeff, my very own happy-ever-after.

One

Danica Novak wanted a hot shower, cool bedsheets and at least ten hours of uninterrupted sleep after her early morning cross-country flight. Instead, she got a claim form for lost luggage, a taxi driver who hit every possible red light between the airport in San Francisco and her office building in Palo Alto, and yet another phone squabble with her parents' health insurance company about her brother's medical bills. This was the third person she'd talked to since her plane landed, and it wasn't yet 11:00 a.m. in California.

"The treatment isn't covered?" She braced her cell phone between her right shoulder and ear while using her hands to dig through her tote bag for any loose bills with which to pay the fare. Her credit card was useless, as she had discovered when she tried to buy food on the plane. Her sudden trip to Rhode Island at last-minute airfare prices had eaten up what remained of her cushion. "You can't negotiate to bring the costs down? At all?"

The driver stared at her through the rearview mirror, his fingers tapping an impatient rhythm on the steering wheel. When her eyes met his in the mirror, he flicked the meter back on. Danica smiled at him through gritted teeth and held up her index finger in the universal plea for just one more minute, while mustering the strength to keep her voice pitched at a pleasant conversational level.

She learned as a teenager, while helping her father apply for the license for his dry-cleaning business, that getting angry with faceless bureaucracies rarely resulted in a positive outcome. "Yes, I understand you've been told the treatment is classified as elective. Can I talk to a manager about this? Hello?" She stared at the phone. The call had dropped—or she had been hung up on.

A staccato beep from the car's horn ripped her attention back to the driver. "Lady, I gotta go."

"One second, please?" She put the phone down to better sift through the contents of her bag. The emergency twenty she always carried had to be somewhere—aha! She added it to the other bills and thrust the fare at the driver, scrambling out of the car as fast as the vinyl seat would let her. The taxi took off, the late Monday-morning sunshine bouncing off its fenders.

She stretched her neck, the bunched muscles in her shoulders protesting when she turned her head from side to side, and opened the glass door to the office building. It seemed a century ago when she last passed through the entrance, racing out in the middle of the day to pack for an emergency visit home. She was still reeling from the shock of seeing her brother, Matt, a perpetual motion machine since birth, so still in his hospital bed.

Matt had been a surprise baby, arriving eight years after Danica to the entire family's delight. Now a high-school senior, he'd attracted attention from universities for his athletic ability. Until two weeks ago, when a freak three-way collision during a football game caused a massive concussion, a fractured femur and spinal shock.

Now out of danger, his prognosis was good for a full recovery, but his doctors worried he wasn't responding as well as he could to conventional treatment. The experimental spinal therapy the insurance company was currently denying might speed up his return to health, but they wouldn't know unless a way was found to pay for it. And she'd find one. She'd told her parents she would take care of it, and she hadn't let them down yet.

Once inside, she closed her eyes and took a deep breath. Only four companies shared the office building, and the lobby was empty most times of day. She welcomed the quiet, letting it wash over her. Family leave was officially over. Time to switch back to worker bee. The Rinaldi Executive Search presentation to Ruby Hawk Technologies was in two days, and it needed to be perfect. Her promised promotion from Johanna Rinaldi's assistant to search consultant depended on it.

She grabbed a free copy of the *Silicon Valley Weekly off the lobby's reception desk*, hoping to catch up on the latest tech-industry news while she headed down the corridor to the Rinaldi offices. The tabloid newspaper was accessible online, but the print version was easier to read while walking. As if the universe had decided she needed a reminder of just how crucial the next few days would be, a color photo of Luke Dallas, the thirty-three-year-old CEO and founder of Ruby Hawk Technologies, stared out at her from the front page.

Like most people in the valley, Danica followed the meteoric rise of Ruby Hawk Technologies with awe. But the man behind the company held a special fascination for her. She long thought Luke Dallas looked as if he should be brooding on a windswept English moor rather than writing code in a glass-and-steel California office. His strong, chiseled features were a perfect match for the rumors of his hard-nosed tactics. In a town that tolerated eccentric if driven geniuses, he stood out for his demanding demeanor.

A shiver traced her spine as her gaze met his in the photo, the blue of his eyes stunning even in newsprint. She would soon be sitting across the table from that stare. A month ago, Danica discovered Ruby Hawk had terminated their contract with their search agency. She knew Johanna and Luke had gone to business school together, and she'd used that information to land a meeting to pitch Ruby Hawk their services. He was scheduled to sit in that meeting.

Surely, he couldn't be that arresting in real life. It must be a trick of the photographer's, maybe the light—

Her peripheral vision screamed out a warning just in time. She barely avoided colliding with a very broad, very muscular male chest. She swallowed her gasp of appreciation for the obviously fine physique under the tailored button-down shirt, threw the man a quick smile of apology and returned to perusing the article while she rummaged in her bag for her office key.

It took a second before the man's face fully registered. She looked up from the newspaper and stared at him. Then she glanced down at the photo. Then back at the man. Her mouth went dry as her heartbeat thudded in her ears.

Luke Dallas stood in front of the closed door of Rinaldi Executive Search. In the flesh. All six feet, four inches of him, from his wavy dark hair to his rather impressively sized loafers.

She'd been wrong. He was indeed that arresting—and more—in person. A two-dimensional image was incapable of capturing the aura of danger in his stance, coiled tension threatening to spring into action at the slightest provocation. The photo revealed the handsome symmetry of his features, but couldn't impart the sheer sensuality and command. This was a man who got what he wanted and didn't care how. Pinned by the force of his gaze, she shivered as his expression darkened. The air grew heavy, thickening with the ominous atmosphere of two weather fronts about to collide into a supercell.

She was in the direct path of the storm.

This should have been a day for triumph. Instead, Luke Dallas's jaw hurt from hours of clenching his teeth. It was a new sensation. He was always in control, no matter the situation.

But that was before this morning. Before a casual meeting in an out-of-the-way coffee shop, away from prying eyes and ears, to sign the deal memo for his company's acquisition turned into an ambush orchestrated by Irene Stavros and her father, Nestor. His vision still flashed red.

He'd travelled straight from the meeting, the ultimatum handed to him by Nestor running on a constant loop, to Johanna Rinaldi's boutique search firm. Johanna was the only person he could think of under the time-crunched circumstances who could help to extricate him from the trap Nestor had pulled closed so artfully.

Where the hell was she? Her office was locked tight and no one answered the door or the phone. His patience had just stretched past its breaking point when a woman, who couldn't be bothered to look where she was going, nearly ran him over. She stared at him with eyes so wide they threatened to take over the rest of her face. Pretty eyes though. Big and green. A man could get lost in those depths if he wasn't careful.

Then she blinked, breaking the connection, and his anger came back.

"Can I help you?" he barked, partially to cover being caught staring at a stranger, no matter how attractive, and partially because she wasn't Johanna and, right now, Johanna was the only person he wanted to see.

"You're Luke Dallas." Her gaze ping-ponged between the newspaper clutched in her hand and his face. "But our meeting isn't until Wednesday."

"You work for Johanna?" Finally. Maybe his day could get back on track and he could salvage what was left of it.

"Um." Her eyes were still wide as she ran a hand through her messy blond ponytail, then used it to tug on a white shirt that looked like it had been put on straight off the floor. Finally, she held it out to be shaken. "Yes. I do. I'm Danica. Novak. Danica Novak."

He shook her proffered hand. When he pressed against it, her fingers trembled and she leaned back, as if she were Little Red Riding Hood and he the Big Bad Wolf and they were standing in Grandmother's house. An appealing rosy shade appeared on her high cheekbones.

"It seems you know my name."

"Yes, well," she said, waving the newspaper clutched in her left hand, "it helps to have a visual aid." She gave him a tentative smile, and if he thought her eyes pretty before, the smile turned them downright stunning. Then the newspaper headline caught his gaze and made him forget any nonsense about the eyes being the windows to the soul.

"May I see that?" he asked. She handed it over.

He read the article, the hallway walls pressing in further with every word. The *Weekly*'s business reporter Cinco Jackson somehow had received wind of Luke's talks with the Stavros Group, despite his best efforts to keep them quiet. The article outlined the rumors surrounding the acquisition, calling it a done deal with the papers due to be signed imminently. Luke would be lucky to make it ten feet past Ruby Hawk's front door without his employees questioning him about timing and next steps.

Thanks to his family, plus some savvy investments of his own, Luke could've retired after college graduation and still lived an extremely comfortable life. But that was due to being born to the right parents. He hadn't earned it.

He refused to be like his stepsiblings, living off the fat of their inheritances. He wanted to build something, like his great-grandfather had. He wanted it to last, *unlike* his great-grandfather's legacy. The Draper & Dallas department store chain was long gone. The advancements made by Ruby Hawk in biofeedback and neural technology, however, could make lives better for generations.

He crushed the newspaper in his hand. Ruby Hawk Technologies was *his*. He'd created the company, pouring his own money into it. Now he needed additional capital for the company to reach its full potential, to prove to those who wrote him off as a rich dilettante that he had what it took to be a tech visionary.

He'd explored options for raising more money but none provided the combination of financing, ownership control and corporate independence Luke sought. Then Irene Stavros suggested he talk to her father. A month ago, Luke received a deal term sheet from Nestor.

On paper, it was perfect. The Stavros Group would buy Ruby Hawk and infuse the company with the cash it needed to expand, while allowing Ruby Hawk to continue to operate autonomously. The original management team, including Luke as CEO, would remain intact and he would continue to call all the shots without interference from the acquiring parent company. Anticipating an easy close to the deal, Luke ordered and installed expensive new equipment for his engineers. Then when he went to meet Nestor to sign the paperwork, Nestor revealed his trap. Unless Luke went along with Nestor's demands, he wouldn't have the means to make payroll in six months' time.

And now, the article. Thanks to it revealing the deal terms, his employees would be expecting their stock options to be worth millions upon the completion of the acquisition.

He had to save this deal. "Where's your boss?"

Her green eyes widened at the snap of his words.

"I've been here for half an hour and no one has answered the door or the phone. What kind of a business is this?" He thrust the tabloid back at her. He'd deal with the story later.

"We're very good at what we do. I'm sure there's an explanation." She shook out the crumpled paper.

He raised an eyebrow and looked at his watch.

Color rose even higher in her cheeks. "I just got off a plane. Johanna probably has a meeting off-site." She opened a substantial tote bag and searched inside. "Although that doesn't explain why Britt isn't on phone duty," she murmured under her breath. Her hand surfaced holding a key ring. "Wait here while I make sure the lights are on."

She swung open the door and disappeared inside, shutting it behind her. He heard a stifled exclamation, followed by a loud thud. Just as he was about to investigate the noise, she emerged, slamming the door shut and leaning against it.

Her face made her white shirt seem dark gray by comparison. "Um, maybe you should wait at the diner next door. The coffee is good. It's all single origin, hand poured—"

"No." It would be a long time before he'd be able to drink coffee without the memory of that morning's meeting poisoning the taste. "What's wrong? Is someone hurt?"

She shook her head, her chest rapidly rising and falling.

"I'm going in." He gently took her hand off the doorknob. It trembled in his grasp.

Her chin snapped up. "No, please don't—"

He ignored her protestations. Was it a break-in? Vandalism? Or hungover coworkers, and she didn't want a prospective client to see what really went on at Rinaldi Executive Search?

The last thing he'd expected to see was emptiness. As in, not only were employees not at their desks, but the desks were gone too. The blinds were open and the sunshine revealed a reception area, barren save for a broken desk stool, naked metal shelves and scuffmarks on the bamboo laminate floors marking where furniture once stood. One lonely high-walled cubicle stood outside a door that led to an inner office empty of all furnishings.

"I thought maybe we were robbed." Danica stood behind him in the doorway, her arms protectively hugging her chest. "But…"

He shook his head. Thieves would have left a mess. "This is the work of professional movers."

The hot fist in his stomach began to squeeze again. Johanna's disappearance was total. How could he so badly miscalculate twice in the same day?

"I was gone two weeks." Danica's voice was thin. "Two weeks." Her gaze, wild and unfocused, travelled around the empty space. She shuffled into the office like a sleepwalker who couldn't wake up. Her tote bag lay in her path, its contents scattered across the floor. Before he could clear it out of her way, her foot tangled in the thick strap.

He lunged, grasping her shoulders to keep her upright. This close, her hair consisted of a thousand shades of gold, from honey chestnut to palest yellow. Faint freckles dusted the pale skin stretched over a small, pointed nose. Her lips were softly curved, the bottom lip presenting the perfect amount of plumpness. Vanilla spiked with cinnamon teased his nose. For a second, he was tempted to see if she tasted just as spicy sweet.

Then reality landed a roundhouse to his gut.

His plan for saving Ruby Hawk had disappeared with the office furnishings that used to grace the Rinaldi office.

"Thank you for the save." Danica heard her voice as if it came from a long distance. Maybe she fell asleep on the plane, and this was just a bad nightmare brought on by the pressure of finishing the pitch presentation? But despite the number of blinks, the vision in front of her stayed the same.

Luke Dallas, CEO of Ruby Hawk Technologies. A *Doctor Who* fan had confided in her that Luke was called Luke Dalek behind his back, because he never met a human emotion he didn't try to exterminate.

Luke Dallas, who had very firm muscles under his Silicon Valley uniform of blue button-down shirt paired with khakis. Underneath his clothes, he must put a Greek god to shame. She grasped the silky cotton of his shirt, his biceps flexing under her fingers. He even smelled like she imagined a Greek god would: like the outdoors after a rainstorm over a base of expensive leather and fresh citrus. The room began to spin, faster and faster, and she closed her eyes.

"Breathe," he said. "In and out."

She did as he commanded, allowing herself to lean into him, just a little, craving the intense sense of confidence and security his arms provided. Then he abruptly let go. Her eyes flew open.

"I don't have time to take you to urgent care if you fall and hurt yourself." His jaw clenched as his gaze travelled the barren suite. "I have to leave."

Think, Danica, think fast. But her mind was a jumble of scattershot fragments mixed with bursts of pure panic. All she knew was if he left, he would take with him the chance of pitching Rinaldi Executive Search's services to him. And with that would go her promised promotion.

She needed to find her boss. This had to be a huge misunderstanding.

"Johanna must have moved offices while I was gone. I was a bit hard to reach." It was the truth. Matt's hospital floor didn't allow cell phones. "Let me call her."

She picked up her treacherous tote bag and scooped the fallen items back into it. Where was her phone? She knew she got off the plane with it. She had it in the taxi—

Oh, no. She placed it on the taxi's back seat while searching for the fare. And she never picked it back up. It could be anywhere from Marin to Monterey.

"Something else wrong?" His hard stare caused her skin to prickle.

"Nothing is wrong. I forgot something, that's all," she said, keeping her tone pleasant. It was if he could see through her and wasn't impressed. Just like in high school, when the kids at the top of the social pyramid made sure she knew she would never ascend to their heights.

He folded his arms. "Seems to me a lot is wrong. Starting with the empty office."

"I'm going to my desk to straighten this out. Will you give me fifteen minutes?" Please, she prayed, let there be a working office phone on the premises. And please let Johanna have an amazing explanation that didn't defy logic.

He nodded. She held her head high until she was behind her cubicle walls, out of his view. Then her shoulders crumbled.

Her cubicle was empty of everything but a file box. The lid was off, and inside were the few personal items she kept in the space. On top were the comic-book action figures that used to decorate her shelves. They had been a gag gift from her brother when she moved to California, a reminder she was stronger than she looked.

Her nose stung. She willed the tears away. Crying only caused more problems, a lesson she had learned well.

A note was taped to the outside of the box, the cream-colored envelope embossed with Johanna's initials. The heavy, linen-weave paper was leaden in her hands.

Hey, Danica!
I didn't want to disturb you while you were with your family. But the Stavros Group offered me an amazing opportunity! I'm their new head of Asia-Pacific talent recruitment. I'll be based in Sydney and traveling all over the world. They needed me right away so I couldn't wait until you came back. :-(

Britt already has a new job, yay! Speaking of, do me a favor and make sure Britt forwarded the phones to the answering service? ;-)

I'll try to call you when I get settled, but I'll be super busy so it might be a while. Here's your final paycheck and the number for the lawyer in charge of the business dissolution in case you have questions. Ciao!
Johanna xoxo

Danica pulled out the attached pay slip. Two weeks' severance had been added to it. Two weeks. That was all she was worth to Johanna? After giving her three years of her life, helping her build the company from the ground up, never taking vacation and only the very rare sick day? The emergency family leave had been the first time she'd been away from the office for more than forty-eight hours in a row.

She sank to the floor. This was worse than when her ex-boyfriend left her. At least then she'd had a job and could contribute to the family finances. Now? She didn't even have her beaten-up car. She'd asked her roommate, Mai, to sell it for her to cover her share of the household expenses, since her plane ticket had eaten up her meager bank account. Nor could she ask Mai to let her slide on her rent payment. Mai's finances were almost as precarious as hers.

Danica always managed to find the glimmer of light in darkness, to think her way out of what seemed like insurmountable odds. Until now. Try as hard as she could, her mind remained an opaque blank.

Luke watched Danica march to her cubicle, ponytail swinging as if she didn't have a care in the world. He couldn't help but notice other rounder portions of her anatomy also swaying. Too bad she was lying about reaching Johanna. He'd tried calling her several times himself. No answer, only voice mail.

He should return to his office and come up with plans B through Z. He would just have to sidestep his team's questions about the acquisition the best he could.

A sniffle-like sound echoed through the empty suite. He shook his head. Tears were a cheap, manipulative trick. He reached for the doorknob.

A second sniffle ricocheted through the air, followed by a third.

Damn it. He turned and walked to the cubicle.

The noises were Danica shredding what looked like expensive stationery into tiny pieces of confetti. "Wanton destruction. Effective," he said.

She gave him a quick smile, her eyes suspiciously bright, before returning to her task. "Johanna moved to Sydney."

He couldn't keep the surprise out of his voice. "You got her on the phone?"

She shook her head. "She left an old-fashioned note. I'd show you but it's not legible now." More paper fragments fell from her hands. "I guess the meeting on Wednesday is cancelled."

"Yes." A strange twinge of something like regret hit him at the thought of never seeing her again, but he shook it off. "I'm leaving. Good luck." He held out his hand to be shaken.

She took it. Her palm fit against his as if it was meant to be there.

He cleared his throat. "If you hear from Johanna, tell her I need—"

His gaze fixated on a scrap of paper near his shoe. *Stavr* was written on it in loopy cursive letters. "Why is Johanna in Sydney?"

Danica shrugged. "Her note said she got her dream job." She kicked at the scraps.

"A job with whom?" His stomach muscles contracted as if anticipating a hard blow.

"The Stavros Group. Why?"

The blow landed, square in his gut. He now saw just how thoroughly Nestor and Irene had prepared the trap. He couldn't help but wonder who else in his social circle they'd co-opted. He bet if he called Gwen, the last woman he dated, he'd find she was filming out of the country—for one of the Stavros Group's production companies.

And he'd walked into it like a green MBA just out of business school, all theoretical book learning with none of the street smarts he had honed over the years. His fists bunched, nails digging sharply into his skin. It was either that or punch the wall, and the cubicle looked like one good blow would topple it over. "I can't believe I didn't see this," he ground out.

Danica stopped tearing paper, her gaze fixing on his. "What does Johanna's new job have to do with you?"

He shook his head, the bile closing his throat and bottling his words deep inside. Nestor and Irene were three steps ahead of him, always had been. They took Johanna off the game board, knowing she would be his first move. It was predictable, he had to admit. He and Irene and Johanna had been at business school together. Irene knew his social circle almost as well as he did. Damn it.

He strode out of the cubicle. "I have to get back to my office."

"Oh, no, you don't." Danica beat him to the outer door and stood in his way. "You're not leaving until you tell me what is going on."

He ignored her, veering right.

She dodged him with a grace he hadn't seen since the last time he was dragged to a benefit for the San Francisco Ballet. She set her feet and held her arms out to block his passage. He couldn't help but notice how her stance caused her shirt buttons to strain against her full breasts, creating shadowy gaps that tempted further exploration.

He dragged his gaze away and reached for the doorknob. "I don't have time for this game."

Her hand grabbed his wrist, her fingers landing on his pulse point. Their gazes met, clashed in a lightning strike that sent electricity crackling through the air.

Her chin dropped, and she looked up at him from under dark gold eyelashes. The tip of her pink tongue darted out to wet her plump lips, her breaths coming faster. Her remarkable eyes almost glowed in the dust-filled light. What if he leaned in, like so—

Before he could put his thoughts into action, she snapped her head up. The static in the atmosphere dissipated. She let his wrist go but he could feel the pressure of her fingers on his skin.

"This is not a game. This is my life." Her voice cracked on the last word, and she took a deep breath. "Before today,

I had a job I loved in executive recruitment. I was really good at it too. My title might have been assistant, but I made most of the placements and I was finally about to be promoted. But this morning, poof!" She snapped her fingers. "And judging by your behavior, you're connected to the magic trick that made my job disappear. You owe me an explanation."

He couldn't tell her the truth. No one got the better of him. Especially not Irene and her father.

Then Danica's words clicked. *Executive recruitment.* She was also a recruiter.

It wasn't the most elegant solution. She'd think him irrational, to start, and maybe he was. He certainly wasn't acting like himself, leaning in to kiss a stranger just because he found her mouth intriguing.

Yet when he ran a split-second mental check of the pros and cons, it made sense. In fact, it might work better than his initial plan, which had required Johanna's unpredictable cooperation.

Danica's words made it sound like her entire world had imploded. She needed him. Or rather, he corrected himself, she needed his offer of employment. It was always beneficial to have the upper hand in a business relationship.

Yes, he found her attractive. But his discipline, at both work and play, was legendary. "You say you're good at executive recruitment?"

"The best." Her expression turned wary. "Why do you ask?"

"Because I need a wife ASAP. And you're going to recruit one for me."

Two

"You need a *wife*?" Danica was surprised her legs still held her up. "And you want me to *recruit* one for you?"

It didn't make sense. Luke Dallas should have no trouble finding a wife. His effect on women was well documented. She herself spent only three minutes in his presence before she started tripping over her bag. If she hadn't managed to break the spell his nearness cast over her, she would have thrown all professionalism to the wind and kissed him. And then prayed for an earthquake to swallow her as she'd be the laughing stock of Silicon Valley: the assistant who threw herself at Luke Dallas. Johanna *especially* would—

The shoe dropped, hard.

"Is that why you're here?" Danica stared at Luke. "You were going to ask Johanna to do this."

A ruddy glint appeared on his sun-bronzed cheekbones. "Do you want a job or not?"

She managed to corral her thoughts into something resembling coherency. "I don't know the first thing about finding wives. Vice-presidents of finance? Yes. Lifetime partners? You're on your own."

"What's the difference?" he countered. "I give you my list of requirements. You find candidates who match those requirements."

"But," she sputtered, searching for words to make him understand, "a wife isn't an employee. What about, oh, I don't know, compatibility? Life goals?"

"I look for employees who are compatible with my company's culture and share my goals for its future. I expect the same from a wife." He sounded as if he were ordering a custom car, instead of entering a committed relationship with a human being.

"But you can fire an employee. You can't fire a wife!"

"It's called divorce. Look, I hire employees who are the best of the best. But I don't comb the world looking for them. I hire someone to do that for me." He leaned into the door, his broad shoulder just scant inches from where hers rested against the polished wooden surface.

Her pulse doubled. It had to be from outrage at his ridiculous request. It certainly wasn't caused by having his attention laser focused on her, his gaze demanding she meet his. "I'd be thrilled to be an executive recruiter for you, but—"

"It's the same principle. I don't have time for the necessary getting-to-know-you dates to ensure a potential spouse fits my specific requirements. I'm hiring you to do the vetting for me. Simple."

"Only it's not—"

"The successful candidate will need to sign a prenuptial contract so that I can, indeed, 'fire' her without consequences if necessary. Just like an employment contract, which you and I will have. It's highly reasonable." His direct gaze dared her to disagree.

No wonder he earned the nickname Luke Dalek. He made marriage sound like lines of binary code. "What about falling in love?"

He raised an eyebrow, like a teacher silently reprimanding a student for failing to add two plus two correctly. "The successful candidate will be well compensated for meeting my requirements. As will you for conducting the search. I assume three hundred thousand dollars will cover your retainer fee and costs."

"That doesn't answer my—wait. Three hundred thousand dollars?" At his nod, blood thudded in her ears. This time, his nearness had nothing to do with it.

Three. Hundred. *Thousand.* Dollars. What remained of the bills for Matt's surgery could be paid outright and he could start the experimental treatment. Her parents could stop worrying. Her rent payments would be covered, staving off homelessness for the foreseeable future.

There was even enough money to start her own search firm. Never again rely on an employer's empty promises.

It sounded too good to be true. And in her experience, when things sounded too good to be true, it meant they would end only in tears: hers. "There are lots of people who are professional matchmakers. Like that TV show, *Matchmaker for Millionaires*, or whatever it's called. Why not go to her?"

His upper lip curled. "I would rather replace my laptop with a typewriter. I told you, I don't have time for the conventional courtship a matchmaker would require. I'm hiring you because my criteria include a successful business track record, experience with high-level philanthropy and an elite education. Qualities you should be familiar with in executive recruitment."

"Seems like a rather extreme way to meet women." Exhaustion always caused her mouth to operate separately from her brain's tact center.

His gaze narrowed, then his mouth upturned ever so slightly. He leaned closer to her. "If I just needed to meet women, I wouldn't require your services. Believe me." His low tones rumbled in her ear, causing her knees to turn to water.

She braced herself against the wall. She didn't want to find Luke Dallas desirable. He was easy to look at, sure. His muscles belonged on a museum statue. His eyes could be used as interrogation weapons: one deep gaze into those blue pools and she was sure spies of all genders would be happy to spill their secrets. It was fun following his exploits in the gossip columns from afar—okay, exciting to imagine herself in the designer dresses of his dates. But in person? Intimidating. Arrogant. And asking the impossible.

Too late, she realized Luke continued to speak. She tuned in just in time to hear him say, "If you complete the search in one month, you'll earn a fifty-thousand-dollar bonus."

"Fifty…thousand…" The room began to spin around her once more.

"Breathe," he said. He put a hand on her upper arm to keep her steady. Sparks flew from where he touched her, crackling through her nervous system. "You should work on that."

It was a lot of money. Money her family needed. She searched his gaze, looking for a catch. She saw only determination.

"Well?" He looked at his smartwatch. "The offer is off the table in three minutes."

Finding suitable contenders shouldn't be a problem if she focused on education and work history. Charity work and social affiliations would also help her determine if they met his criteria. Thankfully, she had backed up the firm's database of recruitment targets before she took her family leave. Johanna rarely changed her own email passwords, much less the password to the cloud storage site Danica used for the firm's important files, so access to the information shouldn't be a problem.

The ethics of finding him a bride, however... She bit her lower lip. But he was right. Executive search hinged on making a successful match between the employer and the candidate. What he wanted wasn't too much of a leap. She blurted out the next thing that popped into her head. "I'm not asking about sexual histories. That's all on you."

A swift grin transformed his face. It made him seem approachable, even charming. "Does that mean you accept the job?"

"I have a few conditions." Her voice echoed in the empty office. "I'll find you three women who fit your criteria. However, getting one of them to agree to marry you is your job. And if no one puts on your ring, I still get paid."

"Only three?"

She held up her hand and checked off items on her fingers as she spoke. "You're asking me to identify suitable candidates, investigate their backgrounds, check their references and ascertain their interest in the potential—" she was going to say *position* but changed her mind "—opening."

He raised an eyebrow and gave her a devastating smirk. Too late, she realized the word she chose was almost as suggestive as the one she discarded. "In one month. Three feasible choices are a very healthy outcome," she said, managing to continue.

"Fine. I accept. But I must agree each one satisfies my requirements before I sign off on the completion of your contract." A gleam lit his gaze when he stressed the word *satisfies*.

"You agree they fulfill the requirements on paper before you meet them. Any satisfaction that occurs after is up to you." She bit her lower lip to stop from returning his smirk.

His gaze lingered on her mouth. If he was trying to fluster her, he was doing a good job. She folded her arms and lifted her chin.

That unholy glint of laughter remained in his gaze. "And your other conditions?"

She resisted the urge to wipe her damp palms on her trousers. "An office to work in, a corporate cell phone and an open expense account. Oh, and health insurance. Starting today." She kept her gaze steadily on his through sheer force of will. He really did have the most amazing eyes. Deep blue with flecks of gray—or were they deep gray with flecks of blue? Either way, they reminded her of pictures she had seen of ancient Roman mosaics in her parents' home city of Zagreb, the colors deep and rich and playing off each other.

This time an actual smile dented one side of his face. "Come by Ruby Hawk after lunch and I'll have someone set you up with a workspace, phone, benefits and credit card."

Danica exhaled. It felt good to have her lungs back in working order. "It's a deal."

"Not yet. I have conditions of my own. One, this is confidential."

She narrowed her gaze. "Searches usually are."

"Two, you'll sign a nondisclosure agreement. No talking to the press, your relatives or your partner." He raised an eyebrow. "I assume you have one."

"I never talk to the press. I keep my work and private life separate."

"And the partner?"

"None of your business, but not an issue." Was that a flash in his gaze? Not that it was any concern of hers. Yes, he was attractive, but so had been her ex. Who dumped her to marry a woman who sounded a lot like Luke's ideal candidate.

He nodded. "We'll tell the staff at Ruby Hawk you're a consultant working on a research project for me. And three, while I understand asking certain questions are not in your job description—" he paused and his one-sided smile deepened "—your candidates must be single and free of romantic entanglements."

His phone rang, an insistent buzz. He looked at it, and the CEO feared across Silicon Valley reappeared. "I have to take this. I'll see you in my office at two thirty." It was a command, not a question. Before she could respond, he was gone, leaving eddies in the air.

She let out her breath as the adrenaline surging in his presence slowly retreated. Her gaze swept the bare walls and scuffed floors. It was hard to believe two weeks ago she thought her job was secure. Of course, two weeks ago she also thought her strong, athletic teenage brother would remain in the best of health. Before the accident, Danica thought her life was on a straight road, with maybe the occasional dip or hill. Now? Nothing but blind curves and unmarked hazards.

Like the blind curve Luke Dallas represented. She squeezed her eyes shut. She'd make it work. To help her brother get the care he needed, she'd do almost anything.

She left the office with her box of personal possessions in hand and headed to the nearest library to log into the employee-only portal on the Rinaldi Executive Search website. As she anticipated, the passwords hadn't been changed. She filled out the template agreement for executive search services, changing the words and terms as necessary. After her finger hovered over the keyboard for several heartbeats, she pressed Send.

Luke wasn't sure if he'd made an expensive blunder or hit upon a stroke of genius. The decision to hire Danica Novak to find him a wife so he could jump through Nestor Stavros's ridiculous hoop seemed right at the time. A week later, driving in his car on his way to work, it seemed like a damn foolish idea. Especially since he had yet to see any viable work product from Ms. Novak.

He refused to think he been taken in by big green eyes and a luscious mouth meant to be kissed slowly and thoroughly. He found her physically attractive, yes. But she also exhibited a quick wit and a willingness to go toe to toe with him that suggested she was intelligent and more than capable. He just needed to see the evidence of it. Now.

He parked his BMW i8 in the parking space marked with his name and strode through the glass doors engraved with the Ruby Hawk logo, forgoing the elevator in favor of taking the stairs two by two up to the third floor that housed the main operations. Today was going to be yet another difficult one. Cinco Jackson wrote another article about the Stavros Group acquisition, and this time he mentioned the deal might fall apart if certain unnamed conditions weren't met.

Anjuli Patel met him as he exited the stairwell. He did a double take as he took in her outfit. The chief financial officer of Ruby Hawk and his second-in-command, she normally wore carefully color-coordinated outfits and tasteful jewelry. This morning she looked as if one of her three-year-old twins had chosen her clothing. "Another article just appeared in the *Silicon Valley Weekly*," she said. "My husband texted me from the gym at 6:00 a.m."

"Yes. I saw it. I'm sure everyone has," he answered without breaking stride.

Anjuli fell in beside him and matched his speed. "How much truth is in it? Is the Stavros Group removing you when the deal goes through? *Is* the deal going through?" Her dark gaze sparked with anxious curiosity. She knew as well as he did how much the influx of cash from the acquisition was vitally needed.

"Let's talk." He beelined for his office. Like most tech companies, Ruby Hawk employees worked in an open plan bullpen. No doors, no cubicles, just desks pushed together to form team clusters. But recently Luke took over one of the glass-walled conference rooms that ringed the outer wall for more privacy during the acquisition discussions. He'd need it today.

"Let's talk in a good way? Or let's talk and it's bad?" she asked.

"Just be prepared," he said. "Run the numbers if the Stavros Group stays with the deal, and then run the numbers if they don't."

"Which set do you want first?"

The sooner he knew what he was up against, the better. "The latter."

"So it's bad." Her worried gaze swept over the engineers sitting at low desks. A few browser windows featuring the *Silicon Valley Weekly* website closed as Luke and Anjuli passed by.

"It might be." He increased his stride to pull ahead of her.

His steps slowed as he neared the door to the conference room. A clump of his top executives occupied the space between him and the door. Every single person standing outside his office he had handpicked to be on his team. In many cases, he persuaded them to leave lucrative salaries and promising career trajectories to join him at Ruby Hawk. He owed them, more than he could express.

"There he is." The knot of executives pressed forward. "Is it true?"

"What's happening with the acquisition?"

"Are you leaving the company?"

He caught sight of a messy blond ponytail on the outer fringes of the group. Good. He needed Danica—or rather, he corrected his thoughts grimly, he needed her work, now more than ever.

He held up a hand and the questions quieted down. "Don't pay attention to the rumors. Our response is to keep our heads down and continue to do good work. But I do need to see her." He indicated with a jerk of his chin for Danica to come forward.

Her startled gaze met his. "Me?" she sputtered.

"You. Anjuli, let's meet after you run those numbers. Everyone else, back to your desks. If you want to gossip, do it on your own time." He stepped forward to usher Danica into his office as the small crowd dispersed at his command.

Danica didn't have time to form a protest. His hand on the small of her back guided her, its warmth radiating through the thin cotton jersey of her shirt. He indicated a chair in front of his desk and let go of her arm, not a second too soon for her comfort. The door shut behind them with a resounding click.

"What can I do for you?" she asked, sitting gingerly on the edge of a clear molded acrylic chair. Her back was to the glass wall, but her spine prickled with the heat of at least half a dozen stares aimed straight at her.

He sat down on the opposite side of the repurposed-wood conference table. He pushed a button on a remote control and mechanized shades unrolled over the windows, shielding them from the curious gazes.

The light in the room dimmed, the atmosphere changing from corporate to intimate. She was very aware they were the only two people in the room.

His shoulders seemed to fall slightly. It was a small chink in his usually impenetrable armor of arrogant self-confidence. She yearned to reach out and smooth the faint creases marring his brow. "What's wrong?" she tried again, her tone soft.

The vulnerability disappeared as quickly as it had revealed itself, causing the temperature in the room to fall a few degrees. "Nothing I can't handle."

She resisted the urge to turn around and point at the now-shaded glass wall. "The angry mob searching for pitchforks and torches was just my imagination?"

His eyebrows drew together. "A vivid one. That was nowhere near a mob, and they weren't angry."

"A group of concerned employees, then. Is it the article about the Stavros Group pulling out of the deal?"

"I need your candidate list."

It was a good thing she was already sitting. The shock would have blown her off her feet. "I sent you my preliminary list days ago. That's why I was standing there, hoping to catch you for your reaction." She pulled an email printout from the folder she carried and placed it on his desk.

He glanced down at the paper, and then his head came up sharply. "I thought this was a list of rejected candidates. I deleted it." He pushed it aside. "It's been five working days. I need your results. Now."

He deleted her hard work? Without so much as an acknowledgment he had received it? "I know it's been five days!" she shot back. "Five days of you ignoring my emails, my phone calls, my chat invitations, my texts." How dare he put this on her? "I did everything but parade naked in front of that window to get your attention!"

The light in his eyes changed. Prickles formed on her skin. "I answer communications when I have something to say. No answer from me means 'No.'" A corner of his mouth turned up in a smirk. "Although no one's tried parading naked before."

That treacherous heat suffused her cheeks again. "If this is the way you treat your employees' attempts to get in touch with you, no wonder they talk as if the company needs to be measured for a coffin behind your back."

His lips compressed into a thin line. "They do no such thing."

"I know this room resembles a bubble, but that's no excuse for talking like you live in one." Luke was powerful and wealthy. Perhaps his lofty status kept him from seeing the ground below him. "I'm practically locked up in a converted supply closet because you don't want anyone to know why I'm here, and even *I* know the acquisition is in trouble. You need to talk to your employees. Starting with me."

His gaze was the glacial blue of an iceberg beneath the surface and just as dangerous. "Fine. Let's talk. If you're having difficulty performing the task assigned to you, we should rethink this arrangement."

What? Her breath came in staccato bursts. She'd told her parents she would pay for Matt's treatment. She refused to let that become a lie. "I performed the task assigned to me. That list is the result of hours of impeccable research. Every single person has been vetted and meets your criteria." She returned his arctic gaze with a heated glare. "How dare you delete it?"

He stood up, his broad, muscled form towering over her. "You submitted a list of women already known to me. Therefore, it's unusable."

She sprang to her feet. He would not intimidate her with his stance. The top of her head came up to his Adam's apple, forcing her to tilt her head back so she could meet his gaze straight on. "It may be hard to believe, but every date you've ever had is not on a gossip website. That is why I sent the list to you to vet. I need your feedback." She leaned over and pointed at the printout, her index finger planted firmly on his desk.

He raised a dismissive eyebrow and slid the paper from underneath her finger, crumpling it up and tossing it in a perfect arc into a nearby wastebasket. He then put his hands on the desk and angled his torso over the table. Scant inches separated them.

"The women on your list work in tech. You think I'm not aware of talented up-and-coming executives? I don't need you to tell me who I know and already considered. I need you to find someone I *haven't* considered."

Danica huffed. "Remember what I said about communication? This would've been useful information to have. A week ago."

He leaned even closer. The scent of expensive leather and fresh citrus teased her nose. She got the distinct sense of a tiger playing with his prey. The prey might think it could escape. But the tiger was coiled to jump and tear out the prey's throat in a blink.

"You're the search expert, not me," he said in a low, controlled voice. "But common sense dictates looking further afield than the client is able to do on his own is a prerequisite for the job."

"You—" she began.

Then she stopped and considered his words.

He was right.

She had overlooked a basic step in conducting a search: assess which candidates had already been rejected before she came on board. And yes, he could have explained the problem with her list in a timelier, if not infinitely more tactful, manner. But if he had, he wouldn't be Luke Dallas.

Her gaze fell. His shirt was open at the collar, revealing a triangle of sun-bronzed skin. A pulse leaped at the side of his neck, and for a split second she wanted to rest her lips there and see if he tasted as good as he smelled.

"You…" she started again. "You're right. I'm sorry. If you still want me to work on the search, I'll compile a better list." She snuck a glance at him from under her eyelashes. She expected chilly disdain, but there was something warm and contemplative deep in his eyes. A hot spark kindled in her chest as their gazes tangled.

"I only hire people who perform well at their tasks. You're still on the search. But I expect better results." He sat back down in his chair, taking his appealing scent with him. She stifled her disappointment.

"And you will get them. I promise." She turned to leave the room.

"Have dinner with me."

"What?" She whirled around so quickly she nearly caused self-induced whiplash.

He put down his tablet and looked up at her, leaning back in his seat. "I haven't given this project the specialized attention it needs. It's clear you don't have the necessary inputs to make correct assessments. I don't have time to remedy that right now. But I do have to eat later, so you might as well eat with me."

His words doused the spark's last flickers. "When you put it that way, how can I refuse?"

"I'll text you the address. I trust going into the city isn't a problem for you?" His tone made it clear it was a rhetorical question.

San Francisco was almost an hour each way on Caltrain, depending on the train schedules, and her exhausted brain was already looking forward to putting on pajamas and binging on reality TV with her roommate, Mai. She gave him her best, if forced, smile. "No. Not a problem."

"Good. I have a commitment beforehand, so I'll meet you there." His attention returned to his tablet and he became absorbed in whatever he was reading. She fled before the tiger could realize the prey had left the room.

Three

Danica wasn't quite sure what to expect from her dinner with Luke, but this establishment wasn't it. Surely white tablecloths and waiters wearing black tie were more his style? She glanced at her new phone and reread the email. This was the address. She looked up at the dingy neon sign that appeared as if it hadn't been cleaned since first put into place decades ago. That was the name of the restaurant. Squaring her shoulders, she looked past the layers of graffiti decorating the outside walls and stepped inside.

The taqueria's interior was reminiscent of an ancient cafeteria, with laminate white tables and red plastic chairs lined up on the scuffed black-and-white-checkerboard linoleum floor. A long line of people stood in front of a high counter, orders barked in rapid Spanish and English. The smell of freshly made tortillas and the sound of knives chopping tomatoes and peppers reminded her stomach how long it had been since she ate a protein bar at her desk.

At least she wouldn't be underdressed as she'd feared. Her cream polyester blouse and navy skirt would allow her to blend right into the disparate crowd. She stood off to the side of the front entrance to wait for Luke, her gaze wandering over the restaurant. The wide range of patrons, from teenagers to executives, made it a prime opportunity for people watching. She smiled as a young mother wrangled her toddler by offering him torn pieces of tortilla. But her attention was arrested by a tall, powerfully built man waiting in line to order, his well-worn jeans molded to the tight, muscular curves of his rear end.

Just then, the man turned and waved at her. She quickly glanced away, ashamed to be caught ogling.

"Danica," he called, "over here."

It took her a moment to realize the perfect male rear draped in vintage Levi's belonged to her boss.

She swallowed. Who knew he had been hiding that under his usual khakis? And she had to admit his front view was just as nice as the back. A dark blue shirt matched his eyes despite the tendency of the overhead fluorescent lights to turn every color to a greenish yellow. His hair was swept back and damp, a testament to a recent shower. As if to confirm her suspicions, when she got into line with him she caught of whiff of soap along with his unique scent.

"There you are," he said. "Do you know what you want?" He pointed to the large menu board over their heads. "They're famous for their burritos. But if you want something else, go for it." He flashed his killer smile at her, and her stomach turned several flips.

"A burrito sounds fine," she said, after trying to read the board and failing because the words wouldn't stick in her brain. Not with Luke's nearness occupying all the other senses. "Whatever you suggest. But easy on the hot sauce. Nonexistent easy."

He raised a skeptical eyebrow. "Is eating here okay? We could go somewhere else if this isn't to your taste." His tone implied not enjoying Mexican food was incomprehensible, like still believing in the tooth fairy.

She shook her head. "I like to try new foods. I just have a New England palate, that's all."

"Anything else I should know? Vegetarian? Food sensitivities? Anaphylactic shock caused by peanuts?"

She laughed. He grinned back at her, his expression more relaxed than she had ever seen it. "Peanuts? Just what is in this burrito? No, no other restrictions," she said.

He nodded and began a conversation with the man behind the counter in rapid, fluid Spanish. Luke accepted two long-necked Mexican beers with one hand and used the other to guide her to a nearby table.

She sat down in a red plastic chair. It was just a business dinner with her boss. Something she and Johanna used to do on a regular basis. Only Johanna never made her pulse sing an aria just by touching her elbow.

She cleared her throat. "What's our number? I'll fetch the food."

"Don't have to," Luke said. He pushed one of the beers in front of her and then took a deep swallow from his. "Enrique will bring the food to us."

She looked around. No one else was receiving table service. All the other patrons went to the counter to bring back trays packed high with plastic baskets filled with foil-wrapped food and tortilla chips. "Another perk of being the CEO of Ruby Hawk?"

He frowned. "Because I'm CEO? No. But because of Ruby Hawk?" He used his beer bottle to indicate a boisterous group of teenage boys, joking with each other as they dug into their food. Each one wore a bright gold basketball jersey, with a small red bird emblazoned on the front.

They reminded her of her brother. "You could say that. We sponsor the league, while Enrique lets this team eat here on game days. Enrique got the worse bargain."

She smiled. Feeding an active teenage boy was something her family knew well. Or at least they used to. "I bet. Was the league your previous commitment?"

"How did you know?"

She indicated his damp hair. "I doubt a business meeting would require shampoo after." A vision of him standing under a shower jet, water cascading off that flawless rear end hidden under his jeans, steam rising off the smooth biceps peeking out from the sleeves of his T-shirt, nearly caused her to choke on her beer. She put the bottle down and ducked under the table to rummage in her tote bag.

Once she was sure the color in her face had returned to normal, she resurfaced, a file folder in her hand. "So," she said, attempting to sound brisk and professional, "as I said earlier, you were right. I hadn't looked outside the box. These candidates—" she slid the folder over to him "—should be more to your specifications."

He pushed the folder away. "Maybe. But I never discuss business while hungry. It leads to poor decision-making. Speaking of, here comes our food." The man who took their order placed a tray on their table, carrying on another conversation in Spanish with Luke that ended with both men laughing and shaking hands. When he left, Luke turned back to Danica. "Dig in."

Luke sat back in his chair. The stress that caused his shoulders to be in a perpetual knot since his meeting with Nestor was currently at bay, thanks to coaching a hard-fought basketball game that helped focus his mind outside his company. And, he had to admit: he liked watching Danica's reactions.

She glanced around the taqueria, smiling at the other patrons. He noticed it lingered the longest on the youth basketball team, her expression somewhat wistful, before she turned her attention to her food. He was about to ask her why when she let out a small groan.

"This burrito? Is amazing." She took another bite. The look on her face was pure pleasure. He wondered what else would cause that expression to appear and found himself shifting in his seat.

"It's even better with salsa," he warned, taking his own bite of the cheese-beans-and-rice-filled concoction.

"No way," she said with a sigh of contentment, and took a long drink from her beer. His gaze fixated on her mouth, her plump lips wrapped around the neck of the bottle. When she swallowed, it caused an answering pull in his groin. Good thing she couldn't see under the table.

She caught his gaze with hers. Her eyes were more than just green, he noticed. Flecks of gold rimmed her pupils, while a band of forest green encircled her irises. What if he were to reach across the table, cover her luscious mouth with his, see if he could make those eyes darken to emerald…

She tore her gaze away, snapping the connection. The haze enveloping him dissipated. He sat back in his chair and stirred his salsa with a tortilla chip. *Analyze the situation. Don't let it control you*, he admonished himself.

He was having a physiological reaction to an attractive woman. It was understandable. His last relationship, if it could be called that, had ended three months ago and the quest to find new capital for Ruby Hawk had taken over his time and concentration since then. He liked sex and he missed having it.

But it wouldn't be with Danica. Yes, she had arresting eyes as well as tantalizing curves under her clothes that begged to be explored. And her brain was pretty damn appealing too. She was smart and perceptive, with a fast wit he enjoyed. He respected the way she stood up for her work in his office. And he was glad she accepted his invitation to dinner. They could have easily talked in the office the following morning. But he didn't want to wait to hear her insights, watch her gaze sharpen as she arrived at a new conclusion.

Still, she was his recruiter. For his wife, damn it. An affair with his consultant would not be a sensible prelude to a marriage. For all that he resented the situation Nestor had put him in, it did bring up a point Luke needed to think about sooner rather than later for maximum benefit. What good was creating a legacy if one didn't have offspring to carry it on? But unlike his parents and their multiple trips down the aisle, his marriage would be based on intellectual compatibility, similar upbringings and mutually agreed-upon goals. Should they come to an agreed-upon parting of the ways, it would be because common sense and rational prudence demanded it.

He popped the tortilla chip into his mouth. It made a satisfying crunch.

He still wanted to kiss Danica though.

She cleared her throat, a rosy glow high on her cheekbones, before placing the file folder in front of him once more. "So. Now that we're no longer hungry, can we discuss my work?"

"Fine." He opened the folder and ran his gaze down the list of fifteen names before closing it and handing it back to her. "No."

"What?" she sputtered. "I did what you asked. None of the women work in tech, and they meet your education and work-experience requirements. Yet you barely looked at it."

"I invited you here so you could have the correct input

for your job. This list precedes our dinner. Therefore, it's inherently flawed," he pointed out with impeccable logic.

She took a deep breath and exhaled slowly. "Let's start over and pretend this is an actual executive search. Why is this position now open? What is the business rationale?" When he hesitated, she gave him a quick smile. "Confidential, remember? I signed an NDA."

It still smarted to know he'd miscalculated so poorly, but Danica's judgment-free gaze soothed some of the sting. He cleared his throat. "Nestor and Irene Stavros... The closest word is blackmail."

She blinked at him. Her pen didn't move. "Of all the things I expected to hear, that didn't make the top one thousand."

"Irene and I..." Used each other for sex when no one else was around? Were friends with only one benefit? It sounded crass even to think.

"Had a fling," Danica supplied. When he raised an eyebrow, the spots of color returned to her cheeks. "I did a thorough internet search on you. For work purposes only," she hastened to add.

"Had a fling," he agreed. It was close enough. "It started in college. It was off and on after that. However, when I started Ruby Hawk, I called it off for good."

"Any particular reason?"

"Does it matter?"

She gave him a stern look. It made her appear only more delectable. "I thought the purpose of this meeting was to give me the necessary input."

"Irene is very competitive. So am I. It's what drew us together. We enjoyed one-upping one another. Taking turns on top. In and out of the...classroom."

Her tongue darted out to wet her lips. "I see," she murmured, bending her head over her pad.

"But when I discovered she wanted to extend our relationship—and competition—to Ruby Hawk, that was enough for me."

"Let me guess. If you avoid making decisions while hungry, then business and pleasure don't mix."

"Hunger is a chemical reaction in the brain. So is sex. As a rule, I avoid mind-altering stimulants in business." And he needed to keep that thought front and center. This was a business meeting. Not a prelude to wrapping her legs around him and evoking more of those moans.

Her gaze landed on his beer. He picked it up and took a swallow. "Alcohol is a social lubricant that puts many people at ease. I know my tolerance, so I'm able to observe the common niceties."

"Of course," she deadpanned. "Please, go on. You broke it off with Irene."

"And that was that. Until I sought growth opportunities for the company."

She frowned. "I'm not following."

"Ruby Hawk needs additional investment if we want to meet our benchmarks."

"I thought you were successful."

"We are. Very much so. But to fully reach our potential, we need to hire new staff, invest in new equipment. I've spent the last year researching investors or potential mergers. Then I received a call from Irene's father, Nestor." He frowned at his beer. He wished his tolerance weren't so high. It would be nice to have the edges filed off the jagged memory. "Ruby Hawk developed a revolutionary way to apply biofeedback technology to consumer entertainment. The Stavros Group is seeking to increase its global domination in the video-game industry. Incorporating our patents into their games would give players a whole new way to experience virtual worlds, while our R&D engineers would put them miles ahead of the competition. It's a slam dunk, businesswise."

Her eyes narrowed to a suspicious squint. "If it's a slam dunk and her father came to you, why is Irene blackmailing you?"

How to explain the twisted game his family and Irene's had played for decades? "I said blackmail was the closest word. It's not the most accurate."

Danica put her pen down. "I can't help if you aren't straight with me."

"This isn't just about me and Irene. It goes back at least a generation, maybe more. It's not a secret my mother is a Durham."

Her face was blank. "I don't know what that means."

"The Durhams were one of the first families to make their fortune in San Francisco during the gold rush. They helped rebuild the city after the 1906 earthquake. For a profit, of course. But by the time my mother was born, the Durham fortune was gone."

"Then why do the websites make a big deal about—" she waved a hand in the air "—y'know."

"My money?"

She nodded, shrugging her shoulders in an apology.

"My great-grandfather on my father's side. He founded a chain of department stores. The chain failed. He also owned the land under the stores, and that was valuable. Very valuable."

"Got it. Where does Irene come in?"

He briefly looked up at the ceiling. Nestor's trap still prickled with the sting of ten thousand red-hot pins. "My mother was engaged to Nestor Stavros. She broke it off with Nestor the night before the wedding and ran away with my father. See, Nestor hadn't made his money yet, but my father stood to inherit millions. However, he wasn't invited to join the right country clubs. She restored the Durham bank account and he got to play golf where he wanted."

Danica's mouth had been hanging slightly open. She closed it with a snap.

"Irene and I knew the family history." He laughed. There was no amusement in it. "It was probably what initially attracted us to each other. And Nestor didn't seem to care. I even interned for him when I was an undergrad at Stanford. When he approached me about acquiring Ruby Hawk, it seemed like the rational answer to both our businesses' needs."

"But it wasn't," Danica said softly.

His mouth twisted. "No. He wants to take my company away from me. Like my father took my mother away from him."

It hurt to say the words out loud. He'd worked so hard to distance himself from the toxicity that surrounded him growing up, the constant stream of new stepparents and stepsiblings appearing and disappearing. He threw himself into writing code, the static language reassuring even as he manipulated it to do new things. To have control of his legacy be threatened thanks to a marriage that barely survived his birth... He took a deep breath and returned his focus to his companion.

Danica pursed her lips into a kissable heart shape. "Wait. Did he say those exact words? Out loud? Because if the deal makes as much sense for both companies as you say it does, how can he justify that to his board of directors?" She launched into a respectable Australian accent. "Oi, I'm acquiring a company because I was jilted thirty years ago. Good on me?"

He took another swig of beer to wash down the memory of the meeting with Nestor, the anger burning hotter than any salsa could. "Funny you say that. Nestor said his board of directors insisted on a morals clause in the deal. If I don't meet the board's standards within sixty days, then either the Stavros Group can pull out of the deal or I will be removed from the company. My reputation for, as Nestor put it, 'loving and leaving' means I'm too unstable, too incapable of commitment for the Stavros Group to bring me onboard."

"Unsteady?" Her gaze widened in disbelief. "Luke Dalek?"

He toasted her with his beer for using his nickname. "When I protested, he brought in Irene. She backed him up, listing the times I supposedly used her and then walked away. She failed to mention our relationship, such as it was, had been mutual, including the breakups."

Danica squinted at him. "That sounds like she was upset you ended it. Are you sure this is about your mother's relationship with Nestor? Or is it really about you and Irene?"

His gut twisted. He dismissed it. He knew what he knew. "I'm positive this is retaliation for the past. But I'm not giving up Ruby Hawk. I'm running it, and that's nonnegotiable."

Visions of unpaid bills, the result of ordering equipment before the deal closed, danced before his eyes. He'd never be able to find another investor or potential buyer in time to make payroll. Hundreds of people depended on him for their livelihoods. He had a responsibility to them. He couldn't cause the deal to fail.

But if he didn't meet the Stavros Group's conditions, then he would be removed from the company he founded. The company into which he poured sweat and toil and sleepless nights. The legacy he hoped to leave, taken away. His best chance of proving he was more than his family's name and his inherited wealth.

He slammed down the empty bottle, causing Danica to

jump. At least he didn't break the bottle. He wanted to. He wanted to smash it, then grind the pieces into dust.

She reached out a hand and briefly brushed the back of his. "Everyone knows Ruby Hawk is a success because of you."

He took a deep breath, his emotions settling back into their usual, well-ordered positions. "My lawyers and I did a thorough reading of the clause," he said. "In short, if I do not quote 'curtail my libidinous lifestyle' end quote, by the end of sixty days, then either the Stavros Group can pull out of the deal or the acquisition will go through but I will be removed. The only surefire way to fulfill the terms of the clause is to be married. A real marriage, not a pretend fiancée for a few months."

Danica blinked. "Wow. That's extreme."

"That's Nestor. Therefore, if I have to be married, I need a wife who is equipped to deal with the pressures that come with my world. That's where you come in."

Danica leaned back in her chair, her gaze fixed on the ceiling. He couldn't help but notice how her posture caused her silky blouse to drape tightly over her breasts. The fabric strained against the high, round globes, just the right size to fill his palms—no. Not his. He liked her, yes. But she was not the solution the situation required, but the means to the solution. His company and its future came ahead of any momentary personal pleasure.

"So," she said slowly, as if thinking through a problem, "if you're willing to go to the trouble of hiring me to find you a stranger to marry so the acquisition will go through, why not marry Irene?"

The beer in his stomach roiled. "I asked. She laughed in my face. This is about taking my company away, period." He crumbled his napkin and threw it into the now-empty plastic basket. "You now have the background. Let's discuss how you will find the right candidates. There are fifty-two days remaining."

"I have to admit, when you said I needed additional information, I thought you meant food preferences, favorite vacation spots, et cetera." She blew a loose curl off her forehead.

"Our discussion should make your job easier, not harder."

She laughed, a sharp burst of air. "You have that flipped." She took her wallet out of her purse and offered him a twenty-dollar bill. "I hope this covers my dinner?"

He pushed the money back at her. "That's too much and besides, the company paid. Why is it harder?"

She left the cash on the table. "So far, you've told me about you, your family and the Stavroses. What about the wife I'm supposed to find? Where does she fit into this?"

It was a good question. He'd been so focused on the terms of the acquisition, he hadn't thought beyond standing in front of a justice of the peace. He said the first thing that came to mind. "She'll be well compensated."

Her gaze widened with what he could only call horror. "Money doesn't make a marriage," she stated, her syllables crisp and precise.

He shrugged. "I beg to differ."

She leaned over the table, blond curls tumbling over her left shoulder, her words intense and fast. "When the war broke out in Croatia, my mother and father gave up everything to be together. Their families, their country, their religious communities. They came to the United States with barely a dime. But they had love, and that made us richer than most people I knew growing up."

Luke blinked, once. He had no idea her parents had been war refugees. "That's admirable. It takes strength to start a new life."

Her features relaxed into a smile, a ray of sun peeking

from behind a dark cloud. "Thank you. And love is what gave them that strength—"

"It's a good story. For them. But in my experience, marriage is best viewed a merger between two parties who desire a joint investment." He shrugged. "Usually in children. But the parties also need to protect their individual assets. The right candidate will know that." He gave the folder a decisive tap.

Danica rubbed her temples. She rarely got headaches, but it felt like a woodpecker and a jackhammer had had a baby in her skull, and the baby was throwing a tantrum. Luke couldn't really believe the words coming out of his mouth.

Could he?

"I thought…" She paused. In the aftermath of their conversation, her assumptions seemed so naïve. "I thought you wanted to fall in love with someone. That's why you hired me."

"It's business. That's why I hired an executive recruiter."

"But…love. Don't you want that?"

He looked as if he pitied her. "Humans confuse endorphins released during sex for love, and then they use the confusion to manipulate themselves and others. But it's just a chemical reaction caused by hormones and preprogrammed neurological responses." He held up a hand to stop her before she could speak. "I know. Your family. But trust me. I've seen my scenario play out far more times than I've seen yours."

How did someone with everything going for him—gorgeous looks, genius brain, socially prominent family, Midas's wealth—have such a cynical outlook? It made her soul physically ache. She took her phone out of her tote and opened up the rideshare app.

"I'll have another list of candidates for you in the morning." She swept her notebook into the bag and pulled the bag's strap over her shoulder as she stood up. "Thank you for dinner. I'll see you tomorrow?"

He stood up when she did. "I'd like to discuss this tonight. The clock is running."

The drumming in her skull would make a death-metal band proud. "Your criteria haven't changed, so I'll fine-tune the parameters. The difference will come in how I conduct interviews, to see if I can suss out if their attitude toward marriage matches yours." She tried to smile but was only partially successful. "I'll email you the list of candidates tonight, so you'll have it in the morning. Thanks again for the burrito."

She turned on her heel and exited the restaurant, heading for the nearest street corner. The car she had ordered via the phone app should arrive soon to take her to the train station. And not a minute too early.

How could he not want love? It was a basic human need, as necessary as sunshine and clean water. She knew people married for all sorts of reasons, love being only one of them, but it seemed so...*cold-blooded* the way he'd spelled it out.

"Danica, wait." Footsteps pounded on the sidewalk behind her.

She tamped down on the traitorous anticipation swirling in her stomach and turned to face him. "Did I leave something at the restaurant?"

He stepped under the streetlight. The mist-filled night air caused it to create a halo around his head. The very picture of an angelic devil.

"I know what you're thinking." He ran a hand through his hair, causing it to stick straight-up in patches. It made him look only more approachable and thus more attractive. "You think I'm doing this because of some long-standing feud. And maybe you're right. But I'm also doing this for my team. I hand recruited them. They took stock options instead of salary when we started. Now they can cash in on their leap of faith. I'm not being as ruthless as you think I am."

He moved closer, tripping her pulse into overdrive. "That's not what I'm thinking," she said.

He gave her a one-sided smile. "You're easier to read than you know."

Fine. She *had* been thinking that. She glanced over his shoulder and saw the youth basketball team exit the taqueria. The teenagers were laughing and horsing around as they said their goodbyes. It was a scene she had seen many times before, with her brother at the center of the action. Now her family didn't know if Matt would be able to walk unassisted ever again.

Her parents showed her love was real, but they also taught her family came first. If she successfully completed the search, the money Luke offered would give them much needed relief from financial worry. In a way, she was in just as much of a bind as he was.

Besides, judging by the way he talked about his team, he was capable of caring—if only as the boss.

"I know what it's like to have your dream job disappear. For your team, I'll do my best. But if I can be honest? Any marriage entered into under the conditions you describe is doomed to failure."

"I never fail." A self-satisfied smirk played at the corners of his devastatingly attractive mouth.

"There's always a first time."

He leaned down until his warm breath caressed her cheek. "We'll see."

An answering heat welled deep inside her, an insistent compulsion she needed to stop before she did something stupid, like use her hands to determine if his butt felt as muscular as it looked in his jeans. Thankfully, a car matching the description on her app pulled up to the curb. "That's my ride."

She turned to say good-night at the same minute he reached to open the car door for her. They collided, her breasts colliding with the hard planes of his chest. She instinctively grabbed on to his biceps to hold herself steady, while his arms encircled her.

Their gazes met, held. She couldn't get enough air in her lungs. "Sorry," he began.

She shook her head, once. The fog swirled around them, shutting the world out until it consisted of just him, her and the awareness between them that could no longer be ignored. His gaze turned heavy, matching the heaviness between her legs, asking a question she answered by reaching up to bring his mouth down to hers.

He responded immediately, his lips firm, hot, insistent. Supernovas pinwheeled behind her closed eyelids as his hands settled at her waist and drew her closer.

She had wanted to kiss Luke Dallas since she saw him outside Johanna's office. She doubted she could break away even if the sensible part of her brain managed to gain control. It had been so long since she had last been kissed.

His tongue licked into her mouth, and she returned the favor. Her pulse thumped hard as his firm arms tightened around her. She heard a low moan and realized it came from her. Her skin needed to be next to his, the insistent desire building deep inside demanding to be fed.

A car horn, loud and insistent, broke through the pleasurable haze surrounding her. She jumped away from him, raising a wondering hand to her swollen lips.

He stared back at her, hands thrust into his jeans pockets, his gaze dark and wild.

The horn honked again. Danica wrenched her gaze away from Luke to glance at the vehicle. "I need to go."

Luke nodded. "Right. So." He cleared his throat. "I'll see you in the office. Safe travels home."

She nodded back. "See you in the office." Somehow, she managed to slide into the back seat and sped off. Her last sight of Luke was him standing on the sidewalk, hands in his pockets, staring after her car.

Her mouth still bore the imprint of his, her core aching from unresolved need. Her thoughts twisted and churned, mimicking the roiling in her stomach. She'd kissed Luke! And he'd kissed her back. It exceeded any fantasy she'd ever had. For a second she basked in the recollection, reliving the pressure, the heat, the demand for more.

Then a tsunami of horror washed away the joyous memory. What had they done? He'd hired her. She'd agreed to find him a wife. She needed the contract and the money it promised for her family. Did she just risk her job and thus her brother's access to treatment?

How would she be able to face Luke in the morning?

Her lips would not stop burning.

Four

Danica walked the last few steps toward the main entrance of Ruby Hawk, her stomach doing a decent impersonation of a tumble dryer set on high. What would she say to Luke after their kiss last night? More important, what would he say to her?

It was unprofessional to kiss a client in the best of circumstances. And this client was Luke Dallas, bad-boy billionaire of Silicon Valley, known for his countless flings with models, actresses and socialites. It wasn't only unseemly; it was downright embarrassing.

But he kissed you back. His mouth opened first, his tongue invited hers to tangle and slide against his. She couldn't recall arriving home or getting into bed, but she remembered the perfect firmness of his mouth—not too hard, not too soft—and how his hand on the small of her back had burned through the silk of her blouse. She stumbled on a crack in the pavement and regained her balance at the last second.

It wasn't as if she hadn't been kissed before, she scolded herself. She was very familiar with the mechanics. No need to be so dramatic.

She managed to make it to her office without twisting an ankle and turned on her computer. A message from Luke sat at the top of her email inbox. Her hand lingered over the mouse for a second before she took a deep breath and clicked to open it.

It was short and to the point.

I trust you now have the necessary information to find viable candidates. I'm on a flight to Tokyo but I expect a new list by the time I land.

Any lingering warmth was doused. She clicked on Reply.

Thank you for the dinner. Your input has been taken under advisement as requested.

She attached the list she pulled together when last night's sleep eluded her and hit Send. Really, it was the best of all possible outcomes. She was still employed and could still secure the bonus money he promised her. But when lunchtime rolled around, she realized she couldn't remember a single email she'd read other than Luke's.

The next two weeks were spent chasing leads, the kiss eventually fading from her lips but playing on a continuous loop whenever she shut her eyes. Luke was mostly out of town. He jetted around the world, seeking a backup for the acquisition in case Nestor Stavros reneged as threatened. However, her speech about communication seemed to have sunk in, because he was quick to respond to a text or an email despite any time difference. Before long, the ding of a new text or email arriving became her favorite sound.

She began the Monday of the third week with a satisfied sigh. Two of her candidates finally met Luke's standards. He met the first one upon his return to California and immediately asked to see her again. While she was waiting to hear his feedback from the latest encounter, she went ahead and finalized the arrangements for him to meet the second candidate. All she needed was a third prospective wife, and then she would be out the door with an impressive check in hand and her professional integrity intact.

There was only one glaring problem with completing her assignment. Success meant she'd no longer communicate with Luke. She may have buried the kiss, never to be spoken of again although it starred in her most erotic dreams, but she didn't know if she could bury how much she looked forward to their daily exchanges.

She opened a text message window and typed a message to Luke.

All confirmed for tonight. Felicity Sommers will meet you at seven at the Peninsula Society fund-raiser in Atherton. I told her this is a callback for the community-giving job, and you want to meet her there so the two of you can discuss best practices.

Danica had realized early on she needed a cover story for her search. She couldn't tell the candidates up front they were being vetted as a possible wife for Luke Dallas—not if she wanted to keep the search out of the press. Therefore she told the women she was looking for a director to run Ruby Hawk's community outreach and charitable giving. The job *was* open, so it wasn't completely a lie.

The rest was up to Luke. Thinking of him walking down the aisle with his recruited-to-order wife caused her heart to do flips, and not the pleasant kind. The kind that ended with every surface bruised and battered.

Her computer dinged.

Consider this confirmation of my meeting with Felicity. Remove Jayne Chung from consideration.

Danica frowned at her screen. Jayne was the first candidate Luke had agreed to meet. On paper, she was perfect: Harvard educated, did a stint in the Peace Corps before receiving her master's degree in urban planning and development, and currently worked for a nonprofit providing grants to create city gardens where none existed. Oh, and she'd paid for her education by modeling haute couture in New York and Paris during school breaks.

I thought the first meeting went well. What's wrong? She didn't start the second meeting by swooning at your feet?

Ha.

I think kids these days say LOL.

He ignored her attempt at levity.

She's not right for the position.

If Jayne wasn't right...

More input, please.

A wave of heat settled deep in her belly at the memory of just how visceral his input could be. *Help me help you.*

No answer. She sat back in her chair. Usually he texted her back, even if it was just a curt Later.

She sighed and shut down the text window. There was a simple reason why he didn't respond: he ran a billion-dollar tech company and she was a consultant hired for one task.

Speaking of, if his reaction to Jayne were any indication, she would need the third candidate sooner rather than later. Danica had liked Felicity, Luke's current date, well enough when they met during the initial vetting period. But something had been a little…off. Felicity had set off a tiny warning light in the back of Danica's mind.

She shook her head. All that mattered was Luke's reaction to Felicity. Danica needed to stay focused, finish the assignment and concentrate on helping her brother. The kiss would eventually fade. Eventually. She absorbed herself in answering emails and chasing down promising leads online.

The phone rang, dragging her gaze away from her screen. She looked at the time. 6:45 p.m. Well, that settled it. No more texting with Luke tonight. He should be handing his car keys to the valet at the fund-raiser right about now. A vision of Luke in a tuxedo, the fine black wool jacket tailored to emphasize his broad shoulders, caused her to almost drop the phone before she could answer it. "Hello?"

"Danica! Thank goodness you picked up."

"Aisha?" Her favorite investigator sounded panicked. And nothing panicked Aisha McKee. "What's wrong?"

"Felicity Sommers. We have a problem."

That tiny warning light put out a full red alert. "What kind of a problem?"

Aisha sighed. "I saw something today on her social media that made me ask around. Turns out she's engaged. Has been for a month. But they haven't told her parents, so they're keeping it quiet."

"What?" Danica's stomach dropped somewhere near her knees. "That's bad."

"It gets worse." Aisha audibly inhaled. "Her fiancé? Cinco Jackson."

"Cinco Jackson—wait. I know that name." Danica opened a browser window to the *Silicon Valley Weekly* website, clicked on the top story and then shut her eyes, tight. "He's the journalist responsible for the recent Ruby Hawk stories."

"Yeah." Aisha sighed again. "I'm sorry it took me until now to discover the relationship. Turns out her parents are dead set against it because one of his previous stories was an exposé that took down a friend of her father's, so they keep it very low-key. One of Felicity's former sorority sisters filled me in."

Danica replayed the conversations she had with Felicity. No, she didn't mention marriage. She and Luke agreed he would broach the until-death-do-us-part subject when he felt it was right.

She had to warn him. If he let something slip to Felicity and it got back to Jackson…

"I have to go." Danica shut down her laptop. "Thanks for the warning. Talk to you soon."

"Sorry again," Aisha started to say, but Danica hit End before she'd finished and dialed Luke's number. No answer. Great. She ordered a car while keeping Luke's number on redial. If he didn't pick up his phone, she had only one option: get to him in person as quickly as possible.

The Aylward-Hopkins mansion hummed with laughter and conversation as the cream of the Bay Area elite enjoyed the Peninsula Society's annual Monte Carlo Night. Croupiers spun roulette wheels, the wheel clack-clacking until the ball dropped with a soft metallic thud, while dice rattled against green felt at the craps tables. Although the games of chance were played with faux money, the charity expected its silent auction to bring in over five hundred thousand dollars to help fund its grants for the next year.

Luke stood in the expansive entry of the mansion, a space big enough that it easily accommodated one of the bars set up for thirsty guests. From his position, he could keep an eye on the front door and new arrivals but also survey the gaming tables occupying the long sweep of travertine floors just beyond the entry. French windows lined the opposite wall, their doors open to the mild night air and the sprawling gardens beyond.

Normally, he'd rather waste hours trying to code on an ancient Apple II Plus computer than put on a monkey suit and pretend to be interested in a retired captain of industry's golf game. He sat on the charity's board, which should be enough demonstration of his support. But he knew from observing his parents that strategic networking at social events was almost as crucial to success in business as a good product. His presence here tonight was a simple equation of trade-offs and benefits.

A member of the catering staff in a low-cut black dress offered him a glass of champagne. He took it off the silver tray and she smiled at him, giving him a slow wink as she brushed by a bit too close for social propriety.

At any other time, Luke might have been interested. But he was here to meet...what was her name? Right. Felicity.

Too bad it wasn't Danica.

He did a quick calculation of the probabilities, as he did every time her green eyes crossed his mind. Which meant he ran this particular set of calculations on an hourly, if not even more frequent, basis. But his initial assessment always came out on top. Danica didn't have the right variables he required.

Yes, she was smart. And he liked her assertiveness. Plus, she made him laugh. Her humor shone through in her texts and emails.

Nonetheless, statistical outcomes for maximum marriage success as measured by length of time married as plotted against divorce rates demonstrated he should stick to his original requirements for education, social status and career achievement.

But...

That kiss. She'd fit against him just the way he liked, her curves connecting with his body in all the right spots. Pure responsiveness, hot and genuine, the heat flaring spontaneously. And that moan, low and breathy, when she'd pressed against him... He'd had to walk multiple blocks in the chilly night air before he was comfortable enough to drive home.

If he wasn't careful, the memory would require leaving the party for a similar stroll. He took out his phone to distract himself just as a pretty redhead, more auburn than strawberry blonde, came through the front door. She looked around and when her gaze met his, she gave him a small wave. He nodded at her over his champagne and put the phone, still off, back in his pocket.

He had to give Danica credit. The first candidate had more than met his criteria, and so far, Felicity also seemed like a good match. She wore a navy blue gown appropriate for the occasion, elegantly simple. Her smile was bright and easily given, her handshake firm as they greeted each other. She had no trouble meeting his gaze, her eyes a greenish brown.

Danica's eyes were green. A warm green with flecks of gold. When her temper rose, they transformed to dark emerald. He liked she hadn't hid her reactions during their dinner. She'd expressed them, fully. And when they'd kissed—

With a start, he realized Felicity was speaking. He tuned in just in time to hear her say, "Thank you so much for inviting me to the fund-raiser. I've heard a lot about Monte Carlo Night."

He cleared his throat. "Thank you for accepting." He caught the gaze of the waitress who had given him his champagne and motioned her over. "Something to drink?"

Felicity hesitated. "I have an early morning meeting. I shouldn't—but sure. Thanks." She accepted the glass with a smile from the less-friendly-than-before waitress. "I've never had champagne at a job interview before." She laughed. "But then I've never had an interview at a black-tie event."

"It's unorthodox. But this is an unusual employment offer." There was something in the way Felicity's gaze flashed when he said *unusual* that made him reconsider saying anything further. "Tell me about your job at Friedmann Adams. What's your favorite thing about it?"

He ignored the urge to look at his watch to see how much longer he needed to stay at the party and still be considered socially polite. Leaving early wouldn't be productive, nor help him accomplish his goals for the evening. If Felicity didn't work out, Danica had to provide only one more pre-approved candidate before her contract terminated.

Danica…

He smiled, remembering their conversation after that dinner and how she'd tried to pretend he didn't know what she was thinking. It had been written all over her expressive face. Not that he blamed her for believing in fairy tales like love and living happily ever after. They were pervasive in the prevailing culture. But they were emotional manipulations. Insubstantial.

Sex, on the other hand, was an actual physical phenomenon. It could be scientifically studied. What would it be like if he studied it with Da—

"And that's the difference between a pessimist, an optimist and a financial advisor!" Felicity laughed. "That pretty much sums up what I do."

He'd missed most of it. What was wrong with his focus? "Fascinating."

Felicity pushed a strand of hair behind her right ear and glanced around the temporary casino. The gaming tables were filling up, and the polished travertine floor meant the sound level rose accordingly. "Not really. I could tell by the way you weren't on the edge of your seat."

Caught. "It's noisy in here," he said. "Let's find a quieter spot."

"That would be great. I'd like that." She gave him a generous smile.

Her lips were full and softly curved. But he had no desire to kiss them. Didn't care to learn how she tasted. No interest in discovering how her mouth would feel against his or if her response would be soft and quivering or hard and driving.

There was only one person he wanted to kiss, and that was—

His peripheral vision caught someone frantically waving two arms high in the air. *Danica?*

For a second, he wondered if his undisciplined subconscious had conjured a vision of her. But then a grin lit her face as their gazes met, and he knew it really was her.

No memory could be that vibrant. The details that had become fuzzy over the past few weeks now appeared in solid form. Her hair, so many different colors of gold, the curls tumbling from her ponytail, twisting and turning in the light. The way she walked, her rounded hips slightly swaying as she cut through the crowd with graceful deliberation.

Her eyes matched his memory exactly. They shone with some unexpressed emotion. Was she happy to see him? Or—no. Something was wrong. He narrowed his gaze questioningly as she arrived at his side. She shook her head slightly in response and thrust her left hand toward Felicity.

"Hi!" she said, her voice as bright as the artificial smile on her face. "Nice to meet you again."

Felicity shook the proffered hand, but a crease dented her brow. "Likewise. I didn't know you were going to be here."

"Of course! I wouldn't miss this event for the world."

Felicity ran her gaze up and down Danica's outfit. Her nose wrinkled as if she saw something not to her liking, which was ridiculous. Danica looked beautiful. She had forgone her usual skirt-and-blouse combo for a plain black dress with buttons down the front, like an oversize men's shirt, belted at the waist. He appreciated the way it emphasized her curves. "I see," Felicity said slowly.

"Oh," Danica said with a strained laugh, brushing her palms against the skirt of her dress, "I ran here straight from work. Hope I haven't already missed too much." She turned to Luke. "What have you two been talking about?" Her eyes were opened wide, as if she were trying to send him a message.

"Felicity told a joke about the difference between optimists, pessimists and financial advisors," he said. At least he assumed it had been a joke.

"I'd love to hear it someday." Danica kept her gaze focused on Luke. He didn't mind. "Did you talk about the open position?"

"No," Felicity said. Luke jerked his head in her direction. He'd almost forgotten she was still standing there. "We did not. I have some questions I'd like to ask."

"I'm sure you do." Danica finally took her gaze away from Luke. The absence hit him like bedcovers yanked off on a cold winter's morning. "That's why I'm here. To help answer them. But—" She stopped, her gaze focused on a point over Felicity's shoulder. "Hey, isn't that Cinco Jackson over by the bar? You know, the business reporter for the *Silicon Valley Weekly*? I love his work." Danica waved at the reporter, who remained focused on his drink.

What the hell was she doing, trying to attract the attention of a journalist? Was that why she was here? His gut said no, but he suddenly realized he and Danica hadn't really spoken since the kiss. And they needed to. It was way out of bounds for him to kiss a contractor. He couldn't and wouldn't blame her if she went to the press despite the NDA. "Danica, can we talk first—"

She trod on his toe. Good thing she wore flat black shoes that looked like ballet slippers. "Hmm, he's not looking our way. I'd love to meet him. I don't suppose you know him, Felicity?"

Two spots of red appeared on Felicity's cheeks. "As a matter of fact, I do."

"You're so lucky!" Danica gushed. "I heard from a friend of a friend—on the down low, mind you—that he's engaged. I'm so jealous."

Jealous? What the... He opened his mouth, only for Danica's heel to connect with his foot again. "Felicity, are you okay?" Danica asked. "Did your champagne go down the wrong way?"

Felicity was indeed sputtering. "Engaged?" she managed to get out. "Where did you hear that? No one knows—" She clamped her lips shut.

Danica clasped a hand to her chest, her eyes wide with amazement. "It is true?" she gasped. "But how do you... Oh! Don't tell me! You must be the fiancée!"

Luke managed to move his shoe before Danica could step on it once more. "I gather best wishes are in order," he said, shooting a warning glance at Danica. She needed to cut back on the enthusiasm.

Not that Felicity seemed to notice Danica was overdoing it. The redhead resembled a fish realizing too late the baited hook had been swallowed. "I—I didn't confirm that."

Danica put a conciliatory hand on Felicity's arm. "Don't worry. We won't say anything."

"But I didn't—"

"You don't need to," Danica said. "You haven't stopped looking at Cinco Jackson since I mentioned him."

"I—" Felicity tore her gaze away from the reporter and shrugged. "Fine. It's true. And this is the strangest job interview I have ever been on."

"It is unusual," Danica agreed, her smile still five hundred watts bright.

"It's the Ruby Hawk way," Luke interjected. "If you're not comfortable in out-of-the-box situations, you won't be comfortable working with me."

"Out of the box certainly describes Luke's methods." Danica gave an emphatic nod.

"This was a test?" Felicity asked.

"Luke gets ambushed all the time by people wanting to pry confidential information out of him. We needed to see how you would react in a similar situation," Danica said smoothly. "Do you still have questions for us?"

Felicity's gaze ping-ponged between Luke and Danica. "I have a million, but not about the job. I think we all know I just took myself out of the running." She laughed, her shoulders falling. "It's actually a relief. I guess I can tell you now. Cinco just accepted an on-air job with a New York City station. We move in a few months."

Danica's smile disappeared. "Then why did you agree to the interview?"

"I was flattered. It's not every day you get a call out of the blue to discuss running a foundation. If the offer had been too good to refuse—" she shrugged "—who knows? I might have tried to work out a bicoastal arrangement."

Luke swirled the champagne in his glass. "Jackson didn't ask you to accept the interview in the hopes of getting inside information about Ruby Hawk?"

Felicity bit her lower lip.

Terrific. Thankfully, Danica saved the evening before he could dig himself into a pit too deep to get out of. He reached for her hand and gave her slender fingers a squeeze of appreciation.

Danica jumped, but kept her gaze on Felicity. "There's still a lot of Monte Carlo Night left. Why don't you find your fiancé and have fun?"

Felicity's gaze shifted between Luke and Danica a few more times. "I will. Oh, and, Luke, I know Cinco would love to talk to you—"

"We'll keep that in mind," Danica interjected. "Best wishes for continued success with your career." She beamed at the other woman.

Felicity's mouth twisted. "Right. Well, thank you for the opportunity."

She moved to shake Luke's hand, but Danica maneuvered her way between him and Felicity. She intercepted Felicity's proffered hand with a shake of her own. "It was great meeting you. Have a terrific night!"

As soon as Felicity joined her fiancé, Danica's face fell. She turned to face Luke, her teeth worrying her lower lip. "I am so sorry. I had no idea she was engaged until my investigator called a little while ago. I hope this didn't ruin your evening."

He opened his mouth to reassure her.

Then he reconsidered. Danica was here, in person, not just a voice on the phone or a string of characters in a text message. And suddenly he was looking forward to an evening of socializing. With her.

He straightened his expression and looked down on her from his full height. "I'm out a date. At a black-tie event."

Danica kept her chin raised, but her gaze fell to the ground. "Yes, I know. I will find someone to replace Felicity. I still owe you two candidates."

"Doesn't help my situation right now."

"If I could change the situation, I would—" she began, her eyes wide with apology.

"Good. You're my date."

Five

Danica stared at him. "You want me to be your date? Here? Now?"

She swept her left hand to indicate the crowd dressed in expensive finery, the museum-quality artwork on the walls and the bottles of vintage French champagne being emptied and replaced by more. Then she swept her right hand over her plain shirtdress, a bargain from an outlet store two years ago. "Me?"

He shrugged. The movement emphasized how well his tuxedo jacket outlined his broad shoulders. "I RSVP'd for two. Beggars can't be choosers."

She narrowed her gaze and was about to tell him just how much of beggar he needed to be for her to stay when she caught the slight uptick of his mouth. "Very funny," she said.

"I think the kids say LOL."

She laughed and his grin appeared, his teeth flashing

white against his bronzed skin. "You really want me to stay?"

He nodded, slowly and deliberately. "I do."

She'd heard stories from her previous boss about the Peninsula Society's Monte Carlo Night. The morning after previous years' events, Johanna would arrive hours late to work and then spend the day rhapsodizing about the gourmet food, the designer dresses and, above all, the one-of-a-kind silent-auction prizes that had millionaires trying to outbid each other, using chips won at the gaming tables augmented by very real money.

And now Danica was here. She glanced around at the glittering crowd and caught the gaze of a nearby server, who sniffed and rolled her eyes at Danica before she turned away to offer another guest a glass of champagne. This was Luke's world, she reminded herself. His and that of the wife he wanted her to find. Even the catering staff knew she didn't belong.

Her parents came to America thanks to a small grassroots organization dedicated to helping war refugees. But after her parents arrived and the novelty of welcoming refugees wore off, the organizers' interest waned. Her mother and father were left practically stranded, the promises of professional jobs as empty as the new bank accounts set up for them.

Her parents survived. They found work—not the positions promised, but they made enough money to rent an apartment and buy a fifteen-year-old car. Danica was born a year later. But her parents made sure she knew the story. *Only family can be trusted to look out for each other*, they warned her and her brother over and over.

Like she was doing now. Looking out for her brother, by finishing this assignment. Parties like this were an everyday occurrence for Luke, but they were the unobtainable fantasies of film and television to her. It would be better, when she said goodbye to him in a few weeks, if she stuck to her world and did not even visit his. One dinner and one kiss had consumed nearly every waking hour—and definitely every sleeping hour. A whole evening in his company? She'd never be able to return to reality.

"Thank you so much for the offer. But I should get back to the office. The clock is ticking on my assignment."

His smile dimmed. "If you insist. However…" His sideways glance caused her pulse to flutter.

"Yes?" she asked, using her tongue to wet her suddenly dry lips. Did he think about their kiss as often as she did?

"What cover story do you give your candidates?" he asked, his gaze fixed on her mouth. "And what is this event?"

"The community-giving job…and this is a society fundraiser," she said slowly.

He nodded. "My wife will be involved with the Bay Area nonprofit community and its donors." He indicated the gaming tables. "And the biggest ones are here tonight. As your client, I advise it's in your best interests to stay so your cover story for the search will be as authentic as possible. This is business." His expression was impressively impassive.

"Business," she echoed. Of course. What else did she expect? She would show up and her presence would cause Prince Charming to admit he was attracted to her and throw away his careful calculations for the perfect wife? Fairy tales weren't real. If they were, her shirtdress would have transformed into a glittering ball gown a half hour ago.

"What else is there besides business?" The glint in his blue gaze dared her to answer.

If he wasn't going to mention their kiss, she certainly

wasn't. "You're right," she said, her tone brisk. "My job is to find you a wife who will be comfortable at events like this."

"Precisely." He finished off his champagne. "Therefore, you need to stay in order to complete your assignment more effectively."

"If that's what the client prefers."

Luke's expression relaxed. It was the first time she'd seen him let down all of his guard. It made him impossibly appealing. Especially the warm, appreciative glow deep in his blue gaze, which lit an answering heat in her belly. "He does."

He placed his empty flute on a passing waiter's tray and took two new ones, offering one to her. She accepted it with a nod of thanks. The champagne tasted of bright, sharp honey. "So. What's first on the agenda?" she asked.

"Let's check out the gaming tables. For research purposes, of course." He offered her his elbow.

She'd never been a huge fan of the James Bond film franchise for various reasons, not the least of which was their tendency to make Eastern Europeans the bad guys. But now she understood why Bond had his contingents of female fans. Luke was already an attractive man. Put him in a tux and he was stunning. The fine wool of his jacket was soft to the touch above the firm muscle of his bicep. She kept her grip loose, not wishing to tempt her fingers into exploring what would never be hers. "Of course," she replied. "Let's go."

He escorted her to where the party organizers had arranged the gaming tables. They were organized in long rows, filling a large open space that overlooked the gardens below. Other guests had the same idea, and the seats were quickly filling up. "Pick your game," he said with a sweep of his hand.

She scanned the sea of green-felt-covered surfaces.

While she didn't consider herself a gambler by any stretch of the definition, if she had to stay, she might as well enjoy herself. "Roulette," she said with a nod.

Luke had a slight frown on his face. "What's wrong?" she asked. "Not a fan of things that spin?"

He shrugged and began to guide her with an arm held low on her back toward the nearest wheel. Her shirt dress was a sturdy cotton weave, but the warmth of his touch burned as if he were touching her bare skin. "There's an approximate forty-seven percent chance of winning a bet placed on black or red, but low risk equals low reward. Playing a single number pays out the best, but the odds of winning are one in thirty-eight. Assuming the table isn't biased, of course," he said.

She stopped short, causing another couple to almost bump into them. The man started to give Danica a dirty look, but it turned into a nod of respect when he saw her companion. "How on earth do you know that?" she asked.

"There are thirty-eight numbers on an American roulette wheel. Thirty-seven if it's European. It doesn't take an MBA to calculate the odds."

She smirked at him. "Your math skills are not in question. How do you know this much about roulette? Do you play often?"

"I prefer playing with money when circumstances can be better controlled."

"That doesn't explain why you can rattle off the statistics."

His mouth twisted to the left. "I was given my first computer when I was ten. When I wanted to replace it with a newer one, my father decided to teach me one of his sporadic object lessons and told me I had to buy it myself. But he never told me how he expected me to come up with the money. So, I created an account for a gambling site using my stepmother's credit card." He smiled, but his gaze remained distant. "There were less restrictions on the internet then."

Her eyes felt dry. She was staring at him so hard she forgot to blink. "You started gambling. At ten."

"Eleven. Only to earn enough to buy a new computer." He thought for a moment. "And maybe some peripheral equipment. I stopped when I reached the amount I needed. But to answer your question, I prefer games that require strategy, such as blackjack or poker."

"What did your stepmother say when she discovered you used her card?" Her parents would have grounded her for at least a month if she had used a credit card without permission. Not that she could imagine doing such a thing in the first place. Her family always had food on the table, but money wasn't plentiful. She didn't get her first computer until a hand-me-down came her way during high school.

Luke paused. "She didn't say anything," he finally said. "I know I went to live with my mother, because I had the computer shipped to her house. It must have coincided with my father divorcing that stepmother."

"'That' stepmother? How many have you had?"

"Three. Stepmothers, that is. Four stepfathers. So far." Luke's gaze continued to search the busy crowd. "There," he said. "Empty seats at the third table from the left, toward the back." He resumed guiding her through the throng.

Danica let him take the lead, her mind still processing the glimpse he let slip. She couldn't imagine her parents with anyone else, much less multiple anyone elses. Yet Luke had—she did the addition in her head—nine parents, including his biological ones? No wonder he held such cynical views about marriage.

They took their places at the roulette wheel beside a woman who wore more diamonds than Danica had ever seen outside of a jewelry store. The woman raised her eyebrows when Danica squeezed next to her, but gave Luke a welcoming smile. He handed the croupier a slip of paper and received two large stacks of multicolored casino chips in return.

"Here," he said, passing half of them to Danica. "When it comes to betting, I recommend the D'Alembert system. Start small and stay with even-money bets such as black or red. Increase your bet by one after losing, and decrease it by one after winning. You're favored to come out ahead in the end." He placed a chip on black.

She nodded and selected a ten-dollar chip for her first bet. The strategy sounded like him: smart, prudent, designed to minimize losses and maximize gains. But just as she was about to place the chip on the table, she drew her hand back. Then she swept all of her chips onto the number three.

"What are you doing?" His mouth hung slightly open. She'd never seen him look so nonplussed. Judging by the sideways glances thrown at him by the other players at their table, she wasn't the only one who thought his expression was unusual.

"I'm placing my bet."

He recovered his usual stoic expression. "I wouldn't advise it. The odds—"

"Yes. You told me. Thirty-eight to one."

The croupier dropped the ball into the spinning outer circle, a streaking silver blur.

"You can still change your mind," he said.

"Nope," she said. "I'm all in."

The ball began to fall from the rim and the croupier called, "No more bets."

Danica found herself crossing her fingers, and she relaxed them. Beside her, Luke's disapproval was evident in the rigid set of his shoulders and the straight line of his mouth.

But sometimes risks were worth taking. Her parents took a risk when they left their war-torn homeland. She took a risk, moving to California without knowing anyone. Taking on Luke's cockamamie search for a wife was the biggest risk of all. Certainly to her professional reputation, if word got out. But she wouldn't exchange her time with him for all the regular pay slips in the world.

She just had to remember not to risk anything else around him.

The ball flashed around the roulette wheel, clattering and clicking. Danica held her breath, waiting for the moment when the ball would drop into the slot—

"Three red. Odd," the croupier intoned. She left a marker by Danica's pile of chips and turned her attention to the rest of the table. After the croupier paid out the smaller bets, she began to add chips next to Danica's stack. And more. And still more. When the croupier was finished, Danica could build her own minifortress out of her winnings.

"What was the strategy you recommended?" she asked Luke as she raked the chips toward her, careless of their denominations. "I won, so I should bet one less chip this time?" She grinned up at Luke, catching his gaze.

It was a mistake. She thought he might be amused or perhaps annoyed she had gone against his advice. Instead, his gaze was warmly admiring, a bright glow shining in the dark blue depths. She nearly knocked a quarter of her chips onto the ground.

He probably used that expression with any female in his vicinity, she admonished herself sternly. He was Luke Dallas. He couldn't help it. Besides, he made it crystal clear this was a business outing.

Yet he'd looked at Felicity as if he couldn't wait for a polite reason to leave the party...

"That was bold," he said in his low rumble.

Danica wrenched her gaze away and began playing with a chip. "Nothing ventured, nothing gained, et cetera."

"You could have lost everything."

"Or I could've gained far more than I had before. Which I did."

"You got lucky," he said. "It paid off. But it was a—"

"I know the odds. But sometimes you have to put yourself in the hands of the universe."

"Fine when playing with fake money. But in real life? Not an advisable strategy."

She had the distinct impression they were no longer talking about casino games, but she didn't know if she was up to examining the undercurrents. She grabbed a five-hundred-dollar chip off the nearest pile. "Here. Go ahead, risk it all in one place," she said with a wide smile.

Luke took it from her, his gaze intent on hers. Their fingers brushed, electricity traveling the length of her arm and heading deep inside her. Instead of placing the chip down on the table, he tucked it into the inner pocket of his tuxedo jacket. Next to his heart. "Are you hungry?" he asked.

She was. For what, she couldn't quite put into words. She nodded, and Luke turned to the croupier. A few exchanged words later and Danica's mountain of round plastic circles had turned into a written receipt with nearly more zeros on it than space allowed. He handed it to her. "I'd repeat my advice not to risk it all in one place, but you might break the bank."

She folded up the receipt and placed it into her dress pocket. "No, you're right. I'd probably lose all my money on the next spin. That's what is exciting about it."

He tucked her hand into the crook of his elbow without

looking. The automatic assumption she would go wherever he led would have rankled coming from anyone else. But with Luke, whose usual demeanor was closed off and forbidding, the gesture made her feel wanted, accepted. As if she belonged, now and forever.

He guided her toward the outdoor terrace, where different chefs from San Francisco's best restaurants had set up food stations. "Losing is exciting?"

She laughed. "No. It's terrifying. But sometimes, on a night like tonight... Don't you ever want to be surprised? Take a chance? Not know what's going to happen in advance?"

He shook his head. "I read the last pages of a book first."

She stopped walking, causing him to halt. "That's terrible."

"It's smart. I know I won't waste my time if the conclusion is unsatisfactory."

"What about serendipity?" *Like the serendipity of running into him outside Johanna's office?* "Or fate? Fortune?"

"Fate and fortune are excuses made by the unprepared. I know the odds and play them accordingly." He laced his words with authority, his mouth settling into a firm line when he finished speaking.

She slid a sideways glance in his direction. "Not everything in life can be controlled," she said softly.

He gave no indication he'd heard her, but she had to double her steps to keep up with him as he threaded his way through the crowd. She decided to relax and enjoy herself, creating mental snapshots as they sped through the party. She couldn't wait to tell Matt all about it during their next phone call. This beat any episode of *Real Housewives* they'd watched in Matt's hospital room.

Luke slowed down once they arrived on the stone terrace wrapping the length of the mansion. It was lined by long buffet tables, each one labeled with the name of one of San Francisco's most exclusive eateries. She tugged on his arm.

"Is that Shijo Nagao?" she asked, indicating a chef standing behind a station offering sushi prepared to order. Nagao's restaurant had a yearlong reservation waiting list.

Luke glanced over. "I believe so."

Danica dropped her hand from his sleeve. "See you later."

He grabbed her fingers. "You're ditching your work assignment? For raw fish?"

"Sushi," she corrected, allowing her hand to linger in his so she could enjoy the fizzy crackles his touch sent singing through her blood. "Expertly prepared, delicious raw fish. And omega-3 is vital to brain function. I'm sure you agree this would help me excel at my responsibilities." She flashed him a grin, daring him to find fault with her logic.

He narrowed his gaze. "What happened to the woman with the New England palate?"

"She likes fish."

"Fish served with wasabi. If you don't like salsa..."

She shuddered. "No wasabi. Never trust anything green and pasty."

He raised his eyebrows in horror, but his upturned mouth betrayed his amusement. "If I didn't have other reasons to trust your judgment, I would reconsider our relationship."

The word *relationship* sent shockwaves throughout her body. She shook her head at herself. He meant it in a professional sense. "How can you eat sushi with wasabi? It destroys the flavor," she said.

"What? No. It enhances it. It's a—"

"Let me guess. Chemical reaction." She raised a teasing eyebrow.

"Yep. Some pairings are proven by trial and time to be the only choice for each other."

"I bet if we ask Chef Nagao, he will tell you when diners add extra wasabi to their meal, it is a sign they can't appreciate the chef's subtle flavors and shouldn't be served the best fish."

Luke swung his attention from Nagao's chef station and focused on her. "Really?"

She nodded. "The diner misses out by insisting on wasabi."

Guests began to pack the space where they stood. Luke stepped closer to her, his presence acting like a shield. The beginning of his five-o'clock shadow was making its appearance. "Misses out," he said, his gaze warm on hers.

Something fluttered in her stomach, and she couldn't attribute it to her lack of an evening meal. "Yes."

"By sticking to the preconceived pairing."

She wet her suddenly dry lips. "Yes."

His gaze fixed on her mouth. "If one were to, say, go in another direction, the result might be greater than anticipated?"

The event planners needed to do something about the number of people in the room. She was struggling to take a deep breath. "When it comes to sushi—"

"Or gambling, apparently."

A waiter tried to squeeze behind Danica. The hard edge of his tray jostled her right into Luke. Her hands flew up to brace herself. They landed square on Luke's chest.

His arms encircled her and kept her upright. "Are you okay?"

No. She was not. His chest was hard and muscled under the thin wool of his jacket and finely woven cotton of his shirt. His leather and citrus scent teased her nose. But she would have been able to laugh off the incident if it weren't for his gaze, deeply blue and full of concern. For her.

Sound faded. The laughter and conversation, the jazz trio

playing in a nearby room—all hushed save for the pounding of her heart. His arms tightened around her, creating a cocoon outside which no one existed. His gaze changed, turned deeper, darker. Concern faded to awareness. Then flared into desire.

"Danica." She felt her name more than heard it, a deep rumble reverberating underneath her splayed hands.

Anticipation fizzed through her, headier than any alcoholic beverage. "Yes?" she whispered.

He raised his right hand and brushed a curl off her face, his thumb lingering on the curve of her cheek. Thankfully, he kept his left hand locked at her waist, keeping her upright when her legs would've failed her. "What were you saying about serendipity?"

"I welcome it," she managed to breathe. Luke Dallas was going to kiss her. And she wanted him to kiss her. Wanted it more than she'd ever wanted anything else. One more kiss for her memories. One more kiss to sweeten her dreams and warm her nights.

He smiled but it didn't reach his eyes. His gaze remained darkly intent, hot enough to leave scorch marks as it traveled the outline of her lips. She lifted her chin and tilted her mouth. Her lips parted. His hand tightened at her waist, pressing her closer—

"Dallas!" a man said from behind Luke. "Just the man we were hoping to see tonight."

The bubbly anticipation fled. The sounds of the party flooded back: the clink of the glasses, the hum of voices, the occasional well-bred laugh. Luke straightened up and let go of her waist. "To be continued," he said to her in a low voice. Then his expression changed to one she knew all too well from their first meeting.

The man came up and shook Luke's hand. He was tan and well over six feet tall, his custom-tailored tuxedo revealing a graceful, broad-shouldered physique most commonly seen in champion swimmers. His dark blond hair, streaked with the kind of highlights only constant exposure to the sun could provide, fell into his eyes. He looked like he'd be more at home on the cover of a surfing magazine, but she knew not to judge people by their looks. He was probably a brilliant programmer or a marketing genius.

"I'm Grayson," he said to her with a firm handshake and a slow, highly charming grin. Then he turned back to Luke. "Evan here thinks his start-up is not only a unicorn, it's a decacorn. I say he might be right. What do you say?"

"I say I haven't heard of Evan or his company before," Luke said. "But a ten-billion-dollar valuation? Pretty damn rare."

"I'd love to tell you more," Evan said. "We have a great opportunity for a partnership with Ruby Hawk's tech. Do you have a minute?"

"Thanks, but I have a prior commitment." Luke offered his arm to Danica. "If you'll excuse us?" he said to the men, his words polite but firm.

"Word is Ruby Hawk might miss its acquisition target date. You'll need good partners for your next venture," said Grayson.

"Want advice on your start-up? Never pay attention to valley gossip." Luke's tone was breezy, but under her loose grip his muscles tensed.

"That came from Cinco Jackson. But I'd still like to talk with you," Evan said.

Luke's arm turned to solid steel. Danica dropped her hand. "Why don't you three have a conversation? I'll save some sushi for you," she said to Luke.

"I promised you dinner." His gaze added, "And more."

"I can stand in line for my own food," she replied with a smile. In a tone pitched just for Luke's ear, she continued, "I'm curious what Jackson knows. If the real reason for our search leaked..."

Luke regarded her. "You're concerned."

She nodded, teeth worrying her lip.

"Don't be. I can handle whatever Jackson throws." He turned back to the two men. "Sorry. Maybe some other time. But as you see, I have far more attractive plans right now." He started to tug her away.

She saw a flash of navy blue silk from across the room. When she tried to catch Felicity's gaze, the other woman looked away, as if hoping to not get caught. "This is a charity event, right?" Danica asked. "And a key feature of this event is the auction?"

Three pairs of eyes focused on her. "Yes," Evan said slowly.

She opened her purse and pulled out the scrip given to her by the roulette croupier. "These are my winnings, which I planned to donate during the auction." She showed the total to Grayson and Evan. "I will let you have a half hour of my time with Luke if you each promise to match the amount."

"I wasn't aware I was up for sale," Luke said drily. She flicked her gaze upward, dreading to see the anger directed her way for selling him out. Instead, his gaze sizzled with appreciation. She flushed hot from her hairline to her big toe.

Grayson laughed. "You drive a hard bargain," he said. "But I agree. C'mon, Dallas, let's go find a place to talk. I don't want the other sharks milling about to hear about Evan's company. Not until we're ready, that is."

"Not so fast." She held out her hand. "Your checks, please."

"Smart *and* pretty," Grayson said to Luke. "You know how to pick them. Hope that goes for companies too." He pulled out his wallet and took out a business card. "Here. You bid on what you want during the auction, up to the combined amount Evan and I owe you. When you win, give this to the cashier and say I will pay the balance."

She took the card, raising a skeptical eyebrow. "Really—" she started to say, and then looked at the name. Grayson was Grayson Monk. As in Monk Partners, one of the top venture-capital firms in Silicon Valley. "I mean, really. You will."

Grayson clapped Luke on the shoulder. "Great. Now let's go make another deal."

"Fine," Luke said to the two men, but his gaze rested on Danica, that light still burning. "We'll talk mythical beasts. And even more mythical company valuations."

A large grin spread over Evan's face. "You won't regret it."

"Your five-hundred-dollar chip says I will," Luke muttered for Danica's ears only. His warm breath stirred the sensitive hairs there, sending a shiver through her. "Meet you back here when I'm done?" When she nodded, he turned back to the men. "A deal is a deal. You have thirty minutes."

Danica watched them walk away. Then she turned to get into the ever-growing line for Chef Nagao. Just as she reached the end, a man in a white dinner jacket thrust two empty champagne glasses at her. "Take these, will you?" he said, and turned his back on her. She accepted the glasses out of pure reflex, and then stared dumbfounded at his jacket-clad back.

What the...? She looked around for somewhere to put the flutes down, but no appropriate surfaces presented themselves. The low stone walls surrounding the terrace were roughhewn, the surface uneven. The high round cocktail tables dotting the outer sweep of the terrace were three deep in elegant people. She doubted they would appreciate dirty glassware set down beside their plates of beautifully prepared food. No busing station could be spotted in the vicinity.

Finally, she spotted a waitress carrying a silver tray overloaded with discarded china and glassware striding briskly through the throng and down the terrace steps to a flagstone walkway below. Danica hurried after her, catching up just as the waitress was about enter a white marquee tent set up behind a large, six-car detached garage.

"Here." Danica held out the empty flutes.

The waitress looked Danica up and down, her upper lip curling into a sneer. "Take them yourself," she said. "And where's your tray?" She disappeared behind a pinned-back flap.

If the guest handing her his empty flutes had been rude, the waitress was out of line. But it wasn't the waitress's exasperation that caused Danica to stare after her. It was her outfit. She sported a black dress almost identical to the one Danica wore. They even had on similar shoes.

It was official. She didn't belong at the party as a guest. Looking around the tent, she spotted a table full of dirty dishes. Quickly adding the flutes to the pile, she stepped out before anyone else could mistake her for a slack member of the catering team.

She returned to the terrace, but Chef Nagao's station had a Closed—Gone Fishing sign next to empty sushi display cases. Luke was nowhere in sight. When a woman wearing a gown Danica had seen in last month's *Vogue* approached her, empty plates in her hand and an annoyed scowl on her face, Danica ducked down the terrace steps again.

She should leave. She almost kissed Luke. Again. She was playing with matches, testing how long she could hold on to the sliver of wood before burning her fingers. But if she snuck out now, then her gambling winnings plus Grayson's and Evan's pledges would not go to the charity. She had to stay until the auction started.

Might as well kill the time exploring one of the many gravel paths snaking through the mansion's expansive grounds. When would she get another chance to wander through a billionaire's backyard?

The path she chose meandered through formal gardens of well-manicured bushes and profusely blooming flower beds. Danica took notes of the varieties, knowing her mom would ask. At the end of the walkway was a wrought-iron garden bench, set in a small cul-de-sac formed by shoulder-high hedges.

It was hard to believe a party full of the Bay Area's brightest and wealthiest was being held a scant fifty yards away. She sat down to admire the evening. The sky overhead had deepened to indigo blue, decorated by a shining crescent moon. A light breeze carrying the scent of nearby roses ruffled strands of hair that had escaped from her ponytail. Later it would be too chilly to be outside without a jacket or sweater, but for now the temperature was perfect.

Gravel crunched on the other side of the hedge. She wasn't the only one to escape into the gardens. She stood up to return to the house but sat back down when she overheard Luke's name.

"He said what?" a male voice asked.

Danica frowned. The voice was familiar. "It wasn't Dallas. It was the recruiter," a female answered.

That voice Danica knew. Felicity. The male voice must belong to Cinco Jackson.

"You're missing the point. It's illegal to ask someone about their marital status in a job interview."

Danica's blood chilled.

Felicity protested from the other side of the hedge. "But

the recruiter didn't ask. I was so surprised anyone knew, I confirmed it."

"You're still not seeing the point." Jackson spoke to her as if she were a small child. "Does Dallas have something against employing women who are married? Does he only employ single women? Is this a behavior pattern?"

Danica clasped her hands over her mouth. She needed to find Luke, quick. But if she left her bench now, the couple on the other side might hear her movements and know they had an eavesdropper.

"Something's up. I can smell it," Jackson continued. "The acquisition is rumored to be going south, maybe because old man Stavros has something on Dallas. Let's get back to the party." Rustling came from the other side as the hedges, as if they were standing up. "I want to see who Dallas is talking to and what about." The sound of gravel crunching underneath their feet drowned out anything else he said.

Danica waited until their footsteps faded away. Then she unfolded herself from the bench, scrambling for her phone to contact Luke. The screen already had a message on it.

Where are you? Sushi closed.

She thought for a moment. With the party in full swing and the auction about to start, the entrance would probably be the least occupied space in the mansion.

Meet you in the foyer. I have news.

Good I hope? See you there.

The crowd had grown exponentially in the time she had been gone. A few faces lit up when they saw her heading in their direction, but they turned dark as she pushed past without taking the dirty plates and used glasses they offered to her. It wasn't her fault the hosts didn't hire enough catering staff, even if she did accidentally crash the party dressed like a server.

She reached the foyer, slowing her speed so she wouldn't slide on the polished marble floor. Luke stood near the imposing double doors that led to the front drive and the valet station outside. He smiled, and the bands holding her lungs captive since she first overheard Cinco started to relax.

"Excuse me." Danica felt a hard tap on her shoulder. "You need to take this."

Danica turned her head to see the server who had scowled at her earlier. She held out a tray laden with empty champagne flutes, dirty dishes and crumbled napkins.

"Sorry," Danica said over her shoulder, picking up her pace again. "I'm not—"

The server followed behind her. "I have to be at the bar station. Your hands are free."

"I—you don't understand. I'm here as a—"

"I have to go, *now*. Here." The server thrust the tray at Danica.

Six

The tray left the server's hands. Danica lunged to catch it. Her thin-soled shoes slid, slipping on the smooth floor. Her feet flew out from underneath her. The last thing she saw before hitting the ground was the server's horrified face, her mouth in a perfect O.

Danica belly flopped on the marble floor. The impact knocked all her senses off-line. Black fog mired her thoughts. She concentrated on her breathing, thankful her heart beat by itself. Bells rang in the distance.

She wriggled her fingers to see if they worked. Good. Then she moved her left hand. A shard of glass sliced into her palm.

The sudden pain shocked her into full awareness. Her gaze swam back into focus, and she realized the bells were her ears ringing from the tray and its contents clattering down around her. She inhaled deeply. Then she wished she hadn't. It smelled like a liquor store had exploded around her.

"Danica!" Luke knelt beside her. Evan and Grayson stood behind him. She struggled to sit up.

"Wait," Luke warned. "Look at me. Did you hit your head?"

She stared into his gaze. His eyes were the color of the Pacific Ocean right before a thunderstorm. He was angry. And upset. For her? Or for the scene she'd caused?

"I'm fine." She broke the intense contact, giving Evan her uninjured hand so he could pull her upright.

Guests and members of the catering staff crowded into the space. The server stood nearby, wringing her hands. Danica shook her head at her, to indicate it wasn't her fault, and instantly wished she hadn't. Voices echoed off the surrounding marble, adding to her disorientation.

"I'm sorry—" she started to say to Luke, but her lips—her whole body—started to shake despite every effort to stop it.

He grabbed her hurt hand and examined it. "You're bleeding."

"It's just a scratch." She kept her gaze focused on his shoulder. The foyer was starting to tilt and the last thing she wanted to do was fall again.

"You need a doctor." He handed her the pocket square from his tuxedo jacket to press against her palm, and then threw an arm over her shoulder. It was comforting and solid, and she sank into his side. "We're leaving."

"But the auction—"

"Don't worry about the auction," Grayson said from her other side. "I'll make sure all the money gets to the charity."

Danica started to thank him, but the heavy wooden doors had opened and she was standing in the cool evening air before she knew it. The valet had Luke's car ready and Luke opened the passenger door, guiding her in.

She slid onto the smooth leather seat and buckled in,

careful to keep her injured palm from touching anything, and closed her eyes to stop the last of the spinning. The car accelerated and she opened them to see Luke, his expression grim in the glow of the car's display.

"The closest emergency room is twenty minutes away. You'll be okay until then?" His words were clipped.

She took her head off the pillow-like headrest and sat upright. "Do you know how expensive a trip to the ER is? If you drop me off at the nearest Caltrain station, I'll be able to get home."

"Don't worry about money. Your hand needs to be looked at. And what if you hit your head?"

She took the pocket square off her palm and looked at the cut in the dim light. "I think the bleeding has stopped. And I know I didn't hit my head. I don't need a doctor." Thanks to Matt, she'd had enough of hospitals to last her several lifetimes.

He made a sound in his throat like he didn't believe her. Then he turned the car around in a smooth, tight arc.

"What are you doing? Are we going back to the party?"

"I live a few streets away," he answered. "If you won't see a doctor, the least I can do is make sure your hand is cleaned and bandaged."

"But—"

"I'm not taking no for an answer."

She opened her mouth to insist otherwise, but he cut her off.

"I mean it," he said tightly. "Hang on, we'll be there soon."

She opened her mouth again.

"Don't even try."

She pressed her lips together. He was being ridiculous. She was fine. Well, except for her heart rate beating in triple time. It was quiet in the car and dark, and they sat close enough that she could extend her hand just an inch or two and touch his thigh.

She barely lost any blood. She shouldn't feel this faint.

In what seemed like no time, he swung the car off the road. They passed a sleek iron gate that opened automatically as they approached, and continued up a long, winding driveway that led to a two-story house set among pine trees and cypresses. It resembled a gray concrete box with steel trim, but natural-wood window frames and doors softened the hard materials and made the house feel more welcoming than imposing. Not a bad metaphor for Luke, she thought. Hard and masculine but there was warmth if you looked.

He opened her car door and ushered her into the house. "Go straight and make yourself at home in the living room," he said. "I'll get the first-aid kit."

She nodded, not trusting her voice, and walked down a short hallway into a wide room shaped like a rectangle. The house she rented with Mai could fit in it, with room for their next-door neighbor.

The far wall was clear glass, floor to ceiling, allowing her to see the dimly lit patio and gardens just beyond. It took her a second before she realized the wall was composed of retractable panels. When the weather was nice, Luke could open the panels and the room would flow into the outdoors without interruption. To her right was the kitchen, all polished stainless appliances and warm wooden veneers, separated from the rest of the room by low counters. A metal dining table surrounded by twelve mismatched chairs stood nearby.

To her left, a fireplace tall enough to stand up in dominated the wall. Arranged in front of it were two oversize, cream-colored leather sofas and several comfortable-looking chairs. A plush rug resembling a soft cloud that had landed on the floor completed the look, straight out of a pricey interior-design magazine.

The plump cushions beckoned her to sit down, but she hesitated. Her dress had soaked up several varieties of wine and other alcohol. Last thing she wanted to do was mar his pristine furniture.

"Pick a sofa," Luke said from behind her. His jacket and black bow tie had been discarded, and the top buttons of his crisp white shirt were undone, exposing a triangle of tanned skin. In his hands he held a white box marked with a red cross.

She indicated her stained dress. "The kitchen would be better."

He shook his head and steered her until she sank down onto cushions that were even softer than they looked. Her face must have shown her reaction because he smiled. "Much better than the kitchen. Now, give me your hand."

She extended it, managing to keep the trembling to a minimum. Just as she had informed him in the car, the bleeding had slowed. He took out a bottle of hydrogen peroxide and swabbed the area with gentle, sure movements. She reflexively tried to pull her hand back but he held on, his grip secure and firm.

Her pulse beat in her ears, a rapid flutter. She told herself it was a natural reaction to the sting of hydrogen peroxide hitting the wound. But then he traced his index finger over her palm and she knew her reaction had nothing to do with pain and everything to do with him.

She inhaled, her lungs requiring more air than she could take in. She couldn't remember the last time anyone took care of her. Oh, her parents had bandaged her childhood scrapes and put ointment on her bruises. But as soon as she was old enough to fend for herself, it became a point of pride to cause them as little concern as possible. Between trying to earn enough money to keep a roof over their heads and food on the table and looking after the energetic, never-met-a-dare-he-didn't-take Matt, her parents had enough worries.

She had been more often the caregiver than not, from babysitting her brother after school while her parents were still at work, to doing everything she could to help her college boyfriend ace the LSATs and apply to law school. Tom did get into a top program, thanks to her coaching. Then he attended law-school orientation, announced he had found the woman of his dreams among his fellow first-year students and dumped Danica.

"You can only rely on yourself and family," her father had said when she was still crawling into her childhood bed to cry under the covers three weeks later. When her boss at the time mentioned he knew an executive-recruitment firm in Palo Alto that needed an assistant, she took the money she had saved for a security deposit on an apartment with her now ex-boyfriend and spent it on a plane ticket to California. It was the furthest possible point from Tom and still in the continental United States. She would show everyone she could do just fine on her own.

But with Luke's touch trailing embers in its wake, it felt good to have someone look after her. More than good. A heaviness gathered deep and low, a persistent ache demanding to be relieved that she hadn't felt—well, she hadn't felt since Luke kissed her outside the taqueria in San Francisco. And before that, a very long time.

He took out a gauze pad and sterile tape. "You weren't planning on using your hand much tonight, were you?"

"Um." Good thing it was her left hand, and she was right-handed. She definitely planned on using her right hand later that night while indulging in fantasies. Involving him. "No."

He bent his head down as he worked. It was all she could do to stop her mind from conjuring those fantasies, right here, right now. For example, what would happen if she leaned forward and pressed her lips to his? Would he welcome her kiss, without the music and the bright lights and the buzz of the party creating an alternate reality in which they moved in the same social world?

What would he taste like? Champagne, bright and tart? Or—

Snap out of it, Novak. She didn't belong here, sitting on a sofa that probably cost more than six months of her salary as Johanna's assistant, just as she didn't belong at that party where she barely passed for a guest. She certainly didn't belong in Luke Dallas's arms.

"You don't have to do this," she blurted out.

He finished bandaging her hand, smoothing the tape over the gauze with deliberate strokes of his fingers. Strokes that advanced and withdrew, creating an answering drumbeat rhythm between her legs. "Due diligence," he said with a half smirk, his gaze locked on hers as his fingers continued their caresses. "If the cut gets infected and you can't work, you could sue. A lawsuit might bankrupt the Peninsula Society."

"Oh." The pleasure-pain tightening deep in her belly at the thought of kissing Luke lessened, just a bit. Then his smile deepened, and it roared back. She swallowed her own smile. "Well, we can't have that, can we," she said primly.

"Just controlling outcomes," he agreed, his gaze sparking with humor. Crinkles appeared at the corners of his summer-sea blue eyes.

A teasing Luke was catnip to her libido. She tugged her hand. He frowned but let it go. "Thank you for the bandage. I'll order a car to go home."

He sat back on the couch, his gaze never leaving hers. "What did you want earlier?"

"What?" She wasn't that transparent. Was she? She didn't need to touch her cheeks to know they were burning.

"Before your accident. You said you had news?"

The conversation in the garden felt like a lifetime ago. "Right." Clearing her throat, she forced herself to sound businesslike. "I overheard Cinco and Felicity." She filled him in on the details.

He made a noncommittal noise. "We knew he was nosing around Ruby Hawk."

"But this sounded personal," she said. "He thinks the acquisition is in trouble because Stavros has dirt on you."

"He's not wrong." Luke shrugged. "Nestor is refusing to close the deal until I meet his conditions. But I don't hire my employees based on marital status. If that's the tree Jackson wants to bark up, he'll be hoarse."

She released her breath. "So, what's the next step?"

His gaze traveled to the top of her head. "Take down your ponytail."

Her uninjured hand flew up to protect her hair. "What? Why?"

He leaned toward her, filling the space between them until only a handbreadth remained. "To see if you have any lumps resulting from hitting your head."

She searched his gaze. "I didn't hit my head."

"You were stunned after the accident so you might not be aware if you did or not. Let me check." His lips pressed together in a firm line.

"I'm capable of seeking my own medical attention," she warned.

"I know you're very capable," he said with a rueful smile. He leaned even closer. "Humor me. Please." His low rumble sent a cascade of goose bumps down her spine.

Perhaps he should check. The room was spinning again. "Fine," she agreed with an exhaled breath. Before she could finish speaking, his right hand reached behind her and removed the elastic holding her hair. Her curls tumbled around her face and bounced off her shoulders.

Intellectually, having her hair down should make her feel more covered up, hidden. Instead, it was as if he had stripped her of her armor, leaving her bare to his knowing gaze. She shivered.

His fingers combed through her hair, tracing small circles on her scalp. He was so close she could see the faint shadow of whiskers making their presence known along the strong line of his jaw, and the dusting of crisp black hairs revealed by the open throat of his shirt. Delicious awareness pricked to life. She leaned into his hands as if she were a cat.

He slowed and then stopped his movements, his fingers still tangled in her hair. "No lumps." His eyes were indigo dark, and the coiled tension she could sense reminded her again of a tiger, ready to pounce on its prey.

She very much wanted to be devoured. All she had to do was lean forward, just an inch, and her mouth would be on his.

"Was that the outcome you desired?" Somehow, she was able to form words.

"It was one," he growled.

"There was another?"

His gaze flared with a primal hunger, and his grasp tightened on her curls. "Only if you desire it, as well."

The air crackled with electricity. She could almost see golden sparks leaping between them, illuminating the thread of attraction that wove around them. She lifted her hand to cover his, encircling his wrist. Under her touch, his pulse beat in time with hers.

She should thank him for the medical attention, spring to her feet, find her phone and summon a ridesharing service to take her home. That's what the old Danica would do. The one who worked long hours for Johanna, expecting a promotion that never came. The one who would have listened to Luke's explanation of how to maximize her roulette bets.

Or she could go all in. Risk everything. The Danica who piled all her chips on one number and waited for the ball to drop. The Danica who kissed Luke Dallas and was about to kiss him again.

Just one night. Not a relationship. It could never be a relationship. She knew where she stood with him. So, what would be the harm of giving in to the anticipation curling in her stomach, the throbbing emptiness between her legs demanding to be filled?

She took a deep breath. Her lips were dry, and she wet them with her tongue. His gaze followed its path. His blue eyes were almost black now. She closed the tiny gap between them and pressed her mouth against his.

Luke's history with women was long and varied. He liked sex, and the women he dated indicated they enjoyed having sex with him. But the players knew the cards on the table, making the stakes for all low. He never got involved unless the other party agreed to mutually assured pleasure and fun, nothing more. Still, there were plenty of women who were happy to share his bed on those terms.

Therefore, he thought he knew every variation on a kiss. The gentle kiss, the rough kiss. The soft slide of lip against lip and the thrusting duel of tongues. The nibble, the suck, the grind, the bite.

Then Danica kissed him. And he knew he had missed out on kissing all these years.

Kissing her was a shot of pure adrenaline, a narcotic

hit to his system no manufactured drug could ever hope
to match. It acted like a rocket booster, taking what had
been a very pleasurable activity and sending it into the
stratosphere. A pure jolt of electricity traveled straight from
where their mouths met to his cock. He was rock hard in
half a second.

His fingers tangled in those glorious blond curls. He
loved the infinite variety of golds in its strands. It was as
soft and yet as wildly dimensional as he thought it would
be—alive to the touch.

Seeing her still on the ground, eyes closed, had shut his
throat with fear. He may have used protecting the charity
from lawsuits as an excuse to take care of her, but it was
as transparent as the walls in his office. He'd needed, on
some primal level he still hadn't fully acknowledged, to
ensure she wasn't hurt.

And now he needed to kiss her senseless.

Her mouth was hot and insistent and greedy. He met
her demands with his own, their tongues tangling and exploring. The scant millimeters separating them on the sofa
felt like miles, and he gathered Danica to him, pulling her
until she half lay across his lap. Her scent, vanilla and cinnamon, sweet and spicy, surrounded him. She shifted even
closer, the curve of her bottom just brushing his groin. An
involuntary shudder ran through to his toes, shocking his
brain back to a limited cognitive function.

He should stop. She was his consultant. Her job was to
find him a wife. A wife in every sense of the word. If all
went to plan, he would be in front of a judge with another
woman in a matter of weeks.

He couldn't stop even if a 7.8 earthquake hit the Bay
Area that instant.

Her hands reached out to tug his shirt free from his
pants and moved up to work the buttons of his shirt free.

The brush of her fingers against his chest brought his cock to a whole different level of density.

Turnabout was fair play. He undid the buttons on her shirtdress from throat to waist. Her skin was smooth, warm. He disengaged from her mouth so he could press his lips to where her neck joined her shoulder, inhaling her vanilla-cinnamon scent. He had to see if she tasted as good as she smelled, and he kissed-licked a path across her collarbone to where the dress gaped open. He pushed the top of the dress down, exposing high, full breasts straining against a cotton bra.

He trailed his right index finger over the generous swells, dipped it into the shadowy crevice between. Hard nipples pushed against the bra cups and with his thumbs he traced slow, tiny circles around each one.

"Luke," she breathed and tugged on his hair. He looked up to catch her gaze, wide and wild and dark. "You're still wearing your shirt."

He grinned. "I'm much more interested in removing yours." He kissed her again, his hands busy untying the sash at her waist then removing all the buttons he could find from their buttonholes, until her dress parted in the middle.

She really was beautiful. He shook his head in silent admiration and ran his index finger from the shadowy valley between her breasts to the top of her plain white panties. She shivered and gasped, her eyes squeezed shut.

"Are you cold?" he asked. He wasn't. He was burning up.

She shook her head, but when he undid the clasp of her bra, her hands came up to cross over her chest. "Wait. Before the rest comes off, I think we need to negotiate," she said, her words coming in bursts between gulps of air.

Those deep breaths caused her breasts to rise and fall, the fabric of her bra slipping even as she tried to hold it in place. It took a moment for him to realize she was speaking. "Negotiate?"

"Set boundaries, then. This is just for tonight. Nothing will change," she said. "Right?"

It was hard to think since all his blood had rushed south, but he managed to nod. "Of course."

She searched his gaze for a moment, her lower lip caught by her upper teeth. Then she nodded. "Of course." She stood up and let her arms drop, her bra falling with them. Her breasts were two perfect orbs custom-made to fill his hands. "This is comfy, but wouldn't a bed be preferable?"

Before a coherent thought could form, he was off the sofa. Leading her by the hand, he guided her to his bedroom.

"Put your hands on the bed," he breathed in her ear, and from behind his knee moved between her legs until she stood with them a shoulder's width apart. Then his hands stroked her thighs, starting above her knees and moving higher. His fingers found the waist of her panties, then slipped down farther, into the nest of soft curls.

She bucked against him, her perfect, round ass grinding against his painful erection. His breathing was harsh in his own ears as he found her opening and slid one finger, then two, slowly, deeply inside the wetness.

She gasped, then moaned. It was the sweetest sound he'd ever heard. There was nothing practiced about her response, no artifice or putting on a show. His thumb brushed the tight knot of nerves at the top of her opening—firm, then soft, then firm again—and her gasps came in short, quick bursts. "Luke," she breathed. "I need—"

"I know," he said, because he felt it too. She shuddered and tried to turn to face him.

He held her hips still. "Not yet," he said in her ear. Then he removed her panties and fell to his knees, his mouth closing over her sweet, hot core. Her taste was more exquisite than any food on offer at the party.

"What are you—" she squeaked out, before her words turned into a moan, low and full throated. The primal sound urged him on, harder, faster, deeper. He couldn't get enough. She was a white-hot flame and he yearned to be burned like he'd never been burned before. He could feel her tremble, her climax beginning to build, and he pulled back just in time to witness her scream and shudder before she collapsed against the bed.

He joined her on the king-size mattress, his erection pressing painfully against his tuxedo trousers, and turned her over. Her big green eyes flew open, dark with satisfaction. He grinned down at her. She was gorgeous, although the word was too inadequate to describe the sight before him. Who knew underneath her ponytail and always-appropriate work attire was such a responsive, passionate woman? *You knew. Since the moment you kissed her. You knew she was special.*

"That was…" she breathed, her chest still rising and falling rapidly. "Can't think." He watched her gaze slowly focus. "You. Too many clothes. Take them off."

Her hands reached out, her fingers still trembling, and she tugged his shirt open. At least one button, torn free from its mooring, clattered on the hardwood floor, but he didn't care. He needed to feel her skin against his. Then her hands moved lower and caressed him through his trousers, causing him to buck like a teenager in the back seat of a car. "Inside," she breathed. "Want you inside."

He didn't have to be asked twice. The rest of his clothes came off even faster than he could open the foil packet and avail himself of the contents. Her eyes widened when she saw him revealed for the first time, but her lips curved upward in a wide smile as she opened her arms to him.

He couldn't wait any longer. He had to have her. Not even as a teenager had he felt so excited yet anxious with anticipation. She was so responsive. So alive and present. He slid into her, closing his eyes and biting back a moan at the slick, tight heat.

His control was legendary. He should have no problem holding out. But the rake of her fingers on his back inflamed his senses, her gasps urging him to go faster, deeper. The pressure built, more rapidly than he thought possible. It demanded to be brought to its inescapable conclusion, now. He gritted his teeth. He was not an inexperienced boy with his first girlfriend. But then she cried out underneath him, her vibrations shaking the bed.

Stars exploded behind his eyelids.

When he had recovered, he gathered her limp, pliant body to his, pressing a kiss to the soft dusting of freckles across her nose. She blinked and looked up at him, a lazy smile playing on her lips. "Best outcome to a negotiation I've ever had," she said.

Male pride expanded his chest. He pulled her closer, burying his face in those curls. Cinnamon and vanilla surrounded him, a combination sweet yet warm and spicy. Just like her.

She sighed, her body fitting against his without any awkwardness as she fell into slumber. None of the unexpected sharp elbow or accidental knee to the groin that often occurred on a first night together. He could stay like this forever, he thought as he drifted into the kind of sleep that came only after truly satisfying sex.

Then his eyes flew open.

Forever?

What kind of a thought was that?

Sex was of the moment, experienced in the here and now. Relationships could be mutually beneficial but like most partnerships, they needed to be periodically assessed and reconfigured. Look at his parents. Their marriage lasted five years, enough time to produce him and his younger sister. His father, Jonathan, got entry into the San Francisco society that had previously rejected him for having more money than manners, while his mother, Phoebe, secured access to the Dallas fortune for the rest of her children's lifetimes. Each of his parents' subsequent marriages had further enhanced their financial standing, social standing or both.

Luke raised himself on his elbow to gaze at the woman curled into his side. She wouldn't enhance his family's social status or their bank accounts. She was…

She was Danica.

He fell asleep with her name branded on his thoughts.

Someone shook Luke's shoulder, soft but insistent. "Hey."

He opened his eyes to find Danica standing over him. She was dressed, her black shirtdress somewhat rumpled but buttoned to her collarbone. He pushed himself up on one elbow, but she started to speak before he could form coherent thoughts.

"Hi. Sorry to wake you. But I'm going home." Her gaze didn't meet his. It swept the floor as if searching for something. Suddenly she bent down. When she came back up into his field of vision, he recognized the white cotton panties in her right hand. She thrust them into her dress pocket. In her other hand, she held her cell phone.

He blinked, still struggling to make his synapses fire. "You don't have to—"

"Yes, I do," she said firmly, then chased it with a quick smile her eyes didn't reflect. "Lot of work tomorrow. We both need sleep."

"We were sleeping." He stretched out a hand. "Come back to bed."

She stepped out of his reach. "I only wanted to tell you I was leaving."

"What's wrong?" It couldn't be the sex. No, the sex had been amazing. Mind-blowing. Call him arrogant or just experienced at these things, but he knew she'd enjoyed herself. Twice.

She laughed, two octaves higher than her normal range. "Everything is fine. I only woke you up because it wouldn't be right to sneak out. I mean, you're still my client and I still owe you work. Right?"

"Right." He searched her gaze. She wasn't telling the complete truth. He could sense it. But he never fought to keep a woman in his bed. If she wanted to leave, that was her choice.

He pushed down the unexpected wave of emotion. No, he wasn't disappointed. How could he be? This was the best possible outcome: great sex then his partner leaves. No morning awkwardness, no worrying if she will expect breakfast and especially no verbal dance around the possibility of an encore.

He swung the covers off. "I'll drive you."

"No!" She averted her gaze from his nude torso. "I called a car. You don't need to bother."

"It's not a—"

"Look!" She thrust her phone at him. "My driver is almost here. Silver Corolla. Can't cancel now. It would be rude." She lowered the phone but kept her gaze riveted on its screen. "So, um, thanks for the party. And the…rest. I had a good time. I mean, I hope you had a good time. No, I mean—"

"Danica." He waited until she looked up and held his gaze. A deep line still creased her brow.

He wanted to sweep the curls off her face and tell her everything would be okay. He wanted to hold her curves against him and caress that soft skin until she agreed to crawl back under the covers.

Wait. That was wrong. He didn't want bed partners to stay. He masked his confusion with a tight smile. "I had a great time. Thank you."

Her shoulders descended. "So, I'll see you in the morning? At Ruby Hawk?"

"Of course."

"Business as usual?"

"Yes." Good. They were each appropriately categorizing the evening as a fun, one-time experience. The sour, hollow feeling in his stomach must be hunger from skipping dinner at the party.

Her phone buzzed. She glanced down at the screen. "The driver is outside the gate." She took a step toward the bed, but when he reached out his arm to draw her close for a goodbye kiss, she retreated to the doorway and offered a wave of her hand instead. "Bye."

And she was gone.

He leaned back against the pillows. The bed held her smell, the air quivered with her presence. He waited for the room to settle and return to being his. Still. Quiet. Orderly. He twitched the sheets back into place and punched the pillows into perfect fluffed form. The room was back to status quo, and so was he.

When he woke again, hours before his alarm was set to ring, he was clasping the pillow she'd used tight to his chest. He tried his usual methods for dropping back into sleep, but none of them worked.

There was only one thing to do: diagram the situation causing his insomnia and diagnose the solutions. By the time he stepped into the shower to begin his work day, he'd made three key decisions.

Number one: the search was off. Danica was careful, but the odds had changed. With Cinco Jackson sniffing around, the search was no longer a calculated risk in his favor. He needed Nestor to believe the marriage commitment was real. A front-page story about his pursuit of unmarried females would call that into question.

Number two: he still needed a wife.

Number three: the only logical solution to his dilemma was Danica.

Seven

Luke pushed open the glass doors of Ruby Hawk, eager to put his plan into action. He had examined it from all angles in the hours before the sun rose, not finding a single flaw. And after discovering just how combustible they were in bed, Danica would agree with him, of course.

"You seem chipper," Anjuli said when she ran into him at the coffee bar. "That's not your usual style the morning after the Peninsula Society shindig. Did you not go?"

"I went. Have you heard of Medevco?"

Anjuli raised an eyebrow at the sudden change of subject. "Is that a city or a company?"

"Company. High-tech medical devices."

She shook her head. "No, but I haven't been following the health-care sector too closely."

"Check it out, would you? Evan Fletcher is the founder. Grayson Monk is the key investor." He saluted her with his three-shot Americano. He needed to get some work done before he took Danica to lunch to explain his stroke of genius. In fact, perhaps he should clear his schedule for the rest of the day. Just in case. The hot flare of anticipation at the thought was not unwelcome.

He frowned as he approached the conference room he used as his office. The mechanized shades were down, turning the glass walls opaque. He was positive he had left them up. With all the rumors surrounding Ruby Hawk, it was important to project openness and confidence. He opened the door.

And immediately wished he hadn't.

Irene Stavros sat behind his desk, thumbing through that blasted *Silicon Valley Weekly.* "Hello," she greeted him. "I'm so sorry I missed you at the fund-raiser last night. But it looks like you had a great time despite my absence." She turned the paper around so he could see the double-page spread. A photo of him and Danica talking to Grayson Monk occupied the center. Her manicured fingernail tapped on Danica's face. "What I can't figure out is why you were seen leaving with the help."

What did I do? What did I do? What did I do? The refrain would not stop playing in Danica's mind. She fell asleep listening to its rhythmic beat, and the words provided the background soundtrack for her shower, breakfast and now her journey to work. She barely noticed the scenery as she walked the six blocks from the train station to the Ruby Hawk offices. Images and sounds and scents from the night before occupied her senses.

She slept with Luke Dallas.

No. Strike that.

She had sex with Luke Dallas. Mind-blowing, can't-see-straight, volcanic sex. The kind magazines wrote headlines about. The kind appearing in books she previously filed under fantasy.

That she and Luke had chemistry had been obvious since that first kiss outside the taqueria. But even very, very, *very* good sex wasn't enough to ruin her career over. This... whatever it was...could go no further.

And Luke was sure to agree. After all, he hired her to find him a wife, and she wasn't on the list. Last night was impulsive madness, fueled by champagne and pent-up curiosity.

Now they knew. It was over and done. There wouldn't be a repeat.

Autopilot brought her to the converted supply room that was her office. Taking a deep breath, she sat down behind her desk and wrote down her game plan. She would find Luke the third candidate, she would submit her invoice for a job completed and then she would leave Ruby Hawk and start her own search firm.

Her phone dinged with a text message. Her mom.

Please call when you can? Bank refuses to refinance mortgage but drs. say Matt needs 6 more months minimum of physical therapy. Would like your help to decide if we should sell the house. Love you.

"I'm glad you're here." A deep male voice interrupted her text reading. A very familiar voice.

Luke leaned against her doorway with his arms folded across his chest. It was all she could do to stop herself from staring at how the cloth skimmed and outlined his muscles.

She tore her gaze away to focus on her computer. "It's nine thirty. I'm obscenely early judging by the hours some of your programmers keep." She hit a few keys. She had no idea which ones. Her concentration was shot between the message from her mother and Luke's presence. "Do you need something?"

He unfolded himself from the doorway and walked to her desk until he stood before it. "Just you."

What the— She whipped her head up, thoughts bouncing around at the speed of light. Had he hit his head sometime between now and last night? Was he on drugs? Had he been replaced by a robot with the wrong programming? Before she could come up with another explanation, his long fingers tilted her face farther up. Then his lips closed over hers.

Shock caused her to remain still. And then the electricity that always arced between them took over, opening her mouth wide in welcome, tangling and sliding her tongue against his. Warmth began to tug deep in her belly and pool between her legs. She heard a squeak of a moan and realized it came from her. She couldn't pull away from him if she tried.

She didn't want to try.

He broke contact first. "Good morning. I didn't get a chance to say it earlier." His gaze burned with want. But his mouth was set in a firm line, and tension held his shoulders straight.

"Morning," she stammered, gathering her thoughts from where they had flown into the ionosphere. "What brought—"

He shook his head slightly, as if in warning. "I want to introduce you to someone. An old friend. I don't think you've met." He straightened up and stepped back, and Danica realized there was a woman standing in her doorway. She barely had time to process her expensive haircut and her impeccable designer outfit when Luke spoke. "Danica, meet Irene Stavros. We went to business school together. Irene, meet Danica. My wife."

His...*what?* Danica stared at him as he sat on a corner of her desk. Nor did she resist when he picked up her left hand and held it firmly in his. She'd heard him wrong. Right?

One glance at Irene and Danica knew, no, she had indeed heard him correctly. Irene's face was smoothly noncommittal, but Danica's experience as an executive recruiter meant she was rather good at reading others. Irene vibrated with curiosity.

Luke, what are you doing? Danica tugged her left hand free and stood up, offering Irene her right to shake. "Nice to meet you. I've heard a lot about you." The latter was not a lie.

Irene's handshake was firm, almost bruising. "Charmed," she said. "I wish I could say the same about you. But this bad boy here never said a word. You kept this very quiet, Luke," she chided lightly.

"Oh, well, you know," Danica said with a shrug, hoping to appear nonchalant on the surface. "We're quiet types." Underneath, a bubbling mixture of disbelief, anger and shock twisted and roiled. Besides, what else could she say? She didn't know what Luke had told Irene or why Luke came up with such a preposterous story in the first place. What she did know is she didn't like the amused glint in Irene's gaze as it travelled from the top of Danica's ponytail to her practical low-heeled pumps.

"No, I'm afraid I don't know," Irene said after she finished her visual inspection, with a smile bordering on a smirk. "You're not even wearing a ring. You must tell me sometime how this whirlwind marriage came to be. Perhaps lunch? Are you free?"

"No," Luke said firmly. "She's having lunch with me. Sorry, but the reservation is only for two. You understand."

"Mmm-hmm." Irene continued to regard Danica with

a mixture of appraisal and mirth. "And restaurants never allow reservations to be changed, of course."

Danica unfolded the arms she had been hugging to her chest. For a second, she was back in middle school, her thrift-shop dress and unruly curls the target of girls with shining straight hair and the latest fashions from the mall.

Then she remembered she had weapons of her own.

"Sure," she said. "Come to lunch with us." She picked up Luke's hand and pressed a kiss into his palm. "It would be fun, right, honey?"

His fingers tightened on hers. "I was looking forward to having you all to myself," he rumbled, tilting her chin up so he could press a kiss on her lips. "Irene reminded me we need to pick up our rings."

She was pretty sure he kissed her just to hide his smirk, but she kissed him back anyway, her eyes fluttering closed, before she remembered it was just playacting. "We have plenty of time for that. Wouldn't it be fun getting to know Irene better?" She beamed at the other woman.

"You two are just so adorable," Irene said, her expression still amused. But her smile no longer met her eyes. "I'd be delighted—" A shrill buzz cut off her words. She dug into her Hermès Kelly bag and brought out a sleek new phone. "It looks like I won't be free for lunch anyway. Duty calls." She looked up from the device. "My father can't wait to meet Veronica."

"Danica," Luke said.

"Right." Irene typed the name into her phone. She pulled a business card out of her purse and handed it to Danica. "Do call me. I'd love to throw you a party to celebrate the happy occasion. Don't worry, it will be a small gathering. But there are some people I'm sure you're not acquainted with that you really must know." She smiled a perfect smile of perfect teeth surrounded by perfect red lips.

Danica was abruptly reminded she didn't put on makeup that morning. Still, she returned Irene's expression, bared incisor for bared incisor. "Sounds delightful," she gushed.

"Great! In the meantime, I'll send Luke the details of my stylist. Just in case you don't have your own." Her bright gaze lingered on Danica's blouse, bought on clearance several years ago at a discount store. "But now, I better run. So nice seeing you, Luke. Congratulations, again. Danica, lovely to meet you. Talk to you soon." She waved, a slight bending of fingers at the tips, and left the cramped office.

Danica waited until Irene disappeared. Then she went to the door and peered down the hallway.

"She's gone," Luke said.

"I wasn't looking for her," Danica said, shutting the door and whirling on the balls of her feet to face Luke. "I wanted to make sure no one could hear me yell at you." Her pulse beat in her throat, threatening to close off her airways. "I may have slept with you last night, but that doesn't give you permission to pull me into your game with Irene!"

Luke took a step toward her, his hands held out. "Danica—"

"Don't come closer," she warned. The last thing she needed was to be overcome by Luke's nearness. Or for him to kiss her again. She was angry, damn it, and she had the right to be angry.

"I know you're upset," Luke began.

"Understatement of the century. Try furious, livid, rage filled—"

He held up a hand. "And you deserve to be. But think about it. It's a win-win."

She scoffed. "This may come as a shock, but every woman who sleeps with you doesn't automatically want to marry you."

Despite her warning, he took two steps toward her.

She moved backward until her rear end hit the door. She took comfort from the solid material. She could be just as unyielding. If she tried.

"Think about it," he said. "It's the right solution to the search."

"Luke—" she warned.

"I know you're not happy with me."

"Again, understatement of the century."

A ghost of a smile momentarily creased his face. "The century is still relatively young. I can live with that."

Despite everything, her lips quirked upward.

"And we kill whatever story Cinco Jackson is planning," he continued.

She frowned. "Marrying your search consultant doesn't put out that fire. On the contrary."

"How can I look at other women when I have you in my life?" A spark lit deep in his gaze.

It was amusement. It had to be. But for a brief second, Danica imagined what it would be like if his words were the truth. If she mattered to his life, was the center of his focus. She swallowed, hard, and looked away. "What's the other win?"

"You fulfill the terms of your contract. Before the deadline, so you qualify for the bonus."

"Bonus?"

He held up three fingers and counted them down as he spoke. "Jayne, Felicity and you. That makes three candidates I've accepted."

"But I'm not a candidate." She laughed. It was either that or cry. "Last night was…last night. I wanted to be there. It wasn't an audition. I don't meet the criteria."

"You think fast on your feet, you handled the Felicity situation with grace under pressure, and I received a thank-you this morning from the Peninsula Society. Grayson Monk gave a very generous donation. He credited you for daring him to match your winnings at the roulette table." He moved a step closer, his blue gaze frank and warm. "You more than fulfill the requirements."

Every cell in her body ached to believe him. Then she remembered he was a skilled negotiator, while she was tired, worried for her family and still on sensory overload from the night before.

She shook her head. "I can't be part of a pretend marriage."

"Who said anything about pretending?"

She blinked rapidly, trying to parse his meaning. "Of course we'd be pretending."

"No. We'll be married. As soon as possible."

He spoke in English, but his words didn't make sense. "Married? Like, *married* married?"

"If by married married you mean legally, then yes."

"Married...in every sense of the word?"

His gaze fell to her chest. Her nipples tightened at the visible appreciation in his eyes. "That would be an advantage of this deal."

Would it ever... Wait. He was far too sure of himself. "Again, just because I slept with you once, it does not mean I want to repeat it, much less be legally tied to you."

The hot light left his gaze. He ran his right hand through his hair, leaving it mussed. Just like it looked when she'd stood by his bed and said goodbye. "I know our association started to save the acquisition. And I still need to present a wife to Nestor Stavros."

"I'm your recruiter." Even as she said the words, a memory flash of how he'd caused her to scream his name turned her cheeks to flame. "We agreed last night would not affect our business relationship."

He moved closer. There was a slight bite mark just

below his jaw. She could still taste his skin, the rasp of his whiskers stinging her tongue. If she just leaned forward, she could kiss that reddened area better...or do more damage.

Right now, she was torn.

"We would still have a business relationship. We'll have a new contract. With a marriage certificate as an addendum," he stated.

She narrowed her gaze. "Explain."

"I hired you to find a wife to demonstrate to Nestor I've changed. We'll extend our arrangement to you fulfilling the role of the wife. We act like a faithful couple in public, the goal is achieved, and the acquisition goes through."

"And after you get what you want?" His scent wafted over her. It made her think of rumpled bedsheets and hot skin sliding against hers and his mouth...oh, his mouth.

His gaze searched hers. "That's up to us. To you." There was a note in his voice she'd never heard before. It almost sounded tentative.

But Luke didn't do tentative. He cut relationships and walked away. She suspected that was partly why the current situation with Irene got under his skin. He couldn't shun Irene and still work with Nestor.

The late night, the lack of sleep and the churning turmoil in her nervous system made it hard to think. Although even if she had slept a full eight hours it would still be difficult to think when he stood so close. She could see the streaks of dark lapis lazuli in his ocean-blue eyes.

"Danica?"

Too late, she realized he had continued to speak. "I'm sorry?"

"I said this wasn't the way I wanted to ask you. I did want to take you to lunch. Irene forced the timetable."

"I don't—you mean this wasn't just a spur-of-the-moment plan when you saw Irene?" Her heart leapt, just a little.

"I thought of it last night. After you left." His mouth twisted and he reached out to cup her cheek, a brief caress that shouldn't cause her blood to ignite but… "I couldn't sleep."

She shouldn't, in all fairness both to him and to her, agree to marry him. She deserved better than a marriage proposition with all the romance of an annual report presented to the board of directors. He deserved better too, even if he wouldn't admit it.

She had sworn off being involved with men who cared more about their reputation than they did about her. She had been already hurt, badly, by a boyfriend who used people as a stepping stone to getting what he wanted. She swore to never again let her heart be used in that manner.

But her bed was a different matter, as the liquid heat gathering deep in her belly reminded her. As long as she remembered this was a business deal, why not continue to have the best sex imaginable? She nodded, licking her very dry lips. "Yes," she said, her voice rough.

"Yes?" His gaze traced the contours of her mouth.

"Yes," she repeated, but held up her hand when he stepped closer. "Until Ruby Hawk is acquired by the Stavros Group."

His blue eyes darkened, but otherwise he showed no reaction. Was he elated? Deflated? She wished she knew. Finally, a corner of his mouth dented his cheek. "Until the acquisition goes through."

"Deal." She held out her hand to be shaken. He drew her into his arms instead, enveloping her with his strength and warmth. She fought the urge to place her head on his chest, close her eyes and breathe in his scent.

Don't get attached, she sternly warned herself.

"The clock starts now," he rumbled. Right before his mouth met hers, he whispered, "I'm going to make the time count."

Her last thought, before all ability to form coherent sentences melted away, was her warning came too late.

Eight

In a perfect world, Danica would be thrilled. It was her wedding day. Her groom was a shining star who stood out even in Silicon Valley's crowded galaxy. Her family wouldn't have a financial worry for the foreseeable future. Matt's therapy could continue until he didn't need it, not end when an insurance company cut off the funds. She should be the happiest person walking through the metal detectors at the entrance to the San Mateo County courthouse at that moment.

She was petrified.

In less than twenty-four hours, Luke somehow managed to get a marriage license and arrange for a courthouse ceremony, to be held at two thirty in the afternoon on the dot. The only thing she oversaw was showing up. Which she managed to do, barely, after an hours-long wrestling match with her conscience in the wee hours of the night and a long talk with her roommate, Mai, in the morning.

She inhaled, counted to three, then exhaled. This was strictly business. They had a contract, drawn up after he left her office yesterday. She was walking into this marriage with her eyes open.

She had only herself to blame if she went into it with her emotions wide open too.

"Danica!" Luke was already in the waiting area, early. His crisp azure blue shirt matched his eyes, and his charcoal suit fit him as if it had been made for him, as it no doubt had been. Judging by the looks thrown their way by the others nearby, she was considered to be a lucky bride indeed.

If only they knew.

"Hey. You're here." She managed to sound normal. Inside, she was shaking so hard, she was surprised she could keep her eyes focused.

"You look…" His voice trailed off. "You wore your hair down." He tucked a curl behind her ear, her skin burning where he brushed it. "You're beautiful."

A white lacy gown would have been absurd under the circumstances, but when she saw the pink floral shift dress hanging in the window of a Palo Alto boutique, she went ahead and splurged. "Thanks," she said, suddenly shy from all the eyes on them. She turned her head, so his kiss landed on her cheek. "I don't see Aisha. Let me call her."

"I'm here!" a woman's voice sang out. Danica turned and saw her investigator making her way to them. They needed one witness for the marriage certificate, and when Mai couldn't rearrange her shift at the hospital on such short notice, Danica called Aisha. She was not only a colleague but a friend and the most trustworthy person Danica knew. Aisha was paid well to keep people's secrets private, and Danica was sure she would be discreet about the wedding, as well.

Aisha was stunning in her full-skirted dress, her dark skin glowing against the daffodil yellow fabric. She gave Danica a once-over with her shrewd gaze, then handed a small bouquet of white roses to her. "Brought these just in case. Looks like you might need them."

"I knew there was something I forgot." Danica's smile was only half-faked. "You look great."

"Not every day I get to be a bridesmaid at the last minute," Aisha laughed. "How did you arrange this so fast anyway?"

"Friend-of-the-family favor." Luke said. His phone buzzed, and he looked at the screen. "If you two will excuse me? I'll be right back."

Danica watched him leave. When Aisha touched her shoulder, she jumped.

"That's some bridal nerves," Aisha deadpanned.

"Yeah, well, y'know." Danica's gaze focused on Luke's receding back.

"Actually, I don't. Can we talk privately? Before the groom returns?"

Danica wrenched her gaze away. Aisha sounded serious. And when she was serious, it meant whatever she had to say wasn't good news. "What's up?"

"Cinco Jackson. Why is he calling my office and asking about you? Does it have something to do with this sudden wedding?"

"He's asking about me? What did he say?" Danica's nerves were already scrambled. This put them into a blender set on high.

Aisha shrugged. "How long have I worked with you, did I know you well, how long you have worked for Dallas, general stuff like that."

Danica searched Aisha's gaze. "Did you tell him about the wedding?" Luke planned to put out an announcement eventually, but without mentioning the date. Just a general "Luke Dallas and Danica Novak are pleased to announce their marriage. The bride and groom will reside in Atherton, etc."

"Of course not!" Aisha scoffed. "That's your personal business. But a few days ago, you had me checking on women's marital statuses, and now you're the one getting married? Jackson isn't the only one who is curious."

She sounded miffed. Danica didn't have many friends in California. She didn't want to lose this one. "It's...a spur-of-the-moment decision. But one we've thought through."

"Right." Aisha didn't look convinced, and why would she? Danica's words didn't make sense to herself. "Dallas is incredibly well connected, his mother practically owns Bay Area society, and yet it's just the two of you plus me here for the ceremony?"

Danica tried again. "We didn't want a circus. Just us."

Aisha's expression was still skeptical. "Word on the street is there's some sort of snag with the Ruby Hawk acquisition, and that snag is the Stavros family and whatever they have on Dallas. I don't know what's going on, but I've done some work for Irene and you do not want to be on her bad side."

"Why would marrying Luke put me on Irene's bad side?" Danica widened her gaze.

Aisha regarded her for a beat. "Hey, if that's the way you want to play it, fine with me. Like I said, it's your life."

"There's nothing—"

Luke walked back to them. He offered his arm to Danica, causing the hyperactive butterflies in her stomach to go into overdrive. "Shall we?" he said. "We're up."

From what she was told later by Aisha, it was a perfectly adequate ceremony. She remembered nothing except squeaking out her responses at the appropriate time and the warm pressure, over far too soon, of Luke's lips on hers. The rest was a blur. Before she knew it, they stood outside the courthouse, the crushed bouquet still in Danica's hands.

"Congratulations, again," Aisha said. "I have to get back to work, but you two go celebrate." She hugged Danica tightly. "I was wrong," she whispered into Danica's ear. "He stares at you like you're a rare steak and he's a contestant on a wilderness-survival show who hasn't eaten in a week." She drew back and gave Danica a wide smile. "Call me. But I expect you to be otherwise occupied for a month, maybe two." She waggled her eyebrows as punctuation.

Danica laughed, even though Aisha was wrong. If Luke looked at her with any hunger, it was because he wanted the acquisition and she was the means to achieving it. Aisha waved goodbye and then Danica was alone.

With Luke. Her husband. Her mouth suddenly was parched and the world spun, once, before it righted itself.

He cleared his throat. "I still owe you that lunch. Hungry?"

Since she had barely been able to eat a bite since he'd walked into her office the day before, she nodded.

"Good." He took her hand. The left one, now sporting a three-carat diamond. "Your fingers are cold."

His weren't. "I did just get married. Better cold fingers than cold feet, I suppose." She tried to smile at him. She was somewhat successful.

His grip tightened. "Thank you, again."

"A deal is a deal. And it's only until you secure the acquisition."

A crease appeared between his eyebrows. "But in the meantime, we are married."

"Of course," she said lightly. "We are. But it's not like that was a real ceremony." She was babbling, but she couldn't stop it.

"I have a certificate that says otherwise."

"I know. But—" she threw out her free hand "—my family wasn't there. And no organist playing 'My Shot' from *Hamilton*."

He stopped walking, causing her to jerk to a stop. "*What* is the organist playing?"

"I can't have 'Here Comes the Bride' played at my wedding. I hate everything about it."

He laughed. It made him devastatingly handsome, his eyes crinkling in the corners. "Of course. Who doesn't?"

"It's such a cliché." She could feel herself relaxing, her shoulders descending to their normal position as they resumed walking. "It's practically a parody of itself. Give me something with more personal meaning."

"And the song you mentioned?"

"It's about taking all the opportunities life hands you. Taking a risk. Like—" She stopped, suddenly aware of who she was talking to. And why.

"Like marriage." He nodded. "I get it." They reached his car and he unlocked the passenger door and ushered her in.

"Like love," she added under her breath while he went around to the driver's side and slid behind the steering wheel. The car didn't have the largest interior to begin with. With him in it, all the oxygen seemed to suddenly disappear. All she had to do was move her hand and she could stroke his thigh. "Where are you taking me to lunch?" She winced. It had come out far too loud.

"That's up to you." He pushed the ignition button and the car purred to life. "I know a nice place not too far from here. Or…"

"Or?"

He turned to her. With a shiver, she realized perhaps Aisha wasn't too off base in her estimation. He did look hungry. The tiger was back. "Or," he said in a deep rumble, picking up her hand and pressing a kiss in her palm, "we go to my place."

Heat instantly pooled between her legs. "You weren't kidding about this being a real marriage."

He shook his head, his blue gaze watching her closely. "No. But as I said, up to you." His thumb gently caressed the back of her hand, drawing lazy circles. Her breasts ached to have the same attention paid to them.

He was hers now. Well, legally, and for as long as the contract was in effect. This may be a business arrangement, but she'd agreed because of the perks that went with it. Like a naked Luke Dallas, tangled in sweaty sheets, about to ensure his prowess would leave her unable to see straight. She smiled and let her hand settle on his thigh. "Do you have champagne at home?"

His blue gaze turned indigo dark. "On ice."

She leaned her torso toward him until their mouths almost touched. "I'm in the mood. For champagne," she whispered against his lips.

He raised his hands and tangled them in her hair. "So am I. But not for champagne." Then he kissed her, insistent, demanding, thoroughly ravaging her mouth until stars pinwheeled around her. She whimpered, irrationally angry at the center console that separated their seats, and he broke away, his breathing heavy. He put the car into drive and they sped out of the parking lot.

This—the way she instantly flared into flame at his touch, the taunt excitement that tortured and pleased them both—would be enough. She could make it be enough. She wouldn't have love, but she would have passion. She could be happy with that, for the duration of their time together.

Or so she told herself.

* * *

Danica put down the phone, happy to finish her conversation with her parents and Matt. Then she felt guilty for being happy. True to his word, Luke had paid Danica her promised fee plus bonus the day after the wedding, and she'd sent it to her family. Knowing she secured their house for the time being had been almost enough to make up for the twinges of conscience that had come with announcing her marriage to Luke. Her parents had been shocked she'd wed a man they hadn't met, and she'd finally gotten out of that discussion by promising she and Luke would visit them as soon as Matt, whose recovery still moved too slowly, felt up to it. The weekly conversations since had been still a bit awkward, but so far she'd managed to answer their questions to their satisfaction.

She opened a file on her computer. Since the wedding, life had settled into something resembling a routine, if *routine* could ever be a word applied to life with Luke Dallas. Luke still needed a director to run Ruby Hawk's community outreach, and Danica had several new candidates to interview. She also had to finish a report on the charitable causes the foundation could support, as Luke wanted Ruby Hawk's technology to be involved.

What she should be doing, however, was concentrating on her business plan for her own executive-search company. She wouldn't be at Ruby Hawk forever.

But facing up to that reality meant facing up to her inevitable parting from Luke. When she'd agreed to marry Luke, she'd known sex with him could be mind-blowing fun. She'd had no idea their first night only scratched the surface of the erotic gratification in store.

When work hours were over and they were alone...she shivered, her mind filled with images from the night before. His mouth, hot, plundering, exploring every inch of her skin, his tongue taking her to heights she didn't know existed before she shattered into mindless shards. She never imagined—

As if her thoughts conjured him up, he walked into her office, his head down as he read something on his smartphone. Her heart gave a skip and a hop, noting the way his tailored shirt hugged his chest, skimmed over the six-pack of abs she knew was underneath. It would be the work of only a few buttons and her hands could glide over his skin...

He stopped in front of her desk. "Did you put together this proposal for using Ruby Hawk's technology to make youth sports leagues safer?" he asked.

Ah. He was in work mode. She'd have to save those thoughts until that night. "Is there something wrong?"

"Not at all. It's good." He put the phone in his pocket and sat on the edge of her desk. "Why didn't you say you were passionate about injuries in youth sports? Did you play?"

"Me?" She laughed. "I'm the proverbial wrong-way kid. My first soccer game, I kicked two goals for the other team. I'm much better at providing moral support."

"But you must have some knowledge. This is a very persuasive proposal. You obviously care deeply about the subject."

She wasn't sure if she wanted Luke to probe into her personal life. They were married but their intimacy was strictly physical. The one area she could keep separate from him was her family. If she let him in, all the way, she might not have the strength to walk away when their contract ended. She chewed on her lower lip.

"I've done a lot of reading about concussions and their effect on the brain. Don't get me wrong—involvement in team sports is beneficial. But Ruby Tech has an opportunity to put sensors using its biofeedback algorithms into equipment to make it safer."

He nodded. "The proposal is very clear on those points. You should talk to one of the lead engineers, however. It's hazy when it comes to tech specs."

"See?" She smiled. "I knew there was something wrong with it."

He got up from her desk and started for the door, allowing her to admire his perfect rear end in action. But instead of exiting he turned around to face her. "This is a good proposal. Stop selling yourself short."

A tendril of exasperation curled up her spine. "I don't."

"You do. You could be the foundation director if you wanted."

"I like recruitment."

"You could do more."

This felt like caring, coming from him. But it wasn't. She was merely a convenient means to an end. That the sex curled all their toes was just the cherry on this sundae. She had to keep reminding herself. "I'm good at what I do."

"I didn't say you weren't. I said you could do more. Make a difference."

"Search does make a difference. I find people good jobs."

"I'm giving you a compliment."

"And I said thank you."

"I—" His phone rang, much to Danica's relief. She watched him take it out of his pocket and answer it. Then she watched a shutter fall over his expression, turning it blank and emotionless. "Yes… No… Yes…" he said at different intervals. Then he hung up and turned to leave her office. His movements were rigid, his shoulders held tight.

Her anger was doused, replaced by concern. She got up

from her chair and blocked him from exiting. "Who was on the phone?"

"No one," he said. "I'll see you at home tonight."

She narrowed her gaze. "What's wrong? Cinco Jackson? Nestor? Irene?" The last name tasted like vinegar on her lips.

Irene had been friendly—too friendly. Every day brought a new invitation: lunch, a shopping trip, tickets to a charity event, seats at the San Francisco Symphony. Danica finally attended a tea to benefit a local women's shelter. Much to her surprise, Danica enjoyed herself. Irene was friendly and very charming. No wonder Luke had had an off-and-on "benefits" relationship with her.

He shook his head as if trying to shoo off a winged insect. "An appointment I thought would be cancelled."

The phone screen in his hand was flashing. "You're getting another phone call."

He cursed under his breath. Then he answered. "What? I just hung up with her… I said I would be there… No… I said, no." His index finger punched End, but not before Danica saw the caller ID. Jonathan Dallas.

"Family?" she asked.

"My father," he agreed.

"That's the appointment?" She knew Luke's father had retired to West Palm Beach, Florida, while his mother and her current husband traveled between their homes in San Francisco, Paris and Cape Town. "Is he in town? Should we invite him over for dinner?"

His mouth twisted. "Hell, no. Lunch on neutral ground is bad enough. They're suggesting we meet in Half Moon Bay. Driving over the mountains in the middle of a work day is supposed to be convenient for me."

His phone rang again. This time the caller ID read Phoebe Ailes. Luke hit a button and the ringing stopped.

He put the phone in his pocket and regarded Danica. "You should consider taking the foundation job."

Nice try. She wasn't biting. "If your parents are in town, why haven't I met them?"

"You're being nosy." It was not a compliment.

"I'm always nosy. It's what I do. I pry into people's lives so I can find the right employment fit."

"I have a job. To which I need to get back." His words were reinforced with steel.

She sighed and stepped aside. "Fine. But if you want to talk about your family, I'm here."

"I wouldn't wish that on anyone. Especially not on you." He opened the door.

Danica was no stranger to Luke's moods. He could be cold, dictatorial even, when people tried to cross him. But when the discussions were reasonable or philosophical, he was thoughtful, witty even. In their bed, he could be tender—so tender it caused her heart to ache with a longing she didn't dare dwell on.

Right now he looked bruised. She never thought Luke could be hurt by others, much less his own parents. She couldn't imagine not cherishing family and being cherished by them in return. The realization punctured her heart.

"I want to go to lunch with you."

He blinked. She felt a momentary burst of pride. It took a lot to surprise him.

"No, you don't." His tone was final.

"Yes, I do." No, she didn't. She was scared spitless. And it meant canceling her appointment to look at a promising commercial real-estate site for her agency. But his parents were another piece to the puzzle that was Luke.

"Are you sure? The reason for the lunch is they heard about the marriage." He grimaced. "Not from me."

"You didn't—" Her mouth snapped shut and she took

three deep breaths. "Why wouldn't you tell them about me? It's not like it's a real marriage."

"It's not that. I didn't tell them because..." He shrugged. "Because in the bigger scheme, they didn't need to know."

She silently counted to ten. "Of course, they need to know if you're married! You're their son."

"The only concerns my parents have about my marriage are how much value you bring to the family coffers and/or how much it will take to buy you off when necessary. I was hoping to avoid the confrontation."

Now it was her turn to blink. "You're kidding."

"No. You sure you want to come to lunch?" He obviously expected her to say no.

He forgot she was the one who bet all her money on a turn of the roulette wheel. "I need to meet them at some point. After all, we're married, even if there is an expiration date."

"It's your funeral."

"Oh, come on." She smoothed faint wrinkles from the shoulders of his shirt. "It can't be that bad."

It was, exactly, that bad. Danica and Luke arrived at the upscale bistro at one o'clock on the dot, thanks to Luke's sports car. She gripped the armrest the entire way as he sped along the twisty mountain roads he took to avoid the traffic on the freeways. She was still recovering from the last switchback he took while overtaking another vehicle.

"Feeling better?" Luke asked.

"Save your concern for the driver of the minivan we passed. I think you took ten years off that man's life." She smoothed back escaped tendrils of hair. They bounced back to framing her face as soon as her hand fell to her side. Luke reached out and twisted a curl around his finger.

"I prefer it down." The rumble of his voice and the stroke

of his thumb on her cheek nearly took her knees out. Luckily for her, the hostess returned with a wide smile on her face.

"I'll take you to the rest of your party." The hostess beckoned, and Luke reached out for Danica's hand without looking at her. The automatic gesture caused her to smile. She was still smiling when they arrived at the secluded patio table set for four. Two of the chairs were occupied, but the occupants were busy staring at their phones.

Luke cleared his throat. His grip on her hand tightened.

The older man, who had to be Luke's father, looked up. "Well, hello there! Glad to see both of you," he said with a cheery smile. "I'm Jonathan."

"This is—" Luke began.

"We know who she is," the older woman said, still staring at her phone. "Just not from you." Luke's mother was blonde and fair skinned, but Danica couldn't discern any other distinguishing features thanks to the oversize sunglasses dominating her face.

"This is Danica," Luke finished. "Danica, my parents. Jonathan Dallas and Phoebe Ailes." He tightened his grip on her hand. "Don't say I didn't warn you," he breathed into her ear.

Danica nudged him sharply with her elbow and then removed her hand to hold it out to his mother. "Pleased to meet you, Mrs. Ailes."

Luke's mother looked up from her phone screen at the proffered hand, gave it one firm pump and let it go in favor of returning to her device. "Likewise," she said, not a flicker of emotion on her expression. Her sunglasses remained on.

Luke pulled out the empty chair next to his father for Danica and helped her into it. "Call her Phoebe," he said. "I do."

His father reached for Danica's hand and carried it to his lips. "Very charmed to meet such a lovely lady," Jonathan said after slowly releasing her fingers.

"Thank you." Danica smiled at Luke's father. He was a remarkably handsome man. But there wasn't much of a resemblance between father and son. Jonathan was Teflon slick, from his carefully coiffed salt-and-pepper hair to his impeccably manicured nails. Nor did Danica see much of Phoebe in Luke. His mother resembled a diamond, all polished and glittering surfaces, from her caramel-streaked hair shining like a helmet in the sun to the heavy gold chains wrapped around her neck and wrists.

Luke consisted of rough edges and dangerous angles. His dark hair was tousled, a sure signal he had run his hands through it more than once, his heavy brows drawn together. That was fine with Danica. She preferred the brooding man of the moors to his magazine-glossy parents.

"So." Phoebe finally put down the phone. "This is a surprise. Luke said you were too busy to join us. Danielle, is it?"

"Danica." Luke took the seat next to his mother and across from Danica. His loafer-clad foot nudged hers. "You know her name. And she cleared her schedule for this, so be nice."

His mother waved him off. "Perhaps if you had told us you were married, instead of leaving us to find out from Irene Stavros of all people, I would be better acquainted with my new daughter-in-law's name."

Danica shot a look at Luke.

Luke shook his head, once. His loafer nudged her ballet-slipper flats under the table again, and then he cleared his throat. "Few people knew about the wedding. Danica and I decided we wanted something quiet and private."

Luke's mother huffed and launched into a rejoinder, but

Danica didn't hear her. Of *course* Irene told Luke's parents. Wasn't the reason Luke needed to find a wife because of the Stavros-Dallas feud? They belonged to the same world of high finance and cutthroat business deals, private jets and unlimited bank accounts. While she…she was just a temporary interloper. With a temporary contract.

"Is something wrong, dear?" Phoebe's eyebrows rose above the rim of her sunglasses.

"Not a thing," Danica said, flipping open her menu and running her gaze down the page. "What is everyone having? I can't decide."

"You're so pale." Phoebe's tone shifted, turning so sweet it could be used to trap wasps. "You're not…queasy, I hope? Or faint?"

"No. I'm fine." Aside from the fact that meeting Phoebe and Jonathan thrust Danica's sham arrangement into the light, exposing shady corners she purposefully tried to avoid.

Luke snapped his menu open. "The ceviche here is good," he said to Danica. "You'd like it. Raw fish, no spice."

"Raw fish? I don't think that's advisable," Phoebe said. "Perhaps the petit filet mignon, although of course one needs to be careful of listeria."

"Listeria?" Danica raised her eyebrows at Luke. "Is that like mad cow or E. coli?"

"She's not pregnant, Phoebe." Luke turned to Danica. "Listeria is a food-based bacterium that can cause serious health issues during pregnancy. Care to split the ceviche as an appetizer?"

"How do you know that?" Danica asked Luke.

"Ordering meals with Anjuli when she was pregnant with her twins," Luke answered. "Maybe you should get your own ceviche. I know how much you like your fish."

Phoebe cleared her throat. Danica and Luke turned

to look at her. "If she's not pregnant, then why did you rush into marriage?" She took her sunglasses off, revealing piercing dark blue eyes. They seemed to be the only feature her son inherited. But while Luke's gaze could be cold and distant, it was never as icy as the arctic blast directed at Danica.

"Define 'rush,'" Luke answered. "How do you feel about lobster rolls as a main course?" he asked Danica. "This place is famous for them."

"Wait—you think I'm pregnant?" Danica blinked several times in Phoebe's direction, struggling to wrap her mind around the question. Sure, she and Luke frequently engaged in the activity required for creating a child, but even if she were pregnant—and she wasn't—she would barely be aware of it herself. A chuckle escaped her lips as she turned to face Luke. "Is this a question every woman you bring to meet your parents receives, or just me?"

Phoebe closed her menu and put it down on the plate in front of her, careful to square the corners so they were aligned perfectly with the plane of the table. "My son has never been married before, Danielle. And certainly not to someone whom we've never met, whose name barely shows up in a web search, much less on any social rosters of any import."

"You've learned to use a web browser. Good for you," Luke said. "Let's cut to the chase. You wanted to inspect my wife. Here she is. She even agreed to the inspection, which says far more about her than any internet search could. Now, can we order?"

Jonathan cleared his throat. "It's a rare occasion when I can have lunch with my son and his beautiful wife." He patted Danica's hand where it rested on the table's surface. "It's such a nice day, wouldn't you agree? I do miss living here at times. Tell me, did you grow up in California?"

"No, Rhode Island."

"Ah, Newport! I know it quite well. Do you sail? I've always said there is nothing in a man's soul that can't be cured by an hour of wind in your hair and sea salt in your face. Bracing!" He chuckled, his eyes crinkling in the corners.

"Sorry, I don't sail," Danica said. "And you probably know Newport better than I do."

"Tennis, then. Surely you play. We must have you out to the club when you come to Florida. Doubles, perhaps, although you two kids would wipe us old folks off the court. Speaking of—" he turned to Luke "—your stepmother and I are at the top of doubles ladder this month, again. The interclub tournament should be a cakewalk this year. At the board meeting, I told them the club is going to need a bigger trophy case. Ha!" He guffawed. "The guys at the club are still laughing."

"Danica isn't much for organized sports," Luke said, flashing a conspiratorial grin in her direction.

"No?" Jonathan's eyebrows met in the middle of his forehead. "Golf?"

She shook her head.

"What about skiing? That's not too organized. Especially not the way we do it." He chuckled and shook his head. "By the time we arrive in Vail and open the house, it's too late to hit the slopes. We hit the schnapps."

"Sure. I ski," Danica said. She had a feeling if she didn't land on a sport, Jonathan would continue to quiz her until he found one. And it wasn't a lie. Much. In high school she went on a school trip to a ski resort in New Hampshire and fell down the bunny slope a few times.

"Great!" Jonathan flashed two rows of very white, very straight teeth at her. "It's settled. Christmas in Colorado."

"Dad—" Luke began.

"Oh, please, Jonathan." Phoebe cut off her son. "One,

you just met the girl. Two, no one knows who she is or what she wants from Luke. This…whatever it is…came wholly out of the blue and I can't believe you're swallowing this malarkey. Three, you have no idea if she will still be around next week, much less by Christmas. Four, Irene said—"

"All right." The thunderclouds building on Luke's expression erupted into a storm. He stood up. "You wanted a meeting, you got one. It's now over." He put his hands on the back of Danica's chair, ready to pull it out so she could stand up. "Danica, let's go."

"Lucas Dallas, sit down," Phoebe commanded. "We're not done, and we won't be until we've figured out how to handle this situation you got yourself into. You have very specific obligations to uphold and we need a plan."

"I have a plan," he responded. His gaze caught Danica's. It brimmed with many things, chief among them long-held pain mixed with frustrated exasperation.

And apology. To her. For exposing her to this. Concern, for any discomfort his parents caused her. Her heart squeezed so hard, she was surprised she could still breathe.

He broke contact to look at his parents. "And the plan is we're leaving. Ready?" He offered his hand to Danica.

No. She wasn't ready. She didn't know what to do. What to say. Phoebe wasn't wrong. Danica might still be around for the coming Christmas, but she wouldn't be present for Christmases further in the future. Her relationship with Luke was indeed, from a certain point of view, malarkey.

But not for the reasons Phoebe inferred. Danica didn't want anything from Luke or his family. Certainly not money—although, her guilty conscience piped up, she accepted the consulting gig because of the dollars he promised her. *But it wasn't the reason why you agreed to the marriage*, her libido shot back.

Her heart remained silent, but only because she knew

what it would say. She was in love with Luke. Had been, ever since their dinner at the taqueria.

It was also hopeless.

She rose to her feet, wincing at the loud noise as the metal chair scraped across the tiled patio floor. "Mrs. Ailes, I understand your concern. This is the first time you've met me, and I'm married to your son. I would be suspicious if I were in your shoes too."

Luke's gaze flashed a warning signal she would be stupid to ignore.

She did so anyway. "I'll tell you the truth. Your son—"

"Danica." Luke's tone could have carved granite. He wasn't cautioning her to stop speaking. He was demanding.

"Your son," she started again, despite the typhoon of disapproval aimed in her direction, "is a very special man. I didn't want to fall in love with him. I fought it." *Did I ever.* "But the more time I spent in his presence, the more it was inevitable."

She didn't dare look at Luke. Still, she sensed he held himself ramrod straight, not moving a muscle. "I know this marriage is sudden, but the emotion is real." *On my side, at least.*

She took a deep breath, and then slowly let it out. "I can't impress you. But you should be very impressed by your son. He deserves your trust and support, in all matters. Including who he marries." *Whoever she will be, after I'm long gone.*

Phoebe stared at Danica throughout her speech, her dark blue gaze unblinking. But at the end, she raised one perfectly groomed eyebrow and nodded, ever so slightly.

"That was a beautiful speech, my dear," Jonathan said. "Just beautiful." He turned to his ex-wife. "See, Phoebe, it won't be a problem getting her to sign a postnup even though the wedding already occurred. You always did worry over trivial things." He clapped his hands together. "Well, now that we have that settled, let's have a meal. Sit back down, you two."

Danica barely heard him over the whooshing of her pulse beating loudly in her ears. She didn't dare look at Luke. "I need to visit the ladies' room. You three talk." She walked-ran toward the dim, cool interior of the restaurant.

But once she was inside, shivering in the air conditioning, she did not turn down the hallway the hostess indicated to her. Instead she turned right, through the central dining room toward the main exit to the street, and kept walking.

She would never get used to Luke's world. Could never adjust. Ski chalets in Vail, country clubs, social rosters... she shook her head. It was as if she had spent the last half hour in another country. Scotland, maybe. Or Australia. Somewhere where she understood the basic words, but the context was wholly new.

She took in her surroundings for the first time. The main street was lined with restaurants and shops, the kind that had hand-painted wooden signs on the outside but scarves that cost as much as a monthly payment on her student loans displayed inside. A block away she spotted a turquoise bench, flanked by terracotta pots bursting with red geraniums. It was a bit too cheerful for her present mood, but at least she could sit and contemplate her next move.

The bench was warm from the sun, but an ocean breeze kept the temperature pleasant. Good, because her cheeks were hot enough to be a fire hazard. She cringed at the thought of seeing Luke after she'd declared her love for him to his parents, of all people. What must he be thinking? She drew her knees up, encircling them with her arms, and buried her face on top of them.

"You have a habit of running out of restaurants." Luke's solid presence sat down next to her.

She took a deep breath and raised her head. There was a faint smile on his face. He didn't seem upset she had run out on him and his family. If anything, he was a bit wary. As if he didn't know what to expect from her.

And why would he know what to expect, when that speech had surprised herself? Better to get this conversation over with so they can both pretend it never happened and go back to their previous arrangement. She unfolded her limbs and gave him a lopsided smile. "I didn't run out of the taqueria. I even offered to pay."

"I'm also counting the sushi at the benefit."

"Hey, Chef Nagao was the one who ran out. Of fish."

He smiled, but it didn't reach his eyes. His gaze remained wary. "I'm sorry," he said simply.

He was sorry? For what? She was the one who'd opened mouth, inserted foot, ankle and calf. "You have no need to apologize."

He snorted. "You were already doing me a favor by coming to lunch. You didn't have to give that speech too. Now I really owe you."

"A favor?" She unfolded her legs and sat up straight, turning so she could meet his gaze head on. He thought of what she said as a favor? She didn't know whether to be happy at the out he gave her or upset he thought her words weren't 100 percent real. "I didn't—"

He made an impatient sound deep in his throat. "You know what I mean. But that went above and beyond." He picked up her hand, rubbing his thumb across her knuckles. As always, hot lightning sparked where their hands connected and spread through her veins. "I appreciate it, Danica. I appreciate you."

Appreciate. It was a nice word. In the past, she'd wished Johanna had used it more frequently when applied to her work. But coming from Luke—

It was like being handed a brussels sprout when one craved a steak. She didn't want his appreciation. She wanted his love.

But it wasn't on the menu. She pulled her hand from his and gave him a wide smile. "Just trying to do my temporary husband a solid," she said brightly. "I'm sorry I ran out."

He gave her a one-sided smile. "I'm sorry I put you through that."

His approval wrapped around her like a warm blanket. It should be enough. He gave it so rarely.

But while she enjoyed his appreciation, it wasn't enough. Would never be enough. "You did warn me," she said, plastering a smile on her face. "We should go back to the restaurant, so I can apologize to your parents for being gone so long."

"You mean so they can apologize to you. Which they will. But they left right after you. Seems an earlier tee time for my father just happened to open up, while my mother conveniently forgot she had plans to meet friends in the city." He stood and offered her his right hand. "I know a great burger joint between here and Palo Alto. Interested?"

She nodded and took his hand, his fingers curling around hers, and he pulled her off the bench. It felt so natural to continue to hold his hand as they strolled through the charming downtown on the way back to his car. She paused to point out the terrible wine puns on display in a cheese shop. "Everything happens for a Riesling," she groaned.

"I just called to say Merlot," Luke countered. "Que Syrah, Syrah."

She laughed, turning to resume their journey toward the carpark. But she stopped, just for a second, when she caught a glimpse of their reflection in the shop's window.

They looked like a couple. A real couple. Out for a stroll, enjoying the beautiful weather. Enjoying each other.

But she knew the truth. Luke was engaged in a game of wits with Irene and Nestor Stavros, and she was just a chess piece. She kept her gaze focused on the sidewalk all the way back to the car.

Nine

Luke drove the borrowed truck as fast as the speed limit would allow to Danica's rented house. In the weeks since the marriage, Danica had spent nearly every night at his place, but she still maintained her own place. Finally, he'd put his foot down. It was important this marriage had all the appearances of a real one when Nestor returned to town. She needed to be in full residence at his place, not ping-ponging between two addresses. It surprised him how much he looked forward to seeing her clothes in his closet. Her books on his bookcase. He liked knowing there would be physical proof she was ensconced in his life.

He certainly didn't mind having Danica there at the end of every day. He'd never lived with anyone before—it had never made practical sense—but the longer he spent with Danica, the more the situation appealed to him. Already he could sense his house, purchased for its investment value, becoming a home. A place where he wanted to be, rather than a building in which to store items and sleep. Things were falling into place, neatly and orderly.

Except one. He couldn't tell if Danica wanted to move in as much as he wanted her to. The fisted knot in his stomach tightened. After the lunch with his parents, she had been quiet. Too quiet. He knew it had been a bad idea. But he'd calculated the risk and took it anyway. He'd figured the odds were in his favor, because she had a way of making even the most onerous obligations seem achievable and fun.

Then his parents had had to behave like, well, his parents. As long as he lived, he would always be grateful—and knocked off his feet—that Danica had stood up to them. No, strike that. She'd stood up for *him*. She'd gone toe to toe with the Demon Czarina of Bay Area society and the passive-aggressive charm offensive that was his father—and won.

Luke fought his own battles. He had ever since he could remember. He enjoyed it. He relished the strategy, the countermeasures, the surprise attacks. He thought fifteen steps ahead and eighteen months into the future. By the time his opponents gathered to attack, he had moved onto the next battlefield.

It was unsettling to have a champion. Unsettling, but triggering an almost painful warmth that swelled inside his chest.

He pulled the truck in front of a small, nondescript house. A chain link fence surrounded a patchy yard, littered with children's toys. Danica ran down the front path to meet him. Raising an eyebrow, he indicated the plastic dump trucks and naked baby dolls. "Something I don't know?"

"My roommate occasionally babysits to make extra money," she said, after accepting a kiss. "She has a good job as a pediatric nurse, but costs have skyrocketed the last few years." The front door opened directly into the living room, and she ushered Luke inside. The late afternoon sunshine barely pierced through the curtains lining the windows and did little to dispel the shadows. Still, he could see the room was well kept, even if most of the furniture had seen better days. Several cardboard boxes were stacked neatly against a wall.

"You didn't tell me you shared a house," he said.

"When I moved here, I didn't realize how expensive it is to live in the Bay Area. I was lucky Mai needed someone to rent her spare room and we hit it off. It worked out well. So, um…" Danica played with the bracelet on her wrist. "Thanks for coming over. But I was happy to call movers."

She was being tentative. Just like she'd been after the lunch with his parents. "Glad to help. Besides, I keep missing my trainer appointments. Someone, not naming names, keeps me occupied in bed in the early morning."

She laughed, and he relaxed. Maybe it was just nerves. They were legally married, but living together was a big step.

It didn't take long to load Danica's possessions from the front room. Mai owned most of the furniture, so it remained with the house. He frowned after they placed the last box inside the truck.

"What about the bedroom?" he asked. The ever-present spark when he was near Danica ignited even though now was not the time. No doubt the bed was stripped of its sheets and pillows. Too bad, because he couldn't think of a better way to recuperate from a short afternoon of moving medium-size boxes than by snuggling under the covers. And by *snuggling*, he meant hearing her breathily scream his name at least two or three times before burying himself in her warm depth.

"Um." Danica suddenly couldn't meet his gaze. "Everything I'm taking is in these boxes."

"In case you've forgotten, you're moving in with me today."

"What do you think you loaded into the truck?"

"A partial load."

Her eyes darkened. "We agreed I would live with you as your wife. I'm doing that. The sooner we get to your place, the sooner I can unpack."

Logically, she was right. He didn't care. It smacked of the false reassurances his parents would give him whenever a stepparent moved in or out. *Oh, they're just moving some unwanted things elsewhere, don't worry.* Or, *You can leave a few toys here, but maybe take the rest to your mom's house. What do you say? Just for now.* It was never "just for now." It was always forever.

"Where's your bedroom?"

"Down the left hallway. Why?"

He picked up an empty box and strode off.

"Oh, no, you don't." Danica caught up to him just as he reached what had to be her room. Here the heavy curtains were tied back to let in golden sunshine that accentuated the cheerful profusion of bright colors and floral prints. Artwork decorated the walls, and photos were crowded next to books on the shelves.

He thrust the box at her. "Get packing."

She rolled her eyes. "Stop being ridiculous. I'm keeping some of my things here, that's all."

"Why?"

Her gaze wouldn't meet his. "I honestly didn't think you would mind."

He did. More than he thought possible. "Not answering my question. Why—"

Then realization dropped on his head like an anvil. "Do

you think I will throw you out of my house when the contract is over?"

Red flooded her averted cheek.

It matched the shade filling his vision. "How could you—you don't trust me?"

Her gaze continued to fix on a point far to his right. "It's not that. But—"

"But you don't." The ground shifted under his feet, throwing everything he thought was solid and sure into question.

She sighed. "Our agreement is only until the Ruby Hawk deal is signed. That's less than a month away. So I asked Mai if I could continue to rent the room."

"I've been honest with you at every step—"

"Yes, but the steps keep changing! I was supposed to find you a bride. Not be the bride. Who knows what your next strategy will be?"

The room turned dark and muddled, the color running together in a muddy mess. "I wasn't aware you disliked being married to me," he managed to say.

Her eyes widened. "No! That's not what I mean! I love—" She stopped, and then pressed her lips together. "I am more than happy with our arrangement. But it has an end date. You don't expect me to hang around after it is over." She met his gaze straight on. "Do you?"

Did he?

He hadn't thought much past the completion of the deal with Nestor. By now, he should have gathered up all the data points and run a regression analysis to determine the natural course forward. But he had no plans past signing the paperwork with Nestor.

He and Danica could make a plan. Together.

He opened his mouth but was cut off by a shake of her head. "No, of course you don't. And I didn't expect you to."

Her dismissal stung. Like an entire colony of fire ants. "You won't be tossed aside." He used his CEO voice. "That would be a waste of invested time and resources."

She flinched, just a millimeter, before she recovered with a smirk that didn't reach her eyes. "Spoken like someone who values heartlessness."

That stung even more. "A heartless person would walk away. Not my intention."

"A heartless person is someone who views others as objects only. No emotion. No love," she finished in a rush. "Let's get the boxes over to your house. Then Operation Living Together can commence." She moved to walk toward the front room.

She would not distract him by changing the subject. "You say I'm heartless. So be it. But you're refusing to trust. That's worse."

She whirled around, her hands thrown into the air. "How can I trust you when there's no emotion?"

"It didn't seem to get in your way last night. And this morning." She trusted him enough to shatter in his arms, crying his name as he shuddered inside her.

She flushed. "Yes, the sex is great. I admit it. But sex is a, what did you call it? 'Chemical reaction caused by hormones and preprogrammed neurological responses'?" She quoted his words from the taqueria back at him. "When there's no lo—caring," she corrected herself, "there can't be trust."

"People trust each other every day without being emotionally involved," he pointed out with perfect logic. "Trust is what allows society to function. If we didn't trust firemen to show up when called or banks to hold our money—"

"Or Nestor to hold up his end of the deal?" Her direct stare challenged him.

"Yes," he agreed. "Or business deals."

"And there's the rub. I don't trust Nestor or Irene either."

He shook his head. "There's a difference between blind trust and expecting someone to hold up their end of the deal—"

"Which you can't trust Nestor and Irene to do, because they don't care about you. They want something from you instead."

On the contrary, they *did* care. About winning. About getting the upper hand in the game of one-upmanship their families had played for decades.

He was still furious with Irene for telling his parents about his marriage. That was underhanded, even for her. His parents always looked down on his efforts to be his own man, build his own legacy. It was the twenty-first century, but they held Victorian notions that working for a living would degrade their social position. They would have been the first to urge him to take the offered money and give up his company, even to Nestor, if it meant he would join them in spending the family trust jetting from golf course to ski slope.

Irene knew that. Siccing his parents on him while wrestling control of his company was just an added bonus for her. "That's not precisely true—"

"You know what I think?" Her words tumbled out quickly, as if a dam holding back a swollen river had finally burst. "You don't want to believe in caring—in *love*—because it would mean giving up control. And you can't stand not being in control. You want to corral the entire world, turn it into nice neat equations. But the world doesn't work that way."

What? No. He didn't believe in love because it wasn't real. Oxytocin and other hormones tricked the brain into attachment, and smart humans learned how to manipulate that to get what they wanted. Trust, on the other hand, was a cerebral choice, born of rationality and logic. It was the most powerful covenant possible between two people.

And he trusted her. Not just with the deal, but with his real self. The self who bought his own computer by gambling online while still in middle school. The man who no longer needed his parents' approval but wouldn't mind having it, on his terms.

She'd learn to place her trust in him. They still had time before their prenup came to its conclusion. And he was confident they could make an even more advantageous deal when this agreement came to its end.

The sun outside the windows started its descent, casting a golden glow over the room. It lit her curls, turning them into a halo that framed her heart-shaped face. Hazy rays outlined the curves of her hips and waist, reminding him how well he knew her unique geography but still had more to explore. His gaze dropped to her lips, pursed into an eminently kissable shape. Her cheeks were rosy, her gaze dark and wide.

His groin tightened. He and Danica may disagree on emotion, but when it came to physical activities, they came together. Many times. Each explosion more mind-shattering than the last.

"I thought you liked my control," he said, moving toward her until only inches separated them. He brushed a loose curl off her cheek, allowing his fingers to linger on the soft smoothness of her skin. "A lot," he breathed into her ear.

She blinked. Her crossed arms relaxed, her body tilting toward his. Several emotions, few of which he could identify, came and went on her face. She settled on a half smile, her closed lips softly curving. "You're trying to change the subject."

"Is it working?" He kissed the skin where her neck met her shoulder, breathing in her delectable scent.

She let out a soft gasp and inclined her head to give him more access. "I didn't tell you the best part about rooming with Mai. She has a double shift today. She won't be home until 10:00 p.m."

He grinned. The knot in his gut loosened, untied. Sex was familiar. Sex, he could handle. "Really?" he rumbled.

She nodded, that mischievous pink tongue of hers appearing as she licked her upper lip. "I have the house to myself," she breathed, and wound her arms around his neck.

"Good to know," he replied. He started to remove the elastic from her ponytail, but she moved away.

"No."

He stared at her. "No?"

She nodded. "My house, my rules. And rule number one—" she stood on tiptoe so she could whisper in his ear, her breath hot against his skin "—is no touching. I get to touch you. Let's see how you can handle not being in control."

Danica focused on Luke, her hands gripping his tightly. When they made love, Luke ensured she was awash in pleasure before he would allow himself to take his. Even moving into his house had to be on his terms, the shots called by him.

After meeting his parents, she had a better idea of what drove Luke. Far better to separate love from sex or remove love from the equation altogether when marriage was a game of power. He'd warned her, but she hadn't believed it. Then she'd seen it with her own eyes.

She couldn't change him. She couldn't make him see winning wasn't the only thing. In fact, it didn't even make the top one hundred of things that make life worth living. She couldn't make him believe unconditional love had a power of its own, so great it could move worlds.

But for now, he was in her hands. Literally. She was the one in charge. "No touching," she reiterated, and stepped back. "If you do, I'll stop."

She dropped his hands just long enough to grab a long piece of fabric from the organizer hanging on the back of her door while his hopeful gaze focused on the queen-size bed that dominated the space in her small bedroom. By the time his attention turned back to her, she had finished looping the item around his wrists and tying them behind his back with a square knot.

He looked over his shoulder, straining to see his hands. "What in the world did you use?"

"Hogwarts school tie from a trip to Universal Studios," she said. "I'm a Hufflepuff."

He shook his head. "I have no idea what that means." Then he wagged his eyebrows. "But I like the sound of huffing and puffing."

"I suppose that makes you the Big Bad Wolf."

He growled, making her laugh. She began to unbutton his shirt, pausing to trail her fingers through the crisp hair outlining his pecs. His flat brown nipples just begged to be touched, and with her thumbs she drew circles, ever so softly, over each one.

A shudder racked his body, and he leaned down to kiss her. She stepped back just in time and wagged a finger in front of his tempting lips. "No touching."

"I thought you meant with my hands."

"Don't think," she breathed in his ear, then nipped his earlobe. "Feel."

His blue eyes were even darker. "Don't worry, that's happening."

"If you're talking, you're thinking," she warned and scraped her nails across his nipples. His Adam's apple worked for a few beats, and the erection she could feel against her stomach pressed harder.

She stepped back, just a smidge, so her right hand could follow the dark trail leading down his muscled stomach and disappearing into his khaki trousers. The front of his pants sported an impressive bulge. It took only a second to undo his belt and then both her hands were free to slip between the waistband of his boxer briefs and the firm skin of his lower abdomen, exploring the straining prize awaiting her.

Luke's breath came in staggered bursts. His hips bucked, brushing against her. When she took her hands away, he stopped.

"Danica." Her name was a strangled combination of syllables.

She grinned. Giving his erection one last caress, she moved away to slowly unbutton her blouse, pausing after each one to see if he was watching. His gaze was glued to her chest. She let the silk fabric fall to the floor and shimmied out of her skirt. When her relationship with Luke turned physical, Danica had decided she needed to invest in new lingerie. Today's matched set was nude-colored lace trimmed with black satin ribbons. She chose the bra because it created cleavage for days, while the wisp of lace covering her bottom seemingly revealed everything yet left most to the imagination.

She didn't need to be psychic to know where Luke's imagination was leading him. His hungry gaze followed her as she walked back to him. Placing a hand on his chest, proud of herself for controlling the tremble caused by the near-feral expression on his face, she helped him step out of his pants and underwear. Then she carefully steered him backward toward the wing chair in the corner of the room. He sank down into it, his gaze never once leaving hers.

She could get lost in the heat she saw there. The heat

and the need and the… No. She would not delude herself there was anything resembling caring in his gaze. He liked sex, and he liked having sex with her. That was all. Still, a tiny corner of her heart began to beat in hopeful rhythm.

Keeping her eyes focused on his, she found his erection, even bigger than before. She resumed her strokes, firm followed by soft and going back to firm again. He stifled a sound deep in his throat as his eyes rolled back, his head falling against the chair. Then she knelt in front of him and replaced her hands with her mouth, her tongue continuing the rhythm.

His loud groan pierced straight to her core. The liquid heat gathering between her legs burst into greedy conflagration. She pressed her legs together to relieve some tension. This was about him, not her. Still, she wasn't sure if she would be the one to break down and ask for completion.

"Danica, I—" his voice was strained "—need to touch you."

She redoubled her efforts, lost in his scent and his taste and the sheer pleasure of having him at her mercy. He was close. She could feel it.

"Danica," he growled. "Please. Please."

Please? The word was so unexpected, she lost her rhythm and fell backward on her heels. Luke Dallas actually said please?

In one movement Luke was out of the chair, the tie holding his hands gone and his shirt shrugged off. He picked her off the floor and threw her on the bed. She landed on her back, stunned by the sudden change in elevation, her arms and legs akimbo. Before she could gather her thoughts as well as her limbs, she heard the rip of a foil packet.

Turning her head, she watched Luke roll the condom on with record speed before he joined her on the bed, removing all disappointment she hadn't been able to complete her task. He pulled the scrap of lace covering her entrance aside and then he was in her, his full length buried in her hot, needy depth.

She came so hard she saw galaxies of shooting stars, their fiery trails matching the fire trailing in her veins, every nerve on full alert. Luke stilled above her and then he shouted her name, his full weight collapsing onto her. She didn't mind. She gathered him close to her, enjoying the raspy breathing in her ear, the scratch of his shaved cheek. For this brief minute, he was all hers.

Luke was spent. Completely, utterly, fully spent. He could feel his lungs working, so at least he was still alive. He didn't think his muscles would obey him even if the fate of the planet depended on it. But Danica was beneath him and he didn't want to crush her, so with a supreme effort he managed to roll to the side. She made a disappointed sound and followed him, curling against him.

That was...there were no words. Explosive, yes. Amazing, sure. But he'd had explosive, amazing sex before. He prided himself on ensuring both he and his partner left the bed with broad smiles on their faces. But all the superlatives in the world couldn't capture what he just experienced.

What he and Danica experienced together.

She stirred against him and he turned his head to see big green eyes blinking back at him. "Hey," she said with a small smile.

"Hey," he answered, and drew her into his arms. She sighed and put her head on his chest, her blond curls tangling in every direction. He tangled his fingers in them, loving the soft, springy texture. Her breathing deepened, became regular.

His limbs were heavy and he could feel himself following her into slumber, but he wanted to make the most of his time in her space. It afforded him a rare glimpse into the private Danica, which she kept so carefully guarded. Maybe that was why he reacted badly to the idea of some of her things remaining here. He wanted to have all of her.

The surface of her dresser was bare, except for a small collection of comic-book action figures. There was something in the way they stood, smiles on their faces, hands balled on their hips to take on the world, that reminded him of Danica. Her stance had been identical when she took on his parents.

On her nightstand, photos in silver frames showed Danica with an older man and woman he assumed were her parents. He frowned at the photo of a young man, handsome and confident in a football uniform. An old boyfriend? One she kept close to her pillow?

He must have moved, for Danica blinked awake. She looked up at him with a smile on her face, but it faded when she followed the direction of his gaze.

"That's my family," she said.

"I thought they were your parents. They look happy."

"They are." She paused. "Well, mostly."

"And the other photo?" He tried to sound casual.

She shifted away from him. He missed the tangle of her bare legs with his. "My brother. Matt."

"I didn't know you had siblings."

"Just the one. He's eight years younger. My mom said he was her best surprise ever. I think so too."

"You sound close."

"I was old enough to help with his care. Sometimes Matt jokes he doesn't have a sister, he has another mother."

He indicated the photo. "He plays football?"

She nodded. "He was a gifted athlete—basketball, baseball, soccer, you name it. But his true love was football."

"You said 'was.' He doesn't play now?"

"You caught that." She thinned her lips into a straight line, and then slowly released them. "Matt is a senior in high school. Colleges started to scout him during last season. Oh, not big programs like Stanford or USC. Smaller schools. His coaches told us if he played well this year, he might get a full scholarship. I can't tell you how much that would've meant to my parents." He caught the glint of tears in her eyes.

"What happened?"

She brushed the moisture away. "His helmet—we still don't know why, but it flew off when he took a big hit. He lost consciousness and when he woke up, he couldn't move his arms and legs. The doctors said he suffered partial cervical spinal-cord shock. It was a miracle he didn't break his neck."

"I'm sorry." He picked up the hand closest to him and held it tightly, hoping his grip would say what his words were too inadequate to convey.

She exhaled deeply. "The doctors don't believe the effects will be permanent. But he hasn't responded well to conventional treatment. And, obviously, the schools have stopped calling."

He pulled her to him, nestling her head against his chest. "Why didn't you say anything before this?"

He felt her shrug. "It's not anyone's business but ours," she said after minute. "Mine and my family's."

"I could've helped." His mind raced with avenues to explore, favors to call in. Medevco, the company Evan Fletcher and Grayson Monk pitched at Monte Carlo Night— weren't they involved in cutting-edge medical research? He was sure he'd read something about rehabilitating spinal-cord injuries in the prospectus they sent him.

She raised her head. "You have helped. Why do you think I accepted your job offer? We needed the money."

"I thought..." He stopped. The truth was his parents showed him everyone had a price. He thought he'd named hers. "I needed your skills, I made you an offer, you accepted. It's not a complicated equation."

She sat up and looked down at him. Golden curls hung in her face, begging him to twist them around his fingers and pull her face to his so he could kiss her senseless. Before he could suit action to thought, she gathered her tresses into a bun and tucked in the ends so it stayed put. "Your offer was preposterous."

Now it was his turn to sit up. "You said yes."

"Because I love my family and want to help them." Her gaze, which had been pinning his in place, dropped to the bedspread. "And, yes, now I can start my own executive search agency. But if we hadn't been desperate to pay for Matt's therapy, I wouldn't have jumped like I did."

Her sheets, which previously had felt silky smooth, began to chafe. He couldn't find a comfortable spot. "It was a generous offer."

"I agree. And I appreciate being able to help my family. I owe you a lot."

"But you wouldn't have accepted otherwise." Not only were the sheets itchy, but the room was too hot. He pushed the covers down.

"No. I like taking bets, but finding you a wife? That would have been too professionally risky, even for me." She smiled at him, but it quickly turned into a frown. "You seem restless. Anything wrong?"

"No." Yes. Danica accepted his original offer only because of her family. Not for her own financial gain. It was counterintuitive to everything he knew to be true.

And he believed her. Her room spoke loudly of her affection for her family. Clusters of photo frames and mementos, cheap in price but cared for as if they belonged in the Louvre, told a clear story.

His carefully ordered world, already wobbling in its orbit, started to tilt. So, when Danica declared her love for him to his parents, did that mean…

No. It was a ploy. A feint in the bigger war. She said that only to win the battle.

Didn't she?

A shrill noise came from the direction of his discarded trousers, crumpled where they had been thrown. They both looked in that direction. "That's the ringtone for Anjuli," she said. "You should pick up."

He got out of bed and stalked to his pants. "Yes?"

"Check your texts," Anjuli said and hung up.

Frowning, he looked at his screen. Several texts crowded the display. Nestor Stavros had unexpectedly returned to Palo Alto. He wanted to see Luke. Tomorrow.

He opened his mail app. His inbox was a jumble of new spreadsheets, press requests from his corporate communications team and questions about catering for the meeting. Too many details he had to get right. Now.

Danica cleared her throat. "What did Anjuli want?"

"I have to leave."

She blinked. "Right now?"

"Nestor Stavros came back to town early." He picked his shirt off the ground and buttoned it, then rebuttoned it when he realized he was off by a buttonhole. "He wants to meet in the morning."

She became very still. "The acquisition."

"Yes." He looked around for his socks. He found one by the door and the other under the bed.

She started to push back the covers. "Let me throw some clothes on and I'll go with you to the office."

"No need." He thrust his feet into his shoes and tied the

laces, and then tried to give her a smile. He wasn't certain he succeeded. "Enjoy what's left of your time off."

Her gaze locked on his. "Are you okay?"

No. "Yes." Patting his pockets to make sure he had his wallet and keys, he straightened up and tried to give her a smile. It felt more like a grimace. "We'll know tomorrow if the marriage is a success."

"If the marriage is a—oh. Right." She sat back against the pillows. "So, do I say good luck, break a leg or...?"

"Let's hope for the best possible outcome." He wanted to kiss her, but he was afraid it would cause him to stay with her for, oh, at least a week. Or whenever the food ran out. He settled for resting his lips against her forehead, allowing her scent to envelop him one more time before he left. "I'll drop the truck by the house and pick up my car before going to the office. It will probably be an all-nighter."

"Of course." She gave him a bright smile. "I might stay here, then, so I can see Mai when she gets home. One more girls' night."

There was a note in her voice he'd never heard before, but he shrugged it off as he hopped into his car. The prize he had been chasing for so long was in his grip. His employees could look forward to a very lucrative payout. Everyone would win.

But he couldn't help feeling he was missing a very big chunk of the game he was playing, and he'd left the clue to discovering it lying in a warm bed.

Ten

Danica walked the short distance from the train station to the Ruby Hawk offices, her gaze focused on the sidewalk. The weather had taken a chillier turn overnight, mimicking the cold descending on her heart when Luke exited the afternoon before.

She spent last night wide awake, trying to solve the mystery of why Luke had left so suddenly. Yes, he had to prepare for the meeting with Nestor, but something had been bothering him before he ran out of her home as if it were a condemned house. Had it been a mistake, allowing Luke into her private space, surrounded by her photos and mementos? Did it make him see the gap between them as insurmountable? There weren't a lot of ski medals and golf trophies hanging in display cases and littering her shelves after all. She pushed open the glass doors, barely hearing her coworkers' cheery hellos.

Maybe she'd revealed too much about her family? She

didn't speak much about her brother or her parents' flight to the United States to escape a war determined to tear them apart. Her family long learned words of sympathy came quickly, but soon faded and disappeared—or even turned to annoyance—while problems lingered. So they stayed quiet and smiled as if they didn't have a care when asked, leaning only on each other.

Or maybe she was the problem. The few times she trusted someone enough to let them in, they left. Tom, her college boyfriend, hadn't wanted a partner whose family couldn't help support them. He'd discarded her for a fellow law student, whose biggest concern had been choosing which white-shoe firm to work for after graduation. Her former boss Johanna took off as soon as something shiny was dangled in front of her, heedless of the employee she knew was counting on the promotion. It was only par for the course, now that the acquisition was almost a reality, that Luke would be eager to finish this pretend marriage as soon as possible.

She pushed open the door to her tiny supply closet. Then she stopped short, her hand still on the doorknob. Her office was already occupied.

Irene Stavros leaned against a corner of Danica's desk, reading something tucked in a manila folder. "Hi!" she said with a cheerful smile. "I couldn't concentrate in the engineering bullpen, and my father is in Luke's office."

"Hi," Danica responded automatically. Irene looked spectacular. Her teal jersey dress clung in all the right spots, the color complementing her glowing olive complexion. If she wore any makeup to enhance her skin's flawlessness, Danica couldn't detect it. "Make yourself at home."

Irene beamed. "Thanks." She hopped off the desk and took the guest chair in front of Danica's desk. As soon as

Danica sat down behind it, Irene began to speak. "I have so many things I need to discuss with you."

Danica switched on her computer, holding her sigh inside. Small talk with Irene was nowhere near her list of top ten things to do. "I'm all ears."

Irene clapped her hands and rubbed them together as if they were coconspirators. "Brilliant." She handed Danica the folder. "Let's start with what to say to the media."

Danica put it down on her desk without looking at it. "The corporate-communications department handles the press."

Irene shook her head, her shiny black tresses tossing as if they starred in a shampoo commercial. "We need to talk about Cinco Jackson and the story he is chasing." She raised an impeccably groomed eyebrow. "You're a big part of it."

The amorphous dread that had started to gather when Danica first spotted Irene coalesced into a hard, painful ball in Danica's stomach. "What story?"

Irene tapped the folder. "The one about Luke hiring you to be his wife to secure the acquisition, of course."

Luke greeted Nestor Stavros and ushered him to the conference table occupying the corner of Luke's office. "I hope you had a good flight?" he asked, taking the chair opposite him.

Nestor smiled and adjusted the cufflinks on his white linen French-cuff shirt. In contrast to Luke, who wore his usual work uniform of khaki trousers and a blue-checked button-down shirt, Nestor had on a fine wool Italian suit, custom tailored to make the heavily muscled man seem even more imposing. One would be hard pressed to tell Nestor had thirty years on Luke if it weren't for the liberal sprinkling of silver hairs at Nestor's temples and the deep creases at the corners of his dark eyes.

"Comfortable but long." His accent was a surprisingly harmonious combination of his native Greece and his adopted country, Australia. "It gave me time to review the documents. Impressive, the work you've accomplished."

"Good to hear." Luke leaned back in his chair. The welcome rush of adrenaline that accompanied a business negotiation hummed in his veins. The dance had begun, and they both knew the steps. "All is in order?"

"Mostly." Nestor did his own leaning. "Irene told me about your marriage. I am impressed. I didn't think you would go through with it."

"I met the right woman." Luke's words were glib. But as they left his mouth, he realized the truth. He did meet the right woman. Danica didn't have an Ivy League degree or come from generations of money. But she was...

Danica.

And that was all she needed to be.

The realization sank in, like a stone thrown into a lake. But the ripples it caused weren't upset or denial. On the contrary. For the first time in weeks he was supremely confident in his insight. Danica was his wife. The only wife he'd ever want.

But did she feel the same way? She didn't tell him about her brother even though he could have easily helped. Forget money. He had connections all over the world. He could have called in favors.

Nestor cleared his throat, snapping Luke's attention back to the meeting. "Lost in thoughts of your bride?" A knowing smirk appeared on Nestor's face. "It's just the two of us. You can drop the pretense."

"There's no pretense."

"You managed to fall in love and get married in such a hurry? You? A Dallas?" Nestor scoffed. "I admit I was reluctant to buy Ruby Hawk if you came with it. You come from a family that does not honor its obligations and is always chasing the next attractive…deal." He took a long sip of water from the glass in front of him, regarding Luke coolly over the rim. "My board begged me to walk away. But then Irene suggested the marriage clause. She said if you wanted the acquisition badly enough, you would find a way to make it happen, thus proving you have the drive and commitment we demand. Well done." He held out his hand to be shook.

Luke didn't take it. "The marriage clause was a ploy."

Nestor took his hand back with a small shrug. "I wouldn't say *ploy*. Think of it as the big battle before leveling up in a video game. After all, that's why we're acquiring Ruby Hawk. To enhance our interactive game technology." He took another sip. "Few have the persistence to make it this far. Much less get married just to secure the deal. That is the need to succeed at any cost I want in my people."

The air conditioning in his office must be set below freezing. That had to be why Luke's lips were numb and his fingers had lost all sensation.

"We have an agreement?" Nestor indicated the papers at Luke's elbow.

Bile started to rise. Luke pushed it down and drew the stack toward him. "Let me take a final look at the term sheet."

The offer was a good one. The stock his employees took in lieu of market-rate salaries would pay out at a rate beyond their wildest expectations. They deserved it for all their hard work. For placing their trust in him.

The hollow pit in his stomach grew into a yawning crater.

Nestor handed him a fountain pen, engraved with the date and location. "I had this made for the occasion." He chuckled. "To celebrate the marriage of our two companies."

Luke dropped the pen on hearing the word *marriage*. It rolled off the table and he leaned down to pick it up, but his fingers encountered something flat and circular instead. He pulled the item up, keeping his hand below the table.

It was a poker chip. A five-hundred-dollar poker chip. The one Danica handed to him at the Peninsula Society fund-raiser.

He stared. He'd been carrying it in his wallet ever since that night. It must have fallen out. A vision of Danica, her eyes sparkling as she watched the roulette wheel spin, danced before his eyes.

Nestor tapped the table. "There's champagne on rapidly melting ice."

Luke slipped the poker chip into his pocket, picking up his pen with his other hand. He sat up and pulled the stack of papers toward him. It really was an advantageous deal for Ruby Hawk Technologies, one that would ensure Luke's legacy would thrive and grow beyond what he could accomplish on his own.

His hand hesitated, the pen hovering over the paper.

Danica did her best to stop gaping like a fish yanked out of the water. "What? I don't—I mean…" She trailed off, still parsing Irene's words. She knew? How?

"I believe you wrote this." Irene took out a piece of paper and showed it to Danica.

It was a printout of her first contract with Luke. The one she created and sent via email the day they met. Danica froze.

"You remember Johanna?" Irene continued. "Of course, now Johanna works for the Stavros Group. When Cinco contacted her about the mysterious recruiter working for

Luke Dallas who married him out of the blue, she was happy to look at the Rinaldi Executive Search files to see if there might be anything...untoward...we should know about." Irene indicated the contract. "That's what we found."

"This is a contract to act as a recruiter." Danica forced the words past her numb lips.

"Read the third paragraph. For a wife. In order to close the Stavros Group acquisition. And it seems one of your candidates was Cinco's fiancée. Bad luck, that."

Danica closed her eyes, but it didn't stop the horrifying visions playing before her. Luke's integrity questioned, her professional reputation destroyed beyond repair...her parents discovering her marriage had been a sham. "You can't blame Luke for trying to jump through the ridiculous hoops you set up—"

"Oh, I don't blame Luke for trying. Nicely done, by the way. Brava."

Apprehension prickled Danica's scalp. "What do you want, Irene?"

Irene smiled. It didn't reach her eyes. "Don't worry. I told Cinco I set you two up, and it was love at first sight. He'll find something else to write."

Irene killed the story? This wasn't a threat? "I don't understand."

"We're buying Ruby Hawk. We look after our own." Irene folded her hands on the desk. "And now you know that we know the truth. Consider it a favor saved in the bank. Just in case."

So it was a threat. "In case of what?"

Irene spread her hands wide. "Luke is happy to acquiesce to us now because of Ruby Hawk, but in the future?" She tapped the folder again. "We have insurance against any future rebellion. I don't need to tell you how much of a scandal we can spin this to be. But please, understand this isn't personal. I very much like you." She smiled, her even white teeth gleaming.

Danica didn't return it. She had to find Luke and warn him. If he signed the deal, he would be under the Stavros thumb. For good. "Anything else? I have work to do."

"Oh, yes, 'work.'" Irene made quote marks in the air with her fingers. "I am sorry, however, that you got dragged into this. You blindly walked into a game you didn't know you were playing. I blame Luke." She shrugged. "Desperate times, desperate measures."

The dry toast Danica choked down for breakfast threatened to make a reappearance. "I married Luke because I care for him."

Irene's smile turned into a smirk. "Of course. He's very attractive, especially in the bank account. And he knows how to use his words to get what he wants. But let's be honest. There's a reason why Luke and I aren't together. He is simply incapable of expressing any emotion that wasn't plotted on a spreadsheet. I'm sure you noticed that even in bed, he leaves after he gets what he wants. But well done on getting the diamond ring. At least you have something of tangible value in return."

Irene rose from Danica's desk. "Now that we're on the same page, my father wants to meet you. After all, as Luke's wife, you'll be spending quite a lot of time with us once Ruby Hawk becomes a Stavros Group subsidiary."

"You're wrong about Luke." Danica kept her chin raised. She wouldn't let Irene see how well her words hit her target. Luke was indeed good at using his words, and his other skills, to get what he wanted. And now that the acquisition was almost done... The memory of how he'd walked away from her bed, without a backward glance, played behind her eyelids.

"I'm wrong?" Irene tsked. "You're smarter than this." She stalked to the door, her long legs making short work of the distance from the desk. "We have a deal to celebrate. Coming?"

Danica could either get her heart rate under control or speak. She couldn't do both. She followed Irene in silence. At least now she had a chance to tell Luke about Nestor's and Irene's machinations, and he would find a way to get out of the deal. He wouldn't sell to the Stavros Group after hearing how they'd manipulated them both.

Would he?

Her heart wouldn't examine the answer too closely.

Luke looked up at the sound of the conference-room door opening, his pen still hovering above the signature page. Irene swept in, followed by... Danica? He sprung to his feet, a wide smile of welcome on his face. It disappeared as soon as he got a good look at her expression. It reminded him of the wide-eyed, stricken stare she gave him when they first met and she discovered Johanna had closed up shop without a word. "What's wrong?"

"What could possibly be wrong?" Irene arranged herself in a chair next to her father. "Shall I open the champagne?"

"When the deal memo has his signature." Nestor indicated the stack of paper.

Luke ignored them. He stepped to Danica's side and took her right hand in both of his. It felt like holding an ice cube. "Is everything okay?"

"You haven't signed?" Danica's gaze searched his.

"I'm about to. Why?"

She threw a glance at the Stavros father and daughter. "Can we speak? Alone?"

Irene took the foil off the neck of the champagne bottle.

"She's about to tell you we know all about your fake marriage and we don't care."

Luke kept his gaze locked on Danica's as he responded to Irene. "Your father made it clear the marriage clause in the contract was fake, as well."

"The clause was a fake?" Danica's eyes widened. "But of course it was. Just another move in the game."

"It worked." Irene shrugged. "Better than we ever could have anticipated. We alleviated our board's concerns about Luke's stability, we own Ruby Hawk, and, thanks to both of you, we have leverage for the future. Oh, that's the other thing she wants to tell you, Luke. We have written proof of your marriage scam." She popped the champagne cork. "Useful, that. Someday, I'm sure."

Nestor looked at his diamond-encrusted Rolex. "Can we get back to business? I leave for Los Angeles in a half hour to meet with my bankers. If we don't have an agreement today, it will be months before the board will approve another offer." He raised an eyebrow. "I've seen your financials, my boy. You don't have months left."

Danica turned to Luke, her hand still locked in his. "You can't sell. Not to them." Her gaze pleaded with him.

"Come with me." Luke ushered her out of the conference room to a small alcove nearby where they could speak somewhat privately. But anyone could walk by, and he was aware they were drawing curious glances from the engineers sitting in the open plan bullpen. He lowered his voice. "I'm signing the deal. I have to. It will ensure Ruby Hawk's future."

Danica's already pale complexion turned ghostly white. "But you heard what they said. You'll never be free of them. You're selling yourself out."

"It's going to be okay." He wanted to push an errant curl

behind her ear. He settled for a tight smile. "This won't change anything between us."

She pulled her hand away from his, her head shaking. "You mean you're okay. I'm not. They admit they have the game rigged but you're still playing." She hugged her arms close, her shoulders hunched. "And things *will* change. Our marriage ends when the acquisition is a done deal. Not that we had to get married in the first place, apparently."

The mention of their agreement caused his gut to contract. "It doesn't need to end. We'll find a way to negate any leverage Irene thinks she has."

Her gaze locked on his. "There you go, changing the strategy again. Don't you understand? This isn't about our agreement. It's about you and the Stavroses. If you take the deal, the game continues. But you can stop it, now, by saying no to them. If you don't—" she took a deep breath "—I will. I will walk away. I won't be a threat held over your head."

"I'll handle it. You just need to trust me."

Danica's head jerked back. "Trust you? Tell me why, Luke. Why should I trust you?"

He was missing something. Something very important. But he didn't have time to puzzle it out. "Because I have everything under control."

"That's what you tell business colleagues. Tell *me* why I should trust you." Her gaze pleaded with him.

"I…" In the corner of his peripheral vision, Irene emerged from the conference room and tapped her watch in his direction. "We'll straighten this out after Nestor leaves. We need to get back to the meeting."

It was the wrong thing to say. He knew it even as the words left his mouth and hung in the air between them.

This should have been a day of triumph. He'd ensured the future growth of Ruby Hawk. His employees would be financially rewarded for all their hard work. But Danica's stunned expression, her eyes wide and suspiciously bright, told him he'd just lost more than he could imagine.

"There's nothing I can say to stop you from this, is there?" She played with her hands. It took him a moment to realize what she was doing. By then, her wedding rings were off her finger and lying on her outstretched right palm. "Here. At least they won't be able to use me against you."

No. This wasn't what he wanted. A bone-chilling freeze rooted him in place.

"Take them. Once the acquisition is done and our marriage is over, they'd be returned to you anyway," she continued. When he didn't move, couldn't move, she picked up his right hand. Her touch burned as they placed the rings in his grasp and closed his nerveless fingers around them.

He got his lips to function. "Danica...don't... I need..."

"No. You don't need me. Turns out you never needed me." She looked over his shoulder, and her gaze sharpened. "Irene is heading our way."

He couldn't get a grip on his panicked thoughts. They bounced and tangled around his skull, refusing to be sorted. "This isn't—"

"Congratulations on the deal. I mean that. Goodbye, Luke." She kissed his cheek, her lips hot against his chilled skin, and turned on her heels. She was through the nearest exit before he could get his feet to move.

Irene put her hand on his forearm, pulling him back when he would follow Danica. Irene's touch reminded him he still stood in the middle of the engineering bullpen. It was more crowded than normal. He recognized people from sales, accounting and marketing, attempting to appear as if they were busy and not eavesdropping.

"Can we sign now?" Irene asked.

He didn't answer, his gaze locked on the rings in his hand, his brain trying to process the image. Every atom in his being urged him to go after Danica. His employees' sideways glances reminded him he was minutes away from securing their futures. A headache gathered behind his eyes. The pain dulled his senses while sharpening his regret.

Irene glanced down at the jewelry. "Too bad. I was honest when I said I liked her."

Her words cut through the aching fog shutting him down. "What else did you say to her?"

She scoffed. "Don't blame your inability to maintain a relationship on me."

"What did you say?" He enunciated each word.

Her gaze widened, and for a second something like hurt entered her gaze. Then she blinked, and her smooth mask of amused indifference was back in place. "Such emotion in your voice," she said lightly. "One might think you have a heart after all."

He didn't react, his gaze continuing to pin her in place.

"We had a discussion about your ability to stay unaffected when it came to affairs of the bed," she said, with an airy gesture of her hand. "Girl talk."

"Danica agreed?" That sliced through the numbness, a full body slam of hurt.

Irene rolled her eyes. "She defended you. Which is why it's for the best she left. If she stayed, she'd be devoured and spit out in less than a year."

Luke stopped listening after the first three words. Danica defended him. She must care. But if she did, why did she leave? Why wouldn't she trust—

When there's no caring, there can't be trust. Her words rang in his head.

He put a hand on the wall to steady himself. Of course. That was the piece he was missing, the clue he couldn't see. She couldn't trust him because he hadn't shown her he could be trusted with her heart. She didn't know how much—

"I love her."

He wasn't aware he did until he said the words out loud. Now he couldn't fathom how he hadn't known. How could he not? He knew how he reacted to her. How his heart rate sped up when he saw her name on his phone's caller ID. How a brush of her fingers against his was enough to arouse him, deep and heavy. How his knees turned to water when she took her hair down and shook the curls free.

He wanted her voice to be the last thing he heard at night. Her face the first thing he saw in the morning. To laugh and argue and sit in companionable silence after stuffing themselves too full during Sunday brunch. The thought of a toddler with golden ringlets took his breath away.

In the past, he might have cataloged these as mere physiological reactions to mental stimuli and nothing more. Even an hour ago, before the meeting with Nestor, he might have argued with himself not to allow intangible feelings to distract him from solid goals.

Now there was only one goal that mattered. He glimpsed a life without Danica and it was a dark and dreary place indeed.

He wasn't his parents. He wasn't his family and their interminable feuds. He could forge his own path, one of love and laughter and growing old with the grandmother of the babies crawling at their feet.

One of trust and commitment.

He strode to the conference room, leaving Irene in his wake. He signed the deal memo below Nestor's thick scrawl, and made sure his lawyers had their copies before Nestor left for his flight to Los Angeles. Then he called Anjuli into his office.

He knew what he had to do.

Eleven

Danica descended the stairs of her parents' home and found her mother seated at the kitchen table. Amila Novak smiled a warm greeting at her, but her expression quickly turned puzzled. "I'm happy you put on a fresh shirt to visit Matt, but why do you need a suitcase?"

The handle of her carry-on bag in one hand, Danica held out her phone, the browser opened to the *Silicon Valley Weekly* website, with the other. "The Ruby Hawk board of directors approved the sale to the Stavros Group. But Luke is no longer the CEO. That wasn't the plan. Something went wrong."

Amila put down her coffee cup. "So you're what…going to California? Now?"

"I have to explain. Get him reinstated somehow. Running Ruby Hawk is all he ever wanted."

"I thought you left precisely because all he wanted was his company." Her mom leaned forward, her chin cupped in her hand. "But I'm glad to see your eyes so alive again. When you showed up here out of the blue, it seemed nothing would get you out of your bed except visiting Matt."

Danica dropped her gaze. When she boarded the plane in San Francisco, she had no intention of ever seeing Luke again. But then Mai called to say that Luke returned all of Danica's things, in person, ensuring everything went back exactly the way she had it. Then he bought Mai dinner as an apology for invading her home—and donated fifty thousand dollars to Mai's pediatric unit at the hospital. He was still an ass though, she was quick to add in female solidarity.

Aisha texted her when she ran into Luke at a local grocery store over the weekend. That was a shock in itself as Luke usually had all his food delivered. Aisha reported he was wandering the aisles, almost as if he was there just to get out of his house.

He came up to me as soon as we locked eyes to ask about you. He still had that hungry look, and it wasn't for anything on the shelves.

Luke did call Danica a few times. She let the calls go to voice mail but sent him a text with her parents' address, so his lawyers would know where to send the divorce papers. A clean break was the best for all concerned, she lied to herself. But ghosting him added to her current remorse. What if he'd needed her to be present for the Ruby Hawk sale? She wouldn't put it past Nestor or Irene to pull a last-minute clause out of their bag of dirty tricks. The guilt of costing him the deal would eat her alive.

She raised her gaze to meet her mother's. "All I know is if I can set things right for him, then I need to do it."

She picked up her bag. "If I leave now, I might make the next flight."

"Wait." Amila sprung to her feet. "You can't leave now. What about—" She coughed suddenly. "What about Matt? You're going to leave without saying goodbye to Matt?"

"I need to do this. Matt knows I love him." Danica moved toward the kitchen door. "I'll be back before you know it."

Her mother grabbed the handle of the suitcase and wouldn't let go. "If you want to leave after seeing your brother, fine. But you must come with us. Look, here's your father now." She nodded at the man coming down the stairs.

"Is everyone ready?" Mirko Novak grabbed the car keys off the table before taking his first look at Danica. "A clean shirt like we asked. Well done."

"She thinks she's going to the airport. To go to California," Amila told her husband.

Mirko's gaze widened. "She can't go. She needs to see—" He stopped, and cleared his throat. "Matt," he finished, sounding slightly...panicked? *But why would he be panicked?* She must be imagining things.

Amila nodded. "That's what I said."

Danica's gaze ping-ponged between her parents. "What's going on? Why is seeing Matt today so important?"

"Visiting your brother is not important?" Mirko raised his dark eyebrows. He took her by the elbow and steered her toward the garage and the car parked inside over her protests. "Tell me more about California while I drive."

"Fine," she grumbled and put on her seat belt. She would go to the airport that afternoon and find another flight. A few more hours wouldn't hurt. Or so she crossed her fingers.

When they arrived at the center, Danica signed in and then turned left at the reception desk to go to her brother's room. Her mother caught her arm. "Matt's doctor wants to see us first, alone."

Danica frowned. "Is everything okay?"

"He wants to go over a new treatment with us, as the parents." Amila shrugged. "You know doctors."

"Uh-huh." Danica narrowed her gaze. First, they insisted she had to see Matt. Now they insisted she not see him? "I'll wait here. For a little bit."

Her mom squeezed her hand. "Thanks, *draga*."

Her parents disappeared through the automatic glass double doors that led to the residential wing, leaving Danica with the security guard for company. Still, it wasn't an unpleasant place to wait. Sunshine streamed in through floor-to-ceiling windows, while comfortable-looking white chairs invited her to sit down. The clean, modern decor reminded her of the Ruby Hawk offices. Which reminded her of Luke. But then most things did. That man coming through the glass doors, for example, was a dead ringer for—

The world stopped spinning. Then it spun too fast. He wasn't a ringer for Luke.

He *was* Luke.

She could only watch, her feet rooted to the ground, as he made his way to her. "Hi," he said, stopping in front of her.

"Hi," she squeaked. So many questions ran through her head, she didn't know which ones to articulate. She settled for staring at him.

He looked good. So good. His dark hair was a smidge longer and as windswept as ever. His blue eyes sparkled like the Pacific Ocean on a calm summer's day. The crisp white shirt he wore was unbuttoned at the top. She took a step closer, to see if he still smelled the same, but jumped back when she realized what she was doing. Then she frowned. His trousers had a shiny stripe running down their outer legs.

"Why are you wearing tuxedo pants?" It wasn't the most brilliant question with which to start. But his face creased into a wide smile. He put both hands in his pockets and came up with two closed fists.

"Because I was wearing them when you gave me this." He opened his left hand. On his palm was a five hundred-dollar poker chip.

The room wouldn't stop revolving. "You flew across the country to return it?"

"No." His fingers closed over the chip before she could pluck it from his grasp. "I came here to ask you to take another risk."

Her heart, which had been beating a hopeful symphony, settled into a more sedate melody. She had been right. He needed her, but to get his company back. "I read about the board of directors removing you as CEO. If it's because I left before the deal closed, I'm happy to speak to whomever—"

"No." He shook his head.

"No?" It was worse than she thought. "But they can't take Ruby Hawk from you! The company means everything to you."

"There is only one thing that means everything to me. And that's my wife." He opened his right fist.

Her wedding ring sat on his palm, shining like a blazing star, sending refracted shards of rainbow dancing around the room.

She stared at it, caught between holding her breath and hyperventilating, as he held it out. "The board of directors didn't remove me. I resigned. Anjuli is the new CEO. She's more than a match for Nestor," he said.

His blue gaze was alight with so much emotion it

made her tremble. "I don't understand. You gave up Ruby Hawk?"

"You were right. I had to stop the game. Stop allowing the past to dictate the future. Stop controlling the present." He smiled, and it was so tender her breath caught. "Allow for serendipity."

Hope started to flower, big, showy blossoms of delight and joy. Her veins sang with it. "What about Irene? And my email about our contract? Cinco Jackson's exposé?"

He laughed. "I called Cinco and told him the whole thing." He held up the hand with the chip again. "Took a risk, but it paid off. He was much more intrigued about the Stavros Group hacking email to find blackmail material on their potential business partners than he was in our contract. Irene is busy fending off his phone calls."

The grin on her face painfully stretched her skin, but she didn't care. "So you're not going to start a new company and sell it under ridiculous conditions?"

"A new company, yes. I've already talked to Grayson Monk and Evan Fletcher about joining Medevco. But no more conditions." He stepped closer, his scent teasing her nose. She yearned to throw her arms around his neck and press her lips to the skin just below his jaw, inhaling more of it, for the rest of time. "I'm never letting you go again. I love you, Danica Novak."

It was a good thing she was in a medical facility, because she wasn't sure her heart could hold all the happiness. She cupped his beloved face with her hands, tracing the faint lines that appeared in his forehead, reveling in the prickle of his five-o'clock shadow against her fingertips.

"You didn't shave this morning," she babbled, scarcely aware she spoke as she bathed in the heat and passion and love—yes, love—radiating from his gaze.

"I was in too much of a hurry to do this." And then his

mouth was on hers and she couldn't think at all, lost in the wonder that was Luke kissing her, reaffirming just how much she meant to him. She melted into him, her lips opening under his, pressing as close to him as the thin barrier of their clothes would allow. She—

Someone tapped on her shoulder. Through the heat and haze, a voice said, "Hey, I hate to break this up, but…"

It sounded like Matt. But he should be in his room.

Danica disengaged from Luke and turned to whoever interrupted them. And then she clung to Luke even harder.

It *was* Matt. And Matt—Matt was standing. As she stared, blinking, he grinned and began to walk.

Oh, he was holding onto a walker, and his progress was slow. But he was moving his legs.

"Look at you." Tears, which had been threatening to form ever since she first spotted Luke, now leaked down her cheeks. Luke handed her a packet of tissues, which she gratefully accepted. Then she frowned at her brother. "Have you been hiding your progress from me?"

"Just this past week. Got access to some new therapies," he said, nodding at Luke.

"From Luke?" She gaped at him.

Luke smiled and tucked her against his side. "It was your idea to use Ruby Hawk technology in sports equipment that got me started. Medevco's products include revolutionary tools for use in physical therapy. Matt was kind enough to be one of our test subjects."

The tears burned hot on her cheeks. But then, joy should feel warm. "Thank you for helping my brother."

"He's family," Luke said simply.

Danica's gaze searched his face. Once upon a time she thought he resembled a brooding man of the moors, solitary, disdaining help from other people. And he still did—

but the aura of utter self-sufficiency was no longer evident. "Family isn't a four-letter word now?"

"My parents are who they are. But love is a four-letter word too. And speaking of…" He turned to face her. Then he dropped to one knee.

She didn't think the day could hold any more shocks. Luke Dallas didn't stoop to others. Luke Dallas walked on top of them. But there he was. Kneeling. In front of her. "What are you doing?" She forced the words past lips numb with surprise and hope.

"What I should have done the first time." He took her hands in his, his grip warm and firm and oh so right. "When you left, you took the sun with you. I want you to come back. Be my light. Be my wife."

Her heart expanded, shutting out doubts and fears with a strength beyond measure. "I love you too," she said, her voice shaking. "I have ever since we kissed outside the taqueria."

He pressed his lips against her left palm. Then he slid the diamond and platinum band on the ring finger. "Will you do me the honor of remaining my wife?"

"Yes. Yes!" And then his mouth was on hers. She gladly opened to him, winding her arms around his neck and pressing closer. She hadn't known just how deeply she missed him until she could smell and taste and touch him once again.

"Hey, guys? People are waiting for the main event," she heard her brother say. Luke laughed and lifted his head, keeping a tight arm around her waist.

"What main event? What could possibly come next?" Her gaze locked on Luke's. She would never grow tired of watching the light dance in those summer-sea depths.

Luke smiled. "You said our last wedding wasn't a real one because your family wasn't there. So…" He took his phone out of his pocket and pushed a button on the screen. The opening chords of "My Shot" from *Hamilton* filled the air. "Your mother has a dress waiting for you. I'll meet you in the center's chapel when you're ready."

She didn't know so much happiness existed in the world. "We're already married." She held up her decorated ring finger. "Another ceremony wouldn't be practical."

He growled, causing her to laugh. "I'm learning to let go when it comes to control, but I'm not letting you go ever again. I'll marry you a hundred times. You can plan the next wedding."

"Just twice will do," she said. "As long as the contract term is forever."

"At least that long," he warned. "Trust me."

Danica smiled. They weren't in the chapel yet, but it was a vow to him that was long overdue. "I do. Forever."

* * * * *

COMING SOON!

LET'S TALK
Romance

For exclusive extracts, competitions
and special offers, find us online:

f facebook.com/millsandboon

🐦 @MillsandBoon

📷 @MillsandBoonUK

Get in touch on 01413 063232

For all the latest titles coming soon, visit
millsandboon.co.uk/nextmonth